"Back!" Ryan yelled

He ejected the clip and rammed in another from the supply he'd removed from Panner's corpse. It seemed to him that his people were only reacting. To survive, they had to get these soldiers on the run.

"Dad, get down!" Dean shouted as he saw the drum rise from the center of the wag. It looked like a circle of blasters on a rotating wheel, which began to spin rapidly.

Ryan dived as the rotating wheel spit fire. He felt a plucking at his clothes, small objects whistling past his ears and through his hair.

Trank darts.

His last conscious thought was that someone wanted very badly to take them alive.

Why?

**Other titles in the
Deathlands saga:**

JAMES AXLER

DEATH LANDS®

Rat King

A GOLD EAGLE BOOK FROM

W☰RLDWIDE®

TORONTO • NEW YORK • LONDON
AMSTERDAM • PARIS • SYDNEY • HAMBURG
STOCKHOLM • ATHENS • TOKYO • MILAN
MADRID • WARSAW • BUDAPEST • AUCKLAND

First edition September 2000

ISBN 0-373-62561-8

RAT KING

Printed in U.S.A.

May we not who are partakers of their
brotherhood claim that in a small way
at least we are partakers of their glory?
Certainly it is our duty to keep these
traditions alive and in our memory, and
to pass them on untarnished to those who
come after us.

> —Rear Admiral Albert Gleaves, USN,
> 1859-1937

THE DEATHLANDS SAGA

This world is their legacy, a world born in the violent nuclear spasm of 2001 that was the bitter outcome of a struggle for global dominance.

There is no real escape from this shockscape where life always hangs in the balance, vulnerable to newly demonic nature, barbarism, lawlessness.

But they are the warrior survivalists, and they endure—in the way of the lion, the hawk and the tiger, true to nature's heart despite its ruination.

Ryan Cawdor: The privileged son of an East Coast baron. Acquainted with betrayal from a tender age, he is a master of the hard realities.

Krysty Wroth: Harmony ville's own Titian-haired beauty, a woman with the strength of tempered steel. Her premonitions and Gaia powers have been fostered by her Mother Sonja.

J. B. Dix, the Armorer: Weapons master and Ryan's close ally, he, too, honed his skills traversing the Deathlands with the legendary Trader.

Doctor Theophilus Tanner: Torn from his family and a gentler life in 1896, Doc has been thrown into a future he couldn't have imagined.

Dr. Mildred Wyeth: Her father was killed by the Ku Klux Klan, but her fate is not much lighter. Restored from predark cryogenic suspension, she brings twentieth-century healing skills to a nightmare.

Jak Lauren: A true child of the wastelands, reared on adversity, loss and danger, the albino teenager is a fierce fighter and loyal friend.

Dean Cawdor: Ryan's young son by Sharona accepts the only world he knows, and yet he is the seedling bearing the promise of tomorrow.

In a world where all was lost, they are humanity's last hope....

Prologue

The old man was going to die soon. He knew it, and so did the others. They could feel the pain of old age, of a body's survival systems shutting down one by one.

They could feel it within him, reaching out to spread over them. One chilled, all chilled.

Inevitably they panicked and wanted him detached, their mute cries coming through on the readings as a sudden increase in electrical activity. Readings the like of which no one in the redoubt had ever seen before.

MURPHY GLANCED over the shoulder of the hunched tech. His hands were slow on the keyboard, laboriously tapping in a code to trigger a programmed instruction.

Except that Murphy knew there wasn't a code. Wasn't a program.

"Wallace will have to know," he said.

The tech said nothing. He just kept tapping. Tap-tap-tap...even though the screen repeatedly told him that there was no response from the mechanism.

Murphy hit the man on the shoulder. He didn't often come to this level, and sec men of his standing didn't bother to fraternize with the other ranks. That was just the way it was. He felt the small rankle of irritation grow to a full-blown itch of anger. An itch he had to scratch.

"Hey, stupe, why don't you answer when I say something? You know you have to answer to superior officers.''

Murphy swung the tech around by the shoulder and drew back his arm to deliver a backhand blow. It was his favorite form of mild reproof, as each of his four fingers had a thick silver or steel ring rammed down beyond the knuckle joint. The index finger had a ring with the head of an old god called Elvis, his name embossed underneath. The middle finger had a skull and crossbones—the edges of the crossbone motif would make a satisfying tear on many an impudent mouth—and the third finger had a five-pointed star that had been awarded to him by Wallace in recognition of the manner in which he had led the defenses on the last outsider attack. Many of the scum had been chilled on that day.

But it was the little finger that held the prize—a diamond cut into many sharp razor edges that could lacerate with only the most glancing of blows. The metal that held the ring on his finger was thin compared to the other rings, but the jewel was a prized weapon, handed down his line from the days before skydark.

Murphy relished taking out his anger on the stupe tech, but halted when the man's face whirled to look into his. The eyes were empty and dull, the nose misshapen into a blob of flesh with no septum. The mouth was open, jaw slack, drool on the receding chin.

Murphy gave a sigh of disgust, his anger temporarily retreating. The tech had to have gotten some mutie blood in his line somewhere. The colony deliberately stole women and some men from the outsiders in order to try to keep the gene pool from getting too stagnant. The trouble was, the rad-blasted valley still suffered from intense chem storms and the irradiated dust brought in by the whirlwinds. The poison became trapped within the valley's confines and just circulated again and again, spraying whatever crops the outsiders could grow, seeping through the food chain into the animals the outsiders caught and ate.

Murphy's men tried to get clean specimens on their raids, but sometimes it was just so hard to tell.

The only way you knew was when you got this....

"Stupe bastard, you don't even know what I'm saying, do you?"

There was no answer. Just the empty eyes.

"I'll just have to tell him myself, I guess." Murphy sighed. With exaggerated care he turned the tech so that he faced his terminal once more. He started to tap in the nonexistent code again.

With a last look through the Plexiglas shield that separated the mechanism from the banks of terminals, and a shudder at the sight that lay beyond, Murphy left the tech alone with whatever thoughts went through the head of a triple-stupe mutie bastard.

MURPHY FOUND Wallace in his office. As always. Sometimes it seemed that Gen Wallace didn't move outside of the office, not even to piss or shit. But if that was the case, Murphy had no idea where he stowed his waste products.

"Sir, permission to report possible code red," Murphy said in staccato fashion, knocking on the door as he spoke. He clicked his heels and saluted, his arm raised in front of him. As prescribed, he didn't look at Wallace until his superior spoke.

"Sarj Murphy, report received and understood. What's the matter?"

Wallace was a big man, spilling out of his uniform, which was frayed at the cuffs and shiny with age. For all that, it was well and regularly laundered, like Murphy's uniform and the tech's white coat. The colony believed in God and cleanliness, like it said in the good book.

Murphy, given permission to look at Wallace by the superior's reply, directed his gaze at the big man as he stepped into the room.

"Trouble, sir. It's the mechanism. One of the components is finally succumbing to obsolescence."

Wallace steepled his fingers and stared at them. He didn't answer for what seemed to be a long time. Then finally he spoke.

"No such thing as obsolescence, Sarj. Recycle is the law. We have parts we can use."

It wasn't a question.

Murphy pulled at his collar uncomfortably. It was too tight, his father having had less of a bull neck. The pants, on the other hand, were too big, where his grandfather had carried a paunch. Right now he'd like to be able to swap one for the other. He felt blood suffuse his face.

"Sir, not so sure about the parts."

Wallace looked at him. His eyes were cold, flinty in the shadowless glare of the fluorescent lighting.

"You daring to argue with the good book, Sarj? You recycle. It works. Always."

Murphy kept his jaw tight. Stupe bastard. Wallace was in command because his father had been Gen Wallace, and his father before him. Just like Murphy's father had been Sarj Murphy, and his father before him. That's the way it was. But Murphy wondered about the strict reg on heredity. There was too much danger of mutie blood infecting the ranks to keep it that simple. The tech was a good example. Dammit, Murphy knew he was smarter than Wallace—smarter than nearly everyone in the redoubt. But the regs couldn't be broken. Never had been. That was how they'd managed to stay as the colony while skydark decimated the outside—the rad-blasted and scarred world the outsiders called Deathlands.

Problem was, it left them with a triple-stupe bastard like Gen Wallace, too inflexible to believe that anything new could ever happen. He'd never actually been outside.

Murphy had. He knew that things changed all the time.

Like now.

"Sir, I really think you should come and see the mechanism."

Wallace snorted. "Sarj, if this is a pointless trip and the recycling can go ahead as usual, then you're on a charge, mister."

Murphy said nothing. He let the big man heave himself out of the chair and waddle after him as he headed back down the corridor toward the tech section. He walked fast, knowing it would make following hard for Wallace and enjoying the small piece of revenge for the Gen's lack of concern.

WHEN WALLACE REACHED the tech section, puffing and panting behind the fitter Murphy, he was in a foul mood.

"You, what's the problem?" he barked at the tech.

"Sir, he can't answer you. Mutie blood."

'Goddamn!" Wallace exploded. "How many times do you have to be told, Sarj. That just can't happen."

"No, sir," Murphy said quietly. "Just like this can't happen, I guess." He indicated the Plexiglas screen.

Wallace looked beyond and frowned.

"Vital signs going down on number three. He was the oldest of the bunch when the great experiment began to run. Got most major organs recycled, and some limbs. Doesn't seem to be anything actually in need to replacement. Just seems to be…fading out."

Wallace didn't seem to be listening.

"Sir?"

"Recycle."

"But what, sir?"

"The whole damn component, Sarj. If a part of the component can be replaced, then why not the whole damn thing? 'Cause the man is just one part of a larger organism—the mechanism. Recycle, Sarj."

Murphy tried to hide his bewilderment. "But, sir, the whole mechanism is predark. The old man is 187 years, three months, two weeks by old chron time. Forty years older than the other components, true, but still, where do I find something of a similar age?"

"That's your problem, Sarj. You're in charge of sec corps. You requisition supplies. Not my problem—what the good book calls delegation."

Murphy ground his teeth. The good book was written before the great chilling. What the hell did it know about right now? But he kept it to himself. He didn't want to be put on a charge. As head of sec corps, he knew what that meant. And he'd trained his men too well.

"Is that a problem, Sarj?" Wallace asked, the flinty eyes glittering in the quivering flesh of his fat face. Fat, but still hard and cruel at the jaw.

Murphy was spared from lying by the sudden deafening blare of alarms that hadn't been used since predark times.

Wallace looked around in surprise. The tech whined and covered his ears.

"Alarms—shit, it must be the mat-trans," Murphy said.

Wallace frowned. 'Don't be stupe. No one's ever got it working. Lost the know-how after the great chilling.''

"Who said someone got it working from this end?" Murphy whispered.

Chapter One

The jump had been as sickening as usual. Ryan Cawdor opened his eye and felt a dull ache across the areas of his face that hadn't been numbed by scar tissue. The empty socket behind the eye patch felt as if it were pulsing in time with his heartbeat, and he flicked open his right eye, the bloodshot blue watering.

Mat-trans jumps were painful and disjointing at all times, the atoms of each individual body being disassembled then flung across vast distances until reconfigured by the mat-trans computers at whichever redoubt was programmed to pick up the signal. The time between was taken up by nightmares and wanderings through the dark nights of imagination. The time immediately after awakening was usually filled with nausea and weakness.

Ryan shook his head, trying to rid himself of the pulsing that thumped inside his skull. He looked across the dull green-and-cobalt-blue walls to where the streaked armaglass ended abruptly as the wall met a floor inlaid with the disks that also peppered the ceiling.

He reached out for his weapons, feeling his hand brush the stock of the Steyr SSG-70. Where that lay, his SIG-Sauer couldn't be far away.

His hand touched warm flesh, and he felt fingers instinctively grasp at him. Head still pounding, he turned his eye to focus on Krysty Wroth, her flaming red hair coiled protectively to her head and neck. Her mutie heritage gave her hair a sentience that acted as an early-warning system, coiling close to her head when danger threatened. After a jump it usually took some time to flow freely, but never before had he seen it this defensive.

It set off a triple-red warning in his brain, and he forced his disoriented reflexes to respond. Forcing unwilling calf muscles to brace his legs as he got to his feet, he looked around the chamber.

J.B. Dix, Ryan's oldest friend and a fellow traveler since their days with the Trader, was beginning to regain consciousness on the far side of the chamber. His beloved and battered fedora was pulled down over his eyes, and his right hand moved instinctively toward one of his capacious pockets to pull free his glasses. Ryan could see that his breathing was steady, and that he was recovering from the jump with his usual speed.

The Armorer's other hand was held by Dr. Mildred Wyeth, a survivor of predark days who had been cryogenically preserved before the big blow of 2001, then thawed by Ryan in the postnuclear age of the Deathlands. The stocky black woman's hair hung in beaded plaits around her downturned head. She was beginning to stir, raising her head and opening her eyes. Her Czech-made ZKR 551 revolver lay in her lap, and before she was fully conscious her hand closed on it.

Dean, Ryan's son, was still out. A thin trickle of blood ran from his nose to his top lip. He grunted as the effects of the jump began to wear off and the first nausea of consciousness returned.

"Dark night, my head's thumping like mutie drums on a bad day."

Ryan turned, dark spots still exploding in his vision

at the speed of the movement. "Thought it was just me." Ryan winced at the pounding that was still making his empty eye socket throb.

"Everybody." Jak followed the statement with a wretch of bile that splashed onto the floor of the gateway. The jumps usually made him vomit, and he spit out the remains of the bile before rising to his feet, pulling on the patched camou jacket that carried his hidden throwing knives and holstering his .357 Magnum Colt Python blaster with a fluid grace.

"The bells, ah, the bells, Esmerelda. Ask not for whom they toll. The bells toll for thee, my Emily...my Esmerelda...."

Doc's eyes were open and staring, but they shared the same faraway quality as his voice. The jumps always proved the hardest for Doc Tanner, whose white hair hung in soaked strands around his face, streaked with perspiration and the blood that flowed from his nose and trickled from the corner of his mouth. No one knew how old Doc really was. Trawled from the 1890s into the immediate years preceding skydark by the whitecoats of Operation Chronos, a part of the Totality Concept, which had also furnished the redoubts with the mat-trans units, Dr. Theophilus Tanner had proved to be a problem. Such a problem that the whitecoat scientists had decided to use him for a further experiment, shooting him forward in time—ironically only a short time before their own lives were ended by the madness of skydark—and landing him in the maelstrom that was the Deathlands.

According to records the companions had come upon in the whitecoat hell of Crater Lake, Doc had been in his early thirties when snatched. The stresses of time trawling had made Doc physically resemble an old man, and his mind had a similar fragility that sometimes tipped him over into temporary madness.

His speech was stopped by an urge to vomit, and he spewed the blood that had run down his throat.

Mildred went over to him.

"Crazy old fool. Sometimes I don't know how his mind ever snaps back from the strain of these jumps," she said as she ran a quick check on his vital signs.

Doc smiled. "Perhaps it never does, and this scenario is nothing but the product of a disordered psyche."

"Big words. Feel better," Jak commented shortly. "Right about bells."

"Gaia, I've never heard a bell quite like that before," Krysty said as she moved toward Ryan. Now fully recovered from the jump, and with a resilience that was close to the one-eyed warrior's, she spoke in a low, urgent tone. "Sounds more like a siren. A warning of some kind, mebbe?"

"New redoubt," J.B. commented, looking at the walls. "Could have an old alarm system. Mebbe working off the same power supply."

"Never heard one before. Why now?"

"Why not?" Dean asked. "Stupe comp systems get faults all the time."

"Not that often, son," Ryan replied, his mind racing. "There's something else—"

"The chamber," Krysty finished. "We've never seen one this spotlessly clean before. Almost like it's been swept out."

"Which would mean someone lives here," Mildred added.

Electrostatic air-conditioning also kept the dust from the floors and walls of most redoubts—in theory. But in truth there had been occasions where time had led to at least one part of the system failing.

"Your grasp of logic is most admirable," Doc said weakly. "Would it therefore be remiss of me to suggest even more than our usual caution?" He was still shaky on his feet, but had the heavy LeMat blaster ready, his lion's-head swordstick thrust into his belt.

Ryan nodded grimly. "Last thing we need just after a jump. Going into a situation cold like this is the best way to get chilled."

But already his fighter's brain was going into action. Whatever lay behind that door would expect them to come out blasting…if it was anything like other inhabitants of Deathlands. But what if it wasn't? What if it was like Alaska, where gatekeeper Quint had been using the redoubt as a refuge from the harshness of life outside?

He dismissed the option. The only way to stay alive was to assume that everything was hostile until proved otherwise. And maybe even then you'd have to chill it.

Ryan looked at J.B. and could see that the Armorer had been thinking the same way. He had the M-4000 in his hands and was checking the load.

"Think what I'm thinking?" he asked laconically.

"Guess so," Ryan replied. "Mebbe one or mebbe many. Either way, they'll expect us to come out blasting. It's our only chance. Bastard door is so narrow it doesn't give us a chance to spread quickly."

"Can't stay like rats in trap," Jak said.

In a trap or walking into a hail of blasterfire. Not much of a choice. The Trader used to say there was only one choice: choose to live or choose to die. Ryan knew that they couldn't stay in the chamber forever.

"J.B., you lay down covering fire when the door

opens. I'll head out and try to find cover. Mildred, Krysty, you follow. Jak, bring up the rear.''

"What about me, Dad?"

Ryan turned to his son. "You and Doc take longest to recover from the jumps. Mebbe buy you a few seconds. You come out after J.B. blasts again. Door that narrow, it's difficult to come out with covering fire unless you want your head blasted."

"Bad enough that some other bastard wants to chill you, without us chilling ourselves," Mildred commented with a dark humor.

In just a few seconds, the group had loosened the chains of torpor and fatigue that the jumps usually left binding them, and were all running on adrenaline.

Krysty's hair still clung protectively to her head.

"I've got a bad feeling about this, lover."

"So have the rest of us," Ryan replied.

She shook her head. "No, not like that. I just get the feeling that this is going to be the easy part."

"Fireblast! If this is the easy part, then I don't want to be around when the difficult part arrives."

He turned to the Armorer. "Ready?"

J.B. nodded.

"Backs to the wall, people. This is it."

With caution Ryan tried the wheel lock that opened the chamber door. They hadn't seen a chamber door like this since the old military installation in Dulce, New Mexico. Was this going to be a regular redoubt, or something different? The door was unusual but the rest of the chamber was the same as most—armaglass, not concrete like Dulce. The wheel gave easily under his grip, far easier than he expected. Yet more evidence that this redoubt was in regular use.

Did this mean someone else knew the secret of the gateways?

The wheel spun, and the door opened smoothly.

Only a fraction. Ryan stopped it and braced himself for any immediate attack. J.B. was at his side, the scattergun up and ready.

Nothing.

"So far, so good."

"Doesn't mean much," the Armorer added. "They're not stupe enough to rush us. Could make them more dangerous."

Ryan nodded. They would proceed as planned.

As they flattened themselves to the green-and-cobalt walls on the left side of the chamber door, Ryan reached out a hand and steadied himself to fling it open. J.B. stood slightly away from the wall, to one side of his friend, ready to step out and fire a covering blast as the one-eyed man flung himself through the door.

Many years of traversing the Deathlands and encountering death, staring it in the face before blasting it away, gave the two friends an almost telepathic bond. Ryan gave only the slightest of nods before flexing his wrist and flicking the door.

As he had expected from the ease with which the wheel lock had worked, the door opened freely, as though smoothly oiled and with no friction to impede the motion.

J.B. stepped in front of the door at an oblique angle, aided by the hexagonal shape of the chamber, his finger closing on the Smith & Wesson's trigger and squeezing until the cartridge exploded with an almost deafening impact in the enclosed space. The fléchettes of barbed steel were driven from the barrel in an ever-widening arc. Anyone standing in the room beyond wouldn't be standing for long.

Ryan sprang through the doorway, rolling across the floor, trying to get a fix on any possible cover. He moved so quickly on the back of J.B.'s shot that the hot air from the blaster seemed to brush his cheek as he passed.

His eye took in the surroundings at a glance as he rolled. The throbbing pulse of the siren still pounded in his head, but otherwise conditions seemed normal. The usual anteroom was missing, but the control room was fairly standard. There were the usual free-standing comp terminals, as well as desks, chairs and terminals that blinked on and off in the controlled atmosphere. The harsh fluorescent lighting cast no shadow on the room, leaving no place for anyone to hide.

Ryan came out of the roll into a crouch behind one of the desks, which he pushed on its side to provide cover. It would be no good against heavy blasters, but the steel would act as a shield against small-caliber handblasters, as well as providing a visual blind.

It was only when the clatter of the uprighted desk and comp terminal died away that he realized the alarm had stopped.

Krysty, Mildred and Jak sprinted from the doorway to cover, risking their speed in the enclosed space against the reactions of anyone training a blaster on them.

There were no blasters; there was nothing.

Behind a desk on the far side of the room, Jak picked up a framed photograph that had been knocked onto the floor. The glass had cracked, throwing a web of lines across the smiling face of a young woman long since dead. There had been similar personal mementoes on desks in some of the other redoubts they had seen.

They meant nothing to Jak, but it didn't escape his notice that there was no dust on the frame. It had been regularly cleaned.

Without pause he threw the frame high in the air, over the top of the desk and out into the unknown territory that was the rest of the room.

There was no response. No blasterfire.

Following through in one motion and using the momentary distraction of the airborne object, Jak aimed the Python over the top of the desk; bobbing up briefly to locate any enemies.

The room was empty. Seemingly.

Mildred had taken advantage of the diversion to scan the room.

"Damn place is empty, Ryan," she called.

"Mebbe. Mebbe only seems." Jak smiled across at her. "Mebbe not stupes."

The last thing any of them expected was the voice that came from the corridor beyond the door at the end of the room.

"Right so far, Sarj. Let's see if they're officer material."

WALLACE WAS WATCHING the outsiders on a vid monitor positioned in the corridor. He could see two men and two women strung out in a line behind their temporary cover. The camera was behind them, positioned on the wall above and to the right of the mat-trans chamber door, on the angle of the hexagon.

He now knew that there were at least four of them. They were sharp and showed intelligence. Were there any others still in the mat-trans chamber? The armaglass was too opaque to be sure.

Murphy stood behind the big man, watching over his shoulder. He was irritated that Wallace had taken over management of this operation. As head of sec corps, it was Murphy's job to handle attacks of any kind.

Even if they came from within.

"Temporary stalemate, Sarj. We go in, they blast. They get blasted back. Need them alive, but we got more men. Numbers, Sarj, that's the key. That's why the mechanism is so important."

Murphy didn't respond. The problem with the mechanism was bothering Wallace more than he wanted to let on. Why else mention it?

This could be the break that Murphy had been waiting for. The circumstances when the regs could be broken. But that was for another time. Right now there were more-pressing problems.

Like how many were left in the chamber.

RYAN SCANNED the empty room.

"How many people beyond the door?" Mildred asked.

"One is one too many," Krysty replied. "I feel like a complete stupe behind this." She tapped the edge of the desk with the barrel of her Smith & Wesson .38.

"Any cover is better than no cover. And if we don't know how many of them, they sure as hell don't know how many of us." Ryan kept his attention fixed on the doorway at the far end of the room, watching for the slightest movement.

Jak took the opportunity to recce the area to the rear, knowing that Ryan had the front covered.

"Not sure. Vid behind. Mebbe watching us."

Mildred looked around and saw the camera above Ryan's head.

"Smile, you're on TV."

One round from her ZKR 551 took out the camera through the lens in a shower of sparks. They rained over Ryan, but the one-eyed man ignored them, keeping his attention fixed on the redoubt doorway.

"Just as well I held the second shot," J.B. said quietly from inside the chamber. He kept his voice as low as possible in the eerie quiet that had succeeded the siren. "If they know about you, then there's three of us they don't know about."

"So what do we do? We can't stay here forever, just like we couldn't stay in there," Mildred said grimly, gesturing to the mat-trans chamber.

"One trap for another." Jak had his back to the table, checking his blaster. He looked over at Ryan, smoothing the milk-white hair away from his scarred albino skin. His red eyes were piercing.

Ryan smiled tightly. "Read something once about what they used to call a Mexican standoff. Bastard stupe name, but I guess this is what they meant."

WALLACE CURSED as the monitor went dead.

"Sir, what do you want me to do, sir?" Murphy said in a flat monotone, trying to keep the amusement out of his voice.

"I want them alive. No casualties. I want to know how they used the mat-trans."

"It might be that they don't see it that way, sir."

Wallace turned toward Murphy. The sec man shivered as he looked into the heart of his superior and saw a glimmer of insanity too close to the surface. He knew that the Gen would be a hard man to usurp, and hoped that Wallace couldn't in some way know his plans. The Gen was a true believer, fired by the regs. He had the fire of generations burning in his veins.

"They will, Sarj. You make them."

The fat man turned on his heel with an astonishing precision for someone his size, and waddled off down the corridor.

Murphy looked after him, then turned to the five sec corps personnel he had with him. They were all trained by him personally, and were the cream of his corps. Their uniforms were crisp and well laundered, although still carrying some stains from the chilling they had accomplished on the raids to the outside. They were well drilled from the manual, and also had a few tricks Murphy had picked up along the way.

They were the elite he would use when the time came.

But how was he going to break this stalemate?

Chapter Two

Inside the chamber both Doc and Dean had taken advantage of the time bought by Ryan's actions to recover fully from the effects of the jump. They stood, blasters ready for action, to one side of the Armorer.

"John Barrymore," Doc whispered, "if I may hazard a suggestion. We three are something of a Trojan horse, and could perhaps be of some use in that manner."

"No sense there, Doc. Tell me a little more."

"When the Trojans were at war with—"

"Not the history, Doc. Not now. Just what you mean for us," the Armorer interrupted. Like Ryan he was easily irritated when Doc's lectures appeared at the worst moments. Like now.

"My apologies," Doc said with a short bow. "I shall endeavor to explain in simple terms, in order to save precious moments. If we are in here, and our opponents have no idea about us, then our companions can act as a decoy by appearing to surrender—"

"That's a stupe idea," Dean said angrily. "Sure way to get everyone chilled. Why don't we just jump again?"

J.B. shook his head. "Came across a chamber like this before. The door isn't the trigger...maybe an earlier mat-trans, I don't know. This'll need triggering from out there." He gestured to the outside with the M-4000.

Dean was unconvinced. "I still say Doc's idea is double stupe."

"Mebbe not. Not if we're all quick enough," the Armorer replied. Raising his voice slightly, he continued, "Ryan, you hear that?"

"We all heard," the one-eyed warrior replied. "A slim chance is better than no chance, and I'll go bastard crazy unless we break this deadlock." He turned to the others. "It's the only way to draw them—whoever the hell they are—into the room. But we need to be triple alert here. Scatter as soon as the others appear."

He was greeted with three nods of assent.

Ryan called out. "Hey, you out there. How are we going to end this?"

"Only one way," came the voice from the corridor. "You outsiders throw down your blasters and we come and get you. No way you can get out, and there's more of us than you. Besides, we're under orders to keep you alive."

Ryan looked across at Krysty, whose hair was still protectively clinging to her.

"Sounds like shit to me," he whispered.

"Amen to that," Mildred added.

Krysty shook her head. "No, I think he's telling the truth. It's what comes after that worries me." She shook her head as she noted Ryan's puzzled expression. "I can't explain it, lover. It's just not clear enough."

"Move or sit?" Jak asked. The inactivity was making him restless. A born hunter and predator, Jak had the ability to stay still and patient for hours when tracking and hunting. Patience wasn't the problem. A decision had been made, and now he was itching to spring to action.

"Let's do it." Ryan threw the Steyr over the top of

the upturned desk. He kept the SIG-Sauer, holstering the blaster, and checked automatically for the panga, secured in a sheath against his leg. Beside him Krysty threw her blaster out into the middle of the room. Mildred threw hers with reluctance.

The last to throw out his weapon was Jak, the heavy Python thudding loudly on the floor. Like Ryan, he chose to keep something close to hand—the leaf-bladed throwing knives stayed secreted on him, hidden in the folds and patches of his jacket.

"Okay—sounds good to me," Murphy said from beyond the door. "Now come forward slowly."

Almost as one, the companions stepped around the flimsy barriers of the overturned desks, Ryan fractionally ahead of the others. All kept their muscles as tight as whipcord, nerve ends jangling for the slightest sign of movement. It was a fairly large room, looking identical to the ones in all the redoubts they had come across. It was cleaner, and had less of an empty, desolate feel than the others. For all that, it was just a standard control room.

So there was that advantage. They knew the territory. Whoever they were facing wouldn't expect that.

It wasn't much of an advantage, but it might be all they needed. Behind them, in the chamber, J.B. clamped his fedora on his head and adjusted the wire rims of his glasses. He could feel, rather than see, Dean tense up for action with the same granite stance as his father. Doc raised the LeMat, tension transforming him from a seemingly mad old man into a taut killing machine.

They were ready.

MURPHY HEARD THE MOVEMENTS around the blind corner. He had sharp ears, honed by a lifetime of avoiding stickies and the ambushing gangs of outsiders he encountered every time he led a party from the redoubt. It was part of the hereditary chain that he had been trained for this since birth.

When he knew they were in the center of the room, he nodded to one of his sec corps.

"Okay, Panner. Now."

Pri Firclas Panner was a short woman with hooded eyes and a heavy body build. In spite of the extra weight, her uniform was too large for her. It showed the marks of being altered and gave her a deceptively unbalanced and clumsy look. In fact her father had been a born killer, and her mother an outsider who had slit her throat after her daughter had been born, as though knowing the psychotic offspring she had produced. Panner liked her work. Too keenly. Panner was Murphy's most trusted ally, and it was only gene-pool regs that stopped him joining with her.

A flicker of a sadistic smile crossed Panner's face.

"Those fuckers'll wish they'd never tried to invade, Sarj," she said in a lusty, throaty voice. The thought of what they were about to suffer excited her. She'd seen these grens at work before. They didn't kill, but were far more subtle in their pain. It lasted longer and left the sufferer alive for other tortures.

Before Murphy had time to take in Panner's arousal, the stocky sec woman soldier swung her body in front of the doorway with a rebel yell that had been passed down her line since the days of skydark.

As she yelled, she adopted a classic firing stance, bracing her legs apart. The gren launcher in her hands was of an experimental type rarely seen in the Deathlands, and was one of only two that were left on the redoubt.

AT THE SOUND of Panner's voice, the friends scattered across the room, diving for whatever scant cover they could find. Jak flipped over and landed on his feet behind a desk, one of the leaf-bladed knives balanced in the palm of his hand, perfectly weighted for throwing. Ryan also sought cover, rolling and coming to a halt with the SIG-Sauer in hand, his eye trying to sight the woman in the doorway.

But she was already gone.

The yell had covered a loud popping sound as the gren had launched. It hit the wall above the chamber door and bounced in front of Krysty.

"Shit…" She threw herself away from the strangely shaped gren, which was oblong with a squared end and unlike anything she'd ever seen before. Not that it mattered—a gren was a gren. It didn't have to be just one shape to be able to chill you.

J.B. appeared in the chamber doorway, holding his Uzi, preferring its accuracy to the less controlled M-4000, which could hit the rest of his party as easily as any enemy sec men.

"Gas gren of some kind. Try to cover your mouths, breathe as shallow as possible," he yelled, pulling a kerchief from one of his pockets and thrusting it over his nose and mouth.

A pale white mist, similar to that preceding a jump, started to infuse the room. It had no smell, but an immediate effect. Ryan felt his eye mist with tears as the gas pricked at it.

"Fireblast! Need to get the hell out of here." His words came slowly. It seemed as though his brain were cut off from his body, the thoughts traveling miles to reach limbs that felt heavy and leaden. The SIG seemed to weigh more than usual, the weight dragging his arm down.

The others were now out in the room, and they seemed to be moving in slow motion.

"Nerve gas. They must be able to seal the room— otherwise the air-conditioning system would spread it through the whole place." Mildred gasped out the words, trying hard to breathe shallow as she sunk to her hands and knees. "John, they must want us alive. Why?" She collapsed unconscious as she forced out the question, trying to look around for the Armorer.

J.B. was close to the floor, figuring that the gas would rise, being lighter than air, and that the air nearer the ground would be clearer, at least giving him a chance of staying conscious long enough to see what their captors looked like.

Ryan was on the floor beside him. Both men were struggling to stay conscious. J.B. swum in and out of focus in Ryan's good eye.

"Well organized. Not crazy muties for sure. Precise, like well-drilled sec men," the Armorer forced out.

It sounded to Ryan as if J.B. were talking in slow motion, the words drawn out and distorted. Blackness closed in at the edge of his vision, as if he were entering a long, dark tunnel.

The Armorer was the last one to pass out. He didn't last long enough to see the door open.

WHEN J.B. OPENED his eyes again, he found that he was staring at the ceiling of a dorm. Hauling himself onto the edge of the bed, he could see that all six of his companions were laid out on the beds, as well. It was one of the smaller sleepers in a redoubt, usually accommodating only four beds. But even with the extra three beds, there was still room to move around and stretch aching muscles. Outside the closed door, he could hear distant activity. From the sound of it, a large number of people inhabited the redoubt.

Figuring it a certainty that they were heavily guarded on the outside, he looked around for a sec camera like the one Jak had spotted above the chamber door. The dorms didn't usually have them, but then this was obviously no ordinary redoubt.

The sec camera was above the door, pivoting on a bracket and covering the entire room in a sweep. The only blind spot would be right up against the door, which was next to useless. Its steadily flashing red light showed that somebody was watching them.

A quick search of his pockets while he gained his equilibrium on the edge of the bed showed the Armorer that his pockets had been stripped of all ammunition, and that his knife had also been taken. That his blasters would have been taken from him he had assumed as a matter of course.

He stood and found that his muscles were sluggish, and that his arms and legs felt as though all the tendons had been sliced through. Pain lanced through them, and they failed to respond immediately.

His first, tentative steps were toward Mildred. She was still out cold, as he could see when he thumbed back her eyelid to reveal the eyeball rolled up in the socket. At his touch she moaned slightly and shifted in her deep sleep.

Moving with increasing ease and speed among the rest of the party, J.B. was able to determine that all of them were still unconscious. Jak's coat and knives had been taken from him, as had Ryan's SIG-Sauer and panga. Both Dean and Doc had also lost their blasters.

But surprisingly they had neglected to take Doc's swordstick. The dark ebony cane with the silver lion's head looked like a walking stick from pre-dark days, and perhaps their captors had assumed it was an aid to the old man. He had already seen that Ryan still had his scarf wound around his neck. It was heavily weighted at the ends, and was a deceptively useful stealth weapon. It, too, also had the advantage of seeming to be innocuous.

Two weapons left, then. Their first mistake. That was encouraging. If there was one error, then there would be the opportunity for others.

Suddenly feeling overcome with a wave of exhaustion, J.B. made his way back to his own bed, trying not to show surprise at the discovery of Doc's swordstick.

He sat on the edge of the bed and took a deep breath, which sawed his lungs.

"Dark night," he croaked through dry lips, "what was in that gren?"

He figured that he had awakened first because he had managed to avoid gulping as much of the gas as the others. And yet it had still had this effect on him...how would the others feel when they began to come around?

He took off his wire-rimmed spectacles and polished them with his kerchief. Their captors knew he was awake. They'd figure the others wouldn't be far behind. And they'd know that they wouldn't be in any condition for a fight.

The only thing to do right now was sit it out.

BY THE ARMORER'S wrist chron, it was just over fifteen minutes before Ryan stirred.

"Feel like a nuke shit in a pox-riddled gaudy house," he muttered in a low, quiet voice, forcing his eye open.

He still felt as if he were separated from his body. His eye focused on J.B., sitting on the edge of his bed.

"Effects take a little while to wear off. Feels like you've had every tendon in your body severed and then soldered back together. Otherwise it's not too bad."

Ryan forced a smile. A joke from J.B. was a rare thing, and could only mean that his old friend had the situation as assessed and secured as was humanly possible. Ryan's hand instinctively slipped down to his waist and leg, feeling for the panga, touching only the empty sheath.

"They took everything. Only left Doc his walking stick." J.B. spoke carefully, indicating with a slight tilt of his fedora the sec camera behind him.

Ryan took it in at a glance. He didn't know whether they could be heard, as well as seen, but he wasn't taking any chances with predark technology that was in the hands of people who obviously knew how to use it.

Krysty moaned as she raised her head behind them. J.B. repeated his warning about the aftereffects of the gas gren.

"Gaia! This and a jump in the same day... It's no wonder I feel like a herd of mutie pigs has trampled over every bone in my body."

"Tell me about it, girl," Mildred murmured as she began to tentatively move her own limbs.

Jak had obviously taken in more of the gas, as it was some time before he recovered consciousness, during which time Dean had opened his eyes.

"Anyone know who did this?" Jak asked finally, shaking his head to clear his vision. "Tell me and I chill with pleasure."

Only Doc remained unconscious. Mildred grabbed her backpack and went over to him. In addition to bits of cloth used as bandages, it usually contained medical supplies traded at villes or plundered from redoubts and ruined sites across Deathlands. The bag now revealed itself to be empty.

"Shit. Whoever they are, they've taken everything."

"Figured they would. The bastards are thorough." J.B. pushed his fedora back on his head. "Mostly," he added.

Mildred felt Doc's pulse, which raced out of control. The old man was sweating and moaning, his REM making his eyelids twitch uncontrollably. The physician cursed the people who held them, and cursed the Deathlands. Why had they taken the few medical supplies she had?

"Is he going to be okay?" Dean asked. "He doesn't look too good."

"I wonder how much more he can take," Krysty added.

"So do I. It's hard enough to figure out what's happened to his metabolism anyway, without the stresses of a mat-trans jump and a nerve-gas gren adding to it in such quick succession."

She was still holding Doc's wrist when his slack hand suddenly made a grab for her arm, holding it tightly with a strength belied by his skinny frame. His eyes opened wide, staring glassily into the light above her.

"Ah, Emily, my dear. Is it teatime already? I fear I am studying too hard, as I seem to fall into the arms of Morpheus far too quickly. So tired... Tell me, did you toast me a muffin, and is there honey for tea? I promise that I will take you and the children for a picnic when the weather improves enough."

Doc's rambling didn't disguise the click of the door as it opened behind them.

Ryan turned slowly. No need to turn quickly and make jumpy trigger fingers itch on their blasters.

A man and a woman stood just inside the room. Both sec guards held 9 mm Heckler & Koch MP-5 K blasters, with the casual air of the regular user who was used to little opposition. Light grip, ready to brace and tighten on the trigger in an instant. They felt they didn't have to keep on the alert, as the blasters would take out the closely gathered group in front of them with ease.

In Deathlands you always kept on the alert or got chilled.

Ryan noted it as mistake number two.

Chapter Three

"Is there any point in asking where you're taking us?" Ryan asked as they exited the room.

"Shut up and walk," Murphy replied, a smile playing across his face.

His captain reveled in having the upper hand. Ryan could see that it made him sloppy. The Heckler & Koch was pointing downward at an angle of about sixty degrees. It would take him precious fractions of a second to level it.

The corridor was a typical redoubt corridor. Long, with a dull floor and walls broken only by the installation of vanadium-steel sec doors.

It was bizarre to see shuffling figures attending to maintenance tasks. One man was mopping the floor; another had the control panel off a sec door and was staring blankly at the wires, as though trying to remember why he had taken it off in the first place.

"John, is it me or is this ridiculous?" Mildred whispered from the side of her mouth to the Armorer, who was walking slowly beside her. "They call this an armed guard?"

"They're either triple stupe or it's a trap of some kind," J.B. replied. "Problem is, I can't figure out what kind of trap."

"Or why... I'll go for the stupe option. Maybe they just need to get out more."

Panner heard the whispered conversation and yelled, "Hey, shut the fuck up, you black bitch. And you, four-eyes."

Mildred's lips tightened, and J.B. could feel her body tense beside him. Not that he was exactly pleased at being insulted by someone who was made brave by a blaster.

"Oh-oh," Dean murmured to himself, exchanging a shifting glance with Jak. Both were aware of Mildred's intense hatred of stupes who picked on her color. Both knew it would be stored up for a future occasion.

Which came sooner than they expected.

Doc had been lagging behind. He walked slower than the rest of the party, and Panner had gleefully jabbed him in the ribs with the barrel of her weapon, spurring him on. Looking over his shoulder, Ryan wasn't sure if the old man was planning something or if the effects of the jump and the nerve-gas gren still debilitated him. He tried to look at Krysty, to see if she could give him some indication. To see if she could sense something.

There wasn't time.

Doc was still shuffling, and Panner shoved him again. Harder, this time. Hearing her braying laugh, J.B. looked around at the same time as Ryan.

Both men knew instinctively that Doc was giving them an opportunity to move. He had timed his last shuffle until they passed the point where one of the maintenance men was washing the floor with an old, almost bald mop. Suds and water were gathered to one side of the corridor, and Doc contrived to stumble away from Panner and slip on the soapy water.

He fell in a manner that appeared to Murphy and Panner to be clumsy, but was in fact a perfect pratfall. Spinning on his heel so that he reversed position and faced the two sec personnel, Doc fell backward. Although it would seem that he was out of control, both J.B. and Ryan noted that the old man relaxed his muscles, spiraling to the concrete floor with a floppiness that protected him from breaking bones.

He also knew exactly the way in which he would land. He contrived to get the lion's-head walking stick on one side of his body, shielding it from the view of the sec corps.

Panner was laughing so hard that her flabby jowls wobbled, and her eyes ran with tears.

"What are we worried about, Sarj? These outsider scum are no danger. This old fucker can't even stay on his feet!"

Even the otherwise taciturn Murphy stopped scowling long enough to crack a grin. Panner stepped forward, her Heckler & Koch blaster now lowered to the concrete floor, and idly prodded the prone Doc with her combat boot.

"C'mon, get up before I chill you and mess the floor, you old fart."

With a speed that would seem surprising for his age, Doc flicked his right arm from the position over his body where he had been grasping the hilt of his stick. Instead of ebony, a rapier-thin double-edged blade of the finest Toledo steel whistled through the air, catching the light from overhead.

It would have mesmerized Panner if she'd had the chance to see the light reflected. However, by the time this happened, she had already dropped her blaster and was clutching at the blood pumping from her torn throat. With the most delicate twist of his wrist, Doc had stroked back and forth, the blade ripping at the exposed area of flesh between Panner's chin and the beginning of her combat armored vest.

"'Manners maketh the man.' I would venture to suggest that bad manners can be an undoing," Doc murmured.

The blade had cut through her carotid artery, ripped tendon, fat and muscle and severed her jugular. It was a perfectly judged stroke, avoiding jarring the blade on bone and throwing the timing of the attack. Blood spilled from her mouth, open in an "O" of surprise. It pumped over and between her fingers, spilling down her combat vest and covering the newly washed floor. It also splashed onto Doc, already climbing to his feet with a limber spring that was spurred on by an adrenaline rush.

Murphy dropped his own blaster, barrel to the floor, unable to believe his own eyes. Panner was his second-in-command, his loyal lieutenant. She had the instincts of a killer, and yet an old man had chilled her in front of his eyes. Furthermore he couldn't work out where the blade had come from.

In slow motion he watched her blaster fall toward the floor.

Before it had a chance to touch the concrete, J.B. sprang toward it and caught it, his forward momentum carrying him into a roll, which pulled up painfully short against the wall of the corridor. The Armorer grunted as the blow knocked the air from his lungs, but regardless he pulled himself into a sitting position. The Heckler & Koch was positioned in his hands, finger taut on the trigger, directed at Murphy's head. The Armorer would have preferred a body shot, but knew it would be useless with the combat vest. At this range it wouldn't stop a burst of fire fatally injuring the sec man, but it could slow his death enough for him to chill his opponent.

J.B.'s snap aim wasn't to be tested. Murphy had allowed his full attention to be directed toward the Armorer, and hadn't noticed Ryan step forward just two paces.

That was all it needed. The one-eyed man unfurled the scarf from around his neck, wrapping one end around his right hand. The weighted end swung down loosely, and with a snap of his wrist he jerked the scarf so that the metal weights were propelled like a slingshot, catching Murphy on his right temple.

The sec man grunted and collapsed in a heap on the floor, his blaster falling from his grip and clattering to the concrete. Ryan retrieved it, checked it and had it in hand ready for use in one fluid motion. Without a closer check, Ryan couldn't tell if Murphy was still breathing. Certainly he was out cold, and for some time. There was an indent in the side of his skull, a depression that was already turning blue and weeping blood slowly.

That only left any possible danger from the two maintenance men. Jak took the one nearer Doc, the one who had been cleaning the floor. The man had been looking blankly at the action unfolding in front of him, and didn't even notice Jak until the wiry albino had his hands around the man's throat. Then he slackly turned his head, his dull eyes staring into the youth's glowing red orbs with an incomprehension of what was happening to him.

Jak twisted, snapping the man's neck and watching the light in his eyes slowly fade and extinguish. There was little change in his expression, as though he hadn't even taken in his own chilling.

The maintenance man who had been working on the

sec-door control panel was more of a problem. But not much. Just that bit detached from the action, being ten feet in front of Mildred and J.B., he watched with an uncomprehending horror at what was occurring.

Like the comp tech Murphy had tried to talk to earlier in the day, the maintenance man was from a lower level in the colony, a level where mutie blood and inbreeding had been more rife. Somewhere along the line, a stickie had entered his family tree, as evinced by the suckered pads that spread out where he should have had fingertips. It gave him a strong grip on the needle-thin screwdriver he was holding, a piece of sharp, strong metal that would have no problem penetrating bone, as well as flesh.

There was little intelligence in his brain, but a strong loyalty to the colony that had been passed down since the earliest days of skydark. He was aware of Murphy's and Panner's positions in the colony, and that he had to try to help them.

With a wild yell he charged toward the group.

Mildred, like the others, had her attention focused on Murphy and Panner, aware of the immediate danger from their blasters. She whirled, catching sight of the maintenance man out of the corner of her eye as she began to turn. She threw her balance back on one heel, and his wild, running thrust went past her.

Completely off balance, the maintenance man flailed wildly toward Dean, who muttered an oath Krysty would have scolded him for using as he adopted a combat stance.

He was ready for the man when he arrived. Moving under the tall mutie's body, which was bent forward at the waist by his momentum, Dean held his hand rigid and drove his fingers into the man's Adam's apple.

A look of pain and shock crossed the mutie maintenance man's face before his mouth dribbled a pale pink mixture of blood and spittle over sharp teeth that emphasized the stickie genes in him. It was followed a second later by a ribbon of bright blood.

The suffocating man's momentum pulled Dean down to the floor with him. The boy cursed as he tried to get away from the flailing, gagging man.

"Come on, son," Ryan said, pulling the man back by his hair so that Dean could free himself.

"Go now, yes?" Jak asked.

"We should," J.B. agreed, gesturing to a winking sec camera with his newly acquired blaster. "They'll be onto us soon enough. And they'll be able to follow."

"Then shoot out sec cameras."

Doc was on his feet, trying to brush himself off and avoid smearing Panner's blood on his clothes. He looked weary, as though the burst of activity had drained him of energy. "Then, if I may make a suggestion of some use, it would perhaps be best if we were to be moving on. Time to get those, ah, big wheels rolling."

"Doc, you speak some godawful claptrap sometimes, but just occasionally you come out with a gem of truth." Mildred sighed.

"The armory first, then," Ryan said. "We need to get some more weapons and our own damn blasters back. They outstrip us in terms of manpower and blasters."

"But we've got one advantage," Dean said with a wry smile.

"Yeah?"

"Yeah—they're definitely stupe bastards."

Ryan allowed himself a grin. "Yeah, mebbe."

He switched his attention to the corridor. "Okay. I'll take point. Usual formation, people. J.B., cover the back."

The Armorer nodded. "Any other weapons on those coldhearts?" He indicated Murphy and Panner.

Ryan frowned. "None. That's even weirder. It's as if they don't expect trouble, even though they're sec."

They started to move off along the corridor, back in the direction they had come. Jak had taken the needle-thin screwdriver from the dead hand of the maintenance man. It would be a useful weapon in hand-to-hand combat if little else.

In nearly all the redoubts they had landed in, the armory had been located in the same place. There was no reason to assume otherwise here. The long corridors offered little cover for the companions, but equally little cover for any sec men who might try to attack. Ryan figured that they had the advantage in that the redoubt dwellers wouldn't expect them to know the layout.

It was pretty obvious to all of them that the sec men were trained and had the weaponry to do serious damage, but didn't have the combat skills or wit that the friends had acquired during their journeys across the Deathlands. Stealth wasn't something these sec men were familiar with.

"I just don't get it," Dean said as they proceeded with extreme caution. "How come they live here, got all this equipment and they can't fight? And how come they haven't used the mat-trans?"

Doc smiled, tapping the ferrule of his swordstick against his thigh and showing his set of perfect white teeth.

"Ah, young Dean, if only you had finished your schooling with the good Mr. Brody. Your grasp of logic is incomplete. What proof have we that they do not use the mat-trans?" He waited for Dean to answer, and when the youth didn't, he continued, "Furthermore did you learn nothing from your biology classes? I suspect that if these are survivors from a predark community, as seems likely by their mode of dress and some of their speech, then the likelihood is that an astonishing degree of inbreeding has taken place. And there is nothing like that for dulling the wits. Would you agree, my dear Dr. Wyeth?"

Mildred allowed herself a small smile. She remembered the freezies she and Ryan had encountered in the Anthill, hidden beneath the remains of Mount Rushmore. There was no inbreeding involved there, as the survivors of predark times had lengthened their lives with biomechanical body parts and low temperatures. They had mat-trans units, as well as a map of every redoubt across the old U.S.A., but they hadn't used them as far as she knew. This was too long a story to go into. Instead she said, "Your timing for a discussion on genetics is bad, but I guess you've just about summed it up. By the look of it, I'd say these people definitely don't get out enough."

"What about stickie?" Jak asked, his eyes still flickering as he scanned the corridor, screwdriver poised and balanced in his palm.

"Ah, there you have me." Doc shrugged. "Although it isn't beyond the bounds of possibility that some outside blood, particularly of a mutated variety, could have—"

"Doc," Ryan said softly.

"Yes, my dear Ryan?"

"Shut up. Save the school lesson for when we're out of here."

Doc deferred with a bow of the head, realizing that Ryan's words were prompted by their arrival at a junction in the corridors.

It hadn't escaped Ryan's notice that Krysty had been quiet. Too quiet, almost as if something was distracting her.

As the group halted some ten feet from the junction, Ryan whispered, "Something's very wrong with all this. Too easy. They can't be that stupe, can they?"

"I don't know, lover," Krysty replied, resting her hand on his arm. He could almost feel the tension in her fingertips. "Back there I didn't feel like it was a setup. But here it's different. Now that we've got the run of the place, I don't feel danger like they're going to chill us…something different. More devious. Uncle Tyas McCann used to warn us of trying to interpret people who had a different way of looking at things. You always have to be on your guard, as they think in a different way. Makes them more difficult to second-guess."

"And that's what's happening here." It was more of a statement than a question. From the moment they arrived, they had been on the defensive, unable to go on the offensive and gain freedom. Whoever was the baron or leader in this redoubt had a mind that worked on different lines from any Ryan could remember encountering. Until he could work out what this leader wanted, they would be at a disadvantage.

He scanned the area in front of him, straining his ears until he could almost hear his own circulation pumping around his body.

It was deathly silent. The background babble of activity that had accompanied their escorted walk from the dorm and down the first corridor had ceased. Now there was nothing.

"J.B.?"

"I'm with you," the Armorer replied. "Withdrawn all sec men. Every damn man, by the sound."

"Could be trap at armory," Jak stated.

"Only one way to find out," Ryan said. He lifted the Heckler & Koch until its length was parallel to his good eye. He felt the unfamiliar weight of the blaster, adjusting his balance for what was to come. "Dead end ahead. Two blind corners each way. Shitty odds, but all we've got. J.B., keep our asses covered."

"You bet."

"Careful, lover," Krysty whispered. "Even more than usual. This is more than just that…"

Without answering, the one-eyed man steeled himself and launched into the corridor. He hunched into himself to make a smaller target and threw himself across the breadth of the corridor, spraying covering fire first one way and then the other, twisting with a suppleness born of many close-combat situations. He was relying on the fact that any sec men gathered on either side of the junction would not want to fire at random for fear of hitting their compatriots facing them. They would want to aim carefully, and his covering fire should cause just enough confusion to prevent that. And maybe take out a few of them at the same time.

Ryan came to rest against the wall of the corridor, the repeated blasts of the Heckler & Koch still reverberating in his ears, ringing through the empty corridor.

"Fireblast!" he exclaimed under his breath. The corridor was empty on either side for as far as he could see.

He looked across at his companions. They were staring at him with as much bewilderment as he felt.

Ryan shrugged. "Empty. The whole redoubt seems bastard empty. What's going on?"

"Like fighting ghosts," Jak said, stepping into the corridor.

"Mebbe that's the idea," the Armorer said, bringing up the rear of the party and not allowing his watchfulness to slacken.

"That would make sense with what I can feel." Krysty rubbed her brow, sweeping back the flaming hair that clung tightly to her. "They're hanging back on purpose, just waiting for us."

"Why don't they just come out with it and try to chill us?" Ryan cursed. It occurred to him that Krysty had been right when she said that they should beware of people who didn't think the same way. Just what were the tactics at work here?

Doc resheathed his sword and leaned on the stick.

"I have a supposition. It may be the ravings of a fool, but I truly believe that they wish to keep us alive."

"When we've chilled three, mebbe four of their people? Doesn't make sense." J.B. shook his head.

"To us, perhaps not," Doc said. "However, we are not cognizant of whatever reason they may have for keeping us alive."

Remembering the perverse habits of some of the barons they had come across, and the trade in body parts that had centered around old military installations, it was not a thought on which to dwell.

"Stupes may not be so stupe after all," Ryan murmured. "The only thing we can do is keep moving to the armory, then be on triple red for an ambush. Seems to be the only place it can happen."

They advanced in line, still keeping alert. In all their travels they had yet to come across a redoubt where the vanadium-steel sec doors could be closed in any other way than by punching in the code on the wall-mounted panels. It seemed unlikely, then, that they could be trapped by their enemies sealing off a section of corridor by remote triggering of the doors. Then again, they'd never jumped into a redoubt that had a population that was actually maintaining it, or seemed to have any idea how the old comp systems worked.

All the corridors were deserted. The only signs of life were the detritus of people moving out in a hurry: a clipboard and pen that lay on the floor; another mop and bucket similar to the one belonging to the chilled maintenance man; a frayed and worn service cap, with a threadbare insignia.

It seemed obvious that whoever commanded the redoubt had pulled out all personnel to some secure place without sounding an alarm. That indicated a strong sense of discipline among that personnel.

By the time they reached the location of the armory, all of them were feeling strung out. The complete silence was unnerving. In other redoubts it had been normal, but here—where they knew the redoubt was still a base of some kind—the silence was eerie.

The sec door to the armory was raised. From their oblique approach angle, Ryan could see into the room. It appeared unoccupied, the ranks and boxes of blasters, grens and ammunition undisturbed by human presence.

There was, however, still half of the armory that was hidden from view by the angle.

"Too quiet," Jak mouthed into Ryan's ear. "Too empty. Want us there."

Every instinct told Ryan that Jak was correct. The armory, too, was deserted.

Dean stated what they were all thinking. "If it is empty, that's 'cause they want us in there. Once we're in there, we're trapped."

All it would take would be the release of the sec door to the armory, and all seven of them would be trapped inside. They'd have all the weapons in the redoubt, but it wouldn't do them any good against being starved to death, or gassed by a nerve gren or by some kind of nerve-gas supply fed into the air circulation. From bitter experience they all knew that no gren or plas-ex could penetrate the vanadium steel—always assuming that they could have survived the impact blast from inside the armory. Or that it wouldn't trigger off every other gren, shell, cartridge or piece of plas-ex in there.

"Simple solution," J.B. told them. "Half of us stay here on watch. At least that way some of us will stay on the outside."

"Mebbe," Ryan answered. "But mebbe that just leaves us trapped in different ways and our forces halved. Better we stay together right now."

"But for what?" Krysty asked with a shiver. "We've come up against some real evil, but this is triple weird. This is just so...so innocent somehow. There's no sense of pleasure in chilling going on here."

As she spoke, they became aware of the rumble of heavy wheels on the concrete floor, and the high whine of an electric engine.

"Krysty, there's nothing innocent about that baby," Mildred husked in an awed voice as a bizarre wag turned the far corner of the corridor.

IN THE WEAPONS-DEVELOPMENT lab, Gen Wallace perched his enormous bulk on the groaning stool, its wheels squeaking in protest as he rocked the stool back and forth. His fingers hovered nervously over the keyboard, using the keys to guide the remote wag. It hadn't been used for several generations, and it was only thanks to the continued diligence of the weapons-development team that the wag still worked. They hadn't actually developed any weapons for five generations, but the blueprints left by their ancestors were used to assiduously strip and clean all the weapons in their possession. It was their task and purpose. That was how it was in the good book.

Murphy spurned the use of tech weapons, claiming that they would be useless on the outside, and that blasters and a well-drilled sec corps were the only essentials.

Wallace furrowed his brow. Where was Murphy now? Unconscious, maybe chilled, on a concrete floor.

And the outsiders he wanted so badly... Murphy would have chilled them. Wallace wanted them alive. They were recyclable. Especially the old man. He seemed perfect for the mechanism.

The vid screen flickered above the terminal the Gen was using. In shaky black and white, reverberating in time with the movement of the wag, Wallace could see the seven people standing by the open armory door. He knew he had guessed right. They needed blasters, and he had used that need to trap them. That was why he was the Gen.

They were frozen in disbelief for a fraction of a second. Then the one-eyed man in front and the man with spectacles at the rear raised their blasters. The black woman, the one with the strange hair, the boy, the albino and the old man—yes, the all-important old man—stood between.

Gen Wallace stopped the wag and grasped the hand-held microphone that stood by the terminal. He thumbed a switch.

"You people. You will obey the regs and put your blasters on the floor. Hands on heads, then follow the wag. No harm will befall you. We come in peace. It is imperative that we have full and fruitful discussions."

He saw the one-eyed man shout something and open fire with the Heckler & Koch. The sec camera was obviously hit, as the screen went black.

Wallace sighed. Why did they do this? Didn't they know the regs stated all resistance was futile? He keyed in a comp code.

"BACK," RYAN YELLED.

"Back where?" J.B. asked. "Damn redoubt corridors don't have any cover."

"Past the last sec door, John," Mildred cried, passing the Armorer and pulling at his arm. "Maybe they're like all other soldiers and pencil the code under the punch plate."

J.B. figured Mildred had a point—that was usually how they found the sec codes of some doors in redoubts.

"Worth a try," Ryan yelled over the chatter of his Heckler & Koch as he emptied the clip at the wag. "It's the only way we can outdistance this thing, buy some bastard time."

He ejected the clip and inserted another from the meager supply he'd removed from Panner's corpse. It seemed to him that they were doing nothing but react. They had to turn the situation around and act, get these soldiers on the run.

"Dad, get down!" Dean yelled as he saw the drum

rise from the center of the wag. It looked like a circle of blasters on a rotating wheel, which began to rapidly spin.

Ryan dived as the rotating wheel spit fire. He felt a plucking at his clothes, small objects whistling past his ears and through his hair.

Krysty screamed behind him. He tried to turn, but movement was sluggish. His vision narrowed.

Trank darts.

His last conscious thought was that someone wanted very badly to take them alive.

What reason could prompt that risk?

Chapter Four

Dean Cawdor was sure that there was something wrong. It was night, and he was making his way across the marshy grasses that separated the boys' dormitories from those of the girls.

That was weird; in all his time at the Nicholas Brody School, he couldn't recall the area between the dormitories being such a swamp. It hadn't been such a long trek, either. Dean's calf muscles ached, each step tearing at them and sapping his strength. He ground his teeth as he pulled a foot out of the sucking earth and moved on.

The girls' dormitory seemed to fall farther into the distance the longer he walked. His breath came in rasps, and his chest felt as though it were about to burst, a burn crossing his lungs with each painful intake of air.

The more he thought about it, the more bizarre it seemed. He had no idea why he was doing this. Trying to think as hard as possible, to concentrate as much as he could while the distractions of searing lungs and tearing muscles pulled at the edges of his mind, Dean knew that something was wrong.

Was it a nightmare?

No, not that... Dean didn't dream with such clarity. His muscles never ripped and tore in his dreams, and his lungs never felt as though they would explode in his chest as if someone had rammed a gren down his throat.

Vaguely, plucking at the corners of his mind, he could remember the redoubt and what had followed. When he reached the point where the trank darts were fired at him, everything descended into blackness....

Until now. So how did he get here? It certainly wasn't an ordinary dream.

"HIS REM IS GOING totally crazy, Gen. I think we should pull him out before the kid ruptures something."

Gen Wallace fixed the tech with a gaze that spoke of barely suppressed fury. Murphy, watching from a few paces back, noted the way that the small man quailed at the Gen's stare. He seemed to visibly shrink. It was something in the way Wallace looked at you: There was a mixture of ice and fire in that gaze, like the barely controlled impassive skin over a raging volcano of fury. The thought of being the agent that unleashed it wasn't pleasant. Murphy screwed his face into a wry grin, or something close. A genetic problem had resulted in numb facial muscles, so they didn't respond too well. Inbreeding. At least it was minor compared to many.

Murphy switched his attention from Wallace and the tech to the kid on the couch. He suppressed a shiver as his view took in the boy, stretched naked on the PVC-covered foam rubber that molded to the contours of his body. Not that you could see much of him under the trailing mess of wires and electrodes that covered his body, attached to the skin by guar-gum pads that occasionally slipped on the sweaty surface of the boy's twitching skin. The wires entwined across the floor until they reached the opened back of a small comp console that sparked ominously with faint crackles.

This part of the old R&D facility was populated by some of the geekiest specimens Murphy had ever seen. The tech who had just been stared down by the Gen, for example. He was a small, hunchbacked man with a squeaky voice—whiny and irritating even after a few words—who stood at barely four feet tall. His white coat trailed across the floor, and the sleeves were turned up several times so that his tiny hands could poke out of the ends. But worst of all from Murphy's point of view, the geek tech was wearing thickly lensed glasses that still didn't seem strong enough for his vision, as he squinted heavily when he stared at Wallace.

That could account for the sparking and crackling terminals. Although it was almost sacrilege to think, Murphy felt certain that the techs weren't learning anything new, and whatever was supposed to be passed down the family lines was somehow going astray.

Murphy doubted that Wallace would get whatever he wanted from any of these outsiders. Chances were that they would be killed on these machines before the Gen learned anything.

Murphy looked at the kid, jerking and twitching underneath the skein of wire.

He wouldn't last long.

IT TOOK EVERY OUNCE of strength, stubbornness and sheer determination that Dean had, but he finally crossed the swampy grasslands and reached firm earth that felt as hard and smooth as metal beneath his feet.

So far, so good. Dean had no idea why he was doing this, but he was driven by some inner message that pushed him on by instinct.

The night was cold and still, and he could almost see the steam rise from his hot, sweating body by the fallow light of the shrouded moon as he made his way across the earth toward the three-story blockhouse that constituted the girls' dormitory. A veranda ran around the length of the building, with stanchions at each corner that would allow him a swift and easy ascent. Even with the pains that still flowed like the blood through his legs, pulsing in time with his hammering heart.

Almost counting between breaths to keep some sort of rhythm to his actions, Dean trotted across the empty expanse of earth that stood before the building, keeping an eye out for the guards. Yet it was quiet. Too quiet. Not even the cry of the whippoorwill disturbed the air.

Why was there no one else around?

"WHAT DOES THIS MEAN?" Wallace snapped.

The tech squinted at the flickering monitor, where various lines were changing pattern and tone at a rapid rate. He glanced up at the Gen. It was hard for Murphy to discern anything on the strange little face, but he was sure there was an aura of fear.

"I, uh, I'm not too sure, sir. We don't usually register such readings when we run tests."

"Do you run tests on subjects, then?" Murphy asked, trying to keep the sarcasm out of his voice.

The geek tech shot Murphy a glance of pure venom. "There aren't any subjects as a rule," he muttered in his high, penetrating voice. "We only run simulations."

Wallace snapped the technician's head around to him with a blow from the flat of his hand. His fat jowls wobbled in fury. "You mean that we could lose these outsiders?"

The tech shrugged. "I don't think so...."

THE ROOF on the veranda was made of sheets of corrugated metal that allowed any rainwater to flow into the eaves troughs that had given Dean easy foot-and-handholds. The roof was steeply angled, but the corrugation made it relatively easy for him to scramble up, even though his aching calf muscles protested.

Clinging to the rough texture of the dormitory's outside wall, the youth steadied his breathing and counted the number of windows. Three along would bring him to where Phaedra was waiting. It seemed a long time since he had left the school with his father and their companions. A long time since he had seen Phaedra, and since she had kissed him, stirring feelings in him that were still strange.

Stranger still was the fact that, despite he was clinging on to the outside of an out-of-bounds building at a school he no longer attended, with aching muscles that felt as though they could give way at any moment, and that he could be discovered by the guards Brody employed as much to keep the sexes apart as to keep the school safe from outside marauders, Dean felt safe. As if he were coming home to a safe place.

Third window along. Dean edged his way across the veranda roof until he was directly underneath. The tip of his nose could touch the sill, and as the window was open it was a simple matter to push it up and then lift himself up over the sill and into the room.

Inside, Dean was immediately aware that things were, once again, not as they should be. The room was larger than those he remembered, and cleaner. There was virtually nothing in the room except one bed, square against the wall opposite the window. Strange—there were at least two occupants to each room in the dormitory buildings. So why was this different?

The bed was covered with an insect net, draped over

the poles that held the net four feet above the bed, like a canopy, and falling to the floor, gathering in a pool around the feet of the bed.

"Dean? Is that you, come back again?"

Dean's heart raced, but not from exertion. It was Phaedra's voice, just as he remembered.

"I guess it is," he said slowly, trying to control his breathing. "I don't know exactly how I got here, but..."

"It doesn't matter," she replied, cutting across him. "The important thing is that you're here now, and it's safe."

Dean wanted to speak, but some instinct stopped him. Why should she use a word like *safe?* He'd been thinking that, sure, but why would Phaedra say it?

The net over the bed stirred, and was pushed aside. Phaedra emerged from the misty depths, and Dean caught his breath as she rose from the bed and stood in front of him. Her long hair fell perfectly straight, parted in the middle and tumbling over her shoulders and down over her breasts. She was naked, and Dean felt stirrings within him that were still new enough to be alien.

Phaedra stepped forward.

"I knew you'd come back one day, Dean. Back to where it's safe."

She held out her hand. Dean hesitated, then raised his own arm to take her hand.

Again why would she say *safe?*

As Dean's fingers were about to brush against Phaedra's, some instinct made him suddenly pull back his hand.

She immediately changed. Her face hardened, seemed to grow old and lined in front of him. She opened her mouth, and instead of speech nothing emerged but a harsh and sibilant hiss, like a stickie that was about to attack. Her hair seemed to disappear without Dean noticing where it had gone, and her hands grew the ugly suckers typical of the mutie stickies. Her open mouth was filled with sharp, needle-point teeth, and he could smell her fetid breath across the short distance between them.

Although the sudden transformation was shocking, Dean showed the same sharp reactions that had kept his father alive for many long hard years traversing the Deathlands, and snapped onto his back heel, throwing his balance back to roll with the attack. Phaedra—or whatever it was that had pretended to be her—came forward and pitched into him. He used the creature's momentum and his own back-foot balance to throw it over his head.

The creature hit the wall behind with a sickening thud. They were close enough for it to lose none of the initial momentum, and so it hit the hard surface with some force—enough to knock plaster off the wall in chunks, dust filling the air. Dean coughed, tears filling his eyes and blurring his sight.

He swore under his breath, not wanting to shout and risk taking in another lungful of dust.

The stickie came at him, rising from the floor as though it had merely brushed the wall. It hissed and spit at him, rushing at him with arms flailing.

Dean backed up and readied himself in a combat stance, prepared to take the creature. He blocked one wild swing of its arm and followed with a straight-handed thrust at the stickie's exposed right side. He felt his fingers penetrate the soft flesh with a sickening squelch, and he jerked his hand free as quickly as possible, determined not to get stuck in the creature. It yelped in fear and pain, pulling back, its thin blood spewing out of the ragged wound.

Anger, the fear and the pain were just about discernible in the black and glistening eyes as it gave a cry and rushed for Dean once again.

Why, he thought, casting a glance around, was there never anything around to be used as a makeshift weapon when a person really needed it?

It was a momentary lapse of total concentration that his father would never have made: Dean's youth and inexperience teaching him a harsh lesson.

The stickie was on him a split second before he was fully prepared. The flailing arms were just a touch too quick for his defenses, and one of the hands glanced across his face, the blow pulling at his flesh and scoring it.

The pain spurred Dean into complete concentration. He had to end this, and end it now. He lowered himself and dived in underneath the flailing arms, pushing against the stickie with all the power he could muster from his aching calf muscles. It was enough to drive them back against the wall. Dean was ready for the impact, and gritted his teeth as the impact jarred every bone in his body. He heard the sickening crunch of splintering bone, the thin snapping sounds of the stickie's ribs giving way and the high, fluting whine of its cries of pain.

Every breath driven from its unprepared body, it sank to the floor, stunned, as Dean stepped back.

The youth ignored the aches of his own body and focused his attention on the task at hand. While the stickie was still sitting, dazed, Dean stepped forward and took its head in his hands. Tensing his muscles, he jerked the head sharply to the right, and then to the left.

He heard the snapping of its neck a millisecond before the cry of pain and surprise that was wrung from its throat. The light in its eyes dimmed swiftly and faded.

As Dean stepped back, it was no longer a stickie. There, in front of him, with her neck broken and her naked body covered in weals and bruises, blood running over her belly to pool between her thighs, was Phaedra.

Dean howled in anguish.

"THE KID'S GOING CRAZY," yelled the small tech as Dean's jerking, howling body lifted itself off the couch, pulling wires and electrodes from his body, the tangles and terminals coming out of the comp console with an alarming amount of sparks and crackles. A small fire broke out, doused immediately by an alarmed whitecoat with a high-domed forehead and bug eyes. She was completely bald, with her front teeth missing. It would seem that she also had a cleft palate, as she uttered a worried yet incomprehensible noise.

The only calm personnel in the room were Murphy and Wallace. Sarj Murphy studied the Gen very closely.

"Desist this ridiculousness. The good book dictates calm in times of emergency, and I will have calm."

Wallace's voice rose almost imperceptibly in volume as he got to the end of the statement, but the increase was accentuated by the sudden silence that descended on the room, broken only by the hum and buzz of the still fizzling terminals.

Murphy couldn't help but be impressed. And worried. This would be a formidable foe.

"Bring the outsider back," Wallace continued in quiet, authoritative tones.

"I'm not sure if we can.... At least, not that quickly," the geek tech said absently, squinting heavily at where Dean had subsided back onto the couch. His eyes were moving wildly behind the closed lids, and his breathing was labored and shallow.

"I think you will," Wallace said simply.

"Sir." The tech snapped to attention, something in Wallace's voice reminding him of his position.

Murphy, on the other hand, was dubious. And if the kid didn't survive, what hope was there for the old man who lay in the next sick bay, similarly wired up?

"NOT LIKE THIS, Doc. Frightening."

"Worry not, my sweet. There is no puzzle to which there is not a solution, if you care to think of it. Be it logical or lateral, there is always a path that can be followed."

"Don't look to me like there are any paths here at all." Lori looked at Doc Tanner with wide and uncomprehending eyes.

Doc sighed. It was ever the way that Lori, as sweet as she was, failed to understand the simplest allusion. He cared deeply for the girl—a fellow waif in a strange land—but couldn't help but find her obtuseness, at times, irritating.

They were standing in a dark cavern, the only light— if it could be called such—a faint phosphorescent glow from the rocks around them. The cavern seemed to stretch away into an unspecific and threatening darkness, a feeling of fear that was in no way alleviated by the faint roar of a distant gale and the odor of old, burned flesh that hung over them like a curtain.

The pearl handle of Lori's Walther PPK .22 blaster glowed softly as it picked up the reflection of the rocks. Her long blond hair framed her glittering eyes. Doc could see little else of her in the darkness, but as they advanced a few steps he could hear the clicking of her high heels on the rock floor.

In the mind of Dr. Theophilus Tanner, reason struggled to gain the upper hand over the encroachment of fear. Doc knew that the others considered him crazy, sometimes tipping into incoherence. The simple fact was that they were correct. He had seen things and been through mind- and body-wrenching experiences that no one else had shared. And it was unlikely that anyone else would.

He shuddered involuntarily as he remembered things he had seen when the scientists of Operation Chronos had tried to shut him up. He remembered the mewling mess that had been Judge Crater. Perhaps he would have been better dead than to end up like this, prone to lapses into insanity. For a man with Doc's intelligence, it was a strain to know that he walked a narrow ledge between coherence and madness. He had once heard someone say that stupidity had saved many a man from madness. Perhaps that was true.

"Doc, what we gonna do?"

Doc was jolted back to the moment. He looked at Lori, peering through the darkness to focus on her.

"I said, what we gonna—"

"I know, my dear. I heard you the first time. My grasp on sanity may be a little tenuous at times, but my hearing has not suffered. As to the action I propose we take, I would suggest that the best course of action at the present time is to actually take no action."

Lori giggled. "You're crazy, Doc."

Doc smiled to himself but refrained from comment. Slowly, in his mind, the fragments of the puzzle were assembling themselves into a whole. He remembered the fat, evil-looking woman whose throat he had sliced in twain. He remembered the attempt to escape from the redoubt, and the signs of a sudden evacuation by the staff. And then there were the trank darts fired from the strange vehicle.

And now he was here.

With Lori?

Doc felt the weight of the LeMat in his hand, and knew that it was primed to be fired. In his other hand he held the swordstick. It was a sign to him of the changes that had occurred in his life that he, an academic by vocation, no longer felt safe unless he had a weapon or two at hand. Particularly now.

Particularly as, although she was standing next to him, he knew that Lori had been dead for no little time.

Doc was about to speak when a blast of air hit him like a solid blow to the solar plexus, doubling him over and driving the breath from his body. He was aware of Lori screaming, her shrill voice mixing into the roar of the gale as it hit them.

With a sickening realization, Doc knew that they were facing a foe worse than any baron, scavenger or mutie. They were facing the implacable force of nature gone wild, distorted by the rad blast of skydark.

It was a foe against which all weapons were useless.

"Doc! Help me...."

"THE OLD DUDE IS looking a bit wired," remarked Pri Firclas Baker, scratching his head and noting idly that he'd made his tender scalp bleed again, a tuft of hair caught under his nail.

"It's nothing we can't handle," snapped the willowy woman who was the end of a long line of techs for this section. By some fluke, Dr. Tricks was an almost perfect specimen of womanhood. A throwback to a cleaner, less rad blasted gene pool, she had flowing raven hair and sharp, classical features with high cheekbones. As a result she was the target of lustful attention from every male in the redoubt. At first Gen Wallace had high hopes of using Tricks to start a new gene pool and eradicate some of the problems of inbreeding and mutie infiltration.

Until he discovered the one flaw in Tricks's otherwise immaculate makeup: she was sterile. He ruled that she was out-of-bounds. If she couldn't breed, then he didn't want his men wasting their seed on her.

It didn't stop them trying, which made her weary of the attention.

It also made any male soldiers assigned to her section slack in their attention to detail. Baker had been commanded by Wallace to inform him of any change in the old man's signs. He was too busy watching Tricks move around the lab to really pay much attention to the way in which the monitor screen was registering a rapid variety of signals. Like Dean, studied so carefully in the next room, Doc had REM that was going crazy, and sweat poured from his body as the muscles twitched beneath his skin.

"Don't you think you should go and tell the Gen what's happening here?" Dr. Tricks said archly.

"No, it's nothing," Baker replied without giving the monitors a second glance. "The old dude'll probably kick it, but so what?"

"I'm not so sure that the Gen will see it that way," Tricks warned.

"Screw him."

"Brave words when he's not here."

"Screw him. Although I'd rather screw you."

Tricks sighed as Baker moved toward her, and she

reached for the small, palm-sized stun gun she'd taken from the R&D repository some time back for just such an occasion. But despite this distraction, she still kept an eye on Doc, who had started to make small whining noises in the back of his throat.

THE WIND HAD BUFFETED Doc until he was huddled into a corner of the cavern, hunched into a fetal position, trying to protect as much of his aching body as was possible from the sheer force of the air and the myriad small pebbles and specks of dust and dirt that whipped and stung against exposed skin. His eardrums hurt where the roar of the wind drove pressure against them until he felt that they would burst.

And yet he could still hear Lori screaming over the roar of the wind. It was so plaintive, so helpless, that it overrode Doc's desire to protect his eyes and ears. He looked up, screwing up his eyes to try to cut down on the amount of dust that could tear at them. The force of the wind was such that his eyes dried almost immediately, and he blinked painfully.

The phosphorescence provided enough light for him to see that Lori had been blown along almost to a point where she was hidden by the encroaching maw of darkness. She was clinging to the rocks, her clothes almost torn from her body, dark flecks on her skin showing where the flesh had been ripped, raising bloody weals.

Perhaps it was his imagination. Perhaps it was his conscience. Whatever, Doc was sure that he could see a pleading light in her eyes, despite the fact that logically he shouldn't be able to tell from this distance, in these conditions.

He knew that if he didn't go to help her, then she would surely die.

And yet she was already dead. Doc knew that. He could recall with an awful clarity the nightmares he still suffered where he saw her consumed by flames. Lori was dead. She couldn't be here. Yet she was.

And he couldn't fail her again.

As BAKER ADVANCED on Tricks, Doc gave a loud yell and almost lifted himself off the couch.

"I really think you'd better get the Gen," Tricks said softly as Baker turned in shock. "I think he's ready."

IT WAS ALMOST impossible to describe the sensation of moving against that implacable gale. It was like drowning in air, yet the stones and dirt that whipped against him made it at times seem like fighting against a moving, living wall of rock. And still Doc pressed on, his wiry frame pushing every ounce of strength he had into forward progress.

He got to within a few yards of Lori before he looked up again. What he saw made his dry eyes fill with tears, caused him to pull up dead.

There were now three figures being blown into the maw of the tunnel. Lori wasn't one of them.

"Emily?" he whispered. Doc felt as though any sanity he might be clinging to was about to be severed, driven from him by the vision that was now before his eyes: his wife and children being thrown into the darkness by the roar of the gale.

And then the greatest contradiction of all hit him: how could he be fighting against a howling wind that was blowing his family in the opposite direction? Many things in nature had changed since skydark, but not something as fundamental as this.

Doc dropped to his knees and howled.

MILDRED SHOOK her head, her beaded plaits swaying about her shoulders.

"No way. It just can't be."

The doctor sitting opposite her smiled sadly. "You know something, Mildred? If you were sitting here right now, where I am, you wouldn't be in the slightest surprised by what you're doing."

Mildred fixed him with a stare. "Come on, you're not telling me that I haven't got a valid point. More than anyone else you have sitting here, I know that an initial diagnosis can be misleading...."

"Listen to yourself, Mildred. It's typical denial. We've run a full series of tests. You have a cyst. It's not major, and it can easily be removed. There won't be a problem."

Mildred sat back and looked out of the window at the freeway beyond the hospital entrance. All of a sudden she felt so lonely. Everyone out there seemed so carefree, so untroubled by an invasion of possibly hostile cells within their own body.

"Mildred?"

She turned back to the doctor opposite. Strange, but he seemed to know her well, judging by his attitude, yet she couldn't remember ever seeing him before.

"I'm sorry." She smiled. "I was just..."

He nodded in a typically medical manner. So understanding, yet also so impersonal. "Don't worry about it, Mildred. It won't be a difficult procedure. In fact, we could do it right now."

Before Mildred had a chance to react, he pressed a buzzer on his desk, and she heard the oak double doors behind her swing open. She spun in her chair to see, with some shock, a fully operational surgery in the room she was sure had been a reception when... When she came in?

Mildred turned back. "Wait a second here. Don't rush me on this. I—"

She stopped dead. The doctor was dressed in a surgeon's gown, but instead of a surgical mask and cap, he was wearing a Ku Klux Klan hood.

"You're not getting your hands on me, motherfucker," Mildred growled angrily, springing to her feet. But any attempts to escape were stalled by the iron grip of two men who appeared behind her, seemingly from nowhere, to grasp her firmly by the arms. Glancing over her shoulder, she could see that both men also wore surgical gowns and Klan hoods.

"What's this about?" she demanded, conserving any energy for an attempt at escape when their grip was relaxed.

"Simple. We're going to remove your cyst. But as you may have a reaction to the anesthetic, we're going to dispense with it."

Mildred felt a cold sweat break out down her spine. From the tone of his voice, she knew that he meant every word. They were going to operate without an anesthetic. For the fun of it. The shock would probably kill her.

The two men dragged Mildred into the operating room and pulled her onto the operating table. Not for one second did they release their grip. Mildred tried to struggle as she was hauled across the table, but to no avail. They remained completely implacable.

When she was on the table, one of them took full control of her, holding her down with incredible strength while the other secured her hands and feet with restraining straps. She kicked out at him, catching him under the chin and snapping his head back with a force that should have rendered him unconscious.

He didn't even pause in his actions.

When Mildred was secured on the table, the doctor walked into the operating room with an almost obscenely casual air, humming gently to himself. He was carrying a tar-and-gas torch—she could tell by the mixed odor in the otherwise sterile atmosphere.

The sweat gathered in a tiny pool at the small of her back. The smell of the torch reminded her of her father, and the way he burned inside his church. She could imagine him, praying for his soul as the Klansmen gathered outside, watching the building burn. She could imagine his prayers, desperate for his own life but still pleading for forgiveness against the scum who were killing him slowly and painfully.

With a flick of an expensive gold lighter, the doctor lit the torch, which crackled and flared into life. The heat was noticeable even from several yards.

"If we're not going to use an anesthetic, the least we can do is cauterize the wound," the doctor said, his eyes laughing behind his Klan hood.

One of the others picked up a scalpel and advanced toward her. He ripped off her clothes and poised the scalpel, which caught the light of the torch and flickered over her.

Mildred, knowing she was completely powerless and doomed, gave in to her frustration and fear, and screamed.

"I THINK SHE'S about ready. Go and tell the Gen."

The guard nodded at the tech, and turned to leave the room. When he reached the door, it was opened by Murphy.

"Sir, the woman has reached a state of readiness. I was just about to report to the Gen, sir."

Murphy nodded. "Good. The old man and the boy are still alive. And now she's ready. The mutie albino outsider seems impervious, but I guess no process is foolproof."

The tech, feeling that the R&D department was once again being impugned by the Army, was about to say something when a warning glance from the guard silenced him.

The hell with it. Let the Army thugs think what they liked. The outsiders' resistance to interrogation had been reduced to virtually zero in a fraction of the time their heavy-handed methods would take.

"Army bastard," the tech muttered as Murphy and the guard left. The insult was wasted on the unconscious Mildred, but it made the tech feel better.

Chapter Five

Ryan was back in Front Royal, and all hell was about to break loose.

The one-eyed man was in a gaudy house even more run-down than those he usually encountered on the trek across the Deathlands. The old stone walls were scarred and pitted with the marks of a hundred bottles, a thousand fights. Dried blood stained patches of old plaster that the gaudy proprietor hadn't bothered to clean. Perhaps he figured that the marks would serve as a deterrent to anyone fool enough to start another brawl.

Guess he was going to be wrong. The almost deserted "reception" area, where an ugly and multiscarred barkeep served drinks to waiting customers, was occupied by three bored-looking sluts of indeterminate age and two drunken men who looked far past the point where they would be able to perform. And then there was Ryan.

Try as he might, the one-eyed man couldn't recall exactly how he had reached this place. Through a vague fog of memory he could remember the redoubt, the escape and the strange machine firing trank darts. And then?

And then this. He looked at the glass in his hand, filled with a spirit that tasted as foul as the glass looked, and wondered how many he had downed before becoming aware he was in a gaudy house.

Just looking at the glass seemed to be all the cue one of the drunks needed.

"Hey, you, One eye," he yelled across the room.

Ryan tried to ignore him. No point looking for trouble. It was obviously looking for him. Just let it come and roll with it. It wouldn't take long.

"Shit, the fucker's deaf, as well as half-blind," the other drunk yelled, directing the comment at Ryan.

The one-eyed man turned to face them, taking them in and weighing their possible danger areas. The one who started the exchange was tall and skinny, no more than 140 pounds and over six feet tall. He had long, loose, lean limbs, his arms dangling at his sides as he swayed gently in a drunken haze with an idiot grin on his face. An old steel bayonet, rusted but still lethal, hung from his belt. His eyes held a mean gleam.

His companion was about six inches shorter, and fifty pounds heavier. All of it was muscle. He had a home-made knife in his belt, jagged metal attached to a wooden handle with wire. It looked more like a tool than a weapon, but still lethal enough. Like the taller man, he was dressed in cutoff jeans that were stiff with oil, dirt and sweat. Both wore heavy combat boots that, perversely, seemed to be immaculately maintained. The men were naked from the waist up, which only served to draw Ryan's attention to the blaster that hung off the squat drunk's shoulder.

It was a Heckler & Koch G-12 caseless rifle, like the one that had served Ryan well for more years than he cared to remember.

So they were armed, and they outnumbered him two-to-one. But he was sober and had more weapons.

Unconsciously his hand traveled to where his panga was sheathed. A tremor of surprise shot through him when he realized it wasn't there. Neither, now that he came to consider it, could he feel the comfortable weight of the SIG-Sauer or Steyr SSG-70.

So they outnumbered him and he was unarmed. The odds had shifted. Ryan felt a charge go through his body as his adrenaline level rose, and he shifted gears to adjust to the situation.

The bartender leaned across to him. "You pay for any damage caused if you live, fucker. Just like those scum pay if they live. House rules."

"Seems fair," Ryan said shortly. At least he could be fairly certain now that it wasn't three-to-one.

"Hey, I think One-eye wants to fight. Mebbe he can only see one of us 'cause he's only got one eye," the skinny drunk yelled.

As a witticism it wasn't much, but it was enough to make his companion laugh with such a ferocity that he spit a stream of alcohol across the floor, dribbling the remnants down his chin, belly and crotch.

It was just the break that Ryan needed to even the score. The interior of the gaudy was lit by a series of naked torches that hung from the walls. One of them was behind the bar, about halfway between Ryan and the drunks.

The one-eyed man sprang onto the rickety wooden board that served as a bar, his balance delicately poised as the groaning wood swayed beneath his weight. He reached across the head of the startled barkeep and grabbed the torch.

The two drunks were also baffled by this seemingly pointless move. Their surprise, and the alcohol haze, conspired to delay their reactions for just the necessary fraction of a second. If they had been sober, it would have been a close shave for Ryan.

As the skinny drunk drew the bayonet and threw it at Ryan, the one-eyed man realized the rusty metal may be badly maintained, but it was a fair bet that the rust was the result of staining by blood. Instinctively shifting the weight in his palm, the skinny drunk had thrown the bayonet so that the lethal point whistled past Ryan's ear. It nicked the skin and drew blood as the one-eyed warrior shifted his balance to pitch the torch seemingly into the middle of the floor.

The squat drunk was too busy unshouldering the Heckler & Koch to notice where the torch landed. The filthy floor had a line of damp leading a trail of spit alcohol, ending at a midpoint between the two drunks and where Ryan had initially been standing. The torch landed at that midpoint, the raw sugarcane alcohol igniting as the flames touched the dirt.

A tongue of blue flame shot along the floor and up the leg of the squat drunk. He'd drunk so much of the raw spirit that he didn't at first feel the pain as the flames scorched his skin and ignited on the old stained denim. He swung the rifle around to sight on Ryan, drawing on the trigger before the intense heat and pain penetrated his fogged consciousness, roasting his balls and making him squeal.

He moved back, trying to step away from the flames, beat at his burning crotch and fire at the one-eyed warrior all at the same time.

Bullets sprayed into the ceiling, bringing down plaster, wood chippings and dust. The three sluts, who had been watching with a mild disinterest, now screamed and disappeared faster than a rat down a hole.

The scrawny drunk had his attention distracted, and half turned to his friend. Ryan, however, didn't let anything deter him from his only course of action. He launched himself from the groaning bar and crashed into the thin drunk, taking him down. A battered plastic chair took the brunt of the impact, and Ryan felt rather than heard the crack of the drunk's elbow as it shattered on the metal frame of the chair.

Bones didn't usually break that easy, and Ryan rode his luck by following up while the drunk was disoriented and distracted by the pain. With the heel of his hand, he forced the man's chin back. A thin, wailing cry of surprise and pain escaped from the drunk's stretched throat. With his free hand Ryan chopped at the man's exposed Adam's apple. He felt cartilage crack beneath his granite hand.

The drunk choked and coughed blood. He was limp with shock, and it took Ryan just one twist to break the man's neck.

An angry cry from behind Ryan alerted him to the possibility that the squat drunk had become a danger once more. He rolled to one side to see the drunk coming toward him, holding the handmade knife. His legs were blistered and charred, and the denim appeared burned into his skin, but above the waist he seemed to have escaped damage from the fire. The rifle lay across the room, discarded in drunken anger.

Good. Ryan stayed calm, despite the adrenaline race of his pulse. The more angry an opponent, the more likely he was to make mistakes.

Like lunging at a man and committing his strength and balance to one direction, when his foe was moving in another.

With a wild yell the squat drunk threw himself toward Ryan, who moved back across the slumped corpse of the skinny drunk. His muscle-bound opponent wasn't expecting Ryan to head in that direction, so the knife hit empty dirt, sticking in the floor.

Momentarily confused, the squat drunk was torn between going after Ryan and retrieving his sole weapon. It was a mistake that enabled Ryan to spring to his feet. The squat drunk turned his head to see where his opponent was just in time to receive the toe of Ryan's combat boot at the point of his jaw. The bone shattered like delicate porcelain china, splintering in the drunk's face.

Ryan stepped back as the drunk hit the floor for the last time, and turned, expecting to see the barkeep ready to argue about the damages.

Instead he was greeted with a sight that made his senses reel. Harvey, his dead brother, the cause of so much trouble in Front Royal and the reason Ryan had been forced to leave the ville, stood behind the bar, flanked by sec men.

"Congratulations, Ryan. Now see what you can do against my boys...."

WALLACE AND MURPHY had left Dean, now disconnected from the comp, and stood over his father, watching the signs on the monitor.

"He's ready," Wallace said, nodding.

J.B. HAD THE WORST nightmare of his life come true. The Armorer was defenceless against a horde of stickies. All his weapons jammed. All his grens had refused to go off. His fedora was lost, as was his minisextant.

But most importantly of all, his spectacles had been knocked off at some point that he couldn't quite recall. So he was fumbling in a blurry mist.

Dark night, but he never lost his spectacles. It was

something he went out of his way to avoid, and he couldn't understand where or how they had gone missing. All he knew was that the Uzi had jammed as soon as he squeezed the trigger, the M-4000 scattergun had no cartridges and his capacious pockets were suddenly, mysteriously empty except for grens that failed to detonate. His knife was stuck in the body of the only stickie he had so far managed to chill. Stuck so hard that he couldn't move it, and couldn't waste time devoting his full attention to it as the horde of muties overran him.

J.B. couldn't even see where he was as they pinned him to the ground. He could smell their foul odor and feel the heat of their bodies as a multitude of suckered fingers grasped his body, wriggling obscenely across him as he was secured in a tight mass grip and lifted from the ground.

He felt the quality of the air change as he was lifted above their heads and carried along. The light increased, and he guessed that he had been sheltered somewhere, but was now out in the open. The landscape blurred as he was jarred up and down on the uneven ground. He could hear the debased chattering of the stickies as they moved en masse.

He struggled, even though he knew it was pointless. There were too many of them, their grip was too tight and he was severely impaired by the loss of his glasses. Despite this, his acute sense of survival impelled him to try. A slim-to-nothing chance was preferable to no chance at all. The Trader used to say that there was no such thing as no chance, only people who couldn't spot it.

As J.B. flexed his muscles, some of the stickies stumbled beneath him. One caught a foot on a stone and lost balance, careering into others, who also lost balance. Among the unintelligent creatures, this caused a mass panic, and J.B. was pitched forward into their midst.

He landed on his feet and hit the ground running. Vague shapes and blurs stood in his way, but were soon knocked aside by sharply aimed blows.

He was off and running, but didn't know where.

The ground was bumpy, stones rolling under his boots as he ran, trying desperately to put some distance between himself and the stickies. His breath came hard, and he could feel the blood pounding in his ears. It was pounding so hard that it took a few seconds for him to realise that he wasn't being followed. There was no sound from behind him.

That was even more worrying than being chased by the stickies.

What was stopping them from following? The answer came to him as he slowed. His feet began to sink into the marshy earth, which became more of a quagmire as he continued, dragging one painful leg after another, until his calf muscles began to tear.

"THAT'S REALLY INTERESTING, sir," the small tech said to Wallace.

"Is it? Explain, boy. This tech stuff isn't part of my duty."

Pulling back one of his sleeves so that his tiny hand could point to a series of flowing lines on the monitor, the tech turned to Wallace and Murphy.

"As you may know, sirs, our ancestors were in charge of developing new weaponry for the cold war between—"

"Spare the history lesson and cut to the chase, runt," Murphy snapped. "The military has work to do."

The tech sighed and continued in pained tones. "Well, before skydark and the great isolation and the time of recycling, there was only a certain amount of the preliminary work that was completed. There are only so many image stimuli that can be fed to the subject for them to feed and respond to. The idea of the swamp has been fed to this subject and the boy we were watching a while ago. And both seem to have interpreted this stimuli at different points in the cycle."

"So?" Wallace asked blankly.

"Well, it suggests... It... It's just kind of interesting to us down here, sir," the tech finished weakly.

"Son, it don't matter bodiddly-squat how they see it, as long as it gets us results," Wallace said blandly.

Murphy suppressed a smile. He still believed that his methods could have softened the outsiders with greater speed, but the Gen loved his toys.

Wallace turned to Murphy. "He's ready now. Just the red-haired bitch to go."

GAIA, BUT THESE NIGHTS were cold.

Krysty huddled into herself, trying to preserve some body warmth in the darkness. She could feel that her flowing red hair had tightened like a steel spring until it was close to her scalp, coiling tightly against her nape.

She didn't need this sign to tell her there was danger about. She could hear it in the rustling of the leaves, the scratching of the undergrowth as it moved, disturbed by the predators that were always just out of view.

They weren't human. She knew that because she had never heard any sec men or hunters who could move that quietly. If not for the fact that so long on the road had attuned her to danger, she would have taken the noises for nothing more than the movement of the night air.

But this night there was no movement. Despite the cold, it was as still as the hottest summer day. So still that the air seemed to solidify around her.

Krysty knew that she was on her own, that she was outnumbered. That the odds were against her making it to morning.

Even more so when she checked the pockets of the bearskin coat that, despite its bulk, was still failing to cut out the chilled air. Her Smith & Wesson Model 640.38 was with her, but there was no ammunition. And a blaster without ammo was as useless as a man with no dick in a gaudy house free-for-all.

The crescent moon cast little light, but there was enough to shine off the silver-winged falcons and points on her boots, and to catch her misted breath in the air. It was enough to cast shadows across the copse, where she sat on the rotted stump of a felled tree, and into the forest beyond. The forest rustled with barely concealed danger.

It briefly occurred to her that the danger came not from there but from something else. There was no reason why she should be alone and unarmed. There was no recollection of arriving here. None of it added up.

It flashed through her mind that the real danger was whatever was making her think she was at this place.

"NOW, THAT'S an interesting reaction," Dr. Tricks mused.

"In what way?" Murphy asked, using it as an excuse to move closer to her as he looked over her shoulder.

"You see these lines here?" she continued, ignoring his heavy-breathing presence and indicating a sudden flattening of the signal on the monitor. "It means a decrease of tension and adrenaline."

"So?"

"So, the clever little mutie is onto us. She may be as hard to crack as the albino."

Murphy smiled and put a hand on her shoulder. "You see, you R&D personnel always put too much trust in science. Brute force and ignorance is what wins battles. Always has been."

"We'll see."

KRYSTY KEPT HERSELF ALERT, despite the sudden doubts that sprang through her mind about the veracity of her senses.

To her left, just out of her range of vision, she heard an increase in rustling and spun to meet it.

"You?"

"Yes, me." Uncle Tyas McCann stepped into the sparse light of the moon. He looked just as he had when she had last seen him. How long ago was that now?

"Too long," he said, seeming to sense her thoughts, before breaking into a throaty chuckle.

Krysty's hair coiled even tighter, straining against the muscles of her neck. It was a little like him, sure, but there was something here that just didn't make sense. He was dead, and this—apparition, for want of another word—wasn't that much like him at all in the faint light.

"That's very perceptive of you," he replied to her thoughts. "You always were too damn smart, Krysty. Just like Sonja."

Tyas McCann never mentioned Sonja, either. Krysty's mother—perhaps dead, perhaps not—had always been a topic he would avoid.

Krysty stood, feeling the cold air invade her as the

movement drove the scant warmth from under her coat. She shivered, and not just from the cold.

"That's right. You should be very afraid, because this is a scenario that you can't control or defeat. You know your mind is being manipulated, and I'm here because I'm what you fear most of all."

"I never feared Uncle Tyas," Krysty replied, trying to keep a tremor of cold and fear from her voice.

"True. But then again, wouldn't that be your worst nightmare? For me to suddenly turn against you, to attack you? How would you react? Would you try to defeat me in order to save yourself?"

"Are you going to try to find out?"

He smiled. "You know the answer to that."

Krysty nodded, as much to herself as to the thing that called itself Tyas McCann. If what she suspected was true, then he couldn't harm her.

"Are you sure about that?" he asked.

"Try me."

Tyas smiled. It was harsh and evil, not at all like the man she remembered, which would make sense. If this was her nightmare, then he would be the opposite of the loving father figure she had once known.

Krysty stood perfectly still as he advanced upon her. If she was right, then nothing could really happen to her.

She closed her eyes and waited for the moment to come. With a roar of anger, Tyas McCann reached out and grasped her left arm. He wrenched and pulled with a barely controlled fury, twisting her arm at its socket. Krysty felt the tendons and muscles tear inside her arm, blood vessels exploding and veins and arteries rupturing.

With the sickening, crunching squelch of bone and

flesh mixed with the tearing of fabric and fur, Krysty's arm came off in Tyas McCann's hands. She opened her eyes to see him fling it away into the trees. There was a rustle, like animals descending on carrion.

She looked down at her exposed shoulder joint, blood pulsing onto the earth, steaming as her body temperature met the cold night air. She should feel pain, shock…but nothing penetrated her consciousness. She was perfectly calm.

Tyas McCann looked perplexed.

Krysty smiled. It was beatific. Even though she had not called upon the power of Gaia to give her strength, she could feel the energies running through her veins, helping her to see through her course of action.

Tyas McCann snarled at her and repeated the procedure on her right arm. Once again she heard the severing of the limb but felt nothing.

A haze began to descend over her, something that she put down to the loss of blood. Even though it wasn't her real physical self, or a real death, she knew that she had to see it through to the end. She had to call the bluff of whoever was playing with her mind.

"You will not fight?"

"I will not fear," she replied, her voice sounding distant in her own ears.

The darkest night slipped away into a blackness darker than anything she had ever imagined.

"SHE'S BEATEN THE COMP," Dr. Tricks remarked, watching the signals on the console.

Wallace pulled a face, his tightly pursing lips making his multiple chins wobble.

Tricks raised an eyebrow. "Two out of seven isn't bad." She looked at Krysty, naked and encased in a skein of wires and electrodes. Unlike everyone except Jak, Krysty had not one drop of perspiration on her body. "It's probably something to do with their mutie blood. I'd like to study them some more, Gen. The mutie outsider scum we usually get die very quickly. These show more resilience."

Wallace shook his head. "No deal. These will be recycled in another manner. They're necessary for my plans, and as Gen I pull rank on you every time, Doctor."

"Just what are your plans, sir?" Murphy asked.

"Now that they're suitably softened up, I want you to extract their backgrounds from them. Particularly the old one. He may be of the greatest use."

"If I may beg your indulgence and ask, sir, why didn't you just hand them over to me?"

Wallace fixed Murphy with a sneering stare that bespoke contempt. "Time is of the essence, Sarj. To get quick results you may have to harm them physically. And I cannot have that." He turned to survey Krysty with a cold, emotionless eye. "At least, not yet."

Chapter Six

The disorientation and mental stresses of the brain-washing process softened them all. It was distressingly, boringly easy for Murphy to interrogate them. The level of resistance was low, and some of them he hit just for fun. Particularly the one-eyed man, whose name he discovered was Ryan Cawdor.

The interrogation room was constructed just as Murphy's forefathers had wanted it: like something out of the crumbling pages of the books that he kept in his quarters and would sometimes thumb through. It made him feel more in touch with the world before skydark, the world on which his world view was based.

Ryan was tied to a metal chair with a cane seat. He was stripped naked, his hands bound behind the back of the chair, wrists pulled low so that his posture was slouched, his shoulders wrenched if he tried to move on the seat. It was a simple torture tactic, and one that didn't take a lot of effort while becoming quickly effective.

"It's quite simple, you murdering son of a bitch," Murphy said quietly, wiping the blood from the rings on his fingers after slapping Ryan backhanded. "You just tell me all about yourself, and I release you from the seat before your balls strain through the little holes. Uncomfortable, isn't it?" he continued, as Ryan tried to move on the seat and ease the pain that was starting to spread into his groin.

Ryan breathed deeply, using his iron will to control the pain. The scar that ran under the eye patch, from the empty socket and down his cheek to his jaw, was white and puckered, the flesh drained of blood as he gritted his teeth. He was storing up the resentment. If he ever got the chance, he'd finish Murphy. But he'd rather get out. One of the things the Trader taught him was the uselessness of bearing grudges. Concentrate too hard on that, and you wouldn't notice the enemy creeping up behind you.

Murphy watched Ryan through slitted eyes, trying to work out how far he could go. The one-eyed man was sitting beneath the only light in the room, directly above him. Murphy stood half in a pool of shadow. Behind him, obscured from Ryan's view, was an armed soldier. Murphy could watch his prisoner's reactions with clarity, but Ryan could see little beyond the pool of light in which he sat.

"You won't get anything from me," Ryan muttered, spitting blood from his torn mouth.

Murphy nodded. "You're a big man. You've proved to me how hard you are. Now let's get real. That kid, he looks like you, One-eye."

Ryan looked up. Slowly, trying to mask his concern.

It didn't work. Murphy grinned at him slyly. "Yeah, figured so. Your sprog, right? How'd you like him to be tied to the chair? I figure he's only...what, twelve? Thirteen? Maybe his balls ain't dropped yet. It'd be interesting to find out."

Ryan winced. In his mind he tried to weigh up the options. What would it lose them at this stage if he told this scum who he was? The redoubt seemed inbred and isolated, so the chances of them hearing about him were low.

A chance he would take to save Dean the pain.

"Fireblast, you win this round, fucker. What do you want to know?"

"Who you are. Why you're here. How come you can use the mat-trans. And the old guy is..."

Ryan's brow furrowed. Why were they so interested in Doc?

"LOOK LIKE SHIT," Jak said quietly.

"Feel like it, too," Ryan replied, stretching out on the bed, his legs apart to ease the pain that throbbed into his groin. The act of speaking opened up one of the cuts in the corner of his mouth.

Krysty took a pillowcase from one of the beds and wet it under the faucet before using a corner of it to dab gently at the edges of Ryan's mouth.

J.B. looked up at the sec camera over the door. They were all back in the room in which they had originally been confined. He pushed his fedora back on his head and scratched idly along his hairline, frowning.

"Got an idea, John?" Mildred asked quietly. She had been the most subdued since they had all awakened on the beds, and had so far kept quiet about her dreamlike experiences. The others had shared some details in order to try to work out what had happened to them.

J.B. shook his head. "No, I was just wondering what exactly it is they want from us."

"Guess find out soon," Jak commented, indicating Ryan with a curt nod of the head. "What they do with Krysty and Mildred?" he added.

"I'm sure they'll have thought of something," Mildred said bitterly.

Ryan raised himself on one elbow and told them exactly what had happened to him. When he had finished, Doc rose to his feet. He made as though to strike a lecturing pose, leaning on his cane, until he remembered that Murphy's men, once bitten, had taken it away from him.

Doc cleared his throat. "Their behavior is most perplexing. I think we can agree that our experiences while unconscious were an attempt to in some way play with our most primal fears, possibly with the notion of reducing our resistance."

Krysty nodded. "For some reason, it didn't affect Jak and myself in the same way as it did the rest of you. Perhaps there's some kind of mutated gene running in us that—"

"What they used to call psychological warfare, but taken up a notch," J.B. interrupted. "I saw some old vid once about it. They've got so much stuff in this redoubt, most of it in some kind of running order. Why not a comp of some kind that could show us our fears?"

"It worked all right," Ryan reflected. "I tried to hold out, but when Dean was threatened, I just caved in."

"You shouldn't worry about me," Dean cut in angrily. "I stand or fall as one of us like everyone else. Don't treat me like a kid."

"Point one, you *are* still a kid. Point two, Ryan's not saying he did it because of that. Are you, lover?" Krysty waited for Ryan to acknowledge before continuing, "The point is simply that he couldn't hold out because something in his mind wouldn't let him."

"And that worries me," Ryan said, looking at J.B., who returned his gaze.

"I'm with you there. If we get a chance to break, what's it going to do to us all?"

"May I offer the suggestion that the only way to find out is to actually make that break?" Doc mused slowly. "I would hazard a guess that part of the effect is simply to make us doubt ourselves."

"That makes sense," Mildred said with a nod.

Jak shrugged. "All talk, need action. Mebbe make some?" He glanced at Ryan.

The one-eyed man was about to answer when the door to the dormitory swung open, and Murphy stood in the doorway, flanked by two sec men. He had obviously learned a lesson from Panner's death, as both sec men had their blasters trained on the prisoners.

He pointed at Mildred. "You're next." He crooked his finger and beckoned her. "Come on, baby. Time to answer a few questions. If you answer them right, then you may get a reward." He leered at her, and the two sec men flanking him broke their impassive stares to smile cruelly.

The black woman stood without a word, and walked out of the room, between the two sec men. Murphy closed the door, but not before muttering "You just be good" in a sneering tone to those left behind.

MILDRED WAS TIED to the cane chair, just as Ryan had been. Murphy stood on the edge of the pool of light, partly shrouded by shadow.

"So what comes next?" Mildred asked with a bravado she didn't really feel. Despite her efforts to quell the uneasiness in her and keep the fear at bay, it crept up on the corners of her mind. Such had been the strength of her dream state under the trank darts that she almost believed Murphy was wearing a Klan hood in the shadows.

"It's quite simple. We want to know all about you and your friends. Particularly the old fart."

"You'll have to ask him about that. I don't know squat about him. And what could there be about a black bitch to interest you?" she spit with sarcastic venom.

Murphy stepped forward into the light. Despite her better intent, Mildred flinched.

Murphy laughed with sardonic glee. "Oh, I love it. The geeks in R&D are gonna love the way their gadgets worked. Don't worry, I ain't gonna violate you as part of the interrogation. We don't know enough about how rad-blasted your genes are to risk that. But I always say that there ain't nothing that works like good old fashioned pain."

With a backhand slap he jerked Mildred's head back, the rings on his fingers ripping her flesh. She kept her head back to one side, breathing heavily and trying to conquer the sudden flash of pain and anger.

Gently Murphy took her chin in his fingers and pulled her head around until he was looking her in the eye.

"Now, when I had you stripped, we found medical supplies in your pockets. I'd swear that you were a medic of some kind. Is that so?"

"You're a clever mother, aren't you?" Mildred answered through the taste of blood, mustering as much sarcasm as she could.

Murphy smiled to himself. "Thought so. That being the case, you won't want those hands of yours damaged in any way, will you? Like losing those nails, for instance?"

Mildred's stomach lurched. She remembered a book she'd read when she was at college: a history of the French Resistance in World War II. There had been a chapter on Odette, the spy dropped by British intelligence who had been captured by the Gestapo. Part of the torture she endured was to have her fingernails and toenails pulled out by pliers, each one wrenched out by the root, so that the exposed nail bed would remain uncovered. It was, in many ways, such a small thing to do. Yet the pain had been almost unendurable, leaving her unable to walk or use her hands properly for months.

If this happened to Mildred, not only would it be more pain than she could stand in her current psychological condition, but it would also be a great obstacle to her in any escape attempt.

Fighting the conditioning, she figured that this was the equivalent of using Dean against his father. What could she lose by telling them about herself at this stage?

"Well?" Murphy queried. Mildred was unaware that she had been silent for so long.

"Okay," she said finally, "I'll tell you what you want to know, although you may not believe it."

IT WENT AS Murphy would have expected. A little pain, the promise of more, and they crumbled. He had to hand it to R&D—the short-term effects of their machines were damn good. Even the mutie woman had given in pretty easily. He hadn't expected it, but had guessed the way to get at her when he mentioned the one-eyed man and noticed how her hair coiled tight around her neck and head. Damn giveaway, those mutie traits...

The albino hadn't been so easy. He was taciturn and as stubborn as hell. When Murphy first leaned over him to threaten him, the insolent little fart had spit in his face.

By the time Murphy had finished with him, the albino's hair was running red with his blood, and he had a few more scars on his face to match those that already crisscrossed his pale skin, now hidden beneath red weals and livid scabs.

And still he'd got nothing from him. Not even his name. That was okay; he knew that from the others.

The only one he hadn't questioned had been the old man. For reasons best known to himself, the Gen had wanted to do that in his office. All they had was a name: Doc Tanner. It didn't seem much, but when Murphy made his report, Wallace had been excited.

The Gen had a plan that he didn't want anyone else to know about yet. That was plain to Murphy as he and the two sec men assigned to the prisoners escorted Doc Tanner to the Gen's office. Murphy studied the old man. His eyes, set in a wrinkled and tired face framed by his flowing white hair, seemed to glitter with the same mixture of cunning and madness as Wallace. The thought of the two of them in the same room made Murphy shudder, and he was glad when the Gen ordered him to stay outside.

The corridor was almost deserted. The maintenance tasks were completed, and the whole redoubt was still on yellow alert, with everyone at their designated posts. Murphy was pleased, as it gave him a more than reasonable excuse to dismiss his sec men, dispatching them back to their posts, and stand guard himself.

In the empty corridor, Murphy was able to stand guard and also eavesdrop, thankful that Wallace was inclined to raise his voice when excited.

And boy, was he excited....

WALLACE FLICKED through Murphy's report as Doc Tanner was left alone with him, standing in the middle of the room with a distracted air as the sec men left.

"Sit down, Doctor," Wallace said without looking up.

Doc took a seat opposite the Gen, remarking, "I would assume that there is some particular reason why you wish to interview me yourself, and outside the confines of the hellhole in which my companions have been interrogated."

Wallace looked up. "Oh, yes, Dr. Tanner. I couldn't risk you being harmed. Not before recycling."

Doc shuddered. There was something about the way Wallace looked at him as he said it that made a lizard crawl slowly and coldly down his spine.

The Gen looked down at the report, then picked up a sheaf of paper.

"There are things about our lives here that only I am aware of, Doctor. We are the only true Americans left, you know—"

"I can think of some native tribes—remnants of whom survive—who would argue that point," Doc interrupted. Then he added with a gracious gesture, "But I am interrupting you. Pray continue."

Wallace suppressed his anger and forced a smile before continuing. "In this base we have managed to keep the traditions of the U.S. Army flying high like the Stars and Stripes. We have maintained the American way against the scum outsiders. We were entrusted by our forefathers to keep the research pure, and to maintain the mechanism that this base was created for. Thanks to the great plan, we still have access to many preskydark records."

"I am surprised that you use such terms, as cut off as you are," Doc interpolated.

"We sometimes have contact with some outsider scum in an attempt to keep our gene pool healthy, and thus we have a tendency to pick up some of their slack speech habits. It's regrettable, but inevitable. And please refrain from interrupting me," Wallace added with a warning glare that shot an electric jolt down Doc's spine. There was barely disguised psychosis behind the man's gaze.

"My apologies," Doc muttered.

"Very well. As I was about to say, we have records of before the great war between the Reds and the democrats. It is unfortunate that, as time progresses, we find ourselves moving further and further away from the technology of the preskydark era. The good book says recycle, but sometimes there aren't things to recycle with. We improvise, but that is all."

Doc wondered idly if there was a point to all of this. Then Wallace's words brought him up short.

"Some of the old comps still work, however, and through them we can access the records of the Totality Concept as a whole, and not just our own role as weapons R&D. And so it was of some interest to me to find out that you were Dr. Theophilus Tanner. The name seemed to me to be familiar. My father, the Gen before me, had an old family tale about my ancestor who was involved with another branch of Totality, a thing called Operation Chronos. Is that familiar, Doctor?"

Doc reasoned that it was pointless to lie or bluff. "Of course it is," he said as calmly as he could, but already the memories were beginning to flood back, the horror and pain dragging him to the brink of insanity. "You know about the madness that lay at the root of it, the way in which I was dragged away from my beloved

Emily and my children and how I was flung forward into the chaos and evil that stalks the Deathlands.''

Wallace studied the papers in front of him in an off-handed manner, seeming not to notice the hysterical pitch creeping into Doc's voice.

"As a matter of fact, the last reference to you just states that you were projected into the future.'' He looked at Doc curiously over the top of the paper. "Did you know that you were the only success? Quite remarkable.''

"There are other words for it.''

"I'm not really interested in your opinions. Only your survival. It just so happens that a vital component in one of our machines has broken down for the last time. There are no repairs that can be made to it, so we need a replacement part. You can be of some use to us.''

"I? How can I be of use?'' Doc scoffed. "An old man out of time, prone to fits of melancholy and madness? What do I know of machines?''

"Perhaps more than you know,'' Wallace said softly. "As soon as you and your companions arrived, I knew you would be of some use. Your great age brings the necessary wisdom. The fact that you are who you are is an unexpected bonus. For that reason you will live. If you agree to help, then your companions will also live. If not...'' Wallace shrugged.

Doc's face cracked wryly. "You hardly give me a choice. So be it.''

Wallace nodded. "Good. I will get Sarj Murphy and his guard to escort you back to your companions until we're ready for you.''

As the Gen bellowed Murphy's name, and the chief sec man opened the door, Doc wondered what horrors awaited him.

Chapter Seven

"Stupe move. Never give anything."

Jak's sharp opinion was echoed by Dean, who shook his head when Doc, safely returned to the dormitory by Murphy, told them of the outcome of his interview with Wallace. It amused Doc that Murphy, obviously still remembering Panner's fate, had kept his blaster trained on him from five yards distance, not allowing the old man any scope for an attempted assault.

"I disagree," Mildred said. "The crazy old buzzard has done nothing more than buy us time, but at least he's done that."

Doc inclined his head. "I shall accept that with the graciousness that you no doubt intended," he murmured.

"You're both right," Ryan snapped. "It was stupe in some ways, but what else could Doc do? What we need now is to work out how we get out of here."

The one-eyed warrior surveyed his friends. His biggest concern was the lasting effects of the psychological weapons they had endured. Physically they weren't in too bad shape. His balls still hurt like hell, but the rest of his wounds were nothing more than abrasions and bruising. Running and fighting would make his balls feel like they were about to fall off, but he could stand that if it was a choice between resting them and being chilled.

J.B. and Mildred were in a similar condition. Minor abrasions, nothing more. When Ryan mentioned his own injuries, J.B. winced, so he, too, may be slowed by the injuries inflicted by the cane seat. They would have to take that into account. It could make the split-second difference between escape and buying the farm.

Dean had been left more or less alone, his "reward" for telling Murphy who he was, Ryan figured. Doc was okay. That was a weird one. What did these coldhearts have in mind for him? Old tech could mean anything, if it was still working.

Ryan looked across the room at Krysty, who was lying on a bed, trying to get some sleep. She was bruised and had a split lip where Murphy had whipped her with that ring hand he loved to use. Ryan idly wondered if he would have an opportunity to cut it off and ram it up the sec man's ass before they left. It was only a passing thought. Revenge was a luxury they couldn't afford.

It was Jak who worried Ryan most. He was a born fighter, with reserves of stamina and strength that belied his slender frame. But Murphy had enjoyed working on Jak. His face was marked with new scars and scabs, his lips swollen and one eye totally obscured where the flesh had puffed and discolored. His body had mostly been left alone, but he, too, had been tortured on the cane chair, and at one point he remembered being cut loose and kicked across the floor of the interrogation cell. Mildred had examined him and had found no evidence of broken bones, but she was concerned that he might have a hairline fracture of at least one rib that could cause problems.

Jak caught Ryan's stare with his one good eye. He seemed to know what Ryan was thinking.

"We break, leave me if slow us up."

"You know better than that, Jak," Ryan said, but it was what he would have said in the circumstances. It was what any of them would have said.

But he'd be damned if he'd do it.

Ryan sank back on his bed. Now to wait.

It was Wallace's move.

IT WAS HARD to know how much time had passed. No one had a wrist chron, as they had all been taken away, and the seconds dragged. J.B. in particular found his fingers itching without blasters to strip and clean, ammo to indent and grens to check. Jak was lost without his leaf-bladed knives to clean and practice throwing.

The only members of the party who seemed not to notice the time passing were Mildred and Doc, both of whom were lost in their own thoughts. Mildred was still trying to exorcise the ghost of the Klan that now haunted her dreams, while Doc was lost in some reverie of jumbled memories, the labyrinthine twists of which only he could follow.

Ryan mentally ran through methods of escape. Every scenario he could imagine was played out in his mind, trying to weigh the odds and take into account their debilitated physical condition and lack of weapons.

Each time he came up with the same observation—things were going to be tough, and chance would play a big factor in their success or failure. Ryan had been a fighting man long enough to know how big a role chance could play...for either side.

If only he could think of a way to shorten those odds in his favor...

His train of thought was cut short by Dean's sudden complaint about his grumbling stomach.

"I guess it is some time since they last fed us," Krysty replied. "Time does fly by when you're having fun, doesn't it?"

Ryan grinned. "Guess Dean's just a growing boy."

"Aw, Dad..."

"Ah, but you must feed the inner child," Doc chided, joining in the ribbing. "After all—"

But Doc's comment was to be forever lost as he was interrupted by the click of the lock, and the door swung open. Murphy was standing in the doorway, a small blaster in his left fist. J.B. noted that it was 9 mm Beretta, and was blue rather than matte black. Not standard Army issue, most likely an heirloom handed down Murphy's family line. It looked pristine. Murphy may be a bastard, but J.B. couldn't help admiring the care he took of his blaster.

It was something the sergeant had to have imparted to the sec men under him, as the two soldiers flanking the man also had blasters that looked to be in pristine condition. Whereas the sec men they had previously encountered had been armed with 9 mm Heckler & Koch MP-5 K blasters, these sec men had Uzi's. The H&K was a handier blaster, more compact, but J.B. had a soft spot for the Uzi. Always reliable, and quite deadly at short range.

Especially if well maintained. And these blasters were gleaming. If the rest of the armory was this well maintained, then J.B. would have given anything to see it.

Murphy, surveying the room, had noticed J.B.

"Mr. Dix," he said, "I must apologize for the manner in which you were questioned earlier. In war there is no time for niceties. And we've been at war for a long time now. I have to say, boy, that you are a man after my own heart. You care about your weaponry, and realize that the key to any effective defense is the maintenance of a good armory. I salute you, sir."

"Nice words, but they don't get me shit," the Armorer replied.

Murphy bellowed a loud belly laugh. "Right on! Okay, you people, face up. Your belongings are to be returned to you—without your weapons, of course—and the Gen will give you the lowdown on our outfit and why you're needed…especially you, old man," he added, nodding in Doc's direction.

"You need all that firepower just to talk to us and tell us that?" Krysty asked.

Murphy inclined his head. "Lady, you may be a mutie, but even you should have worked that one out. I'll bet Mr. Dix here has it sussed."

J.B. fixed Murphy with a stare. "If you mean what I figure, mebbe it means that you respect us too much to take chances."

"Damn, but you're a sensible man." Murphy smiled. "It's a pity you're not one of us. I could really work with someone like you. Okay. In five minutes you'll be ready to move out."

With that, Murphy stepped back and nodded to his right. Two orderlies with the slack jaws of inbreeding shuffled forward carrying piles of clothing, which they flung into the room. One of them grabbed the door handle and pulled it shut.

"Hurry up y'all, just five minutes," was Murphy's parting shot as the door slammed.

THEY WERE READY IN LESS.

All were glad to get into their familiar clothes, rather than the standard-issue Army underwear they had found when they had first awakened. Doc greeted his frock coat like an old friend, but bemoaned the lack of his walking stick.

"Not expect everything," Jak remarked as he hunted through his patchwork jacket for any of the leaf-bladed knives that might have been overlooked.

The sec men had been as thorough as could have been expected, once bitten.

Now they had their wrist chrons back, Ryan noted that it was almost five minutes to the second when the door burst open, and Wallace walked into the room. He entered without taking any precautions, and with the air of a man who was used to his every word being obeyed. In his own kingdom he had no need to be careful. Behind him Murphy and a troop of four sec men kept the Gen covered.

"Listen up, people," Wallace intoned. "We need your man Dr. Theophilus Tanner to assist us in our work, which must continue for the day when the Reds will rise again. Make no mistake, those Russkie Reds are cunning bastards and may just be lying low. In return for the doctor's help, you'll be allowed to stay here and stay alive. There's always a need to recycle, and you'll all be useful sooner or later—"

There was something about the way he said it that made Mildred shiver. Back in the preskydark days, when she was involved in cryogenics, many of the medics and technicians she had worked with had used such terms, and in a similar tone of voice.

"In the meantime I want you to see the facilities we have here. Just so you people know what you're up against. Now follow me."

Wallace spun on his heel and waddled out of the room. As he passed Murphy, the sec chief gestured with the Heckler & Koch he was grasping. Sizing up the other four soldiers, J.B. saw that two of them clutched H&Ks, and two were holding Uzis. All five blasters were trained unwaveringly on their captives.

There was a boastful and proud quality to Wallace's voice that fired hope in Ryan's heart. He was so keen to show them how strong he was that he might unwittingly reveal a weakness. A quick glance at J.B. and an almost imperceptible nod of the Armorer's head showed that he had had similar thoughts.

Ryan led the way out between the sec men, who were well spaced by Murphy in order to insure that any attack couldn't be focused on more than one armed man. The group fell into their normal recce pattern, with J.B. staying back while Jak took the middle, Krysty and Dean in front of him, Mildred and Doc behind.

In front, Wallace had already embarked on a long-winded lecture about the history of the redoubt, and how it had served as a research-and-development unit while still fulfilling its main purpose as part of the Totality Concept. Ryan listened with interest to this part of the lecture. Over the years he had picked up shreds of information here and there about the Totality Concept, and also about the various weapons and operations that had been part of it. He was also interested in the way that Doc fit the pattern, his interest having been piqued by the information they had discovered at Crater Lake.

In many ways, this community reminded him of Crater Lake, the old scientific complex under an extinct volcano that had housed a community of inbred, mutated whitecoats. Except these people were insane in a more dangerous way, and still had a strong military discipline that would make them difficult to best.

As Wallace led them through the redoubt, both Ryan and J.B. tried to keep a mental note of where the corridors led. It looked to be laid out in a similar way to most of the redoubts they had visited, but there were extra sections and more levels. They went down five levels, enduring the hostile gaze of the redoubt inhabitants, going about their daily business, as they passed. All the while Wallace kept up his litany of praise for the work his ancestors had started and that his people were continuing.

"…and this is where we softened you up for interrogation. There are eight obs rooms in all, each one equipped similarly. Which was quite convenient, when you think of it, as there are seven of you…" He allowed himself a laugh. "As you know only too well, the techniques developed here are far ahead of anything you outsider scum may have."

He stopped them as he reached this point in the lecture. They were in the obs room where Dr. Tricks was collecting data spilling from a chattering printer. She looked around at them and raised an elegant eyebrow. Krysty looked her up and down with a perusing eye. She wouldn't have expected to see such physical perfection in an environment where even the muscle-bound sec men and their seemingly healthy chief showed some signs of mutation or inbreeding. Was she a mutie in some way that she didn't understand?

Trick had caught the end of the lecture. "There is one thing," she purred at Wallace. "For so-called outsider scum, they've proved rather adept at traveling. I'd love to know how they've learned to use the mat-trans, especially as our people have never quite worked it out."

Wallace glared at her. "You know why," he

snapped. "They have Dr. Tanner, and you know what is to be done with him."

Tricks smiled. Krysty felt a shiver run down her spine, and her hair snapped tight to her head, coiling protectively around her. She suddenly felt very afraid for Doc, and wondered at what cost he had bought their temporary reprieve.

Wallace led them through the redoubt. They moved down another level to the R&D labs, where the advanced armory was maintained. Here he showed them the remote-control trank tank that had taken them out in the corridor, and other mobile and remote-controlled weapons. J.B. was interested despite himself at gren firers and large-caliber blasters mounted on tracks. There were flamethrowers and laser weapons that looked as though they might, at one time, have been deadly, but were now just highly polished junk.

Ryan and Jak exchanged a look. It was easy to see how the weapons had been allowed to descend to this degree of tidy disrepair by taking one look at the maintenance techs, many of whom were slack-jawed and drooling, or showing signs of too much inbreeding. The mutie genes were less obvious among these personnel —certainly nothing like the chilled maintenance man with the stickie heritage—but there was a large degree of insularity that had led to a mechanical repetition of tasks rather than understanding what they really meant.

Ryan found that interesting. If they were used to a mechanical routine, then anything that threw them off might cause confusion rather than spur them into the same military and drilled action that he knew the sec men would be capable of. That was a good sign.

On the eighth level they passed a laboratory that was sealed off by double-glazed and reinforced fire doors with-a comp coded sec lock similar to those used on the electronic sec doors in the corridors.

Strangely Wallace became reticent when they reached this point. All of a sudden he clammed up on them.

"This level is where the mechanism is maintained. It was the great work for which we were trained and for which we all live. This is the work in which Dr. Tanner can help us."

"Aren't you going to tell us what this is?" Doc queried.

Wallace shot a venomous glance at him, and Murphy stepped forward to prod him in the ribs with the H&K.

"Shut up, you old fuck. You'll find out soon enough."

"Strange that you're so quiet now, though, isn't it?" Mildred asked Wallace.

"There are things about the mechanism that must be kept secret for now," he said sharply. "We'll move on."

It didn't escape anyone's notice that the garrulous fat man had something nasty to hide. What it was, no one could guess. One thing was for sure, it was a worry as to what was in store for Doc.

Where Wallace led them next put all such thoughts out of their minds. They went up several levels, then through a maze of corridors.

"And this, people, is the armory," Wallace announced proudly.

Despite himself, J.B. whistled softly at the array of weaponry and ammunition on view. Boxes upon boxes of rifles, grens, ammunition, gren launchers and mortars were carefully stacked around the base of the armory walls. Hanging on racks were the in-service weapons—

Uzi, MP-5 K, M-60 machine guns, grens primed and ready for use, boxes of ammo for the greased and gleaming blasters and a variety of smaller handblasters.

It was rare for an armory to still contain such an array of blasters and grens, let alone in such perfect working order and condition. The armory was a credit to Murphy and his forefathers.

Jak tried to move forward to get a closer look inside the armory, but he was nudged back into place by the barrel of an Uzi. He glared at the sec man with his good eye, hatred flashing across his scarred features.

"Watch it, mutie," the sec man growled.

"That's enough," Wallace snapped.

The sec man clicked his heels to attention and looked straight ahead. "Sir, my apologies."

"Very good," Wallace murmured before turning his attention to J.B. "Mr. Dix, I understand from Sarj Murphy's report that you are the weapons expert in this little band."

"Mebbe," the Armorer replied guardedly.

"Come now, there's no need for modesty. A good man with a gun is always needed."

J.B. raised an eyebrow. It was a long time since he'd seen or heard anyone refer to a blaster by its preskydark name.

"You notice my use of the term *gun*?" queried Wallace. "I find it less crude than *blaster,* the scum outsider term for weaponry. Too basic, too all-encompassing," he mused, shaking his head.

J.B. caught a glimpse of Jak out of the corner of his eye. The albino had an expression on his face that spelled out his opinion of Wallace. It wasn't good. Ryan, on the other hand, was seriously considering the possibility that Wallace was so far gone into insanity as to just wipe them out where they stood.

The big man seemed to taper off, lost in thought. Then suddenly, as though snapping back from worlds unknown, he said, "Okay, Sarj, take them back to the dorm and contain them. I'll consult the techs on the mechanism and inform you when I require Tanner."

He looked at them with a detached disdain that bordered on contempt. Then, without another word, he spun on his heel and left them standing in front of the armory.

Ryan watched the man waddle around the corner of the corridor, then turned his head to Murphy. The sec chief was also watching Wallace with a look of bemusement. He caught Ryan watching him, and immediately blanked his face.

But not quickly enough for Ryan to wonder about his loyalty to Wallace.

"Right, people, move out like the Gen said," Murphy barked, gesturing with his blaster.

They turned and allowed themselves to be marched back to the dormitory. All kept their eyes wide for any sign of slack on the part of the sec men, any opportunity, no matter how slight, that might enable them to mount an escape bid.

There wasn't even the whisper of a chance. Murphy's men marched them efficiently back to the dormitory and locked them in.

"How CAN THAT GUY Wallace be so stupe?" Dean asked in amazement. "He's shown us the layout of the entire redoubt and where the armory is."

"It doesn't really appear to make sense," Krysty mused. "It's hardly great sec."

"It doesn't, but then why should it? Wallace is crazy. This whole redoubt is riddled with stupidity. You know that, even if you don't know why," Ryan said to Krysty. The blue of his one eye burned into her.

Krysty screwed up her face. "You're right there, lover. I've got a really bad feeling about the whole situation."

"So better do something," Jak added.

Mildred moved over to the door and looked up at the sec camera that surveyed the room.

"Yeah, but what?"

"YOU, SOLDIER, get that damn door open."

The soldier on guard outside the dorm snapped to attention as he heard Murphy storming toward him.

"Sir?"

"Don't you ever pay attention when you're at your post, soldier? What does the good book say, son? Vigilance is the sacred duty of the Sons of Sam. If the old fart is dying, then the Gen will have the both of us on a fuckin' charge. And I'm not patrolling the rad-blast wastes for a month just because you're a fuckwit."

"Sir," the soldier replied uncertainly to the stream of vitriol, "but what is it, sir?"

Murphy was carrying a Heckler & Koch, which he cranked up level with the door.

"Monitor, son," he said shortly. "The old bastard is writhing on his bed and the medic isn't getting far. Might have a better idea if the friggin' sound worked properly, but all I can make out is friggin' static. If the old fart dies, I'm dead meat, and without anyone to succeed me yet. Open the bastard door, boy."

"Sir…"

Leveling his Uzi, safety off, the guard punched the

lock code into the door and turned the handle. He flung the door in and adopted a combat stance, rapidly counting the figures standing in front of him.

Six…and the old man was lying on one of the beds, moaning softly and clutching his guts. Damn, why hadn't he heard anything? He didn't want Murphy on his back.

Seeing that all of the captives were in plain sight, Murphy rushed into the room, sweeping his blaster in an arc to cover them.

"Okay, what's going on here? What's the matter with Tanner?" he asked, barely keeping the panic from his voice.

Mildred turned slowly from where she had been leaning over Doc. "Appendix, I think. Unless you have the right medical facilities and allow me to operate immediately, then he'll probably die."

Murphy focused on the last three words and panicked.

"The hell you'll operate," he shouted. "We've got our own medics. Think we'll trust some outsider?"

Ryan shrugged. "Okay, you get one of your inbred muties to do it and kill Doc off. Doesn't bother me."

Murphy opened his mouth to snap back a sarcastic answer, then considered his options.

"Let me take a look at him," he said, the nervousness now apparent in his voice.

The sec chief's indecision infected the guard standing in the doorway. Twitching slightly, and training his blaster on the largest grouping of prisoners—the trio of Krysty, J.B. and Dean, who stood to the left of the bed—the guard ignored Jak.

An upbringing in the swamps hunting nervous and

sensitive wildlife had given Jak the ability to move without seeming to do so.

Murphy's attention was locked on the bed, where Ryan and Mildred stood over Doc. The guard had his attention focused on the trio clustered to the left-hand side of the room. The forgotten silent albino teen glided around the room until he was just behind the guard, in the man's blind spot.

Ironically it was the sudden awareness of something being out of place that made him look around.

Too late. The plates from their last meal were still piled on a plastic tray, with the plastic cutlery heaped beside them. Remnants of the inedible meal still dirtied the surface of the plates. Pieces of stringy meat from an indeterminate animal, covered in a tasteless goo that passed for a sauce, were hard and stuck fast on the surface of the plate that Jak picked from the tray and in one fluid motion flicked toward the guard.

The albino was small and wiry, but years of practice with his knives had given him an incredible strength and dexterity in his wrists. He also had an unerring eye for distance, even with his vision reduced by his injuries. Instinctively he weighed the plate in his hand and directed it with the required amount of force.

It may only have been made of plastic, and had an edge that was blunt, but it was also a thin plate. Tilted to a forty-five-degree angle and propelled at great speed, it had no problem in crushing the guard's septum as it hit him on the bridge of his nose. Jak was about six inches shorter than the guard, and had also crouched slightly when throwing the plate. The upward trajectory drove the septum up and into the frontal lobes of the guard's brain.

Consciousness ceased almost immediately. His motor

functions were a little behind, and as the guard went down, his trigger finger twitched. A spray of shells left the Uzi, scattering in an erratic arc as his dead arm was jerked around by the recoil of the blaster.

"What the fu—?"

Murphy never finished the curse. Blind instinct told him to hit the deck as the spray of fire flew across the room. As he went down, he cracked his head on an iron bedstead. Perhaps he would have considered it unlucky to have hit the very spot that Ryan's weighted scarf had injured earlier, but he should have considered it good luck. If he hadn't been rendered unconscious, he would most certainly have been chilled.

Leaving him in an attempt to save time was something that Ryan thought he might later regret, but at that moment, the one-eyed warrior was concerned only with getting his people armed and out.

"Good throw, Jak," Dean called admiringly as J.B. retrieved the Heckler & Koch, checking the downed sec chief for spare ammo.

"Teach you sometime," grunted the albino as he tossed the Uzi to Ryan with one hand while searching the dead guard for additional ammunition and weapons.

Doc stuck his head over the edge of the bed. When the shooting began, he had immediately ceased his agonized groaning and thrown himself over the side of the bed, taking cover beneath.

"I would assume it is safe to come into the open?" he asked innocently before baring his gleaming white teeth in a wry grin. "By the by, was my performance of an acceptable standard?"

"Oscar winning, Doc," Mildred replied. Then, noticing Doc's inquiring look, she dismissed the comment. "Before and after your time at the same time, Doc."

The old man nodded solemnly. "A temporal reference, I have no doubt."

"Stop talking in riddles, you two," Krysty said as she joined Ryan. "Any other weapons on the coldheart bastard?"

Together they surveyed the paltry sum of J.B. and Jak's trawl through the pockets of the sec men—Murphy's blue 9 mm Beretta and a pocketknife from the sec chief, and a Glock 17 from the dead guard.

J.B. examined it with interest. "Not usually a predark sec blaster," he mused, rapt in his subject. "Mebbe another heirloom, like the blue Beretta. Kept in good condition. Which one would you prefer, Millie?"

"I'll go for the Beretta," Mildred said decisively, taking the blaster and judging the weight in her palm. "Much more accurate over a longer distance," she added.

"You take this." Ryan took the Glock and handed it to Krysty. She sighted along the snubby barrel in order to gauge the weapon.

Jak picked up the pocketknife and examined the blades and attachments before flicking out the one that he could inflict the most damage with. "Hope get better stuff soon," he said.

It left both Dean and Doc without weapons. Ryan would rather that all his team be armed, but in the circumstances the available weapons had been distributed as well as they could be. He and J.B. switched the H&K and Uzi as each preferred the other's blaster. Mildred had been a champion shootist in her prefreezie existence, and Krysty was no slouch.

They had gone about the task of distributing the available arms in an unhurried manner, but all the while they were aware of the camera, unblinking, that watched over the scenario as it was played out.

Only seconds had passed, but each second was valuable.

"Let's move out," Ryan ordered curtly. "I'll take point. We're heading for the armory. If we've got any chance of getting out of here, then we need to be armed. Mebbe get our own weapons back."

Chapter Eight

They moved out into the corridor, which was deathly quiet. There was no alarm, and no signs of life.

"Same as before," Mildred breathed gently, almost afraid to break the silence.

"Seems to be Wallace's favorite tactic," Ryan commented. "Try to give us enough rope for a lynching."

"To hang ourselves," Krysty murmured, unconsciously correcting the one-eyed warrior whilst suppressing a shudder.

Ryan could feel the tension in her as she followed directly behind him.

"Get any feelings about this?" he asked.

"Only bad ones. But that's all I've had since we've been here, lover—you know that."

"No harm in asking," Ryan murmured. "J.B., what do you think?"

"Wallace's not as stupe as he seems," the Armorer whispered from the rear, covering their backs as they proceeded down the maze of corridors. "Our own nerves'll screw us over in this quiet."

"An astute point, my dear John Barrymore," Doc said at a more normal volume, which, in the exaggerated silence, sounded like a shout. "The good Gen's apparent stupidity in showing us around was perhaps just the pompous pride and illusion of a man who has had his own way too long. He thinks he is invincible, and so has no need for security within the confines of his own kingdom.''

"What does that mean?'' Dean asked, puzzled. ''You mean he's got too confident 'cause he's got no enemies in here?''

"Precisely, young man.''

"I wouldn't bet on him not having too many enemies in here,'' Ryan commented, remembering the expression on Murphy's face when they stood outside the armory.

No one added a comment. The atmosphere was too tense for speech. In the outside, in the mutated jungles and scrub of Deathlands, there was usually some sound, some sign of life. But in here, there was only the oppressive weight of silence, hearing strained to catch the tiniest of sounds, the slightest of giveaways as to what Wallace's plans may be.

With no obstructions they were able to progress rapidly from level to level, taking the elevators.

Jak was unhappy about that. "Bastard stand on roof, we chilled,'' he commented, shifting his weight uneasily from foot to foot as they entered the empty car.

"Yeah, but it's the fastest way. I'll take a look,'' Ryan replied. He gestured to the service door in the roof of the elevator with the barrel of his blaster. Krysty moved underneath and cupped her hands. Ryan put one boot firmly in the stirrup she had made, and boosted himself up to the roof. He pushed up hard with the tip of the blaster and flicked open the cover. The black maw of the elevator shaft gave nothing away. Unwilling to waste ammo, Ryan paused, expecting some fire in reaction to the movement…if the roof of the elevator was covered.

Nothing. J.B. glanced at Jak, who nodded and flicked

open the knife he had taken from Murphy. With silent grace he vaulted into Krysty's still cupped hands as Ryan hit the floor of the elevator. Before the one-eyed man had the chance to put his second foot on the floor and regain his balance, Jak had lithely disappeared through the opening, his white hair flashing in the gloom as his camou jacket blended into the darkness.

He was gone for only a few seconds, during which time his movements sounded as nothing more than a skittering on the elevator roof.

Just as lithely, just as silently, Jak slid back into the car, dropping to the floor with an almost noiseless impact.

"No." He shook his head.

"Mebbe they expect what we're going to do," J.B. said.

Mildred agreed. "They'll be watching us every step of the way with those damn cameras. It must be obvious. Wallace could lay a trap for us at any place."

"Mebbe we should confuse the stupe and head straight for the outside. He can see us going but mebbe won't have time to change his plans," Dean added.

Ryan shook his head as he hit the elevator button for the level that housed the armory.

"If we had our usual blasters and ammo, then that'd be a good move. But with all we've got? And not knowing what's on the outside of this redoubt? We'd have to be triple stupe."

"Instead of double stupe by going right where he wants us?" Dean retorted.

As the elevator ascended, Ryan glanced sharply at his son. He was the leader by virtue of his experience and by the consensus of the others. If there were to be challenges, then it was the wrong time for divisiveness, especially from his own son.

Dean returned his father's glare with an equally heated expression of his own.

Ryan's anger retreated into amusement. The boy could have been him. There was so much of Ryan Cawdor in his son that he would have to watch him in a few years. The lad would want to assert himself.

But that could be dealt with when the time came. Right now they had to get the hell out of this fireblasted pesthole.

Ryan grinned. "You know I'm right. You said it yourself, son. Heading for the armory is only double stupe. That's one less than heading for the outside."

Dean shrugged. "Mebbe you're right," he said grudgingly.

The elevator shuddered to a halt at the right level. As the door slid open, the levity of a few seconds earlier was forgotten. Split into two, the friends flattened themselves against the sides of the car, taking advantage of the scant cover provided by the control panel and intercom on each side of the elevator doors.

The corridor in front of them was empty.

Moving out in formation, falling into position with familiarity, they headed down the corridor.

When they reached the unguarded armory, they received a shock that was more jolting than a surprise attack. The doors to the armory had been left open, and after J.B. had run an expert eye over them to check for any booby traps, Jak made his way inside while the others surveyed the corridors.

Jak reappeared with a baffled expression.

"What is it?" Krysty asked.

"Better see for self," Jak replied.

J.B. and Krysty entered the armory.

"Well, what can you make of that?" Krysty whispered, bemused.

J.B. shrugged. "Not worth thinking about—just act on it."

He moved forward to the collection of objects that had been the cause of their bemusement. The walls and floors of the armory were, for the most part, stripped bare—with the exception of a small pile of blasters and ammunition that lay in the center of the floor.

J.B. hunkered down and poked at them with the end of his blaster, in case there was any hidden trap. As he had expected by now, there was no catch. The pile consisted of the weapons they had possessed when they entered the redoubt.

"What is it?" Ryan whispered, glancing over his shoulder at the armory.

"Expect the unexpected," J.B. replied cryptically.

Ryan furrowed his brow and looked at Doc, who shrugged.

"John Barrymore—as elliptical as ever," Doc told him.

The Armorer ignored the comments from outside and concentrated on the blasters in front of him. Ryan's weighted scarf was neatly coiled, and the SIG-Sauer and panga were gleaming, while the Steyr SSG-70 had been greased and loaded. His M-4000 was similarly overhauled, and the Uzi was ready for action. His knife was gleaming and freshly whetted. Best of all, his minisextant, which he had thought lost, was in the pile. He pocketed it before proceeding to examine the rest of the blasters—Mildred's ZKR, Krysty's Smith & Wesson 640, Doc's lion's-head swordstick and LeMat blaster, Dean's Browning Hi-Power, Jak's .357 Magnum Colt

Python and—best of all—the full collection of leaf-bladed throwing knives, all freshly whetted.

J.B. allowed himself a small smile, knowing how the taciturn Jak would be pleased to have these returned to him, but wouldn't show much sign of his pleasure. He called over his shoulder.

"Wallace's up to something strange. All our blasters are here, all cleaned and loaded. Come and get them."

They collected their weapons one at a time, gradually gaining confidence as the guard in the corridor increased in firepower. Yet at the same time they were all puzzling over the central problem—what was Wallace's intent in leaving nothing but their own weapons in the armory, all in full working order.

It was almost as though he wanted them to escape, despite the noises he had made about needing Doc.

There had to be some kind of warped thinking behind it all, but it would have been foolish not to take the opportunity to get their blasters back. J.B. finally emerged from the armory when everyone had collected his or her weaponry.

"Feels better," Jak grunted, adjusting to the change in weight the knives made in his patched jacket as it hung on his lean frame. Like the others, he had discarded the weapon he had acquired earlier.

They all agreed with Jak, but saved their breath, concentrating instead on staying razor keen for the slightest indication of Wallace's plans.

Whatever they may be…

"REMEMBER WHAT the good book says, Sarj—never shoot till you see the whites of their eyes, or eye in Cawdor's case. It's all metaphorical, of course."

"Yes, sir," Murphy answered, wondering what on

earth the fool was babbling about. He thought that Wallace's idea to let the others go by making them believe they were escaping and then snatching back Tanner at the last moment was a complete crock of shit. The Gen might believe that he was the cleverest man in the whole of Deathlands because of some insane hereditary right, but Murphy was sure that the outsiders wouldn't be fooled for a second. They were too battle scarred, too clever to fall for it.

It galled him immensely that he had let them escape from their dormitory cell—even more so that he had lost a perfectly good man in the process. Of course, the most galling aspect was that they had taken the initiative before he had had a chance to effect his own fake escape opportunity. There was no way that he had intended to put his own man at risk, let alone himself. His head still ached, but not as much as his wounded pride. Given half a chance, he'd wipe out that one-eyed bastard and his bunch of muties and scum—the old fart included.

But the work had to continue. The machine demanded a sacrifice.

Murphy and Wallace stood in front of a bank of monitors in an anteroom to Wallace's office. The Gen wore his prized .44 Magnum pistol with the eight-inch polished barrel. It was a family heirloom and spent most of the time locked away in the safe that hid behind a picture of Elvis on the wall behind his desk. It was only worn in times of the most intense redoubt activity.

The anteroom was the only part of the redoubt that wasn't covered by a sec camera—even the Gen's own office had a camera to survey what went on inside. The anteroom was also the only part of the redoubt that had monitors for every single camera. The sec operations were concentrated on three monitor rooms that had some overlap between them, but didn't cover the entire compound.

Murphy had spent many a sleepless night pondering this when Wallace first showed him the anteroom. In the end he decided that it had to have been a preskydark directive to concentrate base power entirely in the hands of the Gen. After all, he who knew everything had ultimate power.

And now he was standing here, watching the outsiders make their way toward the doors that stood between the redoubt and the outside world.

The room was completely dark, lit only by the flickering images on the banks of screens. Third row down, fourth screen along, the outsiders made their way into the frame. Their body language was tight and intense.

Wallace's face was illuminated by the screens, his jowls cast into shadow and the pudgy flesh under his eyes lit almost white.

"They're getting closer," he said, almost to himself, pointing to the screen. "A remarkable facility for remembering direction there, boy. It's a pity we've got to let them go."

"Why can't I just chill them?" Murphy asked, looking at the Gen rather than at the screen.

Wallace turned sharply. "You questioning my orders, boy?"

Murphy winced at the way the man's eyes bored into him. "No, sir, just curious."

Wallace sighed and spoke in the tone of voice he used for the severely mutated and inbred maintenance techs.

"Tanner is extremely important if the mechanism is to survive and prosper. The other outsiders could be extremely dangerous if allowed to stay. In order to separate them, it is necessary that the outsiders be allowed to escape. Any attempt at chilling them could lead to a last stand, and the possible elimination of Tanner. This would be an extremely bad thing. Do you follow me, mister?''

Murphy chewed his bottom lip. There was a screwy logic to what Wallace was saying, but there was still a good chance that the old fart could get chilled. He was sure that if that happened, he'd be next.

The outsiders moved across one screen and disappeared onto another, third on the right on the next row down. They were nearing the exit ramp.

Wallace nudged Murphy in the ribs.

"Go get 'em, boy," he said softly.

Murphy managed a sickly smile.

DEAN PUNCHED IN the code on the last automatic door. It opened smoothly. They were still alert, still expecting sec men behind every door.

But there were none. All that lay ahead of them was the gentle incline of the exit ramp, leading up to the reinforced doors of the redoubt.

"Too easy," Mildred murmured, "just too easy."

"I hear you, Millie," J.B. replied quietly.

Ryan didn't bother to ask Krysty what she was feeling: just one glance told him. He signaled to Dean to raise the door while he went flat to the floor, covering the gap at the bottom of the door as it began to rise.

A blast of warm air, swirling with dust and grit, hit him as the door began to rise. He screwed up his eye against the stinging spray and shouldered the Steyr, ready to pick off any enemies as soon as they appeared.

The door rose higher, and the wind became a gale,

became a virtual hurricane. One thing had rapidly become clear: it was a bad time to mount a recce on the world outside the redoubt.

It was about to get worse.

ONE OF THE SIDE EFFECTS of the shift in topography that had followed the early days of skydark was that many new valleys had been formed. This was one of them. The shifting of tons of earth, rock and clay had damaged some of the lowest levels of the redoubt, but had generally left the structure untouched. If nothing else, that was a tribute to the skills of the engineers who had designed the military complexes.

However, there was one thing that had happened as a result of the earth shift: A small series of honeycombed caves had been formed that had intersected with the air ducts and bore holes that had been engineered for the redoubt. For several years these had been closed off, but when the air was clean enough for them to be opened once again, the military personnel had soon discovered the uses to which they could be put. Guarded by a set of sec cameras, they acted as a useful secondary route out of the redoubt for any raiding parties. This had been of particular use when early outside settlers had laid siege to the main door of the redoubt.

Although such tactics hadn't been necessary for some time, Wallace was a keen student of history.

Murphy cursed this aspect of his commanding officer's personality as he led the small troop of sec men through the narrow maze of tunnels. The dust hanging in the air was choking and bit at their eyes. Some of the men were coughing heavily, and Murphy suppressed the urge to vomit as the dust caught in his craw.

It was typical of Wallace to think of such a labyrinthine plan. Let them raise the outer door, then ambush them from above, making sure to pick them off or drive them away while separating Tanner.

Murphy kept up his stream of invective as the troops reached the mouth of the cave, suspended on a ledge over the entrance to the redoubt. He indicated to his men to fan out onto the rocks on either side.

He heard the door start to rise above the howl of the wind. It was a metallic sound as the edges of the metal door caught on the reinforced-concrete-and-steel frame.

Murphy lifted the barrel of his Uzi and kissed it for luck.

Chapter Nine

"Fireblast! This is the last thing we need!"

Ryan's angered roar was lost in the howling of the dust storm as it hit them full force. J.B. jammed his fedora firmly on his head and inched toward Ryan, every step impeded by the sheer force of the dust and grit as it whipped around the lenses of his glasses and hit him in the eyes, drying and scratching them.

"Can't go back now," he yelled into the one-eyed warrior's ear. "Have to fan out and take whatever cover there is."

Ryan nodded his agreement, although without any degree of enthusiasm. J.B. was right, but Ryan knew that the Armorer was suggesting this course of action for the same reason that he would adopt it: there was no option.

He gestured with the Steyr, and the group moved out with the ease and practice that came with long survival in the chilling fields of the Deathlands. Ryan went first, squinting against the dust storm to identify any kind of cover. He saw it in the form of a small hummock of earth with a sparse covering of grass. He headed for it, waiting for an attack from any source.

The swirling dust made everything disorienting. Ryan rolled behind the hummock, taking cover and sighting over the spare blades of grass with the Steyr.

There was nothing.

Looking back toward the entrance of the redoubt, he could see that it had either sunk into the earth, or the earth had risen around it, so that they were in a small enclave that rose at a fairly steep gradient. He had guessed as much from the pull on his calf muscles as he ran.

Despite the opaque air, filled with dust and grit, it was possible to see that a bright sun burned down on the enclave despite the cooling effect of the wind. It illuminated the dust in rays of light and enabled Ryan to get a better view of the rock face that lay above the redoubt entrance.

While he had been scanning the area, Mildred and Jak had moved out to seek cover. He lost sight of them in the shadows and frowned. It wasn't good practice not to know where his friends were stationed.

The storm was so noisy that he couldn't call to them if necessary. Krysty and Doc moved out, then Dean and finally J.B., bringing up the rear. They should all be undercover, in a rough V shape, radiating from the entrance to the redoubt. From there, they'd move together at the head of the enclave and group together.

Which would be a whole lot easier if not for the dust storm.

Ryan scanned the rocks above the redoubt. It all seemed calm and empty, but his eye pierced the opacity of the storm with a burning suspicion. If this was regular weather for this stretch of land, then it wouldn't surprise him if the local baron and his sec men were out patrolling their land.

His sharp vision saw the glint of a blaster barrel as it caught a glimpse of sunlight that filtered through the dust. A fraction of a second later came the sharp crack of Mildred's ZKR.

Obviously Mildred had the same suspicions.

Chips of rock joined the grit and dust in the swirling air, and the barrel disappeared.

The staccato rattle of a Heckler & Koch MP-5 K cut through the howl of the storm, the short burst kicking up chunks of dry earth and pebbles from around the sparse cover Mildred had been able to find.

The spray of bullets fanned in such a way that Ryan was instantly aware that they had come from the opposite direction to that in which Mildred had fired her blaster. So they were covered from above by a group of sec men in a formation similar to their own.

Tactically it was almost a stalemate. The problem was, they were underneath the other group, closed in.

"Dad! They're moving down!"

Dean's yell cut through the storm, and Ryan was aware of his son as a blur across the floor of the enclave, tracked by sprays of H&K and Uzi fire that crisscrossed. It was only because of his speed in changing direction that Dean was able to attain cover about twenty yards from where his father was positioned.

"What the hell are you doing?" Ryan yelled at the boy. "Never break cover."

"There wasn't any, and they were moving behind me," Dean snapped back. "And they're sec men from the redoubt!"

For a fraction of a second, Ryan was taken aback, wondering how they got out of the redoubt and into position. No point wasting time thinking about that, though. They were there, and that was enough.

He whirled, his hand snaking to the panga on his thigh and clutching the handle as he became aware of a shuffling sound behind him.

The panga was raised to strike when a flash of white

hair and red eyes made Ryan drop the weapon to his side.

"Closing in," Jak said, hunkering down beside Ryan. The Colt Python was in his fist, looking huge and heavy in that small hand. "Moving in like pincer. Their land, too," he added meaningfully.

Ryan nodded. "How many?"

"Count seven, mebbe eight. No more."

"Even numbers, then. More or less. Okay, we've got to get through that channel before they can close us down," Ryan said, indicating the narrow inclined path leading out of the enclave.

Jak pursed his lips. "Move quick, shoot fast. Sec men slack enough for us see, so mebbe chance."

It was a good point. Ryan looked back over the hummock. There was a sporadic crackle of Uzi and H&K fire punctuating his brief discussion with Jak. He could see that J.B. and Krysty had moved up to join Dean and Mildred so that they were only twenty yards away.

There was no sign of Doc.

"Where's Doc?" he whispered.

"Lost in storm?" Jak mused. "Let me look." Then he disappeared from Ryan's side and into the swirl of dust and grit.

And into someone else's trouble.

MURPHY'S MEN HAD the advantage of old tech radios that kept them in touch. The compact devices spluttered and buzzed in the rad-riddled air, cutting out where old transistors began to fail, but they gave Murphy an edge he knew Cawdor and his people didn't have.

This should be simple. And if the outsiders just happened to get chilled by accident as they recovered Tanner? Well, that was just too bad, wasn't it? As long as Wallace got the old fart, he wouldn't moan too loudly.

Murphy raised the radio to his mouth. "Pergolesi, can you hear me?"

"Yes, sir," came a tinny voice, crackling over the static.

"Try and pick off Cawdor. Chill the one-eyed fucker."

"YES, SIR... And fuck you, too," Pri SecClass Pergolesi muttered as he slid the radio into the pocket of his combat vest. He raised his H&K and took sight at the one-eyed man. How the hell did that madman Murphy expect him to pick off anyone in these conditions with the first shot? And face it, that was all he'd get before fire was returned.

He saw the blurred figure move around as he started to squeeze the trigger, unaware of the sun glinting off the H&K's snubby barrel.

The crack of the ZKR and the whine of the bullet as it took chips off the rocks in front of him made Pergolesi fall backward, swearing to himself. He heard the radio squawk in his pocket and the chatter of H&K fire from the other side of the enclave.

Damn, Murphy would have his hide for this.

MURPHY WAS TOO CONCERNED with his mission going to hell to worry about Pergolesi at that moment. After ordering return fire from the other point of his patrol, he directed his men to form into a pincer and close on the group in the enclave, forcing them toward the narrow exit from the small valley. It would be relatively easy to pick them off from there.

"Leave the old fart to me," he yelled savagely into

his radio. "I can't trust any of you mothers to get it right, can I? Shit, if you want something done, you just have to do it yourself... Now jump!"

He slid his own radio into a pocket and checked the clip on his Uzi. It was full. He kissed the barrel again, even though it hadn't brought him much luck first time around, and left the cover of the rocks.

One thing Ryan had been correct about was that Murphy and his sec men were used to the conditions, each generation having been blooded in the enclave by their forefathers as they learned the hard art of defending the redoubt and the mechanism. Despite the discomfort of the conditions, each man moved confidently across the terrain, making much better time than any of the outsiders.

For his own part, Murphy was down on the floor of the enclave before Doc even had a chance to move out. The conditions and sudden blasterfire had a bad effect on Doc, taking his fragile psyche back to the psychological battering of the trank darts and comp torture. As he shielded his eyes from the dust storm, he felt as if he were back in the dark, wind-battered tunnel with Lori...or was it his beloved Emily?

"By the pricking of my thumbs, something wicked this way comes...or does it, indeed? Are you, perchance, the Snark my friend, or merely a Boojum?" Doc, quietly chuckling to himself, asked the figure that gradually took shape in the dust.

"Madman," Murphy muttered dismissively, raising his Uzi to barrel whip the old man into submission.

Like many another enemy, he had underestimated the seemingly old man. Despite his apparent fragility—both of mind and body—Doc Tanner had reserves of whipcord strength that could, in an emergency, prove to be of use as a surprise.

Murphy brought the barrel around in a down-sweeping arc, aiming for Doc's jaw. As the old man brought his lion's-head swordstick up to parry, the barrel of the Uzi was deflected, hitting the edge of a rock and sending a painful jolt up Murphy's forearm until it hit his elbow. The weakened joint buckled, and Murphy yelped in pain and surprise.

Doc rose to his feet, drawing the LeMat pistol and pointing it in Murphy's direction.

The sec chief stumbled as he tried to regain his balance and level the Uzi. It was only blind fortune that saved him. A bit of grit from the floor of the enclave caught in a crosswind and whirled viciously between the two men, catching Doc in the eyes. It disturbed his aim enough for the loud and resounding explosion of the shot to discharge harmlessly over Murphy's head as the sec chief regained his poise. He crouched, coming under Doc's outstretched arm with the stock of the Uzi turned toward the old man, angled upward as he drove forward.

The stock caught Doc under the ribs, driving the air from his lungs and jarring his heart. Doc's eyes widened, his mouth grotesquely distorted as he exhaled every breath of oxygen within him. The only thought he could muster was to try to start breathing again as he hit the rocks and the dry earth in a sitting position. He dropped the LeMat and swordstick, his arms clutching at his aching guts.

Murphy pressed home his advantage, bringing the barrel around to crack Doc's jaw. A light went out in the old man's eyes as he slumped into unconsciousness.

Shouldering his Uzi, sticking the LeMat into the

waistband of his camou pants and stowing the swordstick in his belt, Murphy leaned over and picked up the
old man with a strength that made Doc's deadweight
seem like a feather.

He was paying little attention to the fighting that was
sporadically breaking out at the head of the valley, and
so didn't notice the white wraith that drifted toward
him....

JAK WALKED PAST the sec men as though they weren't
there. Their attention was focused on attaining the head
of the enclave. As a result they weren't expecting anyone to go through their ranks in the opposite direction,
heading back to the redoubt.

Jak had spent his whole life hunting or being hunted,
and so found it simple to take the scattered rocks and
the opaque storm as cover, flitting across the ground
and blending with the rocks and hummocks along the
way.

The gathering of sec men at the head of the valley,
and their attempt to stop the group attaining open
ground beyond, wasn't his problem. Like the rest of the
companions, Jak trusted the abilities of the others implicitly, and knew that they would either overcome the
obstacles or perish in the effort. Life was that simple.

His task now was simply to find Doc and try to get
him back to the others.

Jak's impaired vision meant that he heard the fight
before he saw it, and he zeroed in on the noise. He heard
Doc's loud exhalation, Murphy's grunt of effort and the
crack of the Uzi on Doc's jaw. Small noises told him
that Murphy was in no rush to finish his business. The
scufflings were unhurried, and Jak crouched low to the
ground, moving noiselessly across the earth. He paused

behind a hummock to see Murphy heave Doc over his shoulder and turn back toward the redoubt's entry door.

The albino teen leveled his Colt Python, sighting along the silver barrel. He cursed silently through gritted teeth as Doc's swaying and unconscious form blocked his line of fire. He wouldn't risk hitting the old man.

Holstering his blaster, Jak moved out from behind the hummock and across the enclave with a fluid and silent grace.

Murphy was slowed considerably by carrying Doc, and so Jak was able to catch up on him quickly. Like magic, a leaf-bladed knife of lethal sharpness sprang into his hand seemingly from nowhere. It would be simple for him to spin the unsuspecting sec chief as he reached the redoubt entrance and chill him before taking Doc back to the others.

He was within three yards of Murphy, poised as the sec chief fed in the sec code to open the redoubt door, when he heard the slightest noise behind him.

Jak whirled to come face-to-face with an ancient, battered and home-repaired blaster. The black hole at the end of the barrel was pointing straight between his eyes.

"I've got no love for that bastard, cully, but if you don't put that knife away now, your brains are going to be just so much water on the soil."

Chapter Ten

If, as he suspected, they were evenly matched in terms of numbers, then why the fireblasted hell were they suddenly getting volleys of blasterfire coming from behind them?

Ryan ducked behind the hummock, uncertain of which was the greater enemy. The new blasterfire was coming from the head of the enclave, and by the manner in which it flew over the heads of the group, kicking up no dust or earth around them, it was clear that it was aimed at the sec men from the redoubt. There was no chance that the newcomers' aim could be that bad.

No one survived long in Deathlands without the ability to shoot at least reasonably.

Ryan cursed the dust storm that seemed unwilling to relent for even a second. The fragments of stone and earth whirling through the air stung his good eye, wormed their way under the patch that covered the empty socket and bit into the dead flesh. A line of sandy deposit formed, which irritated the long scar that bit into his cheek, from empty eye to jaw.

Worst of all, the clouds of dust, earth and stone moved around in the air, obscuring the movements of his enemies coming from the redoubt, making it impossible to see where these newcomers were positioned.

Ryan made a head count—there was just enough visibility in the air to enable him to do that. Doc was missing, and Jak had gone in search of him. Two down.

To his left he could see Krysty behind an outcropping. She was trying to pick off sec men, using her blaster sparingly in the poor visibility to preserve ammo. He couldn't be sure, but it seemed that her mane of red hair wasn't so much being tossed by the storm as fighting against it, whirling wildly around her head.

A few short yards away, Dean was taking cover behind a grassy hummock. His Browning Hi-Power was a good defensive weapon, but not the best blaster for these kinds of conditions. He, too, was using his blaster sparingly, trying to pick off the opposing sec men as they appeared through the confusion caused by the storm.

On the opposite side of the enclave, Mildred and J.B. were almost completely obscured from his view. He knew they were slowly moving toward his position, as their blasterfire was gradually changing direction.

He caught a glimpse of J.B.'s fedora, and the glint of a stray ray of sunlight on his spectacles. The Armorer was grim faced, the battle to maintain a defense in the face of the prevailing conditions etched into the concentration on his visage. He was walking in a low crouch from a small crop of boulders toward a pile of bare earth and rock that couldn't even be graced with the title hummock. It would be barely enough to cover him, but it would suffice.

If he ever got there.

Through the obscured floor of the valley, Ryan caught a glimpse of someone moving parallel to J.B. along a small rut that was cut into the almost sheer hillside. No human being should have been able to move along the rut as this man did—he ran almost heel-

and-toe with a grace and poise that wouldn't have disgraced a mutie goat, even presuming that a mutie goat would be able to keep its balance on such a narrow rut in the first place.

The man was about five-two or -three, and dressed in a collection of rags that seemed to swathe rather than clothe him. The layers could hide any number of weapons, although from what little Ryan could see the man was, at the moment, unarmed.

He was about a hundred yards behind J.B. when Ryan first caught sight of him. But while the Armorer was stumbling slowly across the terrain, the man on the narrow ledge moved swiftly and was sure of foot. He seemed to pay no attention to the storm raging around him, nor to the blasterfire that echoed and ricocheted around the enclave.

He was single-minded about his target.

As the man drew level with J.B., Ryan raised the Steyr and tried to draw a bead on the Armorer's ragged pursuer.

It was then that he felt the cold metal on his neck, a round, hollow shape pressing into the carotid artery. Not enough pressure to hurt, just hard enough to know that it was there.

He smelled the stale breath before the whispered words echoed in his ear.

"I wish you no harm as yet, my friend, but if you don't drop your blaster, then your blood will fertilize this tainted earth for no avail."

"DARK NIGHT," J.B. muttered under his breath as he stumbled yet again on the treacherous floor of the enclave. Trying to reach the head of the small valley was an option that now seemed like no option at all. His spectacles were covered with dust, and his eyes stung. He held the Uzi across his chest as he ran, ready to spin the blaster in any direction should the need arise.

But what direction? The storm was making everything a disorienting experience. So far he had been able to make out Murphy's sec men in the fog of dust and grit. He had a bearing for where Ryan was holed up at the head of the small valley, and he made for it. Millie should be somewhere behind him, and he had heard Dean call out at some point. The youngster was like his father—keen to take responsibility for his companions, expecting the same of them in return.

A shower of pebbles and earth from above and to his right snapped J.B. back from the reverie into which he had unwittingly fallen—a sign, perhaps, of fatigue.

The Armorer spun to his right, pulling the Uzi into position and squinting into the storm. He would fire if he was certain, but he didn't want to chill Dean or Jak by accident, and that was exactly the sort of move they might pull.

J.B. had expected to see either of those two, or more likely one of Murphy's sec men whom he could chill in an instant. The very last thing he had expected was what appeared to be a flying bundle of rags that leaped from off the seemingly sheer face of the valley and hurtled toward him with a shrill scream that cut through the whirling howl of the dust-storm wind.

It was impossible and had to have been a trick of his reflexes blunted by the storm and shock, but it seemed as though the bundle of rags increased its velocity through the air in order to beat him to the punch.

The Uzi was level with the flying figure as it cannoned into him, an arm knocking the blaster to one side. J.B.'s finger flexed instinctively on the blaster's trigger, sending a hail of fire to bite ineffectively into the side of the enclave.

The Armorer didn't notice the waste of precious ammo. He was far too busy trying to fight off the flying bundle, which became a whirling dervish of muscle as it hit him, slamming him to the ground so that his spine jarred and the breath was squeezed from painfully constricted lungs. J.B. felt as though he had to have lost a couple of ribs, the pain was so sharp as he tried to draw breath.

The ragged bundle was now on top of him, pinioning him to the earth. The strips of old clothing were wrapped around the figure in such a way as to obscure its true size. It could have been a small man, or a fat-bellied giant. Certainly the impact on J.B. had made him sure it was the latter at first, but now he wasn't as sure. As the figure lay across him, and the shock of the impact died down to a throbbing throughout his body, J.B.'s instincts kicked in.

The figure wasn't much taller than he was. Their faces were level, and he could feel the other's feet on his own as the attacker lay on top of him. The weight of the attacker wasn't crushing him now that they were hand-to-hand, so he guessed that his assailant was probably about the same build and weight as himself.

The rags were layered and swathed around the figure's head and face so that only the eyes were showing. They glittered with determination and not a little madness as they bored into J.B. And yet there was something in them....

It wasn't a total surprise for J.B. when the voice that emerged from the swaddling was female.

"If you value your life, at least for the short time to come, then you will not resist me."

The voice was sibilant, hissing with a cleft-palate lisp that made it sound even more threatening than the circumstances dictated.

The eyes and voice had momentarily hypnotized the Armorer to the extent that he didn't, for a second, feel her hands as they darted across his body. His knife was unsheathed with a practiced ease, and the Smith & Wesson M-4000 was slipped from its secure moorings. The pockets of ammo that were located all over his body were also probed.

"You will come with me now, away from this hole and into the valley. It is... milder...there. We wish to talk with you."

J.B. found himself nodding agreement with the lilting voice even though all his instincts were telling him to fight back, his muscles refused to respond, almost paralyzed by the hypnotic tones.

Suddenly the woman on top of him stiffened, her muscles contracting. Her eyes lost contact with his for a fraction of a second before J.B. heard a dull thud, and the eyes closed.

He felt instantly as though his strength were restored to him, and he rolled the unconscious body off him.

MILDRED WYETH WAS starting to feel really angry. As if it wasn't bad enough that the idiot Murphy's sec men had them pinned down, and this damn dust storm made it impossible to see more than two feet in front of your nose, now it seemed as though a third faction had joined the fray. She had no idea who they were and where they might have come from. Neither did she care. They were another obstacle between the companions and freedom.

Holding the ZKR with the poise and assurance that

had made her an Olympic silver medallist in predark times, Mildred made her way from cover to cover, knowing that J.B. was in front of her, and—hopefully—Doc behind. How the old man would cope in these conditions worried her. His fragile psyche had taken a battering in the past few days. Sure, all of them had been victim to the same method of torture, but Doc was closer to the edge than most. Hell, most of the time he was well and truly over that edge. And yet the old man had shown time and again reserves of physical and mental strength that had astounded her.

But right now she had herself to worry about. To her right a small pile of gravel littered the earth.

She looked up sharply, leveling the ZKR where she expected to see one of Murphy's sec men. Instead she saw a bundle of rags head past her, tripping along a narrow track that a rat would have trouble keeping a footing on, let alone a human being.

"Well, I'll be..." she murmured to herself. The figure was heading toward J.B.'s cover. If she squinted hard enough, Mildred could just make out the Armorer's fedora and a blurred shape beneath that could be his darkly clad body merging into the cover he had taken. She saw him move off into the open, heading for the next piece of cover.

Then she saw the ragged figure gain ground on him with a sense of purpose.

"Shit, John, do I have to get you out of everything?" she whispered before setting off at a brisk trot in pursuit of the ragged figure.

A sudden volley of shots from above diverted her attention from what was happening in front of her. Spinning on her heel, Mildred dived for cover...except that there wasn't any, the sniper had caught her out in the open.

She hit the ground hard, taking the impact on her shoulder and using it as momentum to pitch and roll. Her heavy coat, pockets burdened, slowed her fractionally as she came up on her knees, holding the ZKR in front of her in a two-handed grip. From the manner in which the ground had spurted around her as she fell and rolled, she had calculated that the sniper would be to her left and about twenty feet up.

Her eyes raked the face of the valley, trying to locate the sec man before he had a chance to get his eye in and chill her.

There...she could see the barrel of his H&K resting on top of a rock, his head clearly visible.

She took aim. The sec man had taken off his protective helmet in order to get closer in to his blaster, resting the stock against his cheek. His sparse, cropped dark hair was rippling in the howling wind.

Mildred ignored the spray of earth around her that joined the storm-tossed detritus as the sec man blasted at her, trying to get his aim right. Gritting her teeth and narrowing her eyes to sight along the ZKR, Mildred got him perfectly within her range. Breathing deeply and slowly to try to counter the adrenaline rush in her guts, she applied a gentle but firm pressure to the trigger of her blaster.

She was quick but wasn't careless. There was no way she was going to waste the two shots that could save her life.

Mildred squeezed off the two rounds. The first caught the sec man on the scalp, making him jerk to one side with pain and surprise. The second had originally been intended to hit him just beneath the right eye—exposed, as he had been sighting her through his left. However, the shock and jolt of the scalp wound caused him to move in such a way that his head shifted toward the line of the bullet, which caught him just beneath the nose. The lead ripped through his top lip, breaking open his palate with a splintering of bone and a pulping of soft flesh. The bone splinters ricocheted around the sinus cavities as his nose powdered under the impact. Bone shards followed the bullet as it drove into his brain.

Mildred didn't have time to watch him die. As soon as she saw him spin for a second time, she knew that he was already dead. By the time his corpse slumped over the rocks and slid down the face of the valley, dragged down by its own deadweight, Mildred was already headed toward J.B. and the ragged figure.

It had taken only a couple of seconds to dispel the danger to herself, but it was long enough for the ambulatory bundle of rags to catch up to the stumbling Armorer and throw itself at him.

Mildred prayed that the howling winds would drown out her footsteps, even though she ran with as light a step as she could manage. The figure was now on top of J.B., facing in the opposite direction to her, so at least it couldn't sight her as she tried to make ground.

She cursed the bundle of rags for being so shapeless and flowing. There was no way she could risk a shot as the rags spread out over the prone Armorer, making it impossible for her to delineate where the attacker ended and J.B. began.

The hissing sounds of low speech reached her ears when she came within range. Why wasn't John trying to fight back?

Without breaking stride or pausing for thought, Mildred tossed the ZKR in the air, catching it by the barrel and preparing to use the butt as a club. As she came within a few strides, she was sure that the bundle of rags could hear her, as it seemed to suddenly pause and incline its head.

But Mildred was quicker, bringing the butt crashing down on where she thought the skull would be located under the rags. She felt some satisfaction as the slumping figure fell off J.B. He looked up at her like a man waking from sleep.

"What was that about, John?" she asked by way of greeting. The smile on her face, however, faded quickly as she felt the pricking of a sharpened blade penetrate through the thick coat on her back and draw a bead of blood in her lumbar region. The warm blood trickled across and down, mixing with the sudden cold sweat.

"Drop the blaster, missy. I don't think Tilly is going to be too happy with you when she comes around—if you haven't broke her bastard skull."

Mildred raised her hands and let her pistol fall to the ground.

She looked at J.B., who was still seemingly dazed, and shrugged.

"Some days you just shouldn't get up. Am I right?"

KRYSTY STAYED behind the rock, keeping as much of the open space as she could see through the swirling dust clouds. Through the roar and howl of the storm she could hear scattered shooting and the yelling of voices. Roughly estimating the size of the enclave from what she had seen so far, she figured that it wasn't that large, which made it all the more frightening that she couldn't see what was going on a few yards in front of her.

But she had heard Dean's shouted exchange with his

father, and watched the boy zigzag past her to find cover. She knew that Ryan was waiting for them at the pass out of the enclave, and wondered how they would all get to somewhere they couldn't even see.

Her ears were sharp enough to detect the distances between the different sounds of blasterfire and movements that she could hear in the enclave. Sharp enough to tell when someone was running toward her.

Krysty whirled to face the direction of the sound and leveled her blaster.

"It's me," Dean whispered as he appeared through the curtain of the storm, his Browning raised and on the defensive.

"Gaia! I nearly chilled you, Dean," Krysty replied, dropping the blaster from its targeted spot over Dean's chest.

"Had to move quickly. They're gaining ground on us all the time," Dean said breathlessly as he slid in next to her behind the rock. "Dad's waiting at the pass, Jak's gone back to try and find Doc 'cause he's gone missing. Don't know about J.B. or Mildred. This storm is slowing us up."

Dean reacted with concern when he saw the way that Krysty's fiery red hair was moving about, coiling in tendrils about her head, neck and shoulders.

"Something wrong?"

She nodded. "Not sure what. But something other than what we're prepared for."

"Murphy's sec men know this land well—and seeing as they got outside before us, I reckon it's not too hard to see how they could get the upper hand on this terrain. We should expect anything from them."

Krysty smiled at Dean. He was learning fast, but still hadn't quite caught up.

"Trouble is, I don't think it's Murphy's men that we've got to look out for."

Dean frowned. "Then who?"

"Good question, young'an. Mebbe I can give you an answer."

Both Krysty and Dean froze at the voice from behind them. Sure, it was possible that one of them, in the noise and confusion of the storm and the fighting, may have missed the sound of an approach from the rear, but for both of them to miss it entirely bespoke a silent enemy to be reckoned with.

"Now, if you want to draw more than one more breath, I'd suggest that you drop those there blasters and turn around real slow, like."

Dean and Krysty both complied, the woman's hair curling tightly and protectively to her neck.

"Say, looks like you're a mutie, lady," said their captor wonderingly.

"Does it make a lot of difference?" she asked, her voice tight with the tension that coursed through her.

"Mebbe, mebbe not," the voice replied. "Guess it doesn't matter a damn. Not really. Just curious. Now, if you'll be so good as to turn around…"

"Guess we don't have much choice," Krysty muttered as both she and Dean turned slowly to face their captor.

He was a giant of a man, nearly seven feet and at least four hundred pounds. The homemade blaster he held in both hands was a gigantic weapon fashioned of what seemed to be two old motorcycle exhausts welded together and bound with wire. The stock appeared to be a burned and scarred old lump of timber, and the trigger was like a rusty old nail.

It seemed to be the sort of device that would explode

in its user's hands when the slightest pressure was applied to the trigger. The trouble was, with a blaster that size, the surrounding area would also get wasted. And that included them.

"Okay, now that we're all friendly, like, I suggest we get the hell out of here before that hell-spawn catch up with either us or you—depending on who they're after."

"Oh, it's us all right," Krysty said.

"Well, now, I guess that's not up to me to decide." There was something about the way he said it as he looked them up and down that made Krysty's skin crawl. Then he continued in a less disturbing tone of voice. "Those sure are nice blasters you got there. Be a shame to waste them, so why don't you just pick them up by the wrong end and carry them stretched out in front of you, like."

He waited until they had done so. "All right, so let's move on out of here."

"What if the sec men from the redoubt attack us now?" Krysty asked.

"Then you get chilled. So the sooner we head out, the better." The giant chuckled cheerfully to himself.

"That makes me feel so much better," Dean mumbled as they began to walk.

The sounds of blasterfire and shouting decreased in frequency and volume as they trudged the few hundred yards to where Ryan was waiting at the head of the only track out of the enclave. Like them, he was covered by an antique and home-repaired blaster.

Ryan exchanged questioning glances with Krysty, who tried to convey to him in a simple gesture that she couldn't figure out what was going on, either.

J.B. and Mildred emerged from the opaque blanket

of swirling dust and dirt, carrying between them what appeared to be a bundle of rags. The giant covering Krysty and Dean shook his head and clicked his tongue softly.

"Wouldn't like to be them," he said softly.

Krysty took one look at the face of the man with the bayoneted Lee Enfield who stalked behind Mildred and J.B. and agreed silently.

Before the Armorer and Mildred had a chance to say anything, Jak emerged from the storm, followed by a squat man whose blaster was trained in the middle of Jak's back.

"Okay, let's move out," said the man covering Ryan, his eyes darting sharply across the dust-shrouded enclave.

They all noticed that Doc was missing. Jak shrugged as their eyes asked the question.

Chapter Eleven

Doc emerged from unconsciousness with a groan. It had been a coma so deep, albeit short, that for minutes he had been aware of nothing. Not even blackness.

The old man realized that his mouth tasted of the sour salt that was dried blood. His eyes felt heavy, and his head ached in a strangely throbbing manner. He opened one eye cautiously, and the reason for the throbbing became obvious.

Doc was hanging upside down over Murphy's shoulder. At least he assumed it to be Murphy, as it was the sec chief who had rendered him unconscious.

Next he was aware of both an artificial quality to the light and the absence of both wind and grit scouring his skin.

They were back in the redoubt....

"I'll say one thing for you, old fart—you've got damn good powers of recovery for someone your age," Murphy said, failing to keep the admiration out of his voice as he felt Doc's weight shift on his shoulder. "Though from what I hear, you aren't as old as you look...or maybe older, if you want to be strictly accurate."

Murphy chuckled and stopped, lowering Doc until the old man was back on his feet. Doc took an uncertain step to try to regain equilibrium. Murphy, sensing that, unlike earlier shams, Tanner was really at a loss to fight back, helped the old man to steady himself.

"I would thank you for your kind assistance, if not for the fact that it is you who is responsible for my current condition," Doc muttered as he gingerly felt the side of his face that ached. It was already swollen.

"Don't worry, I didn't hit you hard enough to break anything. The Gen would have me recycled if I'd harmed you permanently in any way," Murphy said grimly. "You're a very important person to him, so I had my orders. And we always go by the regs down here."

There was something in the way he said it that made Doc start. Was that irony in his tone? A suspicion that may be worth filing away for later.

Doc bowed mockingly—and regretted it instantly. "I always believe on congratulating a craftsman who knows his art," he murmured.

"Better believe it, bub. I could've harmed you without blinking," Murphy said, this time without a trace of irony, as he examined his rings, rubbing the skull ring with a kind of pride. "I know just the right amount of pressure or force for any blow."

"That I can only too well believe," Doc replied ruefully. Then, looking around him, added, "I would assume that you were instructed to bring me back at the expense of my companions because of whatever madness Wallace has in mind?"

Murphy adopted a rueful expression rather than protesting Doc's words.

"I take your point," Doc said simply. "You need have no fears about any form of resistance from me at this point. In the words of old vids, it would be futile."

Doc's eyes strayed to Murphy's waistband, which held both the LeMat and the swordstick.

"Then let's get going," Murphy said, gesturing in front of them.

"Yes, let us," Doc added with a theatrical lack of enthusiasm before starting to walk down the corridor, Murphy's footsteps echoing a fraction of a second behind his own.

WALLACE WAS SITTING behind his desk, agitated and fussing over piles of paperwork when Doc entered his office, preceded by a brisk knock from Murphy. The sec chief brought up the rear, closing the door behind them.

"Sir, prisoner Tanner," he barked.

Wallace looked up from the paperwork, his hands freezing over sheets the relevance of which had ceased to be of importance many decades before. Like everything else in the redoubt, it was something Wallace did as a ritualistic task.

"Prisoner?" he replied softly. "Dr. Tanner is our guest, our honored guest. Without him there can be no hope for the mechanism. He was sent as a sign that there is still a point, a purpose to our existence. He is a sign that our work can still continue."

Doc raised an eyebrow. "And what, pray tell, is this work that I can help you to continue? Why me?"

Wallace smiled. It had that cold, leering quality often ascribed to the shark, but no shark could convey the sinister undertone of madness in Wallace's eyes.

"You will see in time, Doctor. But first—" he turned to Murphy "—I must deal with the guard. Sarj Murphy?"

"Sir?" Murphy clicked ostentatiously to attention

and stared fixedly at a point three feet above Wallace's head. The sudden hardening of the Gen's tone was a grim foreboding.

"Your men were a disgrace out there today. Dead or missing, you are the only one to make it back."

"What?" Murphy's mask slipped for one second, and genuine confusion showed through. "But that can't be possible, sir. These outsiders could never best us in the conditions. We know them, they don't—"

"I fear there was a third party to the slaughter today," Wallace mused. "The valley dwellers—mutie and inbred scum," he added in an aside to Doc, who merely nodded sagely and refrained from adding the view that Wallace might well to consider whether his description could be applied to his own men. "The valley dwellers must have had a scavenging party in the vicinity. They must have intervened."

"How do you know that?" Murphy asked heatedly. If the Gen had this knowledge when they were in the field, why hadn't he passed it on?

Wallace indicated the hidden vid room with an inclination of his head.

"Why didn't you let me know?" Murphy asked.

The Gen's face hardened into a scowl. "Remember who you are and where you are, Sarj. The regs have ways of dealing with impertinence. There are prescribed punishments."

Murphy breathed deeply, slowly, to control his temper. "Sir, I apologize," he said carefully. "But to what purpose was this knowledge kept from me?"

"It always pays to have a little training," Wallace said blandly. "I was interested to see how you'd cope with an assault on two fronts. You were found wanting, my friend."

The tension between the two men had escalated to a point where Doc was almost forgotten. Doc took this opportunity to stand back and observe, filing away character traits exposed in the argument for future reference. Who knew? It might be of use in any escape attempt he could contrive.

"Good men died because you wanted a training exercise based on a random factor?" Murphy railed. "Good sec is based on the elimination of the random factor!"

"No such thing," Wallace snapped back. "Look at the failure of one part of the mechanism. Random. The arrival of Tanner. Random…"

He turned and looked at Doc, a sudden vacancy in his eyes, as though he were searching for something—some strand of meaning that had somehow escaped him.

Then he grasped at it. "Tanner…" he said vaguely, and then with a more assured tone, "Yes, Doctor. Forgive me, I have been neglecting you. You have work to do, and we must prepare you for this. You are our honored guest, sent to us to aid in the war against the Reds."

"But that all ended a long…" Doc tailed off. Yes, it had. But not for Wallace, Murphy and the other inhabitants of this redoubt. And who was he to argue with them? Had the world of his beloved Emily, and of the whitecoats who had kept him captive at Operation Chronos, ceased to be real to him just because they had moved on in time and space?

These men were as much prisoners of memory as he was—the difference being that at least his memories were his own, and not the half-remembered dreams of ancestors distorted through time.

Wallace, seeming not to hear either Doc's tailing off or the long pause that had followed, rose to his feet.

"Please, Doctor, follow me and all will be made clear."

Doc fell into step behind the waddling Gen as Wallace left his office and headed along the corridor toward the elevator. Murphy left a short gap, then fell in behind his prisoner.

Doc wasn't sure whether Murphy's caution in being a few steps behind him was actually a defensive measure or intended to impress Wallace. It would be futile of him to attempt any kind of escape at this point, not until he stood some chance of retrieving his LeMat and swordstick.

As they progressed along the corridor, Doc noted that the redoubt had returned to the semibustling life that had marked it when they were first given the Gen's guided tour. Mechanics and orderlies went about their tasks, sec men moved through the lower orders in their patched, faded and much altered uniforms with a sense of purpose that was as much self-importance as anything else.

Although the redoubt would appear at first glance to be a fully working military operation, Doc was aware of a kind of torpor in the air. They moved, they bustled, but almost as though through water, or in slow motion, as though they had forgotten why they were doing this.

The only one who seemed to know was Wallace. Whether it was the original purpose, he—at least—had a clear idea of what he was doing, what they were all doing.

They were silent in the elevator as it moved to another level. Silent still as Wallace led Doc past the laboratories where the psychological torture had taken place. From the corner of his eye, Doc saw Dr. Tricks noting results from a monitor onto a clipboard. She looked up as they passed. For a fraction of a second her eyes caught his. A gorgeous, melting brown eye with a narrow eyebrow that was momentarily raised.

She was truly beautiful, out of place in this pesthole. Yet it was she who was responsible for their torture. Doc was sure there was a metaphor in there if only he could grasp it.

It was that thought that occupied him until they reached the door that had remained closed to them on the earlier tour. It was an unassuming door, remarkable for nothing except that very fact. Perversely that made it stand out all the more in a redoubt where everything else was clearly marked and delineated. Doc shuddered. What terrors could lurk behind that bland exterior?

Wallace reached for the sec panel at the side of the door, his index finger poised to tap in the code. Then he paused, finger still in midair, and turned to Doc.

"Dr. Tanner," he began, a note of genuine inquiry in his voice, "during your time at Operation Chronos, I understand that you learned a lot about the Totality Concept. Am I correct?"

Doc demurred. "I picked up a little knowledge...." Which was always a dangerous thing, echoed a small voice inside him. He was unsure what to give away, what to intimate, what to lie about.

"Did you ever hear of a project called Operation Rat King?" Wallace asked.

Doc paused before answering. Across the seared and frazzled synapses of his time-tossed brain, he struggled to access any memory, to decide whether to lie.

"I cannot recall for certain," he replied, trying to hedge any bets.

Wallace pursed his lips meaningfully and nodded slowly. At length he said, "I would have been surprised if you had answered in the affirmative, Doctor. It was part of the Totality Concept that was kept ultrasecret."

"I thought that applied to all of the experiments in that maddened scheme," Doc commented.

Wallace graced him with the kind of smile usually reserved for drooling idiots or small children about to be chilled for their stupidity. "That's just the point of view I would expect from your case history, Doctor. I do hope it doesn't mean that you intend to be awkward and noncooperative. That would be most unfortunate for all of us."

"I do not see that I have a choice," Doc said mildly, attempting to mask the acidity in his tone. "It would help if you explained a little more."

"Of course, of course. Some of the finest military, tactical and philosophical brains of the time were brought to bear on the problem of how to outwit an enemy that had the equivalent of our military power in software and hardware. The answer, it was decided, lay in lateral thinking rather than the harsh, cold logic of the computer."

His voice adopted the singsong tone of a man reciting a text learned by heart, a text that he couldn't really know the meaning of, yet felt compelled to repeat to the bitter end.

"To this end it was decided that the way forward lay in the sphere of the biocomputer. Thus was constructed the Moebius MkI—the Rat King."

A feeling of revulsion swept through Doc, churning at his guts and making acid bile rise to his throat. The word *biocomputer* was pregnant with meaning. As for the term *rat king,* Doc suddenly remembered an incident from his past.

It was the middle of March, 1881. It had to have been then, at the cusp of winter and spring, as the young Theophilus Tanner had just turned thirteen. The woods outside South Stafford were still sparse and bare, the foliage not having budded in the crisp air, air that frosted on his breath as he walked through the woods, trying to memorize the periodic table, reciting to himself.

It was before noon, and the sounds of wildlife were small. Few birds sang, and the scufflings in the undergrowth were negated by the sound of his own boots crunching on the dry earth.

''Phosphorous… What is phosphorous?'' Tanner muttered to himself, trying to recall the correct symbol and match it to the element. He shook his head at the stubbornness of the answer, and so was easily distracted by the strange squealing sound that seemed to emanate from a hollowed-out tree trunk about thirty yards to his left.

He paused, furrowed his brow and strode to the tree trunk to investigate.

The squealing seemed to separate out into more than one voice the nearer he got, it sounding for all the world like several animal voices in chorus.

Curious, apprehensive and perhaps just a little scared at what he might find, Tanner leaned over the hollow trunk so that he could see inside.

What he saw gripped him with both awe and fascination. Half a dozen rats were at the base of the tree, struggling and squealing in high-pitched squeals that blended into an awful harmony. Their bodies thrashed together, unable to separate and escape from each other because their tails were knotted, entwined in a spiraling tangle that ascended into the empty space above them.

The knot was so tight—each movement making it tighter—that Tanner knew that nothing short of amputation would separate them. It would also probably kill them.

Yet, bound together in that manner, death was already an inevitability.

Doc came back to reality with a shudder and a cold wave of nausea as he became aware of Wallace tapping in the access code and the door opening.

Back in the woods outside South Stafford, the young Tanner had run away and left the rat king to die.

This time he knew that he wouldn't be able to run.

"THOUGHT SAID storm less?" Jak asked truculently as they emerged from the pass and into the main body of the valley.

"It is less. I didn't say by much, did I, cully?" With which the man laughed so hard that the belly overhanging his ripped and patched camou pants shook and wobbled. The pants looked like those belonging to the sec men, and Jak figured that they were a trophy of a previous encounter.

"Tell the little shit how you came by them, Mac," the now conscious bundle of rags said, noticing how Jak was eyeing his captor's attire.

"Mebbe I will," Mac said, with the air of someone about to launch into a well-rehearsed and much told story. "Y'see, the insiders have always reckoned on how they were so good, and how all the old tech they still have makes them better fighters—"

"But they don't know the conditions, right?" Ryan interrupted, in no mood for self-congratulatory stories.

Mac glared at him. "You're damn right, One-eye. You know that, too. I was watching you. They was fancy moves when you came from the inside, but you didn't know how to deal with the storm."

"Not surprising," J.B. commented. "Never seen anything quite like that."

"Shut up and keep carrying," the bundle of rags grumbled. She was still suspended between the Armorer and Mildred, who glared at her, but managed to refrain from comment...for the present.

Krysty surveyed the land around them. It appeared that they were still in a valley, but a much larger one. The enclave formed around the entrance to the redoubt was a small indent into one side of the valley. Sheer rock walls ascended to a height she estimated at about 100 to 150 feet. The rock curved out in a wide parabola beyond her range of vision, but she figured that the valley as a whole had to be at least thirty square miles.

The dust storm had abated. The sprays of dust and dirt were irritations rather than major problems, and the wind had died down from a gale to a small zephyr that plucked at their clothes and drove grit into their skin. But parts of the valley were obscured by more intense storms, small pockets of violent rage that scoured the land. The skies overhead were a puckered and constantly moving mixture of purple, red and blue, the dark clouds of a chem storm breaking up and re-forming under the buffeting of the winds and letting the sky above shine through.

"I'd guess that you don't get much farming done around here," she murmured.

The giant who had captured Krysty and Dean, and was still guarding them with the homemade blaster, registered almost comical surprise.

"How the fireblasted hell did you know that?"

Krysty suppressed the urge to smile. "Just look at the skies and the storms. It's obvious. Guess we could always give you a few instructions on how to mebbe make more of the land. After all, you must have realized that we don't come from…the 'inside,' did you call it?"

Mac scratched his chin with the barrel of his blaster and furrowed an already well-creased brow.

"Guess we could do with some help. Trading's hard down here. If we could mebbe—"

"You fool!" The growl came from the female bundle of rags suspended between J.B. and Mildred. She was now fully conscious, but had decided that letting them carry her would disable them in conditions they weren't used to. Mildred winced as the harsh voice cut through the surrounding noise of the storm.

"Don't listen to their lies," she continued. "They came from inside—it's some kind of trick. It must be. They can't beat us in any other way, so they want to infiltrate and subvert from within. They want us to take these asswipes to our bosom so that they can smite us like a viper. No, there is only one thing awaiting them—the ritual."

Ryan and Jak exchanged glances. The mention of a ritual meant only one thing to them—a slow and painful chilling.

Mildred dropped her end of the bundle of rags. The woman hit the ground with a hissed, squeaking sound that was part shock and part outrage.

J.B. let go of his end of the woman and looked at Mildred over the top of his glasses, scratching his head and pushing back his fedora.

"Hell, John, if they're going to chill us anyway, why should we give a shit?"

There was a momentary stunned silence, then roars of laughter from their other captors while the female rag bundle fumed in silence.

It could be the one chance they needed. Jak spun on his heel, ducked underneath the barrel of Mac's blaster and aimed a straight-edged blow at the man's gut. He felt his hand sink into the soft, fatty flesh before striking a wall of solid muscle.

Mac wasn't as slow as his bulk would have them believe. Even as Jak ducked underneath him, he raised the blaster just enough to let Jak come underneath, confident that he had enough muscle strength to withstand the blow, and then brought the barrel down sharply at the base of Jak's skull.

Jak's white, flowing hair was stained red as the sharp metal edges of the badly filed barrel tore the skin at his nape. The blow wasn't hard enough to render him unconscious, but it was enough to stun him and send him momentarily to his knees.

Before he had a chance to recover, Mac followed up with his fist, grabbing Jak's hair and bunching it, using it as a rope with which to pull the albino up level with his face. Then he thrust Jak away from him, and the small albino looked even more waiflike and lost as he sprawled in the dust, clinging onto his senses.

"Don't fuck with us," Mac growled, his previously lazy demeanor now lost. "We don't have much, but what we do have we hold to."

"Okay, okay. Joke's over. We'll go with you and no trouble, all right?" Mildred said hurriedly as she went over to examine Jak.

"Too slow." Jak grinned ruefully as he picked himself up.

He glared at Mac. "Thought just fat. Won't make mistake again."

Mac returned the glare with a grudging respect. "You're fast. I'll make damn sure you don't get the chance."

Jak, Mildred and J.B. were now grouped together under Mac's watchful eye. The ragged bundle that was called Tilly now stood at the back of the group, keeping a watchful eye on their rear. Krysty and Dean were covered by the giant, while Ryan had the dubious pleasure of having two of their captors covering him, although, in truth, neither seemed to be taking too much care about how he was covered.

They followed a two-lane blacktop across the valley, the tarmac distorted and warped by the shift of the earth underneath, so that whorls and dips caused them to stumble. Their captors, however, seemed to know every little dip.

Which was why they thought they could be slack with their prisoners, Ryan thought. But it didn't explain why they weren't bothered about attackers.

"Mind if I ask a question?" he said laconically over his shoulder.

"You can ask, One-eye. Doesn't mean you'll get an answer, mind."

"Seems fair. I was just wondering why you're not keeping watch for an ambush."

The question was met with a degree of laughter that Ryan hadn't met anywhere else in the Deathlands.

"Excuse me my impoliteness," Mac, who seemed to vie with Tilly as unofficial leader of the group, said through the tears of humor that rolled down his cheek. "Seems to me that you don't know this place at all. Mebbe we were wrong about you."

"Mebbe you were," Ryan replied. "Still haven't answered my question, though."

"True, true. See, this place is a pesthole. No one much comes here. No one would want to. Mebbe we get some traders once in a purple moon, but mostly that's by mistake. There's only us and the insiders live here. No one else wants to settle here."

"Then why are you still here?" Dean asked, the first time he'd been moved to speak.

Mac shrugged. "Born here. Live here. Die here. That's the way of things."

"We get by," Tilly said. "We'd get by a whole lot better if the mother insiders would leave us alone."

"Why don't they leave you alone?" Krysty asked.

"You tell me, you're one of them," Tilly spit.

Krysty sighed. "If we were one of them, then why were they shooting at us? Why did they want us dead?"

Tilly moved in what might have been a shrug. "Everyone falls out with everyone else. People fight."

"For no reason?"

"There are 'no reasons,'" Mac snapped. "Now cut out the talking and let's move it." He scanned the skies. "I think we're in for another bad one, and I want to get back before it starts."

TRULY, DOC BELIEVED that reason had deserted him this time, perhaps for good.

"You realize that you are in that state that most people ascribe to me? The state of insanity, I mean?" he asked Wallace in a soft, almost disbelieving tone.

Wallace looked genuinely puzzled. "But, Doctor, even with your record of awkwardness and dissent, I would have believed that you would be astounded in these postskydark times that the Totality Concept still operated, still clung to its meaning.''

''Meaning?'' Doc's voice rose to a screech as he whirled away from Wallace toward the glass partition that separated the Moebius MkI from where they stood. He flung out an arm. ''You really believe that has meaning?''

He stood, not expecting an answer of any coherence and not really listening, his eyes glued to the monstrosity that he couldn't truly comprehend.

The slack-jawed, moronic tech stood beside him, still tapping in the codes and keeping the mechanism ticking over. That had to surely be all that it could do. What else was there now? The military-industrial complex for which it was designed had long since crumbled to dust, and any answers it might come up with were for questions that were no longer asked.

Doc pressed his face against the glass, breath misting and obscuring the image that seared on his retina. But not enough...no, never enough.

Behind the glass lay the rat king. At last he understood why Wallace—and the hellish whitecoat minds that had conceived the Totality Concept—had used the term.

In the middle of the sterile floor space stood a master computer. Its terminals were attached to a series of cables that snaked across the floor in six different directions. The screen attached to the mainframe was constantly filled with a series of 3-D images and strings of words that Doc's eyes were unable to translate from blinking lights into coherent sentences. Although, looking at where the images and words had surely to emanate, coherence was the last thing that occurred to Doc.

For the six different directions terminated in six padded chairs. In each chair was something that had once been human, but was no longer—six very old men, their clothes almost perfectly preserved in the sterile atmosphere, but hanging off them where they had become emaciated. They were fed and watered by a series of intravenous tubes that coiled away toward a central bank of a smaller mainframe, located in an antechamber of the room, presumably, Doc imagined, to try to cut down the amount of outside interference in the sterile room.

The six once-human men were blank eyed and staring, their mouths fixed in rictus grins of what could have been agony or ecstasy…or some inhuman mix of the two. Muscle wastage made it hard to tell, as their faces were little more than skulls with skin clinging, papery and thin, to them. Their wrists and hands were painfully thin as they poked from the end of immaculately laundered and starched sleeves.

Two of the men wore Air Force uniforms, one an Army uniform, another the attire of a general in the Marines, and the last two were garbed in suits that were conservatively but tastefully cut in a preskydark fashion. Doc recognized the style from some of the high-ranking security and government officials who had visited him during his brief sojourn in the late twentieth century.

The most horrific sight, however, wasn't their emaciated forms, but what had been done to their skulls above the brow.

In his native Vermont, Doc had been familiar with the practice of trepanning, whereby a hole was drilled in the skull, or some portion of the skull removed, in order to relieve pressure on the brain. It was a medical practice of dubious worth, and was also used by some cultists and followers of ancient religions as a path to release the mind and induce euphoric states. Often, it resulted merely in drooling idiocy, which was, Doc supposed, a euphoria of sorts.

What had been done to these men looked like trepanning on a larger scale. The snaking cables that ran from the mainframe terminals ended in electrodes that were directly attached to portions of each man's brain. It appeared to Doc that the cables disappeared into a network of small holes drilled in the skull.

"And this is what you have in store for me, is it?" he asked, turning back to Wallace.

The Gen nodded. "Uh-huh. You see Secretary of Defense Sethna?" He indicated a figure in a suit whose only defining characteristic left was that he was of a darker skin than the others, possibly an Asiatic origin. "Well," Wallace continued, "he's dead...basically."

"Are not they all?" Doc queried.

Wallace smiled. "Depends what you mean, Doctor. We try and keep them going, as it's the interaction of them all that makes the mechanism work. We recycle body parts, but in this one it just looks like the brain finally gave out. Now, there's no way we could find any part comparable to that...until you arrived."

Doc turned back to the glass and looked at the rat king. "Madness," he muttered. "Sheer folly and madness."

Whether it was a comment directed toward Wallace's plans, or the minds that had originally conceived the rat king was lost as Doc felt a needle plunge into his arm.

He turned to face the drooling, cretinous tech, hypodermic still in hand, as the blackness and welcoming respite of unconsciousness overwhelmed him.

Chapter Twelve

The two-lane blacktop came to a sudden end where the tarmac rose into the sky for a height of twenty feet at an angle that suggested a sudden eruption from the earth had pushed it upward. The ground on either side was divided by a chasm that yawned to a width of twelve feet or so at its widest, narrowing to three or four feet in places.

"End of the line?" Ryan asked as they came to a shambling halt.

"Hell, no," Mac said, gesturing across the divide with his blaster. "We just jump it."

Jak gave him a questioning look, particularly at his drooping stomach.

Mac laughed without humor. "Mebbe I'm just fitter than I look."

"I'm not sure that I'm that fit," Mildred said uncertainly, peering over the edge of the chasm. It descended into a darkness that suggested no small depth.

Mac shrugged. "It's okay by me, missy. You fall down there and get chilled, it just means one less for the ritual. No skin off me."

"Nice to know you care," Mildred muttered laconically.

The giant with the homemade blaster gestured down the divide, swinging the giant pieces of metal as though they were weightless.

''No way we're jumping here. If we go down a little, then it'll be easier.''

''Suits me,'' Mildred replied. ''Lead the way, big man.''

Much to her surprise, he did. Turning his back on them, he wandered along the edge of the chasm like a man leading a Sunday-school outing.

J.B. and Ryan both furrowed their brows, exchanging puzzled looks. Their captors were certainly a contrary mixture. On the one hand, they had kept the group under a close guard with their blasters, yet they were seemingly slapdash about such elementary precautions as turning their backs on their prisoners. Like the sec men in the redoubt, they had spent too long in an enclosed atmosphere—one underground, one trapped by the valley and the freakish weather conditions—to have any conception of outside enemies and their tactics.

Ryan surveyed the surrounding area. The storm had died down to a bluster at this point, the dust on the ground stirring in the small eddies and whorls of the wind. Denser clouds obscuring parts of the valley bespoke of areas where the storms still raged. There was no sign of life, and little cover. The trees were few and far between, stripped bare of life and standing starkly in the landscape. The earth was flat; if not originally this way, then it had been pared down years of storms and harsh hurricanes and zephyrs scouring its surface.

''How do people live in this?'' Krysty asked softly, mirroring Ryan's thoughts.

''They don't,'' he replied quietly. ''They exist.''

''Isn't that what we all do?'' Mildred queried.

Ryan's face cracked in a grimace that could have been grim humor. His scar was puckered white by the elements.

"Some mebbe exist more than others," he said.

The only reply was a shove in the back. The one-eyed warrior, acting on instinct, spun. Tilly stood in front of him, the tip of a long and wickedly jagged hunting knife touching the end of his nose.

Her voice was sibilant and all the more threatening for it. "Philosophy doesn't grow crops, doesn't appease the gods. It does nothing but make you sit on your spreading ass all day doing jackshit. And it may get you cut up if you don't shut up and follow Tod."

If nothing else, at least Ryan now knew that the giant had a name. The one-eyed man held up his hands in a gesture of surrender and turned to follow the giant along the lip of the chasm.

Mac laughed in the humorless, grating way that was beginning to act as an irritant, and gestured with his blaster that they should follow Ryan.

Dean and Krysty fell into step, followed by Mildred and J.B. Jak stayed back to last, dragging his heels and eyeing Mac with barely disguised hatred.

Two of the other captors exchanged looks over their blasters, one of them shivering. Mac grinned wryly.

"You don't say much, whitey," he directed at Jak.

"Action better," Jak replied.

"You ain't shown much," Mac said shortly.

Jak shrugged, then turned his back and followed his companions. It left Mac with a turning stomach and a foreboding that things weren't perhaps to be as simple as he had hoped.

Farther down the way, Tod had come to a halt. The giant waved the heavy blaster in the general direction of the gap between the two sides of earth.

"Guess this is about the narrowest stretch," he said,

spitting over the edge. "It's no ravine at best, but this is as narrow as it gets."

J.B. took off his glasses and polished them on his shirt. He peered over the edge and across at the far side.

"What's to stop us going across first and then waiting to attack you on the other side?" he asked.

Tod grinned lopsidedly, revealing a row of broken yellow teeth. "This…" he said simply before turning and taking aim with his giant blaster at a small piece of scrub that was twenty yards across the gap.

The blaster exploded with a deafening roar that drowned out the background howl of the storms for a second. It belched blue smoke and flame as it discharged a load of shot from the large barrel. The recoil from such a charge had to be enough to break an average man's arm if the blaster was held one-handed, as Tod held it, J.B. thought.

The giant didn't even seem to notice that the weapon had fired.

Twenty yards away the scrub disappeared in a puff of what might have been dirt, but might simply have been the splintering wood of the bushes disintegrating as the mixed load of the charge hit it with tremendous force. The width of the barrel showed in the wide spread of the charge, which pockmarked the ground around the small scrub area.

Some of the debris that made up the load could be discerned as pieces of metal glittering in the weak sunlight that filtered through the dust and chem clouds. Nails, pieces and shards of metal from other weapons, household objects from predark times…anything that could be pared down to pieces small enough to load in the blaster.

Dean whistled, low and soft.

"Point made," J.B. said simply. He had deliberately asked the question in order to try to provoke such an action. Casting an eye around the other captors and their homemade and home-repaired blasters, he made a rough mental assessment of their collective firepower.

It was always useful to know. There was never such a thing as wasted information. You never knew when your life might depend on the minutest scrap of knowledge.

"Cool," Tod said, grinning inanely through his broken teeth as he plucked another cartridge from one of the large pockets on his coat. He snapped open the large blaster, which operated on a simple hinge, like a modified shotgun, and pushed the cartridge into the breech. It was a lumpy concoction of metal wrapped in bulging cardboard that shouldn't, in all logic, have worked. J.B. figured that one day the blaster would just explode in the giant's face.

"Let's cut out the target practice and showing off, and just move," Tilly said flatly, her eyes burning contempt from her layers of rags.

Krysty stared at her defiantly. "Lady, you've got a real problem. You're calling all the shots here, so why don't you lay off? What is it with you?"

"Oh, shit, bad question," Mac whispered to the other two men with blasters. Still they didn't break their silence, just shaking their heads sadly while keeping their blasters ready and aimed.

"You want to know my problem?" Tilly roared, springing forward with a suddenness, violence and grace that took Krysty by surprise. Before Krysty had a chance to move, Tilly had thrust her face into hers.

Ryan stiffened, keeping his eye on the men with blasters. Mildred shook her head almost imperceptibly.

She, for one, would be interested to see what happened. Like J.B., she believed that all information was useful. It was just that sometimes she wanted different information.

"You want to know what's the matter with me? You really want to see why I hate you and your kind?"

"My kind?"

"The insiders," Tilly spit back. "You want to see what your kind has done to me? Just because I didn't fit what you wanted from your gene pool—not that it stopped your sec men fucking me afterward, like pigs."

Tilly began to unwrap the rags around her head. Her eyes burned brightly with hatred, and also with something that Krysty felt sure was self-loathing.

As the rags came away in her hand, a dirty and multicolored bandage that unraveled onto the earth, Krysty could see that Tilly had no hair to speak of, just small tufts of down that appeared on a red raw scalp. It looked as though someone had taken her by the hair and roughly sliced away the skin. Her forehead was heavily lined and crisscrossed by scars.

Around her eyes, the skin was baggy, making her burning eyes seem ancient and old when fully revealed. Her face was scarred with the remains of old burns, her lips almost gone and her nose hollow and devoid of flesh.

"They set me on fire after taking my scalp. They wanted the hair and skin for DNA tests. The burns were for tests on antibiotics. When I was thrown out to die, the sec men took me because they hadn't been allowed to mate and felt the urge...." She uttered the last part with as much of a sneer as she could muster from her broken face.

Ryan kept his gaze steady on the woman, noticing

that Krysty didn't flinch in her face. From the corner of his eye, Ryan could see that the other guards weren't moving. There seemed to be an unspoken assumption that Tilly, if not actually outranking them, was certainly of a higher standing.

Ryan had been at the mercy of psychotics in charge of sec forces many times. It was never a good experience.

Krysty was breathing shallow and fast, trying to stop herself from appearing shocked or disturbed by either Tilly's appearance or her actions.

"Take a good look, bitch," Tilly breathed, her voice reduced to a harsh, venomous whisper. "Take a good look, 'cause you'll end up like this, too. You and the black bitch."

"Tilly don't like women much," Mac said. It didn't escape anyone's notice that the irritating humor was gone from his voice.

"Of course she doesn't," Mildred said quietly. "We remind her too much of what she used to be."

Krysty breathed a sigh of relief as Tilly whirled away from her, trailing rags like banners behind her in the now gentle breeze. With a few strides that seemed to float her across the surface of the ground without touching, Tilly was in front of Mildred, waving the knife in her face.

"Shut the fuck up," she screamed, an edge of madness seeping into her tones. "Just shut the fuck up, or I swear I won't wait until the ritual. I'll chill you now, and it won't be quick. It'll be slow and—"

She was cut off as Mildred snaked out a hand and gripped Tilly's knife wrist. The ragged woman was taken by surprise, a blank look of incomprehension crossing what was left of her face as Mildred twisted her arm. With her free hand she snatched the knife from the weakened grip, at the same time twisting farther so that Tilly had to turn or risk dislocation of her elbow or shoulder joint.

"Hold it right there," Mac snapped, raising his blaster. With an indication of his eyes, he made sure that the other two covered Dean, Krysty and Ryan while he covered Jak, whom he trusted least.

J.B. flicked his eyes toward the lip of the chasm. Tod had Mildred and Tilly in his sights, and a quick estimate told J.B. that the spray from the gigantic blaster would almost certainly chill him, as well.

"Okay, it's okay," Mildred said coolly, dropping the knife and pushing Tilly away from her so that the woman fell into the dirt. "I was just making a point." She looked at her companions and shrugged. "There's nowhere to run yet, anyway," she added.

Tilly picked herself up, claimed her knife and hastily rewrapped the bandages around her head until she was completely swathed. She stood back, a little apart from her fellow valley dwellers, her eyes flashing loathing from within the shadows.

Tod looked up to the skies and sniffed. "I'd say we better get across real soon. There's a change in the air, and we don't want to get caught out here when it happens."

Mac nodded. "Okay. You and Tilly get across and stand guard on the insiders as they come across."

Ryan watched with interest as both Tilly and Tod crossed the divide. The ragged woman was no surprise, bounding across the three-yard gap in the chasm with a lightness of foot and a grace that landed her safely on the other side. Tod, on the other hand, was a revelation. Despite his height, considerable bulk and the size and weight of his homemade blaster, Tod made the leap look like a step into the void, covering the distance with ease.

"Your turn," Mac said when Tod and Tilly were facing them across the gap, the annoying grate of humor returning to his voice.

"Me first," Jak said simply. He took a short run and launched himself into space, arms and legs bicycling to gain those precious few extra inches. He landed on the other side with a puff of dust around his feet.

Ryan looked around at his companions.

"I'll go next, lover," Krysty said, looking less than enthusiastic. She psyched herself up by taking deep breaths, calling on Gaia to give her the strength to propel herself across the gap.

Her concentration was so intense that she didn't even realize that she had made the run-up until she was in midair, sailing across the divide. Her limbs felt weightless, buoyed by the air currents around and beneath her.

It was a feeling so exhilarating that she was almost sorry when she touched down delicately on the other side. But almost immediately her strength felt completely sapped, her limbs heavy. She collapsed into a heap as Jak rushed to her.

He was stopped by a knife that thudded into the dry, hard ground at his feet.

"Leave her, or the next one is in your guts, red-eye."

Jak stared across at Tilly with the eye of one who was keeping the score, but he held his tongue and stayed where he was.

On the far side Dean chewed his lip. He was younger than the rest, in some ways fitter. But he was still growing, his frame sometimes outreaching the strength of his musculature. It would be a real test of his stamina and ability to get across.

"Let me go next," he said. And before Ryan could say a word, Dean ran to the edge of the chasm with measured strides, flexing his knees and getting as much spring as he could into his leap.

As he flew through the air, he could feel his lungs almost burst with the effort and the amount of oxygen he had taken into his body.

As he began to dip, he knew it wasn't quite enough.

On the other side, Jak could see the slight decline in Dean's flight and knew the youngster was hitting trouble.

Dean knew that he wouldn't quite make it. He flung out his arms to grasp at the loose dirt on the edge of the chasm as he slammed into the rock-studded wall. His fingers grappled for purchase as the showers of dirt flew into his eyes, mingling with the sweat of exertion and fear that made it hard to see what he was doing. He moved his feet, frantically searching for some kind of foothold from which to propel himself up.

The rocks under his toes moved as he put the slightest pressure on them, slipping free from the earth and thudding into the darkness, setting off mini-earth slips. The sounds echoed and receded into the distance below, a darkness Dean dared not look down on as the cold, dry earth scored his cheek. He was losing ground, slipping down farther until...

It seemed like an eternity to the youth, but it was only a couple of seconds. A couple of seconds in which Jak would pluck him out of trouble. Ignoring Tilly's sore-throated roar to stay where he was, and taking no note of the badly thrown knife that thudded into the ground on the edge of the chasm, Jak propelled himself forward with a stride that his short stature didn't seem capable of achieving. His snow-white hair whipped out behind him as he flung himself full-length with the second step, one arm shooting out into the abyss, strong fingers grasping for Dean's wrist or fingers.

His eyes stung so much, his vision blurred so much that Dean registered Jak's hand, sinewy fingers extended, as only a lighter blur on the dark surface of the earth and rock face. Jak's fingers groped for Dean's hand and found it as the boy's fingers lost their hold and slipped on the dry, treacherous earth.

Jak's fingers closed around Dean's in a strong grip that bit into the boy's flesh. The pain jolted Dean out of the enclosed world of earth, dark and struggle. Instinctively he knew what was happening, and brought his other hand around, scrabbling all the while on the surface of the almost sheer face to grasp Jak's wrist.

But he was still a long way from safety. His feet were treading air and earth that slipped away beneath him, letting him fall a fraction of an inch with each pedal of his combat boot.

Jak and Dean were roughly about the same size, but if anything the young Cawdor was slightly taller, slightly heavier than the whip-thin albino. On the surface of the earth, while Ryan, J.B. and Mildred watched helplessly from the opposite side, Jak was dragged across the ground by the double pull of gravity and Dean's lack of purchase, dragged farther and farther until the top half of his body began to poke out over the edge of the abyss, the gradual increase in weight balance on the lip accelerating the rate at which he was pulled forward.

Jak grunted heavily with the effort of trying to pull himself back, to pull Dean up and over the edge. His

right arm took Dean's weight, feeling the pull on every
sinew and tendon as the boy's weight strained on the
limb. His left arm was held down at his side, clawing
at the earth as he tried to dig in and gain some purchase
with the toes of his boots.

Krysty shot a glance at Tod and Tilly. The ragged
woman seemed to have expended her anger at Jak's
action, and like the giant was watching the tableau impassively.

Another second ticked past, agonizingly slow. Krysty
decided to take the chance that they would let her assist.
They seemed too keen on their ritual chilling to want
to waste all their captives' lives. So it was worth the
chance....

Krysty hurried to Jak, shrugging off her fur coat. It
was too bulky for right now, and would hinder her
chances of giving aid.

She hit the dirt before the coat, on her knees and
grasping Jak by the waistband of his camou pants. Feeling her strength as she pulled him back from the lip,
Jak redoubled his efforts, toes biting into the ground
and forming small horizontal steps as he scrabbled back.

As Jak's whole torso was once again on flat earth,
Krysty relinquished her grip and moved around to the
edge of the chasm. Looking over the lip, she could see
Dean's face, contorted with the effort of pushing against
the side of the dirt chasm until his legs felt like molten
lead, the muscles burning with a heavy fire. His hands
clung to Jak's whipcord arm, the veins and muscles
bulging as Dean's fingers bit into the white flesh. The
boy had enough sense to reach under the sleeve of Jak's
patched coat, which his weight would otherwise have
dragged off Jak's body. The sleeve had worked its way

up Jak's arm, showing the white flesh going red where Dean's fingers scored into it.

Krysty stretched herself full-length and reached down, taking hold of Dean by his shirt, pulling on it until it came out of his pants and gathered around his neck.

It was enough to help him scramble the extra few inches for Krysty to grab his belt. With that much firmer hold she was able to take more of the boy's weight and relieve the strain on Jak.

As he got closer to the top, and the lip of the chasm gained a slight diagonal incline from the continual slipping of surface dirt, Dean was able to gain more of a foothold and so propel himself onto the plateau at the top, where he collapsed into a heap, panting heavily as he drew precious air into his lungs. The fire in his aching muscles began to abate.

Jak rose gracefully to his feet, rubbing life back into his bruised and numbed limb.

After checking that Dean was recovering, Krysty collected her fur with as much nonchalance as she could muster, casting a disdainful glance at the still impassive Tod and Tilly.

"That was a damn good show," the giant said, nodding slowly. "Reckon as you could mebbe do it again?"

Once Dean was on his feet, Mac gestured to Ryan with his blaster.

"Reckon it's your turn now, One-eye. See if you can give us as much of a show as your brat."

Anger blazed within Ryan, but he kept it hidden, the only outward signs a twitch at the corner of his mouth and a whitening at the edges of the puckered scar under his eye socket.

It was the suppressed fury that gave him the explosive energy to cover the distance with ease.

J.B. was next. As with most things the Armorer did, it seemed to be a matter of little effort and an offhand glance. After polishing his glasses, the wiry weapons expert took a short run and threw himself across the divide.

It wasn't the most graceful landing, but it was perfunctory. The only thing that worried J.B. was the way his ankle twisted as he hit the ground. He felt a slight pull, and a pain that was halfway between a stab and an itch. He noticed the slight sensation of weakness as he walked over to the others. He decided to say nothing for the while, hoping that he could walk it off.

Mildred was the last to jump. Waiting until last had done her nerves little good. There was a small demon inside her that she had never confronted—her fear, not so much of heights but of drops. As a child, she remembered looking at pictures of the Grand Canyon in books her father possessed, and being struck not by the grandeur but by the sheer fall to the bottom.

And now she had to jump across a sheer drop.

"Did you ever hear about a guy called Evel Knievel?" she said to Mac and his silent sec men. She received a blank look in return. "Forget it," she said. "Just an old woman rambling about things you wouldn't know."

She took the jump with a greater ease than she would have thought possible. It was a strong temptation to close her eyes as she soared through the air, but she resisted, knowing that she had to keep them open to judge her landing.

It was close to the edge, but not over. The urge to look over her shoulder and into the abyss was almost overwhelming, and she risked a quick glance over her shoulder.

The drop into blackness zoomed in and out of focus, and she felt herself sway. A hand steadied her. Looking around, she saw J.B. in front of her, grasping her arm.

"Thanks, John," she said, smiled. "Nearly lost it there."

J.B. returned the smile. "About time I helped you out," he said simply.

Tod gestured to them to band together, waving the giant blaster. It crossed J.B.'s mind that with a blaster like that they could be spread in a hundred yard radius and still be picked off by one load of shot, but he kept his peace as they moved together under the watchful eyes of Tod and Tilly.

Mac and the other two sec men crossed the divide with ease, leaping with a surprising grace to cover the distance.

"Mutie jackrabbits, not men," Jak muttered.

"Guess they've just adapted to the conditions," Mildred offered by way of reply.

"Shut up and move," Tilly's hissing tones cut short any further discussion.

"How much farther to your ville?" Ryan asked after they'd been walking for some time. They were going through another whirl of the seemingly constant storm, the wind rising to a howl loud enough to necessitate Ryan shouting. The dirt and dust whipped at them, stinging.

J.B. was aware of the pull in his ankle getting worse. Mildred had also noticed the way in which he was shifting his weight on his left foot, and gave him a questioning glance to which she received a short shake of the head in reply.

Ryan repeated his question. "I said, how far—?"

"I heard you the first time," Mac replied in a slow drawl, cutting across Ryan. "It's as far as it takes."

"You always talk, not them," Jak said, indicating the two sec men who brought up the rear of the party. "They have no tongues?"

Mac smiled again, that lazy saurian smile that was beginning to make Ryan wish he could ram it so far down the potbellied man's throat that it would come out of his ass.

"How did you guess that, boy?" Mac drawled. "Show the whitey, boys," he ordered the other two.

They complied, opening their mouths as they walked. Both men had their tongues torn out by the root, a gaping red gap in the maw of their mouths, obscene and wet.

Mildred winced. It looked like a primitive and painful extraction, even from a distance. "Don't tell me, let me guess," she directed toward Tilly. "The sec men from the redoubt again?"

The ragged, bundled head shook, the voice emanating from within almost quavering with repressed hate.

"Not sec men. Whitecoats who wanted the body parts."

"Nice," Mildred murmured. "And you think we're part of that?"

"You came from there, so it stands to reason," Tod butted in before Tilly could summon the venom to answer.

"You stupe or something?" Dean exploded, fatigued and sick of their seeming stupidity. "Why were they after us?"

"Like I said, to make us think you weren't with them. Make us easy to fool." Mac shrugged. "It figures out."

Dean was about to hotly respond when a gesture from his father stopped him. He trusted Ryan's judgment. Although young, he knew enough about himself to be aware that he had to control his impulsive temper.

"Seems to me that you live on the far side of the valley," Ryan remarked. "We've covered a lot of distance."

"I'd say that was smart, if I didn't reckon you knew that anyway," Mac answered. "After all, seems to me that you should know where we are when you raid us often enough."

Ryan ignored that and continued on his line of thought. "Yeah, I'd reckon you live on the rim of the valley. Can't grow jackshit down here. Never get anyone passing by. Mebbe you can scratch a living on the edge of the valley. And you'd have to live as far away from the redoubt as possible."

"And why's that, One-eye?" Tilly asked, her paranoia scenting an insult.

Ryan didn't want to disappoint her. "Because you're good in these conditions, but you've got no real armory to speak of—not if that shit is the best you can do." He gestured at the homemade blasters before changing tack. "That's okay against foot soldiers, but they've got wags at the redoubt. Good ones. Ones that many a trader would chill for. Mebbe ones that we could help you get."

Tod furrowed his brow, resting the giant blaster on his massive shoulder so that the pipelike barrels stuck into the air.

"You sure are a strange one, Mr. One-eye. Start by cussing us out, then offering to help. Just what do you want?"

"Same thing as you...to survive," Ryan said simply. "Besides, they've got one of our people still in there."

"You'd want to go back?" Mac asked.

Tilly cut across him. "Of course they would," she spit. "Motherfuckers would just be going home."

"Have it your way." Krysty sighed, tired of the way the ragged woman always dented any attempt to build bridges or find common ground, let alone work a means of escape.

Looking around, she could see that escape wasn't a viable possibility. There was nowhere to run to. Perhaps when they reached the ville, on the rim of the valley, they might find a way out, a way they could double back and try to get Doc.

If Doc was still alive.

They sank into silence, trudging across the storm-swept plains, moving slowly from a heavily dust-filled zephyr into a calmer drift and then into the swirl, and subsequently into the calmer eye of another whirlwind. The valley dwellers seemed hardly to notice the changes in the weather. The force of the storm didn't impede the pace they set, and their vision seemed to be unimpaired by the conditions.

It wasn't so easy for the others. At times the strength of the gale-force winds drove them back, seeming to pluck them off the ground and make every step forward seem like two steps back. The sudden flurries of dust, dirt and stones scoured their exposed faces, made their eyes run with irritated tears until they were dry and sore.

It was draining, and Ryan looked around to see how his people were doing. It wasn't encouraging. Jak and Dean were particularly hard hit, both weakened by the effort of saving Dean from plunging into the chasm. They straggled behind, the dumb sec men prodding them into desultory attempts to keep up. Krysty was in front of them, her coat pulled around her to try to ward off the worst of the wind-blasted dirt and dust. The most worrying was J.B. The Armorer was keeping pace with Mildred, his arm around her shoulders as she helped him support his weakened ankle. But Ryan could see that the pace was beginning to tell on him, and his limp had become more pronounced. The dust was sticking to his sweat-stained forehead, and he grimaced at every other stride.

"J.B., how's it going?" Ryan asked as casually as he could.

"Been better," the Armorer replied laconically. "Been much better."

"We should really stop," Mildred interjected. "Get John's ankle bound before we have to cut that boot off."

Ryan took a look at their captors, who were seemingly paying them no attention.

"I'm not sure they'd let us," he commented.

J.B. smiled at the wry humor. "Not the most hospitable of folks," he added.

"Can't figure them out," Ryan continued. "They're slack, like they don't care if we're watched or not."

"Mebbe they're not," J.B. said, glad of something to take his mind off the pain of every other stride, which had grown from an itch to a stab like a rusty nail in the ankle joint. "Where can we go to out here? No weapons to fight with, and not as used to the conditions. Mebbe they've got more to fear from other sides."

"A raiding party in wags from the redoubt?" Ryan mused.

"Could be. Could be something else."

"What the hell could there be out here?" Mildred asked, bemused as she tried to imagine any kind of indigenous life.

"You'd be surprised," Mac drawled slowly, still keeping a watch all around him.

"Yeah, and...?" Mildred asked after she tired of waiting for him to enlarge.

"Weird shit, missy...weird shit. Just pray we don't get sniffed out while we're out here," he answered cryptically.

Mildred raised a questioning eyebrow at J.B., who shrugged. The man with the blaster didn't have to tell if he didn't want to. And there was no way of making him.

They continued in silence for a while, J.B. relying on his good ankle as the pain grew harder and blunter in the damaged joint, each impact on the uneven earth making it increase. He tried to disguise it. There were a number of reasons, not least of which being that he didn't want to be left behind as a liability by their captors, forcing Ryan into a decision about action.

But he knew that if it came to the crunch, he would be found wanting for speed and maneuverability.

WHEN THE MOMENT CAME, it was unexpected.

As they began to march through a slough in the valley floor where a trapped zephyr made the dust storm whip up, scouring and scratching at their bodies, their pace was slowed to a crawl. The wind howled and moaned, and the air was full of earth, small pebbles and even larger chunks of rock that they had to dodge. The surface of the ground became a writhing, shifting mass of loose earth, churned up continuously by the trapped zephyr.

"Couldn't you find an easier route?" Ryan yelled through the encroaching confusion.

"This is the easiest," Tod shouted, somehow imparting this information blandly, despite having to raise his voice.

Although the zephyr could have covered no more than half a mile, visibility in the swirling fog of earth was reduced to a few feet.

Krysty felt her senses tingle, and was at once acutely aware of danger, but not of the source.

She moved closer to Ryan, grasping his arm and pulling him toward her so that she could yell—albeit as quietly as possible—in his ear.

"Trouble coming, lover."

"What kind?" he asked, inclining his head so that his mouth was near her ear as he shouted over the noise of the storm.

Krysty shook her head. "Can't say. It's just getting stronger, that's all." She shivered. "We need to keep alert."

Ryan looked around him. His people were clustered in a small group headed up by Tod and Tilly, with Mac and the two tongueless sec men bringing up the rear. Their flanks were unprotected.

Ryan cupped Krysty's cheek in his hand. "We always need to keep alert," he said. "Let's warn the others."

He moved off and spoke rapidly to Dean and Jak, while Krysty headed for J.B. and Mildred.

"How's the ankle?" she added to J.B. after telling them of the situation.

The Armorer shook his head but didn't speak, the pain bringing him to his most taciturn.

"Dammit John, you shouldn't have to walk on it," Mildred said heatedly. "I should have strapped it up hours ago, at the very least."

"Sometimes we just can't do what we should," J.B.

gritted, leaning a little heavier on Mildred as the pain broke through his concentration.

Krysty and Mildred exchanged glances. It was obvious that the Armorer's injury was worse that he was letting on, and that could make things difficult if they were attacked by anyone—or anything.

Meanwhile Ryan had told Dean and Jak of Krysty's feeling, trying, impossibly, to shout quietly. There was no way that he wanted Mac and his sec men to know— at this stage—that Krysty had mutie traits. Chances were that they were muties themselves—hell, it seemed obvious after their leap across the chasm—but people across Deathlands were suspicious of any mutie traits.

Because of the very weather conditions that made him have to shout, his voice failed to carry back to Mac and the mute guards. They showed no interest in what he was saying, contenting themselves with a desultory glance around the swirling storm fog.

"Mebbe surprises for everyone," Jak said, palming one of the razor-sharp leaf-bladed knives from his patched jacket.

Ryan hid his surprise behind an impassive mask honed through years of experience. Dean didn't find it so easy, and his father looked back to see if his surprise had registered with their captors.

It didn't seem so.

"Hot pipe!" Dean exclaimed. "How come they let you keep them?"

"Just take blaster—not bother search me," Jak commented with a shrug that spoke volumes.

"Triple-stupe bastards," Dean said. It was lost in the storm, but Ryan and Jak got the gist and nodded their agreement.

"Guess they didn't expect you to conceal anything," Ryan mused.

"Not used searching. Murphy's men were," Jak said, palming the blade back into its hiding place.

It was a good point. Ryan had become increasingly aware, as had Jak with his fighter's instincts, that their captors were used to a certain set of conditions and a certain set of enemies. Used to them to the degree that they didn't expect anything outside of their limited experience.

That could be good. If the chance came, Ryan felt sure that his people could take their attackers, despite the advantage they had of carrying blasters.

If the chance came. First they had the possibility of an outside attack.

Ryan, Dean and Jak dropped back a little, until they were level with Krysty, J.B. and Mildred. Ryan viewed the Armorer's stance with concern.

"How bad is it?" he asked.

J.B. grimaced in reply, gesturing with his hand to indicate it was okay, but...

"No bullshit, J.B.," Ryan said carefully. "I think we can take them if the chance comes, so I need to know for sure."

"For real? Might as well dump me now," J.B. said flatly, drawing an appalled glance from Mildred. "Slows me up too much. I'm as much use as a fart in a methane tank."

Ryan merely nodded. It would take a lot for him to leave J.B. behind.

But maybe what they were about to face was a lot. The sudden spray of earth and the inhuman roar as it rose from the ground was certainly no small problem.

Chapter Thirteen

"Dark night! What kind of mutie is that?" J.B. whispered, rooted to the spot as the creature rose out of the earth, showering dirt and dust that caught in the whirl of the storm and formed an almost opaque curtain around the rising shape.

"Fireblast! Scatter," Ryan yelled, pushing Dean away from him and falling in the opposite direction, temporarily blinded as specks of dust hit his good eye, making it sting and close in a mist of tears. He felt the earth beneath him as he hit, rippling with the disturbance of the uprising.

He rolled, blinking and clawing at his eye to clear his vision. As he righted, it returned to him in a blurred and distorted form. He almost wished it hadn't.

It was a lizard of some kind, hideously mutated and grossly enlarged, but probably descended from the Gila lizards that still roamed the desert plains. Its tail flicked out behind it as it emerged from its hiding place and looked around, the cold, blank eyes taking in the scene of confusion, unblinking in the face of the storm and protected by a thick yet transparent skin that covered the eyeball.

Ryan estimated the creature to be about twenty feet in length, stretching up to five and a half feet in height at the tip of its head. About half of the body length was in the tail, which flicked ominously behind. The bandy, scaled legs were planted firmly in the soft, freshly churned earth, sinking deep into the soil.

Casting a glance behind him, Ryan could see that their captors had retreated several yards and were spreading out into a fan formation to try to deal with the creature from a variety of angles, spacing themselves so that it wouldn't be able to take more than one of them with the wickedly vicious tongue that now shot out toward Dean.

Ryan watched helplessly, knowing that he wouldn't be close enough to help his son. The tongue, dripping venom, snaked out at speed. Dean was still on his butt, where he had fallen when pushed by his father as the lizard erupted from the earth.

The boy yelped in shock and surprise, but had sense enough to allow his instincts to take over. Pushing himself up with his feet, balancing by thrusting his arms behind him, he scooted backward in an ungainly crab-like manner. Ungainly it might have been, but it allowed him to get up enough speed to evade the tongue, which lashed at the earth.

The lizard retracted its tongue, screeching in frustration.

Ryan made it across to his son in a few strides, plucking at Dean's arm and helping the boy scramble to his feet. Father and son retreated a few more yards before taking shelter behind a pile of rocks and earth strewed about when the lizard erupted onto the surface.

"Good evasive move, " Ryan panted. "You're learning fast, son."

"Either that or get chilled," Dean replied with a grin. "But why aren't they trying to chill that thing?"

"Mebbe they've just got to take their time. They must be used to them," Ryan answered.

But it was a good point. What were they doing?

It was a question that J.B. and Mildred were also asking themselves. They had dived to the ground and inched toward the scant cover offered by a few rocks. It wasn't much, but on the flat valley floor it was all they could find.

J.B. eyed the fan formation adopted by the outsiders, and also ran an appraising eye over the blasters before taking another look at the lizard.

"They haven't got a hope," he said flatly.

Mildred furrowed her brow. "What do you mean, John?"

J.B. pointed to the lizard. "You see the scaling on that? It'll be like the armor on a war wag. Those home-made blasters are powerful, but they won't have the ammo to get through. Either ordinary lead or the collection of junk that goes in that giant bastard's blaster? Not enough."

"You're right," Mildred said flatly, following his reasoning. "They need steel-tipped—"

"Or some good plas-ex to pitch down its throat," he added with grim humor. "None of the calibers will be strong enough, and the shotgun blast may itch it a little, but otherwise it'll just ricochet off—"

"Right, so heads down, " Mildred shouted as she saw Tod draw a bead on the lizard.

The giant leveled his blaster, then raised the barrels slightly, sighting along them to line himself with the lizard's head. It turned its eyes to him, impassive as he pressed the trigger and took the bucking recoil as though it were nothing more than a feather.

The lizard raised its head and screeched, turning to one side so that the load of metal and scrap discharged by the homemade shotgun hit the scaly, armored skin and flew off at a variety of angles, showering the ground around with hot metal. There was a very slight scorching on the scaled skin, but otherwise no damage.

Ryan saw Tod mouth a curse before the lizard turned to him, flicking out its lengthy tongue.

In order for him to get within a truly effective range, Tod had also moved within reach of the lizard's tongue. He was too stunned by the ineffectiveness of his blaster to move quickly, which was his downfall.

The tongue whipped across the space between them, the venom hitting the giant before the tongue itself as droplets shot off the end, propelled by the speed at which the snaking pink rope moved.

Tod screamed as the venom hit him, eating like acid through his patched denims and dissolving his skin. One drop hit him below the left eye, stripping the skin away on his cheekbone, leaving raw and bloody flesh. The eyeball caught some of the vitriol and seemingly dissolved, the aqueous humor running down onto the exposed and bleeding mess of his cheek.

The scream stopped with a choke as the tongue curled around his head, muffling and choking any resistance. He was pulled forward and onto his belly as the lizard began to retract its tongue, dragging him toward it, his legs kicking in the dust, arms flailing at the tongue that encircled his head.

The fact that Tod was such a big man made the lizard slower than usual in retracting its tongue. Slow enough to allow Tilly to run at it with a piercing scream, wielding one of her knives. Mac and the two mutie sec men covered her with blasterfire that pinged off the lizard's skin as though they were insects buzzing against it.

Ryan thought she'd go for the weak spot on the lizard, but he became instantly aware of the bond that

existed between Tilly and Tod as she headed for the
tongue wrapped around his head, hacking at it with the
knife, trying to free him, regardless of the fact that the
acid had to have already brought him close to death, his
arms and legs becoming more and more feeble in their
thrashing; regardless of the way that the venom ate into
her own rags, scarring skin that was already raw and
weeping from old burn wounds.

The lizard made a rumbling sound in its throat and
moved one large foot, the claw coming loose from the
soil in a shower of dirt and dust. It was in pain, and
concentrated entirely on that which was causing the
pain: Tilly.

Mac and the sec men had no ideas on how to tackle
the lizard. They just kept blasting ineffectively. But the
fact that its attention was focused on the two human
objects occupying its immense tongue meant that there
was an opportunity for someone with a better idea to
act, providing they could move swiftly.

Like Jak.

Ignoring the whining slugs from the sec men's blasters as they rained around him in ricochet, the small and
wiry albino took to his feet, running low to the ground
and zigzagging to keep as much out of the lizard's eye
line as possible. Ideally he would have run straight toward it, taking a path between the side-facing eyes and
so hitting the creature in its blind spot. He remembered
a mutie hare that had run into him when he was young.
Walking across some swamp ground, he had seen the
creature running toward him and had figured it would
move out of his way. But it didn't. Instead, it ran
straight into him, breaking its mutie-weakened neck on
the toecap of his heavy boot. Jak had wondered why,
until he realized that the hare had eyes on each side of

its head, facing out and around…but unable to swivel so that it could see what was in front of its nose.

It was a lesson he had never forgotten. Unfortunately, right in front of the lizard's nose was its acid-venom tongue, wrapped around Tod's head.

The creature's attention seemed focused on its tongue and the irritation caused by Tilly screaming and trying to hack at the pink, thick and veiny length with one of her knives. Her screams were part frustration and part pain as the acid venom ate through her rags and into her flesh.

Tod had stopped moving. She was too late; he was already dead. The only thing that was keeping her going was frustration and hysteria.

Good. Let her distract the creature so that it didn't notice the small albino figure who flitted in and out of the corner of its vision.

Ironically Jak's progress was slowed by the sudden diminution of the storm. The whirling dust had given him some cover from the creature, and now he had to hope that its attention didn't stray to the sides…at least not until he was underneath the body and into another blind spot.

His progress was slowed by the churned-up earth. It slipped under his feet, undermining his balance, making it hard to maintain speed and keep upright. Sweat ran down his matted hair, dripping off the strands that hung over his face, stinging his eyes.

Jak ignored it, focused only on the task he had set himself.

He circled to the creature's left flank, so that he was running parallel to, and almost underneath, its body. He could feel the coldness coming off the scaly skin. He bent as low as he could, coming up the side, boots slipping and sliding on the loose clods of earth and the powdery topsoil.

His companions watched him as he moved to one side, his head just appearing over the top of the lizard's body before he ducked lower, lost to view as the still fighting Tilly and the corpse of Tod blocked their view. The body was getting closer to the mouth, leaving a wet, indented trail on the ground as it was slowly dragged closer to the maw.

Around on the left flank, Jak moved in closer to the drooping belly. His red eyes glittered with concentration as he took in the narrowing gap. It was about twelve inches. He was small and slight enough to make it without having to scrabble out some of the loose earth and so alert the creature as to what was happening beneath it.

Without hesitation Jak sank onto his belly and snaked beneath the creature, slithering like its kind as he prised himself between the belly of the lizard and the loose earth between its splayed feet.

He turned as he moved beneath, coming out under the head of the beast on his back. Drops of saliva and tongue venom dripped around his head, but he didn't notice. If it fell on him, there was little he could do to prevent it. He accepted the risk with his usual unspoken fatalism. In the Deathlands you either chilled or got chilled. There was no other choice.

Free of the lizard's body, Jak was directly beneath the soft throat and jaw of the beast. He could feel, rather than smell, its fetid breath as it filled the air around him.

Jak pulled his body upright, sitting beneath the throat of the lizard with his knees pulled up, ready to spring to his feet. He palmed one of his leaf-bladed knives. They were designed and honed for throwing, but were also useful in hand-to-hand combat. The razor-sharp edge should have just the cutting power he desired. The last thing he wanted was for it to get stuck.

Ignoring the stench that filled his mouth and nose, Jak took a deep breath and thrust down with his calf muscles, propelling himself up with a force that made his stomach muscles ripple and strain with the effort. He rose to his feet beneath the creature, and before he was more than halfway up he made the first sweeping incision in the soft scales that covered the gizzard.

Even the softest parts of the mutie lizard were tough, and Jak felt the resistance jar his arm as the knife bit into the scales. But with a little extra push, he penetrated the skin and felt the knife bite into soft flesh. He pulled across from left to right, feeling the flesh rip and tear as the point moved through the gizzard, the hilt of the knife left behind, following with just that slight degree of drag as it caught on the tougher skin.

Blood started to drip from the wound, a shower that turned into a torrent as Jak hit an artery. The lizard released its tongue from around Tod as it tried to scream in agony, finding that its voice was reduced to a gurgle.

Beneath the lizard's slit throat, Jak was hit by a sheet of stinking, hot blood that turned the ground beneath his feet into a mud bath. It covered him plastering his hair to his head, staining him as red as his albino eyes.

The lizard's tongue whipped through the air in a random series of jerks, any control lost as the creature began to lose control of its motor functions.

Tod's corpse lay on the ground, the head giving off steam as the heat from its enclosure hit the colder air of the storm. All who were looking on were grateful that the storm could obscure their view to some degree, as the giant seemed intact until their eyes reached his neck. There, any semblance to a human being ended. Strips of raw flesh hung off the skull, which in itself seemed to have shrunken and altered shape in some degree. It was as though the acid venom had somehow softened the bone, and the pressure of that immense tongue wrapped around the head had meant that the skull had been compressed so that it seemed elongated, and much too thin for its body.

Tilly took one look at it and fell to her knees, howling in terror and heart-wrenching pain. She rocked back and forth, lost in her own world.

It was to prove fatal. Jak had taken his drenching and stayed beneath the head of the beast for a good reason. While the tongue thrashed about aimlessly but dangerously, it was impossible to try to second-guess the creature's movements. There was a danger that it could collapse on him, but Jak would rather take his chances of using his speed to get free than risk being caught by the tongue.

Such a thought didn't enter Tilly's anguished mind. She just stayed on her knees and howled.

It was only a matter of time until the tongue caught her.

Krysty tore her eyes away from the inevitable, catching sight of Mac and his two mute sec men. They had all stopped firing, and were watching the tableau in front of them in slack-jawed horror. She saw Mac mouth something and shake his head sadly.

Turning her attention back to the direction of the giant lizard, she could see that the tongue had flicked in an arc and caught Tilly around the head. The speed and momentum of the tongue had hit her with a blow strong enough to knock her over. And it would have done. However, the tongue was rough, equipped with suction to grasp its prey. At such a speed and force, the tongue attached itself to her head and wouldn't let go. The momentum of the tongue was greater than the resistance of her neck, and her head was ripped from her shoulders, her anguished howls suddenly lost in the storm.

Tilly's head wasn't firmly grasped in the tongue, and as it reached the farthest point of its wild loop, there wasn't enough suction to cling on to the severed head. It flew off into the storm, tossed by the currents in an irregular arc that carried it out of view.

The wild swings of the dying lizard's tongue began to lessen, and it began to sink toward the earth. Underneath the throat, which was still spurting blood in gouts, Jak felt the lizard begin to tremble and sway. The clawed feet quivered in its death throes, churning up the mud pit its lifeblood had created.

It was now or never. The head of the lizard began to drop, coming close to pushing Jak's head down, pitching him face first into the mud.

The gap under the belly had closed. There was only the one way out—under the jaws and past the arcing, deadly tongue.

Jak went for the narrowing gap, crouching low and pulling his feet from the bloody ground beneath him. He was still clutching the stinking, bloodstained knife that he had pulled from the lizard's throat as he emerged into the open.

Sheltered from the storm by the bulk of the lizard's body, he was hit by the wind with a violence that pushed the air from his lungs. He gulped down clouds of dirt that made him choke, but even this felt clean after the stench and the blood.

Ryan saw Jak emerge, coughing and stumbling, blinded by the storm and the shower of blood that still stung his face. He could see that Jak was trying to avoid the thrashing tongue, but that his vision was impaired and his senses still adjusting to the change in conditions.

The tongue was beginning another arc. It was slower now, with less speed and momentum. It wouldn't rip Jak's head off, as it had Tilly's, but the venom would still be enough to cause him considerable injury.

The arc of the tongue would take it right across Jak's path, and there was no way that he could see it from the angle at which he was headed.

Ryan didn't waste breath shouting. There was only one course of action open to him, and he took it. Breaking cover with a push of his powerful leg muscles, the one-eyed warrior propelled himself across the expanse of earth between cover and Jak. The albino was stumbling over loose rocks, his eyes still partially blinded by the dust and blood.

Noting Jak's position and speed, Ryan decided it would be better to keep his eye on the tongue as it swept toward them with an almost mocking slowness. Mocking because he still had to make up ground on an uneven surface that moved beneath his feet.

Ryan felt his heart pound as he sprinted across the surface. His muscles ached as he pushed them against the resistance of the storm and the yielding earth, aiming for Jak as the albino stumbled, trying desperately to clear his vision.

The tongue swished toward the albino teen who unwittingly turned toward it. Ryan cursed under his breath, unwilling to waste any of the oxygen in his bursting lungs as he launched himself forward.

Jak gasped, the breath driven from his body, as Ryan crashed into him, pushing him back into the earth with a pile-driving force. The lizard's tongue flicked over their heads, reaching the apex of its arc before sliding back across them as Ryan pushed himself into the soil, regardless of the albino beneath him. He could smell the creature's blood on Jak as he crushed his face into youth's hair.

A solitary drop of venom dripped from the end of the tongue and dropped onto Ryan's back, burning a small hole through his jacket and shirt, corrosive on his skin and burning a spot on his flesh. He gritted his teeth at the pain, his eye screwed up in concentration as he tried to blank the pain.

When he looked up again, the creature lay on the ground, twitching violently as the last motor functions ceased to operate and the final sparks of life were extinguished.

Ryan picked himself up, flexing his back muscles and feeling the raw spot of flesh throb. He'd have to get Mildred to look at that later. He reached down and held out a hand to Jak, helping the albino to his feet.

"Owe you," Jak said, wiping the mud from his face.

"Owe you," Ryan replied. "You chilled that bastard and saved us all."

He and Jak returned to the main party.

Mac and his two mute assistants were holding their blasters casually across them, not trained on any of the companions. Ryan gave him a quizzical look.

"Guess I'm mebbe not as suspicious as Tilly was," he said in reply. "Whitey there risked a lot to save us."

"How come you don't know how to fight against those things?" Dean interjected.

Mac turned to the boy. "Son, you tell me how you're supposed to beat a mutie like that. Whitey risked everything, and let's be honest. He wouldn't have stood a chance if the fucker hadn't been busy chilling Tod—"

"Woman took attention away," Jak added. He knew that he could probably have taken the creature anyway, but figured it would do no harm to get on the right side of their captors, now that the blasters were lowered.

"More important, is there anything else like that out here?" J.B. asked.

"Few weird things," Mac said vaguely. "Don't see them that much. We live on the rim—they live down here. Neither gets too interested in the other. You get my drift?"

The Armorer smiled wryly. "Doesn't help us much at the moment, though."

"Can't have everything," Ryan said. He looked past the lizard, in the direction they had been heading, then back at Mac. "We got much farther to go?"

Mac shook his head. "Another half hour, mebbe." He looked at his wrist chron. "Should get us there before sunfall."

"Then let's get going," Ryan said, wondering if Mac had realized that the balance of power had shifted within the group, and that Ryan's people now held the upper hand in terms of numbers and blasters. He noted that J.B. had retrieved Tod's giant blaster, and was carrying it across his shoulder with some effort, his pockets stuffed with the homemade cartridges.

If Mac had noticed, he remained silent. He hadn't even mentioned Jak's knives. The potbellied valley dweller led the way, carrying his blaster over his shoulder.

It seemed to Ryan that he had made a decision without even bothering to put it into words.

"Let's go, people," Ryan muttered as his companions fell into step—with the mute sec men—in Mac's wake.

Chapter Fourteen

Doc's fragile mind was still reeling from shock as Murphy prodded him in the small of the back with his blue 9 mm Beretta, reclaimed from where it had been left in the armory. It was good to have the blaster back, and it gave Murphy a sense of confidence in handling the old man.

"Come on, old fart—out of here," Murphy snapped. "You've got to be prepared."

Wallace glared at him. "Treat him with some respect. He's going to be part of the mechanism. Besides, regs say that a POW should be treated according to convention."

Murphy looked blankly at Wallace for a moment, then it clicked that the Gen was referring to a prisoner of war. He tried to hide the contempt in his eyes for the Gen. He had always believed that Wallace read the regs too literally, but this was just more proof.

Doc dragged himself back into what he laughingly thought of as reality, prompted by the pain in his back where the Beretta's muzzle was digging into him. He assessed the exchange of hostile glances, put it together with what Ryan had said to them earlier about his feelings regarding Wallace and Murphy and shrewdly played the lunatic while he waited for a chance to drive a larger stake between the two men.

"This pathetic old man—treat him with respect?"

Murphy spit. "He wouldn't know if you were or not. He's mad!"

Wallace looked into Doc's eyes. The old man hooded them with a film of madness, ironically using all the sanity and intelligence he could muster to create the opposite impression.

"Hmm... You wouldn't be completely sane if you'd been through all the doctor has been through. I guess a little insanity is excusable. Besides—and strictly off the record—are we sure about the mental stability of each component in the mechanism?"

Murphy shrugged. In truth he'd never even thought about it.

"But it's their unity that gives them strength. The good doctor will actually benefit from being joined to the mechanism. It will help him regain his equilibrium."

Murphy didn't bother to answer. Doc shuddered involuntarily and tried to hide the revulsion he felt.

"Let's just get him prepared, then." Murphy's voice held a weary tone that he couldn't disguise. He pushed the muzzle of the blaster into Doc's back. "Come on—sir," he said with a barely disguised irony.

They left Wallace looking at the rat king. Two tech in vacuum suits had entered the chamber through a decontamination anteroom, and were busy unplugging the dead component from the mechanism. Doc cast a sideways glance as he and Murphy left the observation room.

The sight stayed with him as they walked down the corridor. The component being removed wore a military uniform denoting high rank in the Marines. Like the others, he was glassy-eyed, with skin stretched tight across his ancient skull, clothes flapping loose on his limbs.

In truth the only thing to differentiate him from the others attached to the mainframe was that the vital signs on his own monitors had ceased to function. Just by looking at the once-human frame, there was no way of telling which of the bodies attached to the mechanism were alive and which were dead.

As they left the room, Doc had caught a glimpse of one of the vacuum-suited tech beginning to unplug the diodes and leads from the one-time Marine officer's skull, pulling the ends from the cerebral cortex and frontal lobes, small pieces of decaying gray matter attached to their ends.

With a grim chuckle Doc hoped that they would clean the leads before they plugged him in.

Murphy frowned when he heard Doc laugh.

"What's so funny, you old bastard?"

"Nothing that would amuse you, my dear boy," Doc said sadly. Then, taking the opportunity of a conversational opening, added, "Do you really think that Wallace's plan will work?"

Murphy shrugged noncommittally. "Hell, we all follow regs. That's all."

"Is it really all? Do you not sometimes question a rule book that's over a hundred years out of date? Written for other times than these?"

Murphy allowed himself a wry twist of the lips that might have been a grimace, might have been a smile. "Mebbe you aren't such a crazy old fart after all. You figure that me and the Gen don't exactly see eye to eye on some things?"

"That's a distinct possibility," Doc said as Murphy

led him into a lab and gestured to him to sit on one of
the chairs in the center of the room.

Murphy seemed to relax, but still kept the Beretta
trained on Doc. "I guess there'd be no harm in me
telling you, as you'll be chilled soon enough. Oh,
yeah," he continued in acknowledgment of Doc's
raised eyebrows, "don't think that this bunch of inbreds
and muties is going to be able to wire you up to that
thing."

Doc mused that Murphy himself didn't seem that stable or without the faults he saw in his fellow redoubt
dwellers, but decided it would be more diplomatic to
say nothing at this stage.

Murphy continued. "I think the Gen is barking mad.
Not his fault, not after all this time. But we're getting
nowhere stuck down here trying to keep all this old tech
going. The idea that the Reds will be back, shit that
died with skydark," he said.

"Then why don't you take over?" Doc asked with
as much ingenuousness as he could muster.

Murphy gave another of his twisted half smiles. It
suddenly occurred to Doc that these were a result of his
own inbreeding flaws.

"There is a cabal of us who want to change things,
get rid of the heredity shit and try promotion on merit."

Doc nodded sagely. He had no idea of the social
structure of the redoubt, but wanted Murphy to keep
talking.

Murphy was starting to get enthusiastic. "See, the
main problem we face is that we've got limited resources down here—in real terms, that is. We've got
jackshit in the way of fresh blood, and although blasters
are up to par, we're getting low on plas-ex and grens.
We need to trade more, but that's not in the regs. In-

stead we waste time with old projects that go nowhere, like the rat king. Or all the old tech that stops and starts and can't be used against the outsiders. They're the enemy now, not the Reds. Anyway, R&D ain't that anymore, they're just a bunch of cretins, retards and muties who can barely keep the old shit in working order, let alone make something new.''

''Very fine words, Sarj. Are you going to repeat them in front of the Gen, or aren't you quite brave enough for that yet?''

Murphy whirled at the sound of the cool, sardonic female voice. Dr. Tricks stood in the doorway, arching one of her perfect eyebrows in a way that made Doc go weak at the pit of his stomach. Truly, she was beautiful.

''Don't do that to a man!'' Murphy breathed heavily.

Tricks walked into the room, no, perhaps glided with a hint of a wiggle would be more accurate, Doc thought, and put her arms around Murphy's neck. She kissed him delicately on the cheek.

''What's the matter? Think I'm going to tell the Gen all about your little plan?''

''I know you wouldn't.''

''Why?''

''Because you want me, and you'll only be allowed when the regs are gone.'' Murphy smiled. ''Then it won't matter if you're not good breeding stock.''

''Not like that pig Panner,'' Tricks breathed in his ear.

It didn't escape Doc's notice that a flicker of irritation crossed Murphy's brow at the mention of the name. Remembering it was the sec woman he had chilled, Doc felt it best not to comment. But certainly there was a dynamic going on here that he wasn't, as yet, privy to.

''Why are you telling the old man all this, anyway?''

Tricks continued, not appearing to notice Murphy's brief flicker of irritation.

Murphy shrugged. "What does it matter? He'll soon be chilled."

"But I thought I was to prepare him for the Moebius MkI?" Tricks questioned, drawing back from Murphy.

"Yeah, but he won't survive, will he? I mean, you aren't going to be able to cut open his brain, are you? Not like the others."

Tricks shook her head. "Not like that. But the Gen doesn't want it like that." Murphy gave her a quizzical look, and she continued, "No matter what you think about Wallace, he's not entirely stupid. He's well aware that we just don't have the expertise to open up the skull, to trepan like the others and direct-inject the brain. That was lost a long time ago. I could do it, but there isn't anyone else around here that I'd trust to assist on the operation. You know how I feel about the techs I have to deal with. They're morons who can't be trusted. But Wallace is determined that I link up Tanner to the Moebius, and he wants me to work out a way of connecting the old man without cutting into his skull. He won't die."

"For that, madam, I am in your eternal debt," Doc said with a mocking bow designed to disguise the relief he felt. While he was still alive, there was still hope of escape in some manner.

Tricks gave him a look of pure disdain. "I don't think you'll be saying that when you enter the mainframe and become something other than what you are."

Doc furrowed his brow. "You talk in conundrums, dear lady."

Tricks shook her head. "I can't tell you exactly because I've never experienced it—obviously," she added with a small and musical laugh that was almost perfection. Perhaps, Doc mused, that was her mutation—to appear perfect in the midst of such imperfection. She cut short his thoughts by adding, "All I know is that Moebius takes the intellectual capacity of its components and fuses them into one intelligence. So you become something other than yourself as the others bleed into you."

"I am not sure that I like the sound of that," Doc said quietly.

"Dr. Tanner, you don't have the choice," Tricks said.

She turned to Murphy. "Strap him in the chair, then leave us alone."

Murphy pursed his lips as he strapped the unresisting Doc into the chair, handing his Beretta to Tricks so that she could cover them. For his part Doc reasoned that there was no chance of escape at this time, and so allowed Murphy to manhandle him.

"I'm not sure I like this," Murphy said to Tricks as he stepped back from the secured Doc and once again took charge of his Beretta. "Wallace won't like it."

"The Gen has given me a free hand here," she replied sharply. "I've had to work out this damn procedure for myself, and I can't trust any of the inbreds or muties I have to work with to assist and get it right. I've got my tits on the line here...until we get the chance to change things, I have to go along with the Gen, okay? This is going to be hard, and I don't need any distractions."

Tricks picked up a hypodermic from a tray on her workbench and flicked the end before squirting a thin stream of liquid into the air to knock out any air bubbles.

"Get going, Sarj," she said with her back to Murphy. "Tanner can't give me any problems now, and I need to concentrate."

"Okay," Murphy muttered tersely, investing the word with a multitude of hidden meanings. "I'll be outside. Wallace will expect that, at least."

The automatic door slid shut behind him with a rusting squeal, making Tricks wince.

"I wish the maintenance techs would sort that door out," she murmured before turning to Doc. "Now then, I can't promise this won't be unpleasant. But at least I won't be opening up your brain." She giggled at that, and for a moment Doc saw the creeping edge of insanity that seemed to dwell beneath the surface of everyone in the redoubt.

Any further speculation was cut short as Dr. Tricks rolled up the sleeve of his frock coat, and the shirt underneath, before spearing him in the vein that ran down the joint of his elbow. She depressed the plunger on the hypodermic, and Doc felt a warmth spread through his veins, a velvet softness that hit almost immediately.

During his time in the whitecoat hell that was the headquarters of Operation Chronos, Doc had experienced almost every kind of sedative and painkiller that had ever been formulated.

This felt like the purest heroin…perhaps pure enough to kill him with one hit.

"BY THE THREE KENNEDYS! A nightmare of morphia bliss and sullen joy. Ah, Alice, where is the Mad Hatter now? The Cheshire cat grins at me from beyond the boundaries of space and time. Yet he wears a white coat, my dear. Why is that? And why do you look at me so? For you are beautiful, and I have loved you truly…more truly than the spoken word can tell…''

Doc's hand reached for Tricks's arm, fingers clawing at the air. In his eyes she could see the anguished terror of a man trying to keep a hold on what he believed to be reality while the images of his subconscious ramblings ran riot across his mind.

With a moue of distaste she removed his hand from her arm and let it fall to his side, still clawing in involuntary spasms.

"You poor bastard," she whispered, stroking Doc's sweating brow. "This is a complete waste of time, but at least I won't kill you. I promise that. You alone know what it'll be like for you when you get into Moebius, but at least you'll still be alive…after a fashion.''

Somewhere beneath his fevered ramblings, Doc was aware of what she was saying to him, and realized that there was no escape from being linked into the rat king. But he wouldn't have his skull trepanned, and he wouldn't have electrodes and diodes placed in the soft gray tissue of his brain.

Through a fog of fevered rambling, babbling softly to himself all the while, Doc was able to follow Tricks's movements. Her soft fingers probed across his skull, parting the leonine mane of long white hair to find areas of the scalp that she marked with a stubby indelible pencil, licking the end and murmuring to herself as she found the spots she was seeking.

She turned away, and Doc could hear her moving instruments on her workbench, the clatter of metal and the soft curses as she sought one particular item.

She turned back, and he heard the buzz of electric clippers before he saw them in her hand. Humming tunelessly to herself, she shaved away small portions of his hair, making perfect circles of pink, exposed scalp around the small, purple indelible crosses.

She switched off the clippers and headed back to the bench, returning to Doc with a series of rubber-tipped electrodes, small pads attached to the ends.

"This won't hurt, Dr. Tanner," she said distractedly as she began to attach them methodically to the exposed areas of scalp. "I've been reading up on you from the material salvaged from the computer files. You really are a most remarkable man. It's interesting how your body seems to have taken the immense physical strain. I wouldn't have thought it would have manifested in such a fashion. Still, you never stop learning, eh? There," she added, standing back, "that's that done. There's no way I'm going to open you up, but this should secure you to the mainframe."

With immense effort Doc managed to croak, "Why…others not like…this…?"

Dr. Tricks put a hand on her hip and struck a pose that would have had a younger, less befuddled Doc Tanner thinking of his beloved Emily. Tricks's large, liquid brown eyes stared at him with an intensity that made him feel as if he wanted to melt into them.

"It's quite simple," she said softly. "The original Moebius was made to last longer than it has, really. With the correct maintenance, it could still be going strong. Skydark changed all that. I'd guess the components were—shall we say—coerced into taking part. The removal of part of the skull and the direct inject was to make sure there was no going back. Seems to me that it wasn't strictly necessary, from a scientific point of view."

Through the mist of the drug, Doc recalled the savagery of the whitecoats he had encountered in the twentieth century, and made a small moan of agreement.

"You, on the other hand," she continued without acknowledging him, "are another matter entirely. I can't risk chilling you, not with Wallace breathing down my neck. I have to keep you alive, at least until Murphy gets his act together and we can dismantle the useless projects and utilize our resources properly. So you get the soft option…of sorts."

She smiled, and it made Doc shiver, even through the narcotic haze.

He closed his eyes and took a deep breath. He heard her turn and leave the room. There was a mumbling of voices, too distant through the drug to be coherent. With his eyes still closed, Doc heard footsteps into the room—the heavy clatter of combat boots. For one delirious moment he hoped it may be Ryan and John Barrymore, leading an attempt to free him.

A slim hope, which was dashed as he heard Murphy's voice bark an order. The chair was unbolted from the floor, slipped onto a frame that jarred him, and he was wheeled out of the lab.

He opened his eyes to see the strip lighting of the corridor ceiling slowly flash by above his head. He tried to look around, but his head felt too heavy and stuffed with cotton wool to respond.

He was wheeled into an anteroom and left there. It could have been a few seconds, or it could have been a few years. Time was elastic and without meaning. Finally men in biohazard-suits entered the anteroom and sprayed him with what he took to be some kind of antiseptic. That done, they wheeled him into the main chamber.

Doc was positioned where the now-departed Marine

officer had spent the past century. He felt sharp pains in his hands and arms as the feeding tubes were inserted, felt the pressure as the liquid started to drip into his bloodstream.

Was it imagination, or could he already feel his muscles start to atrophy?

The tech finished attaching him to the apparatus that would keep him alive and prisoner in this room. Now came the moment he had been dreading. They took the cables attached to his head and inserted jacks into the mainframe computer. A series of codes was punched in.

Doc felt a tingling sensation begin at the back of his brain and braced himself.

Suddenly he was no longer in the room. A rush, a blinding light, and an immense spasm of pain that ran through his entire frame, making him convulse in spasms that passed slowly. The lights began to settle into shapes, the oppressive silence melted into white noise that resolved into pulses of static sound that eventually shaped into words.

"Welcome to the torture machine, Dr. Tanner. Welcome to our nightmares."

Chapter Fifteen

Even though the storm was abating, and the conditions meant that they could see more than a few yards in front of them and weren't scoured by sprays of dirt and dust, it was still a long, hard slog toward the ville.

"Don't these storms ever stop?" Mildred asked as she shook the dirt from her braids.

Mac shook his head. "Not in the valley. That's just the way it is."

They continued in silence through the relative calm. Limbs ached, skin was sore, resistance was low. Escape was the last thing they could think of at the moment. Despite the talk of a ritualistic chilling, Ryan felt they needed to reach the ville and assess the situation from there.

And then there was Doc. If there was a chance they could get him back, then this would have to be taken. It would also give them access to a mat-trans.

But before all else they had to actually reach the ville.

The terrain was still flat, but there was a gradual incline on the distance. Looking ahead, Ryan could see the lip of the valley begin to form. They had to be only a few miles from the ville by now. It seemed to Ryan that the wild storms were contained within the bowl of the valley, and as they reached the edges the winds were allowed by nature to dissipate.

There was more foliage and growth here. Not enough

to support farming, but certainly a scattering of scrub that was more than they had seen so far.

The natural corollary of this was there had to be wildlife of some kind. Ryan glanced at Jak, who was scanning the brush.

"Things move—not dangerous…yet," the albino added with a lupine grin.

J.B. turned to Mac. "What lives here?"

Before the sec man answered, Ryan noted that the Armorer's limp had grown worse. J.B. was almost dragging his left foot, relying more and more on Mildred to support him.

Mac gestured expansively with his blaster. "Could be anything lives out here in this rad-blasted hole. Don't rightly know, as we never stick around long enough to find out. You follow my drift?"

Ryan nodded, a wry grin cracking his dried and chaffed lips. For the first time he felt empathy with their captors. "Best way. Imagine the worst and you don't get surprised."

"Right, One-eye. There are stories of strange creatures that live here, between the outside of the valley and the heart of the storm. Can't ever say that I've rightly seen anything, though. I guess they may just be as scared of us as we are of them."

"That I doubt," J.B. interrupted. "Never seen a wild mutie creature that didn't want to rip your heart out."

"Unless you rip first," Jak added.

Dean didn't seem to be paying attention to the idle chatter, looking over to the left as he walked, with an intent expression.

"What is it?" Krysty asked, noticing his distraction.

"Don't know," Dean commented shortly. "Not yet. Some kind of movement over there."

Krysty stopped and followed the line of Dean's arm. About fifty yards away, still partly obscured by the remnants of the storm, there was something that looked to Krysty like a small hill.

"Gaia! What's doing that?" she exclaimed.

Her cry brought Ryan and Mac back from their position at the front of the group. The two mute sec men, standing to Krysty's rear, made signs at Mac.

Ryan gave him a questioning glance.

Mac shrugged. "Yeah, weird. Looks like that hill over yonder—" he gestured with his blaster "—is making itself as we watch."

Ryan focused his one eye on the distant mound of earth. It was true. It was growing as he watched, a sign of something powerful. To see it grow from that distance meant that a generous amount of earth was being moved.

"Don't like," Jak said pithily. "Anything moving under ground cause lot surprise."

"Good call," Mildred said, looking around at the scrub. "Who knows what's lurking here?"

Ryan turned to Mac. "Can I suggest we get out of here before whatever's doing that decides to come looking for us?"

"Good idea." Mac turned to the two mute sec men. "Let's press on."

Gesturing with his blaster, he led the way toward the lip of the valley and his ville. Ryan noticed that Mac had suddenly increased the pace at which they proceeded, obviously rattled by the sudden appearance of the earth mound, and wondered if J.B. would be able to keep up.

The Armorer was finding it hard. The pain in his ankle was like a hot poker with every step, and despite

Mildred's help it was difficult to keep up any kind of speed. What he desired most was just to sit down, ease his combat boot off his swollen foot and rest the aching limb. Yet he knew that this was impossible until they reached the ville. So he drove himself onward, sweat dripping off his brow, making his spectacles slip on the bridge of his nose and gathering around the brim of his fedora as he gritted his teeth and kept going.

Now that they were near the edges of the valley, and the storm was reduced from a roar to a whisper, it was possible to hear other noises. Dean was aware of a rustling from the brush to his left—the same direction as the mound—and whirled in surprise.

"Hot pipe! What's that bastard thing?" he yelled, taking a sideways step to move more toward the center of the group.

Mac raised his blaster and fired into the brush. There was an agonized yelp, and a creature flung itself toward the group. It rushed at J.B. and Mildred, almost as though it had instinctively picked out the weak link in the group chain.

"Dark night," J.B. breathed, falling back and pulling Mildred with him as the creature, now in its death throes, flung itself at them. As they hit the ground, it flew over them, thudding to earth a few feet away, twitching.

"Take a look at that," the Armorer said, pulling himself painfully to his feet and hobbling over to where it lay.

"That's an evil-looking bastard," Mac said, bending to examine it. Ryan crouched beside him.

"Just look at those," he commented, indicating the creature's teeth. "They could really do some damage."

"And would have done, if John hadn't been so

quick,'' Mildred added, shrugging off the twinge of pain in her shoulder where she had landed awkwardly.

The creature was a sobering sight as it lay on the dry earth. The blood had ceased to flow where the creature had died, but enough had leaked out to color the dull earth, framing its corpse. It was eighteen inches long in the body, with short, dark gray fur. The head had elongated jaws and almost reptilian black eyes that were now hollow and empty in death.

The jaws were what drew the attention immediately. Long and powerful, they had large incisors that were sharpened almost to points. Mac prodded the jaws with the barrel of his blaster and pushed back the dead lips. The other teeth were also sharpened, uneven and yellow with scraps of meat and vegetable matter caught between them.

The body was thin and wiry, with short front paws that had wicked claws and powerful back legs that could spring long distances. The muscles seemed bunched, almost bursting out of the fur. The tail was vast and bushy, almost as long as the body, with a gradation of gray coloring that would probably act as good camouflage in the colorless scrub.

''That's the most bastard evil-looking squirrel I've ever seen,'' Ryan said.

Mildred nodded her agreement. ''Nasty little mutie. Let's hope its little brothers and sisters don't decide to exact vengeance on us.''

J.B. pushed his fedora back on his head and cast a glance around at the scrub. ''If that's a nest of some kind,'' he said, indicating the distant mound, ''and that's the direction this little fucker came from, then I wouldn't give much for our chances if we don't keep moving.''

"Good call," Ryan said, turning to Mac.

"So I guess this is as good a time as any to ask for our blasters back."

The sec man looked at him askance. "You've got to be kidding, One-eye. What guarantee have I got that you won't just chill us and be on your way?"

"None, I guess," Ryan said calmly. "But we outnumber you already, and it wouldn't be too hard for us to try and take you down. We could, but it'd be triple stupe right now. If there are more of these little bastards, then we need to all be prepared, or else none of us are going to reach your pesthole ville."

Mac thought about it, but not for too long, as he cast a worried glance across to the mound. There were rustlings in the brush that could have been more of the creatures approaching, or could have been nothing more than the breeze in that part of the valley. Did he really want to take that chance?

"Okay," he said finally. "Give them the hardware."

The mute sec men unhooked their backpacks and opened them. Ryan received his panga, the SIG-Sauer and Steyr, returning them to their places on his body and feeling at once better balanced. J.B. was glad to see his knife, Uzi and S&W M-4000. Jak received his Colt Python .357 Magnum to go with his secreted knives. Testing the balance of her ZKR, Mildred felt more comfortable with the encroaching dangers. Dean checked his Browning Hi-Power and looked around, scanning the horizon. Last blaster out of the backpacks was Krysty's .38-caliber S&W. She pocketed it in her fur coat, preferring to wait until it was necessary to draw.

"That's better," Ryan said, checking his group. "We can all cover ourselves and each other now."

"Just as long as it is each other," Mac added warily.

"Listen, stupe, if I wanted to blow you away right now, I could," Ryan gritted, leveling the SIG-Sauer at Mac's chest. "But I don't. You want us for this bastard ritual chilling—we want you to guide us out of here. It's equal now. When we hit your ville, it's everyone for themselves. But until then…"

He lowered the SIG-Sauer.

"Guess I can't argue with that," Mac commented, switching his attention to the surrounding brush, where the noise and scufflings were on the increase. "Also guess we've got something to worry about."

They were clustered together on a rough trail that ran through the brush, worn down over a space of decades by raiding and hunting parties that had ventured that far into the valley. It was less than three feet across before the wild foliage started to take hold again, springing up sparsely but with enough clumping of brush to provide cover for something small and deadly, like the mutie squirrel that lay at their feet.

"Okay, let's move off," Ryan whispered, assuming command as Mac seemed unwilling to move, and set off in the direction of the lip of the valley, Mac falling in behind him.

Mildred hung back to support J.B. as he hobbled to bring up the rear.

"I'm a liability, Millie," he said quietly, grimacing through the pain.

"Don't think about it, John. We just need to keep going until we're out of danger. With that psychotic bitch out of the way, and three sec men outnumbered by us, I guess we might have a chance to negotiate with the ville's baron. If we can do that, then I might get a chance to have a better look at that ankle."

"Don't kid yourself, Millie. This isn't going to get

better, and I don't want it to be the reason you're chilled. First sign of trouble, you think of yourself.''

"Like you would?" She raised an eyebrow at him.

Despite the pain, it still raised a smile from the Armorer. "Mebbe."

Looking ahead of her, Mildred could see that already a gap had opened up between them and the rest of the group. Ryan wasn't setting that fast a pace. It was more an indication of how J.B.'s ankle was slowing them.

Mildred was about to call to Ryan to wait for them when it happened.

There was a sudden silence from the brush, as though all the hidden life within had, at a silent command, ceased to move. A moment of eerie silence was then broken by a wild screeching that began as one animal and increased as more and more joined in the cry, a cacophony of screeching that drowned out the fading noise of the storm.

"Fireblast! What the—?"

Ryan's shout was interrupted by the explosive crack of Dean's Browning Hi-Power as the boy sighted one of the mutie squirrels springing from the brush.

The creatures had incredible power in their heavily muscled back legs. It was almost as though the creature had taken flight, its jump describing a sharp arc as it achieved a height of just over six feet, starting to descend with its elongated jaws distended, teeth flashing as it headed straight for Ryan's good eye.

Dean was a good shot. He fired at the creature, judging its airspeed in a fraction of a second. The slug from the Browning ripped through the top of the creature's skull, entering through one eye and exiting just behind its flattened ear, taking a chunk of the skull with it. Its trajectory thrown off by the impact of the bullet, the creature spun in the air, landing just in front of the one-eyed warrior.

Ryan would have appreciated Dean's fine shooting if he had the chance. But he was far too busy taking evasive action against another of the squirrels, which had emerged from the brush behind him. He turned quickly on his heel as the sound of the disturbed brush reached him.

The mutie was coming at him from a lower trajectory, its front paws tearing at the air with its wickedly sharp claws as it sprung toward his groin, looking to tear into his flesh. Ryan crouched and lowered the SIG-Sauer, loosing off a round that tore a chunk of fur and flesh from the side of the creature, spraying a fine mist of blood behind it.

The mutie squirrel bared its teeth in a squeal of agony as Ryan sidestepped the flailing arc of its trajectory and stamped on the skull, his heavy combat boot crushing the bone and smearing the brain on the earth. He was unwilling to waste ammunition when he was unsure of how many of the creatures were lying in wait.

There could have been a few, or hundreds. He couldn't allow the latter option to occupy his mind.

Bedlam had broken out around them as the creatures sprang from the brush in attack. Krysty fell to one knee, keeping a still poise about her as she picked off as many of the creatures as possible before having to take the chance of reloading and being temporarily defenseless.

They seemed to have a group intelligence about them, as they concentrated less on her the more she put down. So when she had to reload as swiftly as possible, she was granted the respite she needed.

Mildred, too, was having no little success in picking off the creatures. She adopted a classic firing stance and peppered the air with slugs from the ZKR, shooting fast and accurately—and thereby buying herself time to reload.

The two mute sec men weren't faring so well. Neither was an excellent shot, and they were missing more of the flying squirrels than they were hitting. As their blasters ran out of ammunition, they found themselves using the rifles as clubs, both reversing the blasters and swatting the creatures out of the air. They were marginally more successful in this, as the number of stunned squirrels littering the path attested. Fortunately most of those hit had their spines or skulls broken, only a few managing to return to enough sense to pose a problem. The sec men had to try to stomp on them without missing those creatures that were still in flight.

Dean picked off the squirrels as they sprang at him from all sides, but was hindered by the mute sec men, who were near enough to cause him problems with their flailing blasters, forcing him to duck and weave on one knee to avoid being caught by the flying rifle butts. His success rate was lower than Krysty's or Mildred's, so more of the creatures concentrated on him, and he was fighting a losing battle.

Jak came to his aid. He had dispatched a flying squirrel with every slug from his Colt Python, and hadn't bothered to reload. His childhood in the Louisiana swamps had been spent stalking and killing wildlife far more dangerous than even these killing machines. The Python was holstered in a blur of silver metal before his hands delved into the patched coat and withdrew some of his knives from their hiding places.

Jak's eyes burned sightlessly, lost in a fearsome mixture of blood lust and intense concentration as his arms became a whirling blur. He held two of the razor-sharp knives in each hand, his whipcord wrists twirling them in a figure-eight pattern that sliced the very air, ripping and tearing at anything that came within range, absorbing any shock that might come from the jar of blade on bone as he disposed of the many creatures that flew at him.

Their almost group mentality caused them to cease the intensity of their attack on Jak, allowing him to help Dean by taking out those squirrels that the boy missed in his attempts to avoid the desperately flailing mute sec men.

But the man facing the most problems was J.B. He had decided to use his Uzi on the creatures. The rapid-fire pattern of the blaster would have been a problem in less skilled hands. The cluster of people near him would have been endangered as he spun to attack the squirrels as they flew at him from both sides of the brush.

The Armorer was no ordinary marksman. He fired in short, controlled and accurate bursts, the pressure of his finger on the trigger both firm and yet gently caressing. Honed by years devoted to the art of weaponry, his instinct took over from his consciousness, and he registered the flying creatures not as a danger but as targets that had to be eliminated. This approach displaced the fear from his conscious mind and enabled him to fire calmly and accurately.

He would have had no trouble if not for the flailing sec men. One of the flying squirrels, dealt a glancing blow by a rifle butt, was deflected in his direction. It landed too far away for the sec man to stomp on it, so he ignored it. Mildred didn't notice it as she fixed her sights on an airborne danger, blasting it in the skull with the ZKR.

The creature landed, stunned, and rolled toward J.B. The Armorer saw it from the corner of his eye, and raised his foot to crush its head.

He raised his left foot.

Acting on an instinct that forgot to remind him about his injury, or take it into account, he slammed the foot onto the prone body of the squirrel.

An agony of red-hot needles traveling up his legs made the Armorer drop his Uzi from its firing position. He screwed up his eyes, gritted his teeth and emitted a small high-pitched scream that was all his tortured and tensed vocal cords would allow. There was no power in the injured ankle, and all the force he had put into his action was translated into pure pain.

His foot was ineffectual on the squirrel, which squirmed beneath his boot, screaming for its life as its powerful front paws dug into the material of his combat pants and into the soft and tender flesh that lay above the top of the boot.

J.B. was beyond screaming at the pain generated by the clawing. He felt little of it, as the agony from his untimely foot stomp was still coursing through his body.

The creature used its purchase on his leg to haul itself from underneath the sole of his foot, clinging on its own injured agony to try to inflict damage with its dying breath.

The elongated jaws opened, the sharp teeth poised as it moved its head back to get a good, firm, darting bite at his leg. J.B. regained enough awareness through the red mist of pain to drop the barrel of the Uzi even farther, until it was parallel to his leg. He put the snubbed, open end of the barrel against the creature as the head darted in.

The mutie squirrel sunk its teeth into J.B.'s leg the

same instant that he fired. He'd had enough presence of mind, through the pain mists, to switch to single shot.

At such close range, he felt the heat of the blaster burn into his leg, scorching the material of his pants. Not that it was any worse than the pain he was feeling through the wounds inflicted by the squirrel. If anything, the pain there was so immense that he felt he would black out at any moment: It was so intense that his leg was beginning to numb, overloaded with agony.

There was little left of the creature as the slug tore its body to bloodied shreds. The remnants of the corpse were scattered around the Armorer's feet as it splattered onto the ground. Most of the skull had also disappeared in the blast, only the snout remaining. One eyeball—miraculously undamaged—hung loose on a tendon. The teeth, firmly embedded in J.B.'s leg, were all that kept it anchored in place.

"John!" Mildred shouted, her attention drawn momentarily from the attacking hordes by the action beside her.

She stepped closer to him in a sideways motion, keeping her ZKR trained to pick off any of the creatures that decided to attack. Eyes still scanning the brush on both sides, she crouched to where J.B. had fallen. He was sitting upright, cradling the Uzi with one hand trying to pick the snout from his leg, a glassy stare coming into his eyes.

Mildred glanced at the wound and winced. "Leave it, John," she said sharply, hoping to get through the mist of shock that was fogging his perception. He stared at her, blankness falling like a curtain over his gaze.

"Leave it," she repeated, gently pushing his hand away from the wound. "Let me look at it in a moment," she said softly.

"Uh-huh," J.B. replied vaguely.

"How bad is it?" Krysty yelled, casting one eye toward Mildred and J.B. while she kept vigilance on the brush.

"Hard to tell," Mildred answered, moving slightly away from J.B. in order to keep her area of brush covered. "I need to get a good look at it. It's the leg he already damaged, and those mother teeth will probably infect the wound." She cursed Wallace and his military lunatics, who had removed most of the medical supplies from her many coat pockets. But they were slack. Maybe she still had something in there. If not, J.B. was in for a rough ride.

The waves of attacking squirrels had slowly decreased.

"Know we winning," Jak said to no one in particular as he wiped the blood from his knives to stop them slipping in his grip.

"Seems to me those little bastards knew our weak links and concentrated on them," Ryan commented, taking the opportunity to reload his SIG-Sauer.

"Hell, Dad, all animals know when they're beat," Dean said wearily, checking his Browning. "Just some of us don't give up."

Ryan suppressed a laugh. Sometimes he could see so much of himself in Dean that it was like having a mirror. "More than that, son," he said, returning to the subject. "It's like they knew who was faring best against them, and somehow targeted the others."

"If Doc was here, he'd give us a rambling lecture about psi powers against natural instinct and observation," Krysty commented wryly as she joined Mildred at J.B.'s side. "How is it?" she asked, switching her attention to the concerned woman.

"Not so good," Mildred answered curtly. "It was bad enough with his twisted or sprained ankle," she continued, indicating the way that the Armorer's flesh was swollen and spilling over the top of his boot, "let alone right here." She prodded with a surprising gentleness at the area ringed by the remains of the snout. J.B. flinched, even though she never made contact.

"Need get teeth out," Jak commented, coming over to look. "Now. Meds left?" he asked of Krysty and Mildred.

The black woman shook her head angrily, her beaded plaits swinging around her head. "Those asswipes at the redoubt took just about everything when they stripped us. We might have got the blasters back from the armory, but they weren't kind enough to leave everything else in there."

But even as she spoke, her hands were restlessly searching through every pocket of her coat, opening flaps and probing into the corners of cavernous folds of material. With an exclamation somewhere between amazement, disgust and relief, she came up with a sealed roll of medicated bandage and a small bottle of pills. The label revealed them to be nonspecific antibiotics. She worried about a potential allergic reaction, but had no choice. They might help fight whatever rad-altered infections he could pick up from the vicious teeth that were embedded in his leg.

"It's not much, but it'll have to do," she said grimly. "The teeth will have to come out."

"Leave to me," Jak said, producing another of the leaf-bladed knives from within its patched hiding place. With no further comment he set to work, prying the teeth from the wound.

The two mute sec men had moved into position behind the Armorer, and took a firm grip on him, holding him steady as he writhed and twitched in pain.

Ryan looked away, scanning the horizon. "How far now?"

Mac joined him, just away from the group. Despite his impassivity throughout the whole of their trip, he actually looked a little sick at the operation Jak was conducting.

"Not far. Mebbe carrying your friend will slow us down," he speculated.

Ryan glared at him. "We still outnumber you, friend."

Mac gave him a weak smile. "Okay. If you can carry him at a pretty normal pace, then just about twenty minutes more. It'll be past sunfall now, and that's always a danger. But I guess those weird things have had enough for now."

Ryan studied the path and brush around them, littered with the corpses of the mutie squirrels. "I hope so," he said shortly before turning back to where J.B. lay.

Dean and Krysty were preparing lengths of the medicated bandage to bind the wounds, while the mute sec men had J.B. in a firm grip. When they caught Ryan looking at him, both seemed to communicate a kind of sympathy through their eyes.

Jak had almost finished his task, under the watchful direction of Mildred. The bloodied remains of the snout had been sliced away, the knife paring the fur and flesh from the bone so that Jak could get a better view of how the teeth were embedded in J.B.'s leg. The bone was almost as clean as if it had been boiled.

The teeth were firm in the jaw sockets, so there was little opportunity for Jak to pry loose the bone before extracting the teeth from the wound. He cursed to himself, knowing that this would make it more difficult for him to cleanly remove the teeth.

Jak grasped the bone carefully but firmly in one hand, while he began to pry the teeth loose with the other. Mildred kept a close watch on J.B.'s leg, using a piece of bandage to wipe the dribbling blood from the localized area as the teeth moved in his flesh. With the blood wiped away, it was easier for Jak to see what he was doing.

"Fuck mutie bastards," he cursed, as the jawbone seemed to take forever to pry loose. Finally it came away in his hand, and he tossed it over his shoulder, moving rapidly out of the way to allow Mildred to take over.

Mildred didn't have much to work with, but she used another length of medicated bandage to clean around the deep puncture marks. She wiped away the dribbles of blood from the wounds. It was fortunate that the teeth had been sharp, as the wounds they left were like needlepoint rather than large, jagged tears. Consequently they were actually bleeding less than she had feared.

It wasn't much, but at least it was something.

After binding the Armorer's wound, Mildred gestured for the bottle of antibiotics. Mac, who had managed to turn back now that the worst of the operation was over, gave Mildred a canteen of water from his backpack, and she forced J.B. to swallow a couple of the pills.

Semiconscious, he sunk back onto the earth.

"Let's get moving," Ryan said. "The sooner we reach this ville the better."

He left unspoken that once there, they would work on figuring out a way of escaping. It might seem like jumping from one danger to another, but if the talk had been of a ritual chilling, then it wouldn't be likely to happen straight away...and that would give them the most precious of commodities—time.

Ryan took J.B. by the feet, and Jak moved to take him under the arms. It wasn't the best way to carry him, but it would have to do.

They walked in silence.

THE SUN HAD BEEN DOWN for nearly an hour by the time they reached the small ville. If ever there had been a ville that deserved to be described as a pesthole, then this was it. A few fires around the edges of the shacks and huts that comprised the ville were all that protected it from the encroaching dangers of nocturnal predators.

Ryan couldn't see if there were any wags in the dim light, but somehow he doubted it.

Mildred looked at J.B., strung out between Ryan, her heart sinking. She had been hoping to pick up some sort of supplies from the ville to improve J.B.'s condition, but from her first look, it seemed likely that she was better equipped than they were.

They walked unchallenged into the heart of the ville, Mac leading the way. If there were any guards around the outskirts of the ville, Ryan didn't see them.

Mac answered his unspoken question. "No one moves out or across the valley after sunfall. You've seen it in daylight. It's far worse in the dark. Never know where you are. The insiders are as wise to that as we are. They've never attacked us by night, 'cause they wouldn't want to risk crossing the valley."

"What about people from outside the valley?"

Mac grinned with a return of the old sick humor, now that he felt safe on home territory. "They get this far,

then the storms eat 'em up anyway. They're our friend,
as well as our enemy."

They continued until they were in a rough earthen
square that served as the meeting point for the ville
dwellers. In the dim light provided by the lamps and
fires, faces appeared from the doorways of huts, keeping
their distance but peering with interest at the newcomers.

Particularly at Dean.

"Why are they staring at me like that?" he whispered
to Krysty.

Krysty looked in the darkness, and could see that
there weren't many children in view, and those who
were all seemed to have some kind of deformity
springing from either rad-blasted genes or inbreeding—
faces with squat, snuffling noses dripping with mucus;
hare-lipped, gap-toothed grins; slack jaws that hung
open over black eyes.

"I think you're probably the first child without a mutation or genetic problem they've seen for some time,"
she whispered. "This could be a good thing for us if
we play it right."

Ryan was too close to Mac to acknowledge her ver-
bally, but he heard...and agreed.

When they were all in the small square, there were
muttering and rustling sounds from the huts as a small
crowd gathered on the fringes.

Ryan and Jak lowered J.B. gently to the ground. He
was mumbling softly and incoherently. Mildred bent
over him and felt his skin and took his pulse. He was
too hot, and his pulse was racing. If they could have
some water boiled, and a dry, relatively clean place
clear of the ground, she could clean the wounds and re-
dress them, maybe give him more of the antibiotics. She

was uncertain how stable or effective the pills would be after so long, but they were better than nothing.

"John needs to be rested and cleaned up," she said to Mac. "So if you show us where we're sleeping, and get me some hot water…"

She trailed off, noticing that the potbellied sec man was looking at her uncomfortably.

"Reckon it may not be that simple, missy," he said softly. "See, all outlanders or insiders are killed to appease sunup. Without sacrifice to the sun, well, the storms could get worse."

Mildred regarded him coldly, suddenly aware once again of the light scouring of dust and the perpetual breeze. It was much less than at its worst, but still ever present.

Mac flinched before her stony gaze.

"You mean to tell me that after all we did to try and save that freakin' rag woman and that fat giant, after all we did together to fight off those freakin' squirrels, you'll sell us down the river and let us be chilled to try and stop a storm that never ceases?"

Mac couldn't look at her. He stared at one of the huts. "Mebbe Abner will make the decision…under the circumstances. But it's not up to me."

"Not up to you," Mildred spit back, looking at J.B., whose eyes flickered wildly behind closed lids, encountering terrors in his delirium that only he could ever understand.

"It's okay, Mildred," Ryan said softly. They had their blasters and other weapons, but they were a man short and in the middle of the ville. He wanted to buy some time, and if it meant being nice to these bastards, then so be it.

"No, let the black woman speak."

The voice was wheezing, old and had a sly quality that immediately pricked Ryan's suspicion. It came from the edge of the clearing, and the speaker walked through the small crowd as it parted for him.

He was shorter than Mac, and if anything, even more potbellied than the sec man. His breathing was labored, and his long, thinning and straggly hair was a dirty gray streaked with black. His long mustache and beard were similarly peppered.

"Are you the baron of this ville?" Ryan asked him.

The man looked puzzled. "Baron? That's not a word I know for what I am. I'm the leader of this here ville, if that's what you mean. Just like my pappy before me, and his pappy. We always have been, long as there's been a ville. I've heard other outlanders talk of barons, but not the insiders with the stupe uniforms."

"We're outlanders, I guess, certainly not from the redoubt."

"The what?" the old man asked, furrowing his brow.

"He means the place where the insiders come from," Mac offered. "Guess that's what they call it."

The old man nodded, then smiled at them. "Anyways, you can call me Abner. Least I can do, all things considered. Got to be friendly now."

"Why?" Ryan asked.

Abner smiled again, ingenuously. "Hell, boy, the sun don't like it if we're not real friendly to those we chill for him."

Chapter Sixteen

The hut in which they were imprisoned was a round adobe structure of mud and straw. The walls were flimsy, with patches where the mud had caked dry too quickly and not been bound by the straw which was visible in the flickering shadows cast by the old hurricane lamp that sputtered smokily in the center of the hut.

J.B. lay near the center, an equally foul-smelling poultice on his wounds.

"Are you sure this will work?" Mildred asked Krysty skeptically. "Back when I was in med school, they weren't exactly hot for herbal medicines."

Krysty shook her head. "I know, but when it's all you've got... When I was young, back in Harmony, Mother Sonja taught me how to blend healing things from the most unlikely sources. It might smell like shit, and no one knows how it works, but if there aren't any meds, then it's got to be worth a shot."

Mildred joined Krysty by J.B.'s side. In the light of the flickering lamp, his brow was dripping with sweat, matting his already soaking hair and running in rivulets down his face and neck.

Mildred stroked his forehead gently, feeling the heat rise from him. He responded to the pressure of her touch by muttering incomprehensibly, opening his eyes for a second but not really seeing.

Krysty moved the poultice, made from rags she had persuaded Abner to give them. The wound underneath was cleaner than before, pus and a clear discharge being drawn from it and onto the rags. A cauldron of luke-warm water—boiling when left by Mac earlier—stood to one side of the hut. Krysty stripped the pus-covered rags from the outer covering of the poultice and threw them into the cauldron.

"Water's next to useless," she commented. "Too cool to be any good, and we've got no more rags. Time to find our own."

Without comment Ryan, Jak and Dean all started to strip down to their underwear. Having acquired it at the redoubt the day before, it was relatively clean, and hav-ing been under their other clothing, was protected from the ravages of the dust and dirt that had assailed them in the storms.

All three men took off the regulation military white T-shirts and handed them to Mildred. Jak also handed her one of his leaf-bladed knives, with which she sliced the material into strips, handing it to Krysty. The ma-terial formed a new dressing on the poultice, which was replaced on J.B.'s injuries.

"Will he make it?" Ryan asked, speaking for the first time since their imprisonment.

Mildred shrugged. "This gunk is working by the look of it, and he should be past the crisis of his fever before too long. If he gets through that okay, then he'll live. The question then is how fit will he be to move when we make a break."

She tried to keep her voice even, to sound offhand about J.B.'s chances. But she was fooling no one: they all knew how much it was eating into her.

"I'm just wondering if we should make a break," Ryan said quietly.

Dean looked at his father sharply. "We've got to, Dad. There's J.B. to get out of here, and Doc to get after. Besides, I don't want to be chilled as part of some dumb-ass ritual to the frigging sun."

Ryan regarded Dean coldly. His one eye blazed anger. "Remember who's in charge here, boy. The only chance we have is if we work together, not pulling separately. Before you jump to conclusions, hear me out. I've got no intention of being chilled, either. Trader used to say that when your time was up, you had to go down. Well, I don't feel like going down without fighting. But there's more than one way of fighting."

"Sorry," the boy muttered.

Jak put an arm around his shoulders. He was only a few years older than Dean, and yet in terms of harsh experience he was an old man.

"More one way skin mutie rabbit. Mebbe not best blast way out—'specially when no blasters."

Dean bit his lip and smiled. It was a good point. Still stunned by Abner's pronouncement, none of them had been ready for the sudden swarm of ville dwellers, who had taken it as their cue to rush forward and disable the outlanders, moving like a mass of ants that engulfed their enemies, sheer weight of numbers pinning them to the ground and enabling the ville dwellers to strip them of their weapons.

Or almost all of their weapons. Jak's throwing knives were so well hidden in the patches and folds of his coat that it would have taken a long and thorough search to uncover them.

There hadn't been time for such a search. They had been picked up by the swarm and rushed into the hut.

Once in there, Mac and his mute sec men had trained their blasters on them while Abner had told them that he would assist them, in whatever way his people could, to heal J.B.'s wounds. It was important that the sun receive a "whole" sacrifice, and not a damaged one.

And so they had been left here. At least, as he had warned them that the outside of the hut would be guarded, Mac had had the grace to look embarrassed at his behavior.

"Why can't we make a break for it?" Dean continued impatiently.

"Because walls have ears for one," Krysty snapped, losing her patience, "especially walls that are made of mud and straw. And for two, how can we move with J.B. in this condition?"

"I guess...yeah, I guess so," Dean said quietly.

Ryan beckoned them into the center of the hut, where they crouched around the prone Armorer, as though watching him. Ryan spoke low and soft.

"We're better fighters, but this is their terrain, and they're used to the weather conditions. Besides which they outnumber us. We've got a short while to prepare something. They won't chill us in this ritual until J.B.'s at least coherent. Thing is, what exactly do we do?"

"Mebbe," Jak said, scratching idly, "mebbe need take Abner."

Ryan nodded. "They seem to follow him blindly, so yeah, if we have him, that's a powerful bargaining tool."

"How far are we going to get out there with John like this?" Mildred looked down at J.B. and shook her head. "The thing he'll need most is time, and that's just what we don't have."

"Then we'll buy it." Ryan looked his son squarely

in the face. "I've got an idea, and I need to know I can rely on you totally."

"Dad, you don't even have to ask," Dean replied.

THE STARS TWINKLED faintly through the ever present curtain of dust. It was a lighter breeze than usual on this night, stirring motes on the surface of the tracks that comprised the roads of the small ville.

Mac sighed and leaned on his blaster, his arms crossed and resting on the mouth of the long, roughly beaten barrel. It was bored smooth inside, but the outer metal was still pitted and uneven, where he hadn't been bothered to shape or smooth it. The butt rested in the dirt, trigger a long way from his finger. He was supposed to be on guard, but felt tired after the long trek from the redoubt back to the ville. They had been on a scavenger hunt, hoping for some equipment that had been left by the insiders, and hadn't bargained on walking into a firefight between the prisoners and some of the insiders.

And it had been a real firefight. Mac had never really gone along with Tilly's idea that it was part of some plot to infiltrate the ville. After all, how would the insiders know that they were going to be there, let alone that they wouldn't just chill anyone they captured?

He sighed to himself, barely able to keep his eyelids open. It had always paid to go along with Tilly, because she was insane and might just tear your throat out if you said the wrong thing. Tilly and the giant Tod had been two of the best fighters in the ville, and now they were gone. Mac shook his head sadly. They were good to have on your side. What his people would do now worried him.

He yawned. It wasn't his problem. Except that if not

for the outlanders, he'd be as chilled as Tilly and Tod. Even so, Abner had wanted to use them for the ritual chill. It didn't strike him as being a good move. Their skills would be good for the protection of the ville. Besides which, he figured that he owed them for his life.

But he was just a sec man—the chief, sure, but still just a sec man. He couldn't go against the leader.

He was so occupied by his thoughts that he didn't notice the slight scuffling behind him, didn't notice first Jak and then Dean emerge from around the side of the hut, covered in dirt and mud, pieces of straw still clinging to their clothing.

Jak picked up a rock from the ground, a jagged but basically round rock that fit into the palm of his pale hand, and brought it down with a sharp and fierce force on the back of his skull.

"I CAN'T SAY I feel good about sitting on my ass doing nothing while they're out there risking their necks." Mildred's tone was angry, but from frustration rather than anything else, as she soaked strips of cloth in the now cold water, squeezed them out and applied them to J.B.'s fevered brow.

"Can't say I don't agree with you," Ryan said, squatting by the hurricane lamp and drawing patterns in the dirt with his finger. "Fact of the matter is, I'm itching to get out there, but it just isn't possible."

"I know," Mildred whispered. "I just feel the frustration, too, I guess."

Ryan didn't answer. There was nothing to say. The plan had been worked by himself and Jak, but this was one of those rare occasions where Ryan could do nothing but sit and wait.

The albino had noticed that the adobe wall at the back

of the hut had a small gap of a few inches, forming a hollow that bit into the wall and the earth beneath. It formed a small channel into which the inhabitants of the hut had to urinate and defecate, a kind of primitive sewer.

Jak and Dean were small and slender enough to squeeze through the gap without disturbing the fragile wall too much. The albino teen was certain that the back of the hut wouldn't be guarded, and if it was, then the guards wouldn't expect anyone to crawl out through the channel. The sec men in the ville were too used to defeating any enemy using the storms. They had little idea of what to actually do with any captives.

It was a theory in which he had been proved correct. He and Dean had squeezed through and come around to the sole guard at the front of the hut without encountering anyone else.

Now they were on their way to where Abner lay sleeping, while Ryan, Mildred and Krysty stood watch over J.B.

"SO WHERE DOES this guy Abner live, anyway?" Dean whispered to Jak as they slunk from shadow to shadow, in and out of the huts and shacks. It was incredibly quiet, as though all life ceased with sundown. Perhaps it did. If the ville scratched a living from the soil, with only the occasional opportunity to trade, then it was probable that the inhabitants were ruled by the rise and fall of the sun, working the land as long and hard as they could.

If that was so, then it would make it easier for them to find Abner and make him see their point of view.

If they could ever work out where he was.

Jak stood in the shadows, his ruby eyes raking the

darkness. His night vision was better, in some ways, than his day vision. Because his albino traits left him sensitive to the light, he was able to make out shapes in the darkness without an excess of light blinding him.

"Guess look for biggest shack. No baron live in shithole," he answered finally.

"The whole place is a shithole," Dean replied with a grin.

Jak returned the grin. "Some less shit than others. Like that…"

Dean followed Jak's arm. About fifty yards in front of them lay a shack with a veranda. It was the only one they'd seen so far that had such a structure. And there was more—two sec men were seated in old cane chairs at each end of the veranda, cradling handblasters. It was impossible to tell from that range, and in this light, but by the shape of them Jak suspected that one was a .44 Magnum, long barreled and deadly. The other was a .50 Magnum Desert Eagle. Both were deadly blasters, even given that they probably weren't in the best of condition. None of the blasters Jak had seen so far in this ville were well cared for.

"Looks like it could be the place," Dean murmured.

Jak nodded. "Big shack, two sec men…not home of shit shoveler, even in shithole."

They withdrew farther into the shadows to watch and observe. They stayed there for almost half an hour, crouched in the dark and ignoring the cramp in their aching limbs. Neither had been able to rest adequately before setting out to search for the dwelling.

Nothing happened. The guards didn't move, seeming to be sleeping fitfully. There was no movement other than the snuffling of a stray dog.

"These guys are slack," Dean commented eventually, shifting to rid himself of the pins and needles running down his leg. "I don't think they'd know what to do if they were attacked."

"Mebbe not, but no need to take for granted," Jak returned. "Act like best sec men ever seen."

Saying no more, he slipped Dean two of the leaf-bladed knives to use as weapons and gestured to indicate a roundabout pattern for the boy to follow so that he would come up to the sec man on the left from behind, hitting the man in his blind spot.

Dean nodded and set off, leaving Jak to make his way around to the right.

The albino took off, using the shadows as cover. His dark camou clothing kept him well hidden, and his face, hands and hair were streaked with mud, disguising the usually all-too-conspicuous white. He kept low to the ground, running swiftly and lightly in the way he had learned as a youngster in the bayou. He passed shacks where the windows were open to the outside, and could hear the animal sounds of rutting humans or the contented snores of sleepers from within. Whichever, he was careful not to disturb them, nor to kick up dust when he passed the doorways to huts that were covered only by haphazardly hung pieces of old sacking.

It was a twisting route, as the paths through the ville were winding and not in any kind of order that could be described as a road. Once or twice Jak nearly lost his bearings, and hoped that the less experienced Dean hadn't become hopelessly lost.

Rounding a corner, Jak got the sec man in his sights. He was approaching him from an angle and from behind. If he was quiet enough, it was doubtful that the sec man would ever feel the knife as it slipped between his ribs and punctured his heart.

Stealthily Jak moved in. He was less than three feet behind the man, and poised to strike, when he heard a muffled groan from the other end of the veranda. It startled Jak's target out of his slumber, and he sprang to his feet, looking around in confusion.

It was obvious that Dean had found his way to his target and taken care of him. It was just unfortunate that his route had turned out to be a fraction easier than Jak's, and his chill had been achieved more quickly.

The sec man turned toward the far end of the veranda and raised his blaster.

He didn't speak or make a sound, so there was still a chance to keep things under cover, as long as Jak acted quickly.

Springing forward, Jak reached up while in midair. He was shorter than the sec man and had the disadvantage of being on a lower level, the veranda forming a six-inch platform around the house. But he had the element of surprise.

If the sec men in this pesthole had been more familiar with keeping prisoners, and in being attacked from the outside with any degree of regularity, then it was certain that Jak's task would have been well-nigh impossible. The sec man would have been expecting an attack to parallel Dean's on his colleague.

Instead he was an easy prey. Jak's hand snaked out in the darkness, grabbing the man's straggling blond hair and jerking back hard. A surprised gasp was all that escaped his lips before he fell into Jak and onto the knife as it slipped between his ribs and punctured his vital organs.

He tried to scream as he died, but only a harsh gurgling escaped as blood bubbled from his lips.

Jak fell back, the sec man becoming a deadweight as

he slipped into unconsciousness and death. Jak's feet planted themselves firmly as he landed, swiveling so that the chilled sec man's weight was used to Jak's advantage, pitching him past the albino to collapse in the dust.

Jak knew he was dead and didn't bother to look back. He had bounded onto the veranda by the time the sec man was laid flat on the ground.

Dean was waiting for him by the entrance to the shack, grinning. "What kept you?" he whispered.

Jak returned the grin, but said nothing. He gestured to Dean to follow him, then tried the old wooden screen door that hung lopsidedly in the doorway. It wasn't locked, and Jak had almost expected it not to be. They were too sloppy in this ville, protected only by the weather conditions and seclusion of the valley.

Inside, the shack was pitch-dark, the scant outside illumination from the moon and from the protective fires around the ville shut out by the sacking that hung over the windows. It also served to trap the filthy smell of unwashed humans and raw sewage, which seemed concentrated, as though the shack hadn't been cleaned out for a long while.

Jak and Dean slid in the door and up against the wall, flattening themselves into the dark and waiting for their eyes to adjust to the new level of darkness. It took several seconds, in which time both youths used their ears to take in as much detail as they could from the sounds around the room.

Heavy snoring came from one corner of the room, to their left, and at the back. Away from any of the windows. Not so stupe, then. The snores came from two people. One had to be Abner. The other was from a woman. It was higher pitched, lighter, and followed by a small groan that was unmistakably female. There were the sounds of someone shifting in his or her sleep.

Eyes now adjusted to the dark, Jak could see that they were sleeping on an old iron bedstead, raised from the floor. There were few items of furniture in the room, all salvaged from predark and in varying states of disrepair. Craftsmanship was obviously not high on the list of priorities in this ville.

There was no one else in the one-room shack, no other sec men. Even more stupe. Did the old man want to get chilled?

The floor was unprotected boards. To make their way across to the far corner and the bed without making a noise to wake Abner was going to be a hit-and-miss affair, made easier by the lack of extra sec men, but still risky. What were the chances that the old man would sleep with a blaster as readily as a woman?

Jak tapped Dean on the arm and gestured for him to follow the line of the walls around to the bed, keeping low under the window openings. Jak would follow the line around the opposite wall.

It took a matter of seconds for them to skirt the edges of the room, where the boards would be least likely to creak. They met at the foot of the bed. Abner and his woman were still snoring, oblivious.

Without a word Jak strode forward and put his hand over Abner's mouth, pinching his nostrils with his thumb and forefinger. The old man's breathing was cut short, and he spluttered into wakefulness, his eyes staring wide in shock as he began to rise—into the point of the leaf-bladed knife that Jak held with his other hand.

"Make noise, get chilled. Your choice," Jak whispered.

Abner's staring eyes, flicking across Jak and registering fear, said everything.

The woman stirred in her sleep, then awakened slowly.

"What is it?" she asked sleepily, raising herself on one elbow. The filthy sheet and blankets covering them fell away, revealing her young and newly formed breasts. She couldn't have been more than fourteen years old.

Seeing Jak standing over Abner, she opened her mouth to scream, only to suck in her breath and squeal when Dean moved into view, holding the point of his knife to her throat.

"Don't make me use it," he said softly, trying not to stare at her breasts.

Wide-eyed, the girl shook her head.

Jak spoke softly in the darkness. "Come with us. Keep quiet."

Abner nodded. Jak stood back, and the old man rose from the bed. He was naked, his sagging gut hanging over his balls, making him look like a eunuch in the darkness. He reached for his clothes, draped on the end of the bedstead.

"Uh-uh…" Jak reached out to the ragged garments, shaking them before handing them to Abner. An old bayonet fell from the material. Even in the near-black, Jak could see that the weapon had a serrated edge, the kind that tore and splintered bone on its removal.

There were no other weapons in the clothes, and Jak allowed Abner to dress quickly before ushering him toward the door.

He left Dean to deal with the girl.

"You just stay here, stay quiet," Dean whispered. "I

won't harm you unless you shout or scream, so don't do that. Okay?''

The girl nodded, clutching the sheet to herself—more in the manner of a shield from the knife than in any kind of modesty.

Dean left her, turning his back to follow Jak across the room.

He was only a few steps behind the albino when he heard the rusty click. Whirling on his toes, Dean caught the barest glimpse of the girl kneeling on the bed, her nakedness now fully exposed as she grappled with the old blunderbuss that Abner kept by his side in the bed. The rusty click had been the old hammer being hauled back.

She started to raise her head and aim the blaster.

She never made it.

Without pause for thought, Dean judged the distance and range, taking the largest part of the target to get the maximum chance of a hit. The knife left his hand and was embedded in her breastbone before she had a chance to blink.

Eyes still wide in shock, the girl fell onto the stinking mattress, dropping the blaster under her.

Abner started to shout, either in shock or outrage, but was stopped by the sudden pressure of Jak's knife on his carotid artery. He watched in silence as Dean hurried to the now dead girl and turned her over to remove the knife and to make the blaster safe. She had died with the hammer still cocked and ready, not even given the reflex time to squeeze the trigger.

"Good chill—you remember," Jak whispered in Abner's ear. The old man tried to nod, but stopped when he realized that it pressed the blade into his artery.

Dean took the lead as they left the shack, Abner

stumbling momentarily when he saw the bodies of the chilled sec. It was a simple matter to return to the adobe hut where Ryan and the others were waiting. Mac was still lying outside, still unconscious.

Dean pulled the wooden gate open, and Abner walked inside with Jak's knife at his throat. When Dean had shut the gate behind them, Jak withdrew the knife and stood back, at the same time gently pushing Abner so that the baron stumbled into the center of the room, where he came to stand near the still shivering and muttering J.B.

Mildred, bent over the Armorer, looked up but said nothing.

Ryan was standing, arms folded, partially in shadow. Krysty was beside him. They said nothing.

"What is it you want?" Abner asked in a tremulous voice.

Still no one spoke.

"Look, you...you can have anything you want, friends," Abner stuttered in a pitiful voice. "You can leave before morning, with supplies. We don't have much, but it's yours."

"Right, we leave the ville and end up in the valley, where your sec men can outnumber us in an environment where they're more familiar with the conditions. Yeah, that makes a lot of sense," Mildred scoffed without looking up.

Abner gave her a puzzled look. "Why would we come after you?"

"The ritual chilling." Ryan spoke softly, his voice all the more menacing for its relative calm. "You haven't forgotten that, have you? You still need victims for it. Us."

Abner spread his hands and shrugged. "So we don't make a sacrifice to the sun...it won't be the first time."

"Fat man give in too easily," Jak muttered.

Abner turned to the albino. "Why not? You've got me at your mercy. I'd have to be triple stupe to try and hold out on you now."

"But later?" Ryan asked.

Abner shrugged again. "Okay, I could send sec men against you, true enough, I guess. But why waste time on outlanders when we have enough trouble just surviving and coping with the insiders when they come for us?"

Ryan said nothing for a moment. He could see the fear and worry in Abner's eyes, reflecting the smoky glow of the hurricane lamp. He had the baron on the run, if he played it right.

Finally he spoke. "I don't usually do deals. I like to clean the mess up and get out of the bastard ville before the shit starts to spread. But I'll make an exception for you."

Abner looked relieved, but still had to ask. "Why?"

Krysty answered. "J.B.'s sick and needs time to recover. That coldheart Wallace also has one of us still in the redoubt. You want them out of your face. We want them out of the way so we can get our man back and leave this bastard place. So we need manpower. You need more fighting skills."

"A deal?"

Ryan nodded. "A deal. You don't chill us. You help us get our man out."

"And in return?"

"We teach you things you never dreamed of. You'll have a chance of ridding yourselves of Wallace, Murphy and their sec men. More, you'll have a better than even chance of beating away any other attackers you might get.''

Abner scratched his chin through his beard and rubbed absently at his dangling belly.

"Guess I'm not in any position to say no, even if I want to," he mused. "I don't agree, you just chill me and go."

"That's about it," Ryan assented. "Thing is, at least the other way we both get a chance for what we want."

Abner nodded. "That's true, boy. I don't say I trust you, but I guess I'll go along with it."

"I can't say that I trust you, either," Ryan replied. "We'll just have to live with it."

SUN UP CAME as a wan light reflected red through the light mist of dust. The inhabitants of the ville rose to go about their tasks only to find that something radically different had happened in the night.

At Abner's request, the bodies of the two sec men and that of the young girl had been laid out in the rough square at the center of the ville. They lay in the early-morning sun, starting to swell in the rising heat.

Abner stood at the head of the corpses, with Ryan, Krysty and Jak behind him. The old man carried his blaster, and the companions had their own blasters, retrieved from the shack that laughingly passed for an armory. It had crossed Ryan's mind that J.B. would have wept to see blasters stored in such a way, had he been able.

Instead the Armorer lay in Abner's bed, attended by Mildred and Dean. The two of them acted as security for each other, as well as nursing J.B. on his route to recovery. The Armorer had passed the crisis of his fever during the night and was now lying peacefully. Once he recovered his strength, the real problem would be in how long it took his ankle to heal. In the corner, not forgotten, lay Mac. The sec man was still unconscious.

Outside in the rough square, the curious ville dwellers gathered to hear Abner speak.

"Listen here, all of you. These good people, who were to be our sacrifice to the sun, did this last night...." He spread his free hand to indicate the corpses. "They chilled these folk without a second thought, and spared me only because they propose a bargain."

"What bargain could be enough to appease the sun?" came a voice from the back of the crowd.

"Good question, friend," Abner said with a note of ice in his voice that didn't escape Ryan's notice. "What do we need more than anything? To rid ourselves of the mother insiders. These good people have a man inside that they want back. We help them, they train us so that we can grind the mothers into the dirt once and for all. That seems fair to me. After all, the sun must have sent them—look what they did to two of my best sec men without even trying."

There was a thoughtful silence from the crowd. Any doubts were kept unspoken in deference to Abner's underlyingly sinister air of command.

"This should be an interesting experience, lover," Krysty whispered to Ryan.

Chapter Seventeen

Doc found himself standing in a room similar to the one in which his corporeal form was lying prone. Blurring and wobbling at the edges of his vision, the room contained the mainframe computer, the couches, the trailing wires, but not the skeletal forms that were molded to the couches.

These men were now standing in front of him, clustered in the middle of the room. They looked as they had to have when first joined to the mechanism—fat, sleek, well-fed military and intelligence services men, middle-aged and experts in their own fields of diplomacy and conflict.

Fields that were too rapidly rendered barren by skydark.

One of them smiled. They all smiled.

Doc shivered. Their eyes reflected only the same glow of insanity that he had noticed in Wallace.

"Welcome to the mechanism. It wasn't designed to admit fresh blood, but the technicians have done a fine job in joining you. It was unfortunate about our colleague, but we were warned that accidents and acts of nature could occur."

"Acts of nature?" Doc spit, backing away from the man's outstretched and welcoming hand. He checked himself when he realized he was in cyberspace, a virtual reality where they couldn't physically harm him.

"Death can come to us all. From nowhere," the man continued in a bright tone. He lowered his hand awkwardly, feeling snubbed by Doc but not wanting to lose face. He turned the lowering into a sleeve-tugging gesture on his Air Force uniform.

"I hardly think from nowhere. Extreme old age is hardly an unexpected cause of death," Doc said with a heavily sardonic tone.

The Air Force general looked momentarily confused. "Old age?"

He turned to his companions, and they muttered among themselves, obviously excluding Doc by choice. Doc took it as an opportunity to survey the room further.

It was an almost perfect replica of the room in which they were all strapped, with one glaring omission: the wall where the glass observation window into the control room beyond was situated. There was no window. There was nothing but a blank wall.

Doc also noticed that the door into the anteroom was open. What lay beyond that?

He was interrupted from his reverie by a cough. He turned back to find them looking at him again.

"I find that we have some questions to ask you before we accept you into our fold," the Air Force general said softly. "Not the least of which is how you came to be here. My colleague here—" he indicated the sole soberly suited man "—was under the impression that the Chronos operatives had tired of your constant disruption and had used you as part of an experiment in forward time travel. You were their great success in trawling, but as for forward travel..." He shrugged.

Doc felt a bile of anger begin to rise. A "success"? He remembered the obscenities that were Judge Crater and Ambrose Bierce, remembered the pain and agony of being trawled by the cruel whitecoats and was painfully aware of his own mental instability. So that was 'success'?

"Do you know what's happened outside your moribund and absurd machine?" Doc snapped.

"No," the general answered ingenuously, so much so that it took Doc aback.

The uniformed man continued, "We have been cut off from the outside. Some sort of communication breakdown. It happens, even in the best-run complexes, and this is such advanced technology. We've been running through simulations, waiting for the call. But so far there has been nothing. In truth we, ah, have rather been hoping that you can tell us."

Doc was drained of anger by his surprise. For a moment he forgot that these men were part of a project that had ripped him from the bosom of his family and hurled him—twice—into futures that he should never have witnessed. For a moment he looked on them as human souls as lost as himself, trapped by harsh circumstance in a world for which they were not made.

"Have you been fed no information about the world?" he asked. "Hasn't Wallace been giving you the data?"

One of the men—Army by his uniform, and bunching large fists in frustration as he spoke—said, "Wallace is a good man, but it seems to me he's losing his grip. I've noticed a deterioration in his mental capacity over the time period we've been hooked up."

Doc was about to comment that he felt Wallace was bordering on insanity, when it suddenly struck him: the Army man was talking about the General Wallace who had been in charge of the redoubt when they were initially hooked up to the Moebius MkI. He had no idea that he was now several generations of Wallace down the line.

"Do you actually know how long you've been linked together?" Doc asked quietly.

The Air Force man looked puzzled, scratched his head and turned to the others for guidance. They all seemed to be at a loss. Finally he said, "Something you will soon realize Doctor, is that time has no meaning as such in here. Once you become part of the rat king, as you just have, then the outside world and all its concepts become very, ah, abstracted is probably the best word."

"To a ridiculous degree," Doc commented. "There is no need for this computer. There are no Reds anymore. There's little of anything anymore. Your obscene plans caused the end of the world as you know it."

"You mean there's been a war?" the Army man asked after some whispered consultation.

Doc gave a hollow laugh. "You could call it that. Skydark. A total nuclear conflagration that has laid waste to the world. What we used to call the United States is now the Deathlands. And believe me, gentlemen, it more than lives up to that name."

There was more whispered consultation. The Army man turned to Doc.

"So who won?"

Doc felt an urge to giggle. It crept up his throat, making him choke. He began to laugh. At first it was soft and low, but it grew louder and louder, harsher and harsher, verging on hysteria. Tears of laughter ran down his cheeks, turning to tears of rage and sadness.

They watched him impassively, only the occasional puzzled flicker of a frown giving away any emotions.

Doc finished, doubled up and in agony from cramps in his ribs. Which, if he tried hard to concentrate, was absurd. How could he get cramps when he wasn't, as such, real?

He pulled himself upright. "Nobody won, you cretin. Everyone lost. There is no world as you know it. There's nothing. Just outposts of mutated idiots trying to take little degrees of power and justify their pathetic existence. Just a few people trying to make their way in the rad-blasted world without being chilled by those of little sense."

One of the men in suits stepped forward and spoke for the first time. "I'm sorry, Doctor, but that just doesn't make sense. It doesn't fit with any of the models we've used for our simulations over the years. And those models were very carefully planned and plotted to cover any eventuality. There's no chance that anything could have happened outside of that."

Doc sighed. "I've been outside of this mechanism. Have you?"

"Of course. Before we were attached—"

"I'm talking about since," Doc snapped. "You've been in here over a hundred years. How could you possibly know what has happened?"

"Because the simulations and simulatory models fed into our mainframe covered every possibility."

It was a circular argument, and Doc could see no way of countering it. He threw up his hands in resignation and exasperation. "Have it your way, gentlemen. Have it your way."

"Oh, but we will," said the Air Force officer. "After all, there is one flaw in your argument."

Doc was about to explode in fury and say that it wasn't a debating society, he was talking about reality, when he realized that for these men, the rarefied air of abstract argument and simulation had become the only reality they knew. So he said simply, "What, pray tell, is this flaw?"

"Simple. If the outside world is so irrevocably changed, then why do we still exist? Who is keeping us maintained?"

Doc shook his head, refusing to answer, to debate. It didn't matter. Fate had decreed that he be locked inside this machine, perhaps forever. If it came to that, what was forever in a realm where there was no such thing as time?

"Gentlemen, I acquiesce," Doc said with a bow. "As I am here, you may as well show me where I am to live."

"Very well. We know you are Dr. Theophilus Tanner, but we have no names. We are one with the mechanism, and something you will have to realize is that you, too, will become one. You will cease to have the trappings of individual ego and meld into the amorphous brain of the rat king. We are one, and you will be one with us. When that happens, then the mechanism will once again be in full working order."

Doc resisted the urge to ask why the Moebius MkI would need to be in working order when there was nothing for it to do anymore, no world into which it could possibly fit. Instead he merely nodded, and allowed the other members of the rat king to lead him from the chamber.

As one they filed toward the door into the anteroom, moving in a close mass that seemed to shimmer in Doc's mental vision, so that they—at moments—appeared to meld into one creature, rather than a collection of individuals. Doc followed, wondering what was waiting for him through the door....

"REALLY, DR. TANNER, this just won't do."

"Why not? I have nothing to lose, do I? After all, this Alice-in-Wonderland hell of absurdity is not a world that I know. It is not a world that I care to know. My only desire is to return to the bosom of my family...to my own time, to my own world. Is that really so much for a man to ask? If you were in my position, would you not ask the same?"

The whitecoat scientist blew out his cheeks and scratched at his balding pate. He'd been warned that the only success for Chronos was a problem in the flesh, but he hadn't expected an argument of this sort.

"Doctor, you aren't a stupid man, are you?"

"That, my dear man, is possibly my great curse." Doc sighed, settling back on the bench in his cell and hearing the chains on his manacles rattle. It astounded him that, more than a hundred years after his birth, the military was still so unimaginative as to resort to chains when trying to confine one man. He mentioned as much to the whitecoat, who gave a short, barking laugh.

"I like that. You realize, of course, that we only use these on you because you've been such a problem. We've never had to resort to such measures before."

"I'll take that as a compliment," Doc replied.

His captor looked at him with a puzzled frown that was partway between exasperation and admiration before turning on his heel and leaving the room.

"YOU SEE, we can trawl these memories from you," came the voice of the rat king. Unlike before, it was a sinuous voice that seemed to be all of the men talking as one. It wormed its way into Doc's brain, eating at the corners of his mind and reminding him that he wasn't actually in the 1990s, but over a hundred years ahead, not really in this cell, but strapped to a couch with electrodes connecting him to a mainframe computer.

"To what end?" Doc asked of them, speaking aloud, even though he knew didn't have to in order to communicate with them.

"To show you how powerful the mechanism is. To show you what we can do. To show you what you can do, if you join us. Not that you have any choice in the matter. You will be absorbed eventually. We all had our qualms and doubts to begin with, but in the final analysis we became as one. And it is glorious, Dr. Tanner, it is glorious. But allow an indulgence...."

DOC FOUND HIMSELF back in Baron Teague's hellhole ville, strapped to a table and subject to the attentions of the hideous Cort Strasser.

Pain racked Doc's body, even though he knew this to be ridiculous. He was inside a computer, and the computer was inside him. He wasn't in any real danger, although it did cross his mind momentarily that the computer could be stimulating his cortex in such a manner as to simulate pain.

He was unable to detach himself from the searing agony of torture enough to work these thoughts through logically. The memory was too much. Of course they knew that he had ended up in Strasser's hands after being flung forward by the whitecoats at Chronos. Of course they knew that this was where Ryan Cawdor and his band of survivors had entered Doc's life. Of course they knew that this was where he was about to escape, to be set free. They couldn't change that...could they?

Strasser was silent as he prepared the next torture. He had already burned Doc, and the frail man's limbs were aching where he was stretched out on the torture table, tied so tightly that he felt as though his wrists were about to burst with pent-up pressure, and his fingers were numb where the circulation had been stopped.

"It's a pity you've lost the sensation in your fingers," Strasser said quietly as he picked up a pair of pliers. "It won't be quite as effective as it would have been if you still had feeling there. Ah, well, it'll just be a de-layed torture for you, won't it? You'll just feel the ben-efit of the pain when you've been untied and left to rot for a few hours...when the feeling returns."

"What do you want from me?" Doc husked, aware that his throat was dry and sore.

"Want?" Strasser asked in surprise. "Who says I want anything? I enjoy doing this. That's reason enough."

"I know, you ugly, stupid fool," Doc whispered hoarsely. "I wasn't talking to you."

"Not talking to me?" Strasser said, a flicker of a smile crossing his face. "I knew you were crazy, old man, but I didn't think it would amuse me so much."

"Shut up. You will be overwhelmed soon enough when Ryan and Krysty arrive." And the short, rounded Finnegan, with his tall black friend Hennings—good warriors, long since lost but not in this moment of time. A silent tear left Doc's left eye and trickled down his cheek as he remembered their chilling, and the chilling of Lori, and the others who had traveled with them across the Deathlands but had bought the farm before reaching this stage. Good people.

Doc was unaware that he had rambled all of this in an undertone the whole while, and that Strasser was looking at him with a bemused expression.

"You're beyond crazy, old man," he said softly. "I can't enjoy my work if you don't shut the fuck up. So I guess I'll just have to shut you up myself, won't I?"

He took the pliers, and instead of grasping one of Doc's hands, he used the powerful fingers of his free hand to pry open Doc's jaw. Doc was so weak that he couldn't resist Strasser's grip, and moaned incoherently as his jaw was held open.

He felt the cold metal of the tool's nose as it touched his tongue, felt the cool scrape as Strasser opened the nose. The tickle of the metal as it searched for the edge of his tongue, one half of the nose slipping underneath his tongue, the other sliding over the top surface. He felt the pinch as the two halves of the nose started to move together, the pressure on the top of his tongue turn into a cutting edge that drew salty blood as the nose began to bite into the flesh.

The pain shifted gear, moved into another dimension as the pliers took a firm grip, and Strasser started to exert pressure. He pulled on the pliers, the tongue moving out of Doc's mouth, extended at the root until the pulling was painful to him. Until he felt the flesh and tendon at full stretch.

Until he felt the tendons start to tear, the flesh start to rend, the pain start to drive him over the edge…

But this was a false memory. It hadn't happened like this. So why was it occurring now?

"To show you our power to alter reality—to be reality. We are the rat king, we are God. And you will be a part of us."

Doc heard the words echo in his head, louder than

any outside volume; louder than it would take to rupture his eardrums and make them bleed; louder than his own thoughts, drowning them and overrunning them, blotting out his own self.

Doc clamped his hands over his ears, screwing up his eyes to shut out all light. Why, he didn't know. It made no sense, as he wasn't a physical body at this moment. And how could he cover his ears when his hands had been tied but a moment before?

Come to that, why was his tongue no longer hurting?

Doc opened his eyes and let his hands drop. In yet another strange twist, he found he was standing upright instead of lying down.

And he was in a room full of people.

"THIS IS OUR TRUE PURPOSE."

Doc turned, no longer surprised. Behind him was the cabal of men that comprised the rest of the rat king. Doc suddenly thought to ask a question that had been running through his head for some time.

"Just tell me—before we go any further—what are your names?"

The Army man clenched his fist and looked troubled. "We don't have names, Dr. Tanner. Not anymore. I used to, but we are Moebius now, and it is us. You will be part of it, part of us."

"I feared as much," Doc murmured, turning back to the activity behind him. It seemed to be something that he had seen before, in his days as a prisoner of the whitecoats. It was old tech in full flow: banks of terminals, lights winking, phones ringing, answered by men in military uniform or in shirtsleeves, one eye always on the large screen that stood at the front of the room, display rapidly changing.

The display itself was a map of the world, laid flat, with different-colored lines running from continent to continent. Doc wondered idly what shape the continents would show now on such a map, so long after the events of skydark had reshaped them.

This display showed no signs of acknowledging any change. Why should it? Moebius had been cut off from the outside world, had never known the changes triggered by the nukecaust.

The LED display that made up the graphic changed the trajectory of the lines as more information came through. Fresh lines began to spurt from the old USSR and its satellites, traveling toward the U.S.A. Lines from the U.S.A. and some of its European allies began to travel, in different colors, in the opposite direction.

The virtual staff manning the computer consoles looked alarmed, sweat and fear distorting their faces.

"This is how you—I mean, we—amuse ourselves, is it?" Doc asked.

"It's not a matter of amusement. We exist for this purpose, and the simulations are to keep us up to scratch, to keep our minds sharp for every eventuality. The only task we are called upon to perform at present is to keep the redoubt running and in good order. This seems to be harder than previously, and we suspect the technicians are slacking because of the lack of war footing—"

Doc remembered the inbred and mutie technicians he had seen in the redoubt. Of course Moebius, cut off in its own world, could not know of this.

"But still, it takes but a fraction of our power to keep the redoubt in working order, waiting for the call. In the meantime we keep sharp by running these simulations."

Doc held up a finger to silence the collective voice.

"One point," he said softly. "If you are Moebius, and Moebius sets the simulation, then how can it ever outwit you, since you are it?"

He was met with silence. The men in front of him exchanged puzzled frowns, muttered the odd word that he couldn't make out, and seemed to take some time to work out the logic of what he was saying.

Finally the Air Force general turned to speak to Doc.

"You make a valid point, Dr. Tanner. Our very insularity could, it seems, be a disadvantage. This is no doubt where the hand of chance takes a turn. It has given us you at a most opportune time. Come and be absorbed. Join with us now and you will bring in another intellect, another point of view. A fresh input to the mechanism, making it stronger."

He held out his hand in a gesture of supplication.

"Do I have any choice?" Doc asked.

"Only the choice of making it difficult or easy."

Would Ryan lead his friends back to rescue him? Were they even still alive? Doc had every confidence in their ability to survive, but not so much in their ability to reach him. Indeed, as there was no time as such inside the rat king, he had no idea how long he had been inside the brain of Moebius, and how long the brain of Moebius had been inside him.

"I acquiesce," Doc said quietly. "I will join with you, if not willingly then with no resistance. I fail to see what else I can do."

He moved toward the outstretched hand, and as his fingers touched those of the Air Force general, he felt a charge shoot through his whole body...or his psyche, represented as his body.

The universe became a blur of color, too fast for him

to assimilate detail. Inside his head ideas and images whirled too quickly for him to grab hold of them. It seemed that everything was passing him by, and he was marooned in a sea of thought.

The blur stopped. A whirling kaleidoscope of color was fixed and fused in front of him, frozen in a moment of time. It stayed for what could have been a fraction of a second, what could have been a month or a year, beautiful and solid. Then it melted, slowly dissolving to reveal a whiteness born of a brilliant light. A light that gradually decreased in intensity, that gradually dimmed until Doc was able to make out details.

The first thing being that instead of facing the group of men who comprised the rat king, he was now one of them. He stood in the middle of the group and could feel his links to them in this physical representation. It was as though they blurred into one, visually, from the waist down.

More disturbing was the fact that he could feel them inside his head. He had memories and thoughts bubbling to the surface that weren't his own; a kitchen in Washington, arguing with a beautiful woman who was about to throw a juicer at him, crying and asking why he had to volunteer for a mission that would take him away again; a childhood that wasn't his own, riding a bike through suburban streets, disco music blaring from a radio hanging off the handlebars, people washing cars and trimming lawns shouting greetings to him; a fight in a bar, himself and two other grunts holding a long-haired and bearded man over a pool table, taking turns to smash a pool ball into his face, his mouth a bloody mess of broken teeth and pulpy flesh.

DOC RECOGNIZED the area. It was Washington, D.C., and he rounded the corner with the rest of the rat king, adopting the shuffling walk that kept them all together. They were on Pennsylvania Avenue, heading for the White House.

The air was still, almost static and charged with lack of motion. Doc listened, but there were no birds singing. A creeping horror made him feel nausea rise from the pit of his stomach. Still he kept moving with the others.

They turned into the driveway that led up the immaculately manicured grounds to the White House. There was no sign of guards. The immaculately trimmed lawns were dead and brown, scorched beyond redemption. Looking up, Doc could see that there were no windows left in the White House. Glass and frames were all gone: the building was nothing more than a shell, a faint black-and-brown patina covering the surface of the stone.

Without having to ask, Doc knew that they were examining the damage caused by an initial nuke hit. He knew without question that the shadows scorched into the ground were all that remained of the sec men who had guarded the White House, a futile gesture in the face of such destruction.

"As expected. An initial target. Compute follow-up damage from a series of hits at such strategic points. There will be some disturbance of the land—"

"Some?" Doc interrupted. "Half of the continent is unrecognizable out there. The other half is radically changed. In reality this place is nothing but a huge hole. Do you realize what this means?"

"It means that we have to strike back. This is the first strike in the chain. The beginning of the simulation. Now we work."

THEY WERE BACK in the control room, the LED screen winking and changing rapidly as the rat king barked orders to the virtual staff, ordering them to program strikes on East Bloc targets. Doc found himself joining in without thinking, just knowing by some osmotic process what the others were thinking, ideas and strategies flying from mind to mind, altering according to different perspectives and ideas, forming into a single thought that flew to the consoles as an order.

The rainbow patterns of mutually assured destruction sprang up over the globe, running in lines of brilliant color until the whole LED map was a bright blaze of moving color. It reminded Doc of the kaleidoscope that had formed around him when he was being absorbed, and with horror he realized that was exactly what it was supposed to be—a visual representation of the ultimate purpose.

"But don't you fools realize what this means?" he screamed, feeling sure that this time he would surely lose whatever fragile grip on sanity he still possessed.

"This…"

DOC RECOGNIZED the place. It was Moscow. He remembered too well their attempt to recover the soiled and abused American flag that had hung by the tomb of Lenin, in a glass cage covered with generations of phlegm and spittle. He remembered Major-Commissar Gregori Zimyanin with a shiver. A worthy man in his own way, as honorable in his own cause as Ryan Cawdor in his: a man to have on your side rather than fight against.

It was only with some effort that Doc remembered that this was a simulation, a virtual Moscow, where there would be no need for him to fear running across Zimyanin.

Besides which, there were no people around. The city was freshly nuked, too hot for any pockets of survivors to crawl from hiding. Or for most...

Doc felt bile rise in his gorge, an instinct of revulsion as he spotted the mewling, puking thing on the steps of the Kremlin. It was naked apart from a few charred rags. As they drew nearer, he realized that the rags weren't clothing, but strips of skin and charred flesh. It had no face, no hair, and very little in the way of skin. It crawled on the steps, dirt and dust blowing onto the exposed flesh in the storm that was brewing in the aftermath of the bombs, in the beginnings of the nuclear winter that had formed the Deathlands.

The thing that had once been human kept crying voicelessly and incoherently, not noticing the filth that blew into its flesh, all nerve endings stripped away with the epidermis, maddened beyond pain by the experience of being nuked and yet still living.

"Interesting. The fact of survival is in itself a superb demonstration of human tenacity. If this thing—" the voice of the rat king paused, momentarily at a loss whether to describe the now genderless creature as male or female "—is able to survive on ground level, compute the possibilities of underground bunker survival.

"If our resources for a postholocaust survival factor are stronger, then ultimate victory is assured."

Doc found himself agreeing, his mind and intellect being sucked out of him by the greater power of the computer. Remembering Emily; remembering his beloved Rachel and Jolyon; remembering the sweet Lori; remembering the strength of Ryan, J.B., Krysty, Mildred, Jak and Dean; remembering others like Finnegan and Hennings, Abe, Trader and Michael Brother, who had been lost along the way. Remembering all of them, Doc fought to retain a vestige of his own identity.

"No," he screamed, "no. This is all wrong. You—collectively—are mad. A senile, grumbling old machine that remembers battles never fought. Condemned by fate to run down slowly, maintaining a redoubt full of fools, never fulfilling your task. Frustrated by fate, spinning out fantasies of pornographic destruction to appease your impotence."

"No. Our time will come. You will see. You will be."

The voice of the rat king was calm, implacable, as though it expected this outburst and didn't care. Doc was terrified by hearing—he was sure—his own voice in the blended tones.

"You will be one."

He didn't know whether to surrender or fight, whether to hope for the best or give up hoping.

His mind began to slip into the madness of Moebius, to lose the slender thread with which he kept a grasp on his sanity.

He was tired of fighting and tired of giving in.

If only something—someone—would make the decision for him.

"We will. If you let us. Join and be one. Without all the links, we cannot survive."

Chapter Eighteen

Taking the small population of the ville, training them and waiting for J.B. to improve was a slow and painful process. It took almost a week, and a day didn't fail to pass where they all thought of Doc and what had happened to him.

Abner had some old dilapidated predark books salted away in the rusty metal chest that lay under his bed. As a token of his trust in them, he let Mildred and Ryan look at what he kept in this time capsule.

"This is my heritage," he said proudly, in a tone of voice that suggested his father had said it to him and his father to him, and what the word *heritage* meant had long ago been forgotten.

The papers were fragile, yellowing and crumbling with age and neglect. Mildred lifted them out with a delicate touch, hardly daring to breathe. Ryan stared over her shoulder in the dim light of the room, his eye glittering as he strained to see what relics of the past would be revealed. He had always relished the chance to catch a part of the past, to read about the old days.

The first thing Mildred retrieved was a *Hustler* magazine. The pages were stiff and stained, and she looked at Abner with an arched eyebrow.

"Don't look at me, missy. They're all too old for my liking."

She laid the magazine aside with distaste. The next

magazine was an old *National Enquirer* for January 1998, with Pamela Anderson and Tommy Lee on the cover. She smiled as she remembered the soap-opera lives of the rich and famous. She hoped that they had perished quickly in skydark, as they would never have been equipped to survive in the days after. The *Enquirer* joined the skin magazine on the bed, and she came to a pile of crumbling paperback books.

"Stephen King—I've seen some of his books before," Ryan said quietly, gently taking the book with a reverence and gentleness that surprised Mildred.

"That's his analysis of horror on film and in books," Mildred remarked. "*Danse Macabre* indeed. I wonder what he'd make of all this."

"Real terror springs from the same well the storyteller draws from," Ryan stated, remembering the stories he had heard as a child in Front Royal, and how they had scared him more than his first taste of battle.

Mildred said nothing. Ryan wasn't the sort of man to say something so profound unless he had drawn on something deep. She wanted to leave him with those memories, whatever they might be.

"This guy was quite some King fan," she observed, gently lifting out several paperbacks by the author. There were also some old science-fiction paperbacks about a character called Simon Rack and some books about the Hell's Angels.

But the real treasure lay at the bottom—a guidebook to Kansas City, annotated in a spidery hand, the black ink faded to a purple indentation by age and neglect. The trunk had a small hole at the bottom, and some damp had started to seep in, causing the back pages of the book to stick together.

Mildred pried them open as best she could, but soon found that it was at the front that the real prize lay.

"Well, look at this," she breathed.

Ryan peered over her shoulder and saw a map of the state. Scrawled in pen was a roughly circular shape, shaded in with cross-hatching. "We are here" was written in, with a page number. Mildred delicately turned the pages until she came to the right one.

It was an in-depth map of the part of the state shaded in on the previous page. It showed that they were fairly near to Kansas City itself, and the nearest town was Tonganoxie. Outside the town, in the scrub country, small farms and settlements of self-built houses stood along the main roads. There were photographs of some of them. Outside one stood a couple with a small child. The girl was angelic, with golden curls that tumbled over a solemn face with just the hint of a hidden smile in her large blue eyes. The couple was leaning into each other in the way that only those in love could do. He was tall, with short hair and a full beard, a rifle casually canted over his shoulder. The woman was almost as tall, with a full figure, a shining, smiling face and incredibly long, chestnut-brown hair that was whipped around her in the breeze.

They looked blissfully happy.

The photograph was so evocative that it took a little while for either of them to realize that it was the map that was the reason for the page being indicated. It was a relief map of the area around Tonganoxie, and had been altered in the faded purple-black ink to indicate the way that the earth had moved after the upheaval of nuclear war. The valley, the lip of which they were currently inhabiting, had been formed out of a shallow basin, seeming from the scribbled map to have dropped at least a hundred feet, more in places, with the underground construction of the redoubt causing an instability that had led to an additional small drop that formed the enclave.

"Now we know where we are," Ryan said, indicating the area with a chipped and calloused finger, "this'll be a bastard place to move through without a wag of some kind. We need to get back into the redoubt for transport or a jump. Otherwise we're stuck here, and it's a long haul out."

Mildred looked over her shoulder. Abner was making a poor show of trying not to eavesdrop.

"But we don't move until we're through here," she said slowly and firmly.

Ryan guessed whom she was looking at, and smiled wryly. "We've got unfinished business, and so have they. A bargain's a bargain."

MILDRED WASN'T SURE if it was the antibiotics or the poultices that Krysty had slaved over, marshaling the ville dwellers into the collection of herbs before boiling and straining them to make the stinking poultice. Something, though, had been working. In two days J.B. had come out of his fever, slept so much that they feared he would never wake and had opened his eyes to show a glittering, biting edge to his gaze.

"Ryan," he murmured softly, catching sight of his old friend first, "what's been going on?"

Ryan filled him in. The Armorer, more taciturn than usual in his just awakened state, contented himself with a muttered "Dark night!" as his only comment. On Mildred's recommendation, he didn't try to get out of bed right away, although it was obvious from his restlessness that he was itching to get into action.

By the following morning, J.B. could stand it no longer. Yelling at Dean to help him until the youngster gave in, J.B. got up and hobbled out of the shack and into the center of the ville, where he sat on an upturned box and watched in disgust as Jak attempted to teach some of the local fighters the finer points of hand-to-hand combat. Even pulling his punches, Jak had in the past hour injured two of them enough that it would take them several days to recover.

The Armorer pulled his fedora down so that the snap brim shaded his glasses from the ever present swirl of dust. Watching Jak, and remembering something Dean had said to him as he assisted him into the wan sunlight, J.B. commented, "Now do you see why Mac was allowed to live?"

Dean nodded. "I do now, seeing this bunch of stupes." He kept his voice low so as not to antagonize the ville dwellers, but it didn't change the way he felt. "It just seemed weird, 'cause Dad's drummed it into me that you never leave enemies alive. And don't tell me the story of the little girl who ripped out someone's jugular with her teeth, 'cause I've heard that one too many times," he added with a grin, preempting J.B.'s launch into a Trader story.

The only advantage of J.B. telling it rather than Ryan was that the Armorer was more terse in the telling, and it was a much shorter story.

"Trader was right, though," J.B. said softly in reply. "Then there's always one exception to any rule. Being too rigid can be as dangerous as being too slack."

Without answering, Dean knew what the Armorer meant as he watched Mac take on Jak.

The fat man outweighed the slender Jak by almost double, and was several inches taller. His head was still scarred by the blow he had taken outside the shack, and from the look on his face he was expecting to get some revenge in a one-on-one fight.

They circled each other, watched by the crowd of men and women who were there to learn. The tension grew as they circled, until it seemed that no one in the crowd could draw breath until the first strike.

It came from the blue, still unexpected despite the close attention and anticipation of the crowd. Jak feinted to the left, drawing Mac's attention, then followed up to the right with a kick that took the sec man's legs from under him.

Instead of falling heavily, as would be expected, the awkward-looking sec man let himself flop to the ground, relaxing his muscles to avoid the rigidity that broke bones. He rolled as he hit the dirt, out of the range of Jak's follow-up kick. Instead of connecting with his jaw, the albino's foot carved a space in nothing but air. It was only Jak's immense control and balance that stopped him falling flat. Instead he used the momentum of the kick to pivot, taking him out of range of the thundering roundhouse blow Mac aimed at his body. The sec man was more powerful and agile than he looked, but his notion of fighting was basic—he aimed for the body with a succession of kicks and blows designed to cause maximum damage.

Jak avoided all of those with twists and turns of his body, staying out of range and letting Mac expend energy. Then, when the sec man was puffing and blowing, slowing slightly, Jak darted in beneath one of the blows and delivered a hard jab with his extended fingers, sinking them into the soft flesh above the sec man's ribs.

Mac shot backward through the air as though a jolt of electricity had been forced through him. He tumbled over, falling naturally by instinct. Jak stood back, waiting for the sec man to get up.

"Less…more," he said simply as Mac shook his head to clear it.

The sec man gave him a vulpine leer that passed for a smile. "I hear ya, whitey," he grated, his breath still coming hard.

They closed on each other, circling tightly, neither willing to make the first move. Jak feinted, then lunged. Mac second-guessed him and blocked the straight-fingered blow by trapping Jak's arm in both of his own, crossed to strengthen them. He stepped back, allowing Jak's momentum to carry him forward. The albino sailed past Mac, hitting the dirt face first.

Like the sec man, he allowed himself to relax as he hit, but Mac had anticipated that and followed up in the millisecond while Jak was prone and—momentarily—defenseless. His heavy boot thudded into Jak's face, splitting the albino's lip and causing blood and spit to fly into the dust.

"Water the earth, you mutie bastard," Mac whispered, his anger expended. "We're quits."

He stood back, allowing Jak to get up. The albino wiped the blood from his face, hawked up a bloodied glob of phlegm and spit it into the earth.

"Yeah, quits." The albino laughed. "Learn quick, fat man. Why think I let live?"

Mac laughed, a big guffaw that stunned the crowd and Dean. But not J.B.

"Always a reason to break your own rules," he said. "Except that it has to be a good one."

MILDRED AND KRYSTY were given the thankless task of trying to teach the ville dwellers to shoot straight. It seemed almost alien to them that anyone in the Deathlands could survive without any kind of shooting skills. Blasters were second nature to the postskydark generations.

Nonetheless, the dwellers of this pesthole that didn't even have a name—"what do we want names for, friend? We know where we are," Abner told them—had few blasters, and they were in poor condition. Most of them relied on explosive power rather than accuracy, and it was dispiriting for a crack shot like Mildred to have to train such an inept group of fighters.

So she was glad when J.B. hobbled into the fray to offer his services. The Armorer still couldn't get around at great speed, but the ankle was healing as he was resting it. Ironically the time of his fever and semicoma had been beneficial to his damaged ankle, allowing the initial sprain time to mend. The reticent Armorer had once again muttered an oath and little more when Dean had shown him the tumbledown shack that passed for an armory. His response to taking a look inside had been to moan gently and to shake his head sadly.

There wasn't much J.B. could do to assist them. Most of the time he was under orders to do little except sit all day. However, having cursed the way in which the ville dwellers looked after their blasters, J.B. decided that the best thing for him to do would be to try to lick the armory—such as it was—into shape.

A small group of women and children gathered around J.B. as he sat on an upturned box, stripping the blasters and polishing them, greasing them as best as he could and putting them back together. Along the way he found that some of the blasters were entirely homemade, while others were comprised of separate parts that had been forced and welded together to make a complete blaster. Why these hadn't exploded in the faces of those who fired them was a complete mystery to him.

J.B. cleaned the weapons and explained to his audience why it was important to keep the blasters clean and oiled. He tried to explain to them the concept of different calibrations on weapons, the differences in ammo and their respective firepower. His eyes shone behind his glasses, and he didn't notice that some of the women and children looked at him blankly, not understanding him.

It didn't matter. He told them all that he could, hoping that enough would penetrate to keep the blasters in good working order for the final confrontation.

While he did that, Jak and Dean took turns to coach people in unarmed combat; Krysty and Mildred tried to improve the shooting of the ville dwellers. As all this was going on, Ryan was far from idle.

The one-eyed warrior had been thinking and planning. He could see that his forces, even swollen by the ranks of the ville dwellers, would be no match for Murphy's men once they were inside the redoubt. Outside they had matched the well-equipped sec men by virtue of their being adapted to the conditions. Inside they could hit big trouble.

Ryan spent most of his time with Abner, learning all that the old man knew of the redoubt forces, all that he knew of the surrounding terrain. They called in Mac, who had been in more expeditionary raids on the territory than any other sec man in the ville. Ryan picked their brains, put forward his plans, making sure that Abner and Mac thought that they had come up with half the ideas themselves.

Finally the baron called together his people in the

rough ground they called the center of the ville. He outlined the plan he and Mac had come up with to help the outlanders. Krysty, knowing Ryan, smiled to herself as Abner claimed Ryan's best strategies as his own. It didn't matter, as long as they got the result they wanted.

Ryan listened to Abner and looked at the ville dwellers. They were muties, inbred, and not used to hard, hand-to-hand fighting. He felt a twinge of conscience, briefly. Did they realize what they were getting into?

It would be difficult, hard and bloody. That much Ryan knew. But it was necessary, for their long-term survival as much as that of Ryan and his people.

And they were ready. Or as ready as they'd ever be.

Chapter Nineteen

The worst part was the waiting. Ryan and J.B. stood, at night, staring into the darkness beyond the beacon fires that marked the ville's boundaries.

"Think we're ready to attack those bastards and get our ticket out?" Ryan asked.

J.B. took off his glasses. "Ready as ever," he replied, pausing to polish them and replace them on the bridge of his nose before finishing the comment. "Though that's not saying much."

Ryan nodded. "Either we're outnumbered or we hope that they can pull together long enough. Some choice."

"Just don't expect firepower miracles, that's all."

"I know. It's enough to make you cry." Ryan smiled. J.B. answered him with the kind of look that could pass between old friends but would have started a fight between strangers in any bar or gaudy across the Death-lands.

"Question is, when do we move?" J.B. continued.

Ryan stared out into the dark, squinting his good eye to try to focus on the swirling darkness. The storms made the night seem like a solid thing he could reach out and touch, like a physical barrier between themselves and the redoubt. In some ways that's exactly what it was.

"Got to trust Abner on that one," Ryan said quietly.

"If nothing else, his people know the valley. We have to go with them."

"Sure, but excuse me if I get an itchy feeling down my spine when I think of it," the Armorer commented with a dryness that made Ryan laugh out loud.

Wiping a tear of laughter from his eye, Ryan said simply, "Yeah, sure be good to move."

RYAN SOUGHT OUT Abner the next morning, coming on the baron as he was still in the rusty iron bed, with the latest in a long line of girls young enough to be his granddaughter. Hell, for all Ryan knew, they might well be. It wouldn't be the first time he'd come across that sort of sickness. He remembered Baron Willie Elijah and his wives Roonie, Toonie and Poonie, and their daughters Roonie-Two, Toonie-Two and Poonie-Two. Fireblast, they were all from the same wife that Willie had first taken.

"Morning, One-eye," Abner grunted, stretching so that his fat belly wobbled, farting so that the girl next to him giggled. "Shut up, girl," he commented in an offhand manner before returning his attention to Ryan. "So what can I do for you, friend?"

"I was talking to my people last night. We want to move as soon as possible."

Abner pulled a face. "I don't know about that, friend Ryan," he said sweetly. "See, it's got to be the right conditions. Otherwise my people stand a chance of getting chilled big time."

Ryan pulled the panga from along his thigh, slowly so as not to alarm Abner or the girl. Nonetheless the long and wickedly gleaming blade made her eyes widen, and Abner looked distinctly uncomfortable. His hand reached under the covers, and Ryan heard the muffled click of the hammer on the blunderbuss he kept down there.

Ryan began to pare his chipped and hardened nails with the panga, smiling over the top of the blade. "I'd be careful with that blaster, Abner. One day it might go off and blow your pecker clean away. And you wouldn't like that, would you?" he continued, switching his attention to the girl. She shook her head, wide-eyed with complete incomprehension.

Ryan looked quickly back to Abner—not from any sense that the baron would pull the blaster on him, but more to escape the waves of revulsion that overcame him, seeing the young girl next to the old man.

"Just what do you want from us now, One-eye?" Abner growled.

Ryan shrugged, still paring his nails. "Nothing. Just a chance for us both to get what we want. And don't worry, I'm not going to try to kill you. I know Mac's back there just itching to put a hole in me."

A grating, humorless laugh came from the doorway where Mac had his blaster trained on Ryan.

"I like you, One-eye. You and your people got balls, even the women. Sure learned a lot from you. Still more to learn if you don't get yourself chilled too soon."

"I've got no intention of that," Ryan said in a level tone, not taking his attention from Abner. "All I want is to know when we're going to move."

"Can't yet," Abner said tightly.

"Why not?" Ryan asked with a studied casualness. He suspected the baron of cowardice, and he didn't want that to hold up their chances of getting out, perhaps even rescuing Doc if the old man was still alive.

Abner stayed silent. It was Mac who answered.

"The storms, Ryan. We get a nose for them here.

Guess we have to if we're going to survive. They're always here, but some are worse than others. If you look out east from here, you can see the swirls of dust rise up mebbe twenty, thirty feet into the sky. That means we got some real sons of bitches out there. Whip your skin off you in five minutes. Can't move through them at any kind of pace without your legs turning to jelly. No way we'd be in any fit state to fight, even with your training.''

Mac's tone had been level, reasoned. Even the way in which he had addressed Ryan by name rather than as "One-eye"—as everyone in this rad-blasted pesthole had since he'd arrived—convinced the one-eyed warrior that the sec man was leveling with him. Ryan didn't trust him, but he felt certain that the sec man had a respect for his skills that Ryan felt was mutual. Mac was as good as they got in this nameless ville.

Slowly, keeping a watch on Abner's hand hidden beneath the blanket, Ryan resheathed the panga.

"So how long do those kind of storms usually last?" he asked, directing the question over his shoulder at Mac rather than at the baron.

"Hard to say exactly. The storm ain't exactly a believer in accuracy. It doesn't carry a wrist chron, you know.''

Ryan smiled. "Roughly, then."

Although he couldn't see, he could almost feel the sec man shrug. "Mebbe a day, mebbe a week. This one…I dunno, it might not be long one. Can't rightly say why, but when the dust gets that high, it usually means that the storm blows itself out pretty quick. Don't hold your breath, though.''

Ryan nodded and turned slowly to face the sec man. "Don't fret yourself, Mac. There's no chance of me doing that. Every breath is precious," he said carefully before walking out of the shack, past the fat sec man, who shuffled out of the way, lifting the long-barreled blaster to allow the one-eyed warrior to pass.

When Ryan was out of earshot, Abner slowly let back the hammer on his blunderbuss. "Bastard outlanders. I'll be glad when that mother and his people are gone. If we're really lucky, the insiders will chill them while they chill the insiders, leaving it all nice and peaceful for us."

"Don't hold your breath," Mac muttered softly, echoing his words to Ryan.

THE STORM WAS RAGING. The wind whipped dust and dirt through the air, which was almost solid with the force of the howling winds. Small stones and pebbles rattled off the reinforced windshields of the wags, bouncing off the metal-and-canvas covers that Murphy had made his men erect before leaving the redoubt. They had wags that weren't convertible in such a manner, but Murphy—like the Murphys before him—felt safer if his men could see around for 360 degrees. The metal, covered-in wags might protect them better from the worst ravages of the storms, but they sure as hell didn't help them see outsiders creeping up on them. When the storms lessened, the covers came off. They were only used in the most violent of storms.

Murphy sat in the lead wag with a group of five men, a driver beside him and four men on the bench seats that lined each side of the wag. There were three other wags, each with similar personnel, which totaled twenty-four. Not exactly a large task force, but enough for their needs.

The outsiders really were stupid, Murphy mused as

the wag bounced over the terrain. They never expected a raid when the storms were this bad, despite the fact that it was always the time that Murphy picked. He'd have thought that even the most stupid of them might have caught on by now.

It never occurred to Murphy that it wasn't that simple, that the outsiders couldn't see them coming, and that they couldn't mount solid defenses because they didn't have enough old tech to compete.

"Bridge coming up, sir." The driver, Pri Firclas Bailey breathed hoarsely. The dust always got into his lungs, making him hawk and spit and fight for every breath. But he was a good soldier and never complained. Murphy admired that. That was why Bailey was one of his chosen few.

"Very good. Take it slow, as usual."

"Sure thing, sir. Not much chance of there being any of that scum around, not in this," Bailey wheezed between coughs.

"Nah, why else choose a shitty time like this?" Murphy replied with a grin. He picked up the handset of the crackling radio. "Alpha One to Beta, Gamma, Delta. Praise the Lord, there's a bridge coming to take us to the promised land. Follow the one true path. Don't go for the endless sleep. Over and out."

He put the handset back, only half listening to the crackly and distorted replies from the other three wags. He knew that they would be following orders and following him. He trusted his men implicitly in a combat situation. They knew the penalties for deviation—always assuming that they could get back to base.

The bridge across the chasm was camouflaged. Murphy's grandfather had built it about as far away from the old two-lane blacktop as he could, then covered it with a camouflage paint that made it hard to pick out from a distance. He figured that the outsiders always followed the line of the old road, wary of straying too far because of the mutie wildlife. To build the road here made sense, and the camouflage paint was the final touch. Although such paints had already existed in pre-dark times, this was something special. This had a chemical in it that made it adaptable to weather conditions and levels of humidity, with a life of a hundred years.

Which meant that it had a couple of decades left before it became visible for any outsiders brave enough to wander this far. Hell, Murphy thought, in a couple of decades there wouldn't be any of that scum left.

The wags rattled over the bridge, which sagged ominously as the first wag hit the metal. Even though he trusted it implicitly, Murphy's guts still gave a little tremor of fear every time he hit the bridge.

Over the chasm, they headed onward through the storm. Wallace wanted a fresh supply of body parts, and Murphy had a blood lust to quell. The unfinished business with Cawdor and his people was still eating at him. Hell, he might even find them there, if they'd managed to avoid getting chilled by the outsiders. The thought of it made him feel warm inside.

The wags were now careering through the brush where the mutie squirrels lived. The evil little critters evinced a certain death wish. Their territory was being invaded again, and they didn't like it.

The wags rattled and thumped as the bodies of the squirrels hit the sides, high-pitched squeals of pain and anger, fury and death penetrating the canvas-and-metal shell. Small rips appeared where the most tenacious of the creatures managed to get its jaws into the sides of the wags.

"Those little fuckers never learn, do they?" Bailey commented.

"They certainly don't, son," Murphy replied impassively. "Stupe bastards'll probably make themselves extinct at this rate. But you've gotta admire their guts, Bailey."

"Something like that, sir." Bailey coughed, fighting to keep control of the wag as the wheels skittered on bloody corpses.

"It's okay, Bailey. We'll soon be past the brush and into the homestretch. And that's where the action really begins." Murphy unholstered his blue 9 mm Beretta and kissed the barrel.

That had never failed him yet.

JAK WAS SQUATTED on a mound of earth just past the last beacon fire, now damped down for the daylight hours. Dean was with him. While Jak was still and impassive, staring into the storm, Dean was itchy and fidgety, unable to settle.

"I'm still not sure what the hell it is we're supposed to be keeping a lookout for," he complained. "Nothing can move out there, not in that."

"Not want stay, not stay," Jak commented quietly. "Not forcing you."

"I know," Dean replied, struggling for the right words. "I kind of don't want to, but feel like I should."

"Why?"

"Because you feel like something's going to happen."

Jak turned to Dean, and for a moment there was a

hint of suspicion in his red eyes. "Not a doomie," he said tersely. "Just bad feeling. Not know what, why."

"Not just you," Dean said. "Krysty's had a weird feeling today. I heard her tell Dad before he went to see that bastard Abner. Krysty doesn't get bad feelings for nothing."

Jak didn't reply, but now he knew why Ryan had picked today to find out when Abner was actually going to act. The bad feeling returned to him, intensified. It wasn't a doomie feeling, not like those Krysty had.

No, this wasn't a doomie feeling. It was more the kind of gut tension you got before a fight. The feeling that a chilling was in the air.

Jak returned to his vigil, Dean settling in beside him. Both of them ignored the wind and dust that stung their eyes, keeping watch for the slightest sign of activity.

Such as flurries of dust where there were previously none.

"Over there," Jak said pointing, squinting to try to get a better look.

Dean followed the line of Jak's bony white finger, not quite believing what he saw. Out of the dust clouds emerged a war wag. No, more than one. He counted four of them.

"I don't believe it," he whispered. "Four wags?"

"How they cross chasm?" Jak murmured.

"That's what I'd like to know," Dean replied.

That shook Jak from his reverie. He hadn't realized that he was thinking aloud. In one graceful, fluid movement he rose to his feet, placing a hand on Dean's shoulder.

"You keep watch."

"Yeah, you go and fetch Dad and the others. They need to see this," Dean said.

"Already there," Jak replied as he disappeared like a wraith.

Dean kept his gaze locked on the wags as they careered through the dust storms. At that speed it wouldn't be long before they were at the ville.

JAK SPED through the twisting lanes and paths that comprised the streets of the ville, making his way to the adobe hut where his companions were still billeted. Their training of the ville dwellers hadn't led Abner to give them better accommodations. Then again, looking at the sty in which the baron lived, perhaps there wasn't anything better.

When Jak reached the entrance to the hut, he could hear J.B., Mildred and Krysty talking about the possibility of making a mat-trans jump without being physically sick at the other end.

The albino burst into the adobe shack, his sudden appearance causing surprise that turned to a crackling, palpable tension as his body language communicated his urgency.

"War wags coming. Counted four. Dean still watching. Where's Ryan?"

"With Abner, last I knew," J.B. told him, reaching for his Uzi and the M-4000, checking their load and readiness for action.

"I'll get him," Krysty said, heading for the doorway and passing Jak. "You get the rest of these stupes ready. They never said anything about war wags."

J.B., grim faced, nodded. It was true that Abner, Mac and others they had spoken to had said nothing about Wallace's men coming by wag. Because of the chasm, they had all assumed that the attacking forces had to come on foot. That would make them easy to spot and easy to make a head count. But in wags?

"Round them up," J.B. said, striding toward the doorway. He had barely the trace of a limp now, but was still a little concerned about putting too much strain on the ankle. He'd have to watch his positioning as much as was possible in any firefight. "We'll take it in three. Okay?"

Mildred and Jak agreed. The ville was small enough for them to divide and alert the population quickly enough. So far they'd heard no alarm being raised, so did that mean that the ville was usually completely unprepared when Murphy's sec men were sent by Wallace?

J.B. marveled at the fact that there was still a ville at all as he went from shack to shack in his allotted section of town, yelling that an attack was on the way. He could only put their continued and precarious survival down to the protection of the elements that seemed to work against their survival in so many other ways.

RYAN WAS JUST LEAVING Abner's shack when Krysty found him. He was itching for a fight, the baron having irritated him with his offhand manner.

"What is it?" he snapped as he saw her rush toward him. It was a reaction caused by a deep sense of foreboding and the beginnings of an adrenaline rush. Action was imminent. He could tell by the way that her hair had coiled at her nape, and by the depth of concentration in her eyes.

"They're coming, lover. Jak and Dean have seen them approaching."

"How many?"

"Can't tell. They're in wags. Four, they counted."

"Fireblast!" Ryan whirled back toward Abner's shack, mounting the veranda and grabbing Mac through the open doorway. The fat sec man had his back to Ryan and grunted with surprise as the one-eyed warrior pulled him through the doorway. Ryan spun the man so that he faced him. "They're coming. Why didn't you say they used wags?"

Mac looked at him blankly and said ingenuously, "But you never asked. Besides, they've never come in storms this bad. Not often."

Ryan cursed. No matter how much a person trained someone, a stupe was still a stupe. Taking a deep breath and marshaling his thoughts, which raced on a rush of adrenaline and his fighting instincts, Ryan said, "Okay, you know the plan. We let them come and then attack. We need sec uniforms to get into the redoubt, and we need one of them alive. Getting a wag will be a bonus, I guess. Let's go."

Ryan and Krysty left Mac to prepare his sec forces—such as they were—while they raced on the double to the mound where Dean was waiting. Krysty told Ryan briefly how J.B., Mildred and Jak were rounding up the ville dwellers. Indeed, the ville was now a hive of activity, with the armory broken open and the dangerous homemade and altered blasters being passed out among those who had trained to shoot under Krysty and Mildred.

Ryan and Krysty reached the mound where Dean was waiting. He didn't turn as they approached, keeping his eyes focused on the approaching wags.

"A couple of minutes, no more," he said without preliminaries. "They're making good time. No more than four wags. Do we still follow the original plan, Dad?"

"Even more necessary," Ryan replied.

"Right. Got to get the bastards out of the wags first," Dean replied.

"Okay, son," he said. "Let's fall back and get into position."

THE WAGS RATTLED PAST the embers of the beacon fires, past the earthen mounds that circled the ville and along the main track that led into the heart of the ville.

Murphy frowned as he peered out of the dirt-splattered windshield. The heavy-duty wipers were going at full speed, the washers squirting detergent-laced water onto the glass. But all it did was produce a muddy smear that made it hard for Murphy to keep surveillance and for Bailey to drive.

"This is weird shit," Murphy whispered to himself.

"Sir?" Bailey risked a sideways glance at his superior, having to throw the wheel to the left to correct the steering as a result.

"It's probably nothing," Murphy replied, still peering intently through the mud streaks. "It's just too damn quiet out there."

"They're hardly trained soldiers like us, sir," Bailey said intently. "Probably all still in their shit pits, sleeping or rutting like the animals they are."

Murphy grunted. "And we have to use them for stock. Not for long, Bailey, not for long."

"No, sir!" Bailey breathed, bringing the wag to a halt in the center of the ville. The rough circle that served as the meeting place was deserted, the shacks and huts ringing it dark.

"I sniff Cawdor in all this," Murphy said quietly. "I just hope they've left the one-eyed bastard for me." He picked up the handset of the radio and opened the channel between the wags. "Listen here, people. I smell trouble, and if you don't, then what the fuck have you been doing all your lives? I don't know what we should expect, but look alive. Dismount and proceed with extreme caution."

He didn't bother with the call signs, an indication of his own nervousness and wariness. It communicated itself to all the wags, where the military remnants of the old ways gathered their standard-issue Uzis and H&Ks, checking that they were ready for firing. No one spoke.

In the lead wag Murphy turned to the four soldiers behind him, who were also in the process of checking their weapons.

"Let's go, people. Follow me, with extreme caution. Terminate with extreme prejudice. I think we can forget breeding stock this time out, unless we get lucky. Remember, aim for the head. We want those organs undamaged when we gather the harvest. Okay, let's go."

He spun the sec lock on the wag's door and slid down onto the dirt floor of the circle, keeping watch all around him for any signs of life. There were none, not even the mangy hounds that they raised in this pesthole for watchdogs, and meat when the animal grew old. There was nothing at all.

Murphy heard the clicking of other sec locks, as the rear door of the wag opened and the four men in back jumped out, fanning out around the wag to keep it guarded—to keep one another guarded. The men in front and back of the other wags followed suit, until all twenty-four men were in the circle, surrounding their wags.

Still there was silence, as though the very atmosphere of the storm itself was holding its breath, waiting for the first move.

RYAN SETTLED the Steyr against his shoulder, nestling the butt of the blaster into the hollow. His finger caressed the trigger, while he sighted with his eye, drawing on the driver of the last wag into the circle as he dismounted. He'd thought about taking out Murphy first—he had a score to settle with the sec chief from the redoubt—but decided against it as Murphy might be useful in getting them back into the redoubt.

The man in his sights looked around slowly, his Uzi leveled, his eyes glittering and alert. It caused Ryan only a ripple of surprise to see that the driver was, in fact, a woman. And a ripple of surprise only because she was larger, heftier and more muscular than any of the men in the detail.

It might be doubly useful to take her out first. He wanted to chill a driver so that it freed one wag for them to capture. Ryan assumed that the other sec men in the wag wouldn't be able to drive. He'd gathered enough about the redoubt to assume that each handed-down position was specialized and jealously guarded as such. The woman looked stronger than many of the men, so it would be good to get such a formidable opponent out of the way.

"Keep staring right at me," Ryan whispered to himself, so much under his breath that it only emerged as a sigh. Keep staring, keep giving me a great view of your face, a clean and simple target...."

Ryan squeezed gently on the trigger, shoulder braced for the recoil, squeezed until...

Ryan was already on the move when the shot hit home, killing the driver. He tapped the ville dweller next to him on the shoulder to let him know that he was to maintain the position, then jumped off the roof of the shack and headed out along the back alleys of the ville.

He heard the burst of Uzi fire, and the eerie scream of a man with no tongue as the sec man he had left behind caught the ricochet of Uzi fire. There was no way it would be directly fatal at that range, no way anyone could have got an accurate shot in with a machine pistol. The poor stupe had to have just been unlucky.

First blood to Murphy's men.

Ryan had memorized the alleys until he felt that he'd lived in the pesthole for years. The rest of the companions had done the same, preparing themselves for when the attack came.

It wasn't unfolding as he'd hoped. Murphy's men were grouped in the center of the ville. That much, at least, was according to plan. But they had wags to protect them, which would make attack much more difficult.

J.B. was waiting for him at the arranged point, by Abner's shack. The Armorer had been assigned the task of covering the far sector of the ville simply because he couldn't guarantee his mobility would be one hundred percent. By dropping back, he protected himself and also decreased the chances of being a liability to the others.

"Had a look at them?" J.B. asked.

Ryan nodded. "Four wags, six men per wag. Only twenty-three now, though."

J.B. chewed his lip. "Wish we had some plas-ex. The wags give them too much cover. We need to draw them out."

"If you come with me, that's just what I intend to do," Ryan replied, instantly changing plans.

MURPHY FELT the cold sweat of fear run down his back. His eyes stung with perspiration and dust, but he didn't dare relax his grip on the blaster for the fraction of a second it would take him to wipe the sweat away.

After he heard the ricochet of the Uzi fire, and the scream from the direction of the initial shot, there had been nothing. Murphy didn't know that the ville dwellers, hidden away but watchful, had been itching to fire back, stopped only by the knowledge drilled into them by the one-eyed man and his compatriots—the knowledge that a war of attrition would have a better long-term effect than a blind firefight.

If Murphy had known that, he would have gladly told them it was working just to goad them into some action. He glanced around at his men, who were looking as jumpy and wired as himself. Whatever had been going on here, that bastard Cawdor and his crew of scum had trained the outsiders well. He regretted the fact that he and Ryan were so opposed. Cawdor would be a good man to have on his side when the crunch came with Wallace.

The quiet was becoming oppressive, the howling wind seeming to grow in volume, distracting as Murphy tried to listen for any sound that could give the ville dwellers away. There was nothing.

He couldn't hear Jak, silently gliding around the back of the wags, with a leaf-bladed knife in each hand, ready to take out anything that got in his way. He couldn't hear J.B., moving around to inform Mildred, Dean and Krysty of Ryan's change of plan. He couldn't hear the ville dwellers as they moved into their new positions.

Murphy had never had to deal with the ville when it was prepared for action. He had never been on the defensive, and he didn't like it.

RYAN COULD FEEL the tension coming off the sec chief. Murphy knew he was giving it off.

So Ryan felt at ease when he stepped out of the alley, shielded by the back of a shack that faced directly onto the circle. Murphy was to his left, about twenty yards away. There were six sec men between them.

Ryan carried the Steyr on his right shoulder, an H&K hanging by its strap from the other shoulder. He stepped into the rear of the shack, shrugging loose the Steyr and leaving it on the dirt floor while he slid the H&K into his hands, preparing to fire. He looked around at the interior of the shack. It was adobe, reinforced by old corrugated-iron sheets.

He had been counting in his head the whole time. He was up to five hundred. It should have been plenty of time for the ville dwellers to take up their new positions.

Now it was show time.

Chapter Twenty

Mildred was surprised by the silence in which the ville dwellers could move. After receiving word from J.B., she had begun the slow process of quietly informing the armed people under her command of the move around one side of the rough earthen circle. The way in which they had responded was amazing. It was almost as if, realizing that this could be their chance to rid themselves of the menace of the redoubt sec men once and for all, they were determined to be organized and careful.

Mildred brought up the rear following the last of her people in time to catch a glimpse of Krysty down one alleyway, doing the same with her people.

The plan itself was simple. J.B. had directed Mildred and Krysty to one side of the circle, at ten o'clock. Jak and Dean led their people to two o'clock. The two new groups formed a pincer movement to close on the sec men when their attention was distracted, and they had been drawn away from the cover of the wags by Ryan.

Which should be about...

Now!

MURPHY HEARD the familiar click of the H&K and located it in a second.

"There—fire at will," he screamed, opening fire with

his own Uzi on the shack. He sprayed it with rapid-fire rounds, moving forward on the run.

As Ryan had hoped, Murphy's men followed the lead, shaken and rattled by the unexpected response in the ville, and following their commanding officer's orders blindly, as it said in the regs. Not thinking for themselves. Being stupid.

Breaking cover.

"FIREBLAST!" Ryan exclaimed, throwing himself to the dirt floor as the H&K shells started to punch holes in the adobe shack, spraying straw and dried mud around him. There was whining and ricochets as some of the fire hit the sheets of corrugated iron that helped support the shack walls. Ryan could only hug the ground and wait out the barrage.

The walls of the shack were beginning to gape large holes, the mud and straw building up on the floor, covering him. Mud clogged his nose, stung in his eyes, filled his mouth with its bitter and musty taste. Lizardlike, Ryan crawled across the floor, taking the Steyr from where he had left it. In his other hand he still held his H&K—he hadn't even fired a single shot, certainly hadn't expected Murphy to fall for it quite so completely.

The noise in the shack was intensely loud, vibrating on the corrugated iron as if it were directly on Ryan's eardrums. The shots blurred into one continuous noise, the mixed H&K and Uzi fire concentrated on him and his hiding place—a hiding place that was rapidly becoming a filled grave, as the shack tumbled around him, and onto him. They were still firing high, as though he were standing. But the continuous fall of mud, straw and now the sheets of corrugated iron pried loose from the walls they had been supporting, was threatening to engulf him as he made slow progress toward the back door of the shack.

KRYSTY WATCHED in mixed horror and awe as the sec men advanced on the shack where she knew Ryan was holed up, spraying it nonstop with blasterfire, pumping ammo into it as if they had an endless supply. There was no letup. When one sec man had to reload, there were at least ten others who were still on rapid fire.

A bile rose from deep in her gut, burning in her gullet, mixing with the burning that seared her eyes as she blinked back tears. She felt as if she were watching her lover being chilled in cold blood. And she was now helpless to stop it.

There was no doubt that his plan to draw the sec men away from the wags had worked. Murphy had led the way, striding toward the shack, across the circle of earth. The whole crew of sec men had spread out in a fan formation, pumping fire into the shack, forgetting that they were after only one man and that the whole population of the ville was unaccounted for. All led by Murphy's panic.

Some of the ville dwellers, blasters at the ready, looked at her. She looked at J.B., standing at a junction in the alleyways of the ville where he could keep visual contact with both herself, Mildred, Jak and Dean.

The Armorer exchanged rapid glances with both sides, then signaled.

Krysty nodded at the faces turned to her.

The ville dwellers, faces flushed with a mixture of fear and excitement, took their cue. A bloodthirsty yell of revenge and bravado rent the air as the ville dwellers charged, those in front firing their blasters at the sec men.

For a first front-line assault, it was a good result— five sec men hit the ground, chilled or about to catch the last train west, shells from the large-caliber rifles or shot from the scatterguns riddling their bodies.

Two of the sec men were chilled by their own people. Hearing the yell and the roar of blasterfire from behind them, the men next to them had turned while still firing, cutting their own men to shreds.

"Spread out… Lay down a suppressing fire… Chill the fuckers!" Murphy yelled, panicking as the unexpected action left his mind racing. He had no idea what to do. Nothing in the manual or regs covered this. Nothing he had ever experienced, or had been passed down from his forebears, had prepared him for such an action.

He reloaded rapidly, fumbling in his terror as he sped toward the wags, right toward the angry mob of ville dwellers. Looking up, stumbling across the earth, he was sure he saw the albino bastard's white hair and flashing red eyes appear in the crowd.

"No blasters," Jak yelled, "too close. Hand to hand."

Leading by example, one of the leaf-bladed knives left his hand, flashing through the hot, tense air and hitting a sec man beneath the eye, chipping the bone beneath the socket and deflecting upward to lodge behind the eyeball and into the brain. The ruptured eyeball spilled down his cheek as he hit the earth.

Murphy's men didn't eschew the use of blasters. They still tried to fire into the crowds. It was bloody and wasteful. Although several ville dwellers were chilled or injured as the shells ripped into them, the spray of fire also took out three more of their own men.

"Cease fire! Retreat!"

Murphy's voice penetrated the noise, a high, keening, hysterical edge to his yell. He was frightened beyond any capacity for tactical thinking. He just wanted to get the hell out of there.

That was okay by his men. Eleven of the twenty-four were down, nearly half the force wiped out. Two of the drivers were amongst those chilled, which meant that only two of the wags could return.

Some of the ville dwellers pursued the sec men as they piled into the wags, but most remembered that part of the plan was to let them escape if possible.

Because they were the way into the redoubt, even though they didn't know it.

Dean, looking desperately around, caught sight of the ruined shack. "Hot pipe! Dad!" he yelled, running toward it while keeping himself covered.

RYAN HAD MADE IT almost to the back of the shack, and the safety of the open doorway, when a sheet of corrugated iron had fallen from the wall and pinned him. It didn't have enough force in it to knock him out, but it did slow him down. The rusting metal sheet was thick and heavy, but he was glad that the fates had let it cover him, as he felt the impact of ricochets scream off the metal. The force was still enough to make him wince as he felt one slug punch the metal into his kidneys, a wave of hot nausea sweeping through him.

He stayed still for only a moment, allowing the wave to sweep over him and die. It subsided, and he made a decisive move. The iron lay heavy on him because he'd been crawling across the room, but it wasn't so heavy that he was unable to move at all. Bracing his hands on the dirt floor, feeling the grit and stone fragments in the dirt bite into his palms, Ryan began to push down, his biceps straining as they took the whole weight of the sheet. His back ached, the muscles pulling hard as the weight of the iron was lifted on his back. As he gained more height, so the weight spread down the line of his body, the muscles rippling on his torso as they began to relieve his arms and spine of the strain. His thighs lifted off the dirt, his combat boots biting into the earth floor as he pushed up....

The sheet fell off him with a crash, tumbling to his left. Ryan gasped and fell forward, propelled by the sudden lack of resistance to his straining muscles.

Gasping for breath, the one-eyed warrior allowed himself no time to recover, as there was none. He had to get out of the shack before he was chilled. Gathering the Steyr and the H&K, Ryan scrambled to his feet and made the few strides to the back doorway of the shack, the hole gaping open.

He threw himself through it in a forward roll, pitching onto his shoulder and coming up with the H&K in his hand, leveled for any enemy that may be in view.

"You're covered, Dad," Dean said calmly, his Browning Hi-Power in his fist. "I was worried about you. Murphy's turned tail and is ready to run."

"Any wags we can use?" Ryan asked, his mind racing to cover all possibilities. If they could get on Murphy's trail in a wag, he could be their ticket into the redoubt without needing the sec men's uniforms.

"How much of a head start have they got?" he asked.

The boy grinned. "Nothing yet. Take a look."

Ryan followed Dean around the alleyway and onto the edge of the center of the ville. Two of the wags lay abandoned, and through the press of bodies he could see the uniforms of dead sec men. The mass of bodies, however, was gathered around the two wags whose engines were whining in high gear, wheels spinning and kicking up earth at the back, front wheels raised from the ground by the press of bodies.

Ryan grinned. The superior power of the wags would crush the crowd beneath their wheels before too long, but the delay might be just long enough.

Jak appeared like a wraith from the crowd. "Ryan, good you alive. Two wags we use, but need speed."

Ryan nodded agreement. "Get the others, split between the two wags. I can drive one, you or J.B. the other. I need to find Abner and Mac, and quick."

The albino didn't waste time, disappearing into the crowd without a word. Ryan turned to his son. "Try and find Mac or Abner, get them to me. Let's go!"

Dean nodded his agreement and melted into the crowd while Ryan turned his attention to the sector of the crowd not covered by his son. It wasn't hard to spot Abner, as the old baron was relishing the victory over the insiders, gesturing with his blunderbuss and yelling incoherently at his people. He was a sitting target if Murphy or any of his men chose to take a shot from inside the wags. But the sec man didn't make a move.

Ryan fought his way through the crowd to Abner, grabbing the baron and unceremoniously pulling him to one side. The old man was so drunk with the atmosphere that he didn't even show any anger at being treated in such a disrespectful manner.

"We've got the bastards on the run, friend Ryan," he yelled, his eyes gleaming. "They're dead meat."

"But we don't want them to be," Ryan yelled back, desperate to make himself heard above the screams of the crowd. "Listen to me—if we follow them back to the redoubt in the other wags, we can strike inside and destroy them like we planned. Remember?" He spoke in simple terms to try to bring the old man out of his blood frenzy, to remember the plans and strategies they had discussed.

Abner paused. For a moment he looked blank, as though assimilating his thoughts. In that moment Dean appeared with Mac.

"Ryan," the fat sec man said with a face-splitting grin, "it goes well, my friend. I understand from the boy that we follow them back and hit 'em hard. Yeah?"

"Yeah," Ryan said simply. Dean had done a good job of explaining the situation. There was nothing else for him to say to Mac. It just remained to be seen if Abner had caught the drift.

"How many people you want?" the old baron said suddenly, everything falling into place for him.

"You, Mac, mebbe ten others at most. With us that makes eighteen in two wags. It'll be uncomfortable in there."

"I can handle a little of that—you get the best," Abner snapped at Mac, "and tell these mothers to let those wags go!"

"GO, GO, GO!" Murphy screamed at Bailey, his hapless driver.

"Can't, sir. These scum are holding us off the ground, and this is a front-wheel drive, sir."

Murphy cursed. There were four-wheel-drive wags back at the redoubt, but they were totally enclosed. His desire to be as open as possible for recce purposes was going to be his undoing.

"What about Avallone?" he shouted, referring to the driver of the other wag.

"Can't see, sir," Bailey replied.

Murphy swore loudly, picked up the handset for the radio and barked into it. Avallone's fear-struck voice replied that he was having the same problem.

"Shit. We're fucked now, really fucked," Murphy said, almost to himself, realizing that blind panic and losing his cool had gotten them into a no-win situation. What they needed was a miracle.

"Son of a bitch," he breathed in sheer disbelief as the whine of the engine suddenly became a roar. The wag bucked as the front wheels hit dirt and it began to move, skidding across the circle, through the main alley and out past the beacons.

"Sir, we're free and right behind you," Avallone's voice crackled over the radio, relief in every breath.

"Sir, why did they let go?" Bailey asked.

"Don't ask why, just be thankful that they did," the sec chief breathed.

RYAN AND JAK HEARD every word over the radio in their respective wags. J.B. had decided that Jak should drive rather than risk his ankle, which still gave him cause for concern if strained, on the pedals of the wag.

Jak drove silently, concentrating on the trail ahead of him, following Murphy and Avallone in their wags. He carried J.B., Mildred, Mac and five ville dwellers. They crouched and squatted in the back, crushed together as the wag bumped over the plains.

In the other wag Ryan carried Dean, Krysty and Abner along with five ville dwellers. Like the other wag, they traveled in a tense silence. They were going into the heart of the enemy's territory, something none of the ville dwellers had ever dreamed of doing.

Ryan and Jak kept close to the tail of the other wags,

so that they could locate the bridge. Once they were over that, it was a matter of keeping them in sight.

The enclave housing the entrance to the redoubt came in view. In the driver's seat of each wag, Jak and Ryan could feel the tension grow behind them.

They heard Murphy yell over the radio for the sec door to be opened. Ryan and Jak gunned their engines, getting every last ounce of power from the wags so that they could tailgate Murphy and Avallone, beating the sec door as it started to fall.

In each wag fighters prepared themselves. Once the wags rolled to a halt, then all hell would break loose.

Chapter Twenty-One

The wags screeched to halt inside the redoubt. The sec door to the enclave closed behind the four wags, leaving Murphy with the wags driven by Ryan and Jak between himself and the sec lock that would open the door once more. The sec door directly in front of him was also closed.

Wallace's voice came over the radio, now that the wags were inside the redoubt and in the range of the failing old tech. There was little doubt that the Gen had observed the return of the wags, and the manner in which they had screeched to a halt.

"Murphy, what in the holy hell is going on down there? Did you get the parts?"

"You could say that.... Yeah, you could fuckin' well say that," the rattled sec chief replied. "The back two wags have got Cawdor and his scum, with some bastard outsiders, and they've been trained to fight. I lost half my men out there."

"Then don't lose this half. I'll be down with reinforcements," Wallace barked.

Murphy looked at the handset in his sweating grip. It occurred to him that if Cawdor had the radio sets switched on, he would have heard it all—the reinforcements and his own panic.

Shit, blast and damn them all to the deepest rad pit.

RYAN GRINNED as he heard the exchange between Wallace and Murphy. There was nothing like knowing in advance what the enemy was going to be doing. He turned to the back of the wag.

"Okay, everybody out, blasters ready. Keep alert or be chilled. We've got time—not a lot, but just enough—to take up positions. Let's do it."

As they left the wag, he saw that Jak had directed the passengers of his wag in a similar manner.

Reinforced-concrete arches stood near the entrance to the redoubt, buoying the doorway and keeping its shape intact. None of them had seen anything quite like this in previous redoubts, but the workmanship on the arches was rough and ready, not the work of skilled builders. Possibly it was the work of sec men shortly after skydark, refashioning the arch when the first wave of quakes had swept the land.

For whatever reason they had been built, they now proved to be a piece of serendipity. As silently as possible, moving from the back of one wag to another, Ryan came to where Jak had marshaled the people in his wag. As with the front wag, they were currently standing to the rear, covered by the vehicle. Ryan directed them to spread out to the arches, using them as cover, those at the back of the wag covering the progress of those heading for the arches.

The people in his own wag were doing the same.

Ryan swiftly repositioned himself behind the forward arch, where he was joined by Krysty and Mac.

"They're too quiet, lover," Krysty whispered, not wanting to break the heavy silence that had fallen. The engines of all the wags had ceased, and there was no movement from the two wags with Murphy's men.

"Mebbe Murphy's too scared," Ryan mused.

"Mebbe he has a plan that Wallace doesn't know about. When that door goes up, that's when we'll know for sure."

The one-eyed warrior gestured with his Steyr at the sec door beyond the two wags. It had closed as soon as the wags had screeched to a halt. Beyond it lay the rest of the redoubt, the mat-trans they needed to get out, and Wallace....

Ryan cursed the fact that they had lost their contact with the Gen's plans by having to leave the wags and the radio, but they would have been a sitting target. At least out there they were spread out, and Wallace would have a clear shot at the enemy when they came.

MURPHY SAT in his wag, biting his nails and thinking as swiftly as his terror and the changing circumstances allowed him. This could be his big chance. Most of the military was on his side, plus some of the civilian scientists. It was a good opportunity. Wallace had never had anyone invade his base before. Let him make a mess of things, then step in to clean up. That way Murphy could avoid any blame, as well. He allowed himself a brief wave of optimism. This might just go his way.

"Murphy!" Wallace barked, his tone harshened by the reception of the radio. "Get yourself ready, boy— we're coming in...now!"

He turned to the other sec men in the wag. "This is it, men, Operation Munich."

The sec men exchanged puzzled and worried glances. "Now, sir?" one of them asked in a nervous quiver.

"Hell, yeah!" the sec chief exclaimed, trying to hide his own nervousness behind an exterior of bravado. "What better time? These scum can fight it out with the Gen and his people, then we pick up the pieces and take control.''

''Uh, how do we let the others know?'' one of the nervous sec men asked.

''Word of mouth, boy,'' Murphy replied. ''Now, heads up. It's all starting to come down.''

The sec door was grinding to life, rising slowly.

FROM HIS POSITION behind the arch, Ryan could see how slowly the door was rising. And to his amazement he could see the sec men on the other side just standing there, waiting for the door to finish its job. Standing unprotected and without cover. He risked a backward glimpse, catching the astonished faces of J.B., Jak and Dean. It seemed so incredible that for a second they were all frozen to inaction by the idiocy of Wallace's tactics.

Given time to reflect, Ryan would have realized that Wallace considered the outsiders, and the friends, as no better than dirt. He was so obsessed with his own superiority in the position of Gen that he couldn't believe anyone could outthink him. And he was slack from lack of actual combat.

But there was no time to reflect. There was only time for action. It was Mildred who broke the spell. While the others gaped, she raised her ZKR in a two-handed competition stance, feeling sheltered by the arch, and took aim.

The crack of the ZKR was high and clear, breaking across the low rumble of the opening door. It was followed by the high-pitched scream of a sec man hitting the concrete floor, his kneecap shattered into a bloody mess of shards by the high-velocity bullet.

It broke the spell. Falling to his belly, the Steyr raised

slightly on his shoulder, Ryan fired. Simultaneously J.B. had moved forward to get a better sweep of fire with his M-4000, the barbed steel fléchettes loaded into his blaster spreading out in a deadly hail that ripped at the knees, thighs and groins of the sec men on the other side of the door. The fléchettes spelled death rather than pain as they gouged at high velocity into faces and throats, ripping out flesh and artery.

The door was now three-quarters of the way up, the bodies of the sec men still standing now fully exposed. In the confusion and mayhem, some of them still had their blasters down. They died in a hail of slugs and shells from the homemade blasters of the ville dwellers.

The shooting was erratic, and some of the raiding party forgot the tactics they had been taught, lost in the blood lust and the heady excitement of a victory that seemed within their grasp. They stepped into the open and were mowed down by the surviving sec men, Uzi and H&K fire sweeping across the space between the arches and the wags. Four of the raiding party caught the last train west, and in his wag Murphy wondered what the hell was going on. He and his own men were trapped.

Mildred continued to pick off sec men with clean, precise shots, as were Krysty and Dean. Jak was distracted by the need to try to rein in some of the raiding party before they were all wiped out, lessening the chance of recovering Doc and reaching the mat-trans.

"BACK... BACK NOW!" The distorted voice of Wallace, using a bullhorn to issue commands crackled and barked over the noise of blasterfire. In confusion the remaining sec force started to pull back, covering themselves.

"Perfect," Murphy whispered to himself. "Go, go now. Let's get out of the immediate area and get organized. I couldn't have expected more," he said to Bailey, the driver.

"Sir, those are our men," Bailey replied in a quiet, shaken voice.

"Mebbe, but if we don't move, there won't be any left, will there?"

Bailey didn't answer. He slung the vehicle into first gear and touched the accelerator. The wag moved beyond the open sec door, skidding on the concrete floor, which was slick with the blood of their dead fellows. The second wag automatically followed.

It left the raiding party on its own, suddenly cut off without a visible enemy and the echo of the firefight still ringing in its ears.

"HAVE WE GOT THEM on the run, or is there something going on here that we don't know about?" Mac asked Ryan, looking puzzled. "There's no way that this is the end, right?"

Ryan nodded. "Reckon there's something going on between Murphy and Wallace. If we're lucky, then it might help us get what we want."

"And if we're not?"

"Then we might buy the farm," Ryan replied grimly.

They turned back to where J.B. and Jak were trying to subdue the triumphant outsiders. Abner was one of the most vocal. Ryan cast a quizzical glance at Mac, who shrugged.

"The old man hasn't been in a firefight for years. Guess he's just overexcited," Mac said.

"He'd better calm down, or he'll get you all chilled," Ryan murmured.

Mac nodded.

When they reached the group, clustered in front of the wags, Abner and the others had been calmed considerably by words from Krysty and Mildred. For some reason they were more inclined to listen to them than to Dean or Jak.

"It's because they look on them as kids, despite the fact they could outfight most of us," Mac commented.

J.B. stood a little apart from the rest, checking his Uzi, then reloading the M-4000. He beckoned to Ryan, who left Mac and went to join his old friend.

"What is it?"

J.B. took off his glasses and cleaned them, then pushed back his fedora and scratched at his forehead.

"I'm worried," he said simply.

"About these stupes?" Ryan asked, indicating the raiding party with an incline of the head.

"Nope. Me. This ankle. If I get left behind, don't worry about me too much. I'll find a way—"

Ryan clasped his friend on the shoulder. "No. We split up with different objectives, but no one gets left behind. Fireblast, we might even find Doc."

The Armorer allowed himself a wry smile. "You think he's still alive?"

"Wallace wanted him for a reason. He's not likely to have chilled him just like that," Ryan said, snapping his fingers.

The one-eyed warrior turned his attention back to the main group. Going over to them, with J.B. close behind, Ryan said, "They're on the run, but not because of us. There's something else going on here, and we need to find out what it is."

"WE ARE UNDER ATTACK. Wallace is not the man he was. We sense that he isn't the same man. How much time has passed since we were joined together? What has occurred outside in that time? And part of us wants to know why, when we have this capacity, we spend our time using just a fraction of it to run this base?"

The amorphous mass of men moved across a landscape of burned-out rubble and rotting corpses. Doc had discovered that this was how the Moebius MkI spent most of its time—if time was a concept that could exist to something so alien to human experience—moving across the logical conclusions of its purpose, simulated in a vista that continued forever.

And now there was real danger on the outside, and the mechanism was powerless to do anything about it. It flailed about in its imaginary landscape, recording and assimilating impressions from the outside, impotent to do anything except keep the redoubt running…and suddenly realizing its impotence as it came under attack for the first time in its long life.

Doc, knowing from the assembled data, who was invading the redoubt, tried to block that knowledge from the rest of the mechanism, to stop it using all he knew about his companions to defeat them.

"We are dividing. Why does Dr. Tanner wish to leave us?"

WALLACE WAS in his office when Murphy burst in with six armed soldiers behind him. The Gen was sitting at his desk, calmly reading the regs, as though they comprised a holy book, which, to him, it was.

"Ah, I was wondering when you would get here," he said calmly, an edge of ice to his voice.

"You guessed, then?" Murphy asked him, the blue 9 mm Beretta trained on a spot between the Gen's eyes.

"Oh, I knew that you had plans. Very well, you think that you can usurp the chain of command? Let's see what you make of these outsiders."

"More than you have. There were some good men mowed down out there," Murphy replied.

Wallace gave him a stare to chill his blood. "If you expect me to believe that you really care about those men, you must think that I'm a bigger stupe than the outsider scum. You have a wooden heart, and your men will learn the hard way."

Murphy ground his teeth, repressing the urge to rant at the Gen, to pistol-whip him now that he had him at his mercy. Instead he turned to the men behind him. "You and you," he snapped, gesturing at two of them. "Guard him. The rest of you come with me. Spread the word that we're in charge now. Things are going to be different."

He turned back to Wallace. "I'll deal with you when I've dealt with the outsiders."

"I wish I had your confidence in you, boy," Wallace said with a sneer as Murphy left the room.

Murphy's plan was simple—position sec men so that he could guide the raiding party down a certain path, insuring that they could be trapped and chilled with the minimum of fuss. After all, they had only seen the redoubt once, so they would have no idea where they were going.

This overconfident reasoning neglected the fact that he had witnessed their ability to find their way around the base when they had earlier escaped from his guard. But Murphy was high on his own sense of victory, and his memory had become selective.

RYAN AND J.B. HAD SPLIT the forces. The Armorer and Mildred had taken three men and were to try to locate

Doc. Their objective after this, regardless of result, was to secure the mat-trans unit. Ryan and the others, including Abner, Mac and the other three ville dwellers, were to try to eliminate Murphy and Wallace, and use the plas-ex that they knew to be in the armory to mine the redoubt and bring it down once and for all.

The combined party made its way down the corridors of the redoubt, headed for the point at which their paths would diverge. Ryan took the lead, followed by his friends and the outsiders, who were beginning to show their lack of experience in a combat situation. Their initial bravado had given way to nervousness, and their tension crackled from man to man, making them jumpy.

It was something Ryan wanted to avoid: an itchy finger on a blaster trigger, and it was likely to be one of their own party that bought the farm, rather than any of the redoubt's sec men. So his people were there to calm them down, keep them relaxed by their own vigilance.

But so far the corridors had been deserted. A wailing siren cut through the air, loud and insistent. It was a maddening sound, and didn't help the composure of the outsiders. Otherwise there was nothing: no sec men, no tech. Just the debris of a rapid pullback.

It was something that Ryan had expected. The tactics used by the redoubt sec men seemed to be along these lines, if Wallace was running things. But if it was Murphy now? And what if the two factions were at war with each other? Ryan didn't want to contemplate being caught in the cross fire of the two groups.

They came to a junction in the corridors. Ryan halted the line and flattened himself to the wall, edging forward until he was at the corner. He picked up a discarded clipboard from where it had been thrown to the floor. With a flick of the wrist, he tossed the board into the gap where the two corridors conjoined.

The blasterfire was deafening. Mostly Uzi, on rapid fire, thought J.B. His keenly trained ears picked out four men firing. He held up four fingers when the one-eyed warrior looked back at him. Ryan nodded his agreement; his own hearing had picked out the same amount of fire. As the corridor ahead was clear as far as they could see, it was obvious that this was the direction Murphy or Wallace wanted them to proceed.

It was taking them away from the elevators down to the armory, but there were other ways to get there. First they had to get across the junction.

Ryan beckoned Mac and whispered an instruction in his ear. The fat sec man nodded and turned to relay instructions to Abner and the other ville dwellers.

J.B. moved up to Ryan's side. "The usual?" he asked.

Ryan nodded. J.B. shouldered his Uzi and checked the M-4000. The deadly load of barbed steel fléchettes was in place. He pushed his fedora back on his head and looked Ryan in the eye.

"Let's go."

On the count of three, J.B. stepped into the open long enough to let loose a blast of fléchettes. The four sec men were strung out across the width of the corridor, crouched behind makeshift barriers made of tables. Two of them caught the largest cluster of fire, the barbed fléchettes ripping away flesh in searing agony. Their companions flattened themselves to the floor, thankful they escaped the brunt of the charge.

Ryan had flung himself across the gap and stood ready to provide covering fire.

The two surviving sec men opened fire. They were

situated on each side of the corridor, and were well protected. J.B. cursed and wished he had some grens. But as he was relatively ill equipped, he made do with firing another load of fléchettes at the nearer sec man, while Ryan concentrated his fire on the man on his side.

It was enough to allow Mac and Abner to cross as one, the sec man helping his baron to make the crossing quickly, using his bulk to shield the even fatter old man.

The fléchettes were once more effective. By looking up at the wrong moment, the sec man in the line of fire lost both his eyes and most of his face to the barbed metal.

The sec man on Ryan's side of the corridor was proving more tenacious. He kept his head down, and the barrage from the H&K picked holes around him but didn't touch him. He returned the fire sporadically.

J.B. switched to his Uzi, unwilling to waste too much of his M-4000's ammo when it wouldn't be truly effective. But the sec man was lucky and hung on, managing to avoid being hit by the blasterfire from two directions. He also got off bursts of his own, making it a tricky business for the rest of the party to get across the divide.

Mildred finished matters when she made the crossing. She shook her head so that her plaits swirled around her head. "That boy is really irritating me," she commented. Timing herself so that she acted in complete synchronization with Ryan, she flung herself to the floor as he swung out to fire a burst of cover. Bracing her elbows on the concrete to give her aim enough elevation, she sighted in the sec man as his head appeared to return fire.

One crack of the ZKR and he was silenced, a small hole drilled neatly in the middle of his forehead.

"Now let's get on," she remarked casually, getting to her feet.

The remainder of the party crossed.

"If the blasters and plas-ex are down there, why don't we go that way?" Abner asked.

Ryan shook his head. "That way will be well guarded. We're being pushed this way for a reason."

"Then surely we should surprise the bastards by going the way they don't expect?" Mac said with a puzzled frown.

Ryan grinned. It was cold and deadly. "We will. But it won't be that way."

Krysty gave Ryan a puzzled look for a second, then a smile spread across her face. "Right, lover. Wallace and Murphy think we only know the way we went before, so they're guiding us that way and making sure we don't take another path. But all the sec cameras are out along here because we shot them out."

"Right. And these stupe bastards don't know that we've been in other redoubts, or that they're all basically the same."

"You've lost me, friend," Abner said, his voice showing signs of irritation. "As far as I can see, you're just leading us into their trap."

But Mac shook his head. "No, I get it. They can't watch us along here, and expect us to end up at the end. But we won't, 'cause you know how there's another way out." He laughed.

"Got it in one," Ryan replied. "Now let's go."

They proceeded along the corridor strung out in formation, as before. The sec cameras were all inoperable, and there were no more corridor junctions for some way. Nonetheless to relax vigilance for one second was something that Ryan and J.B.'s instincts wouldn't allow them to do.

They came to a bend in the corridor.

"It should be just about here," Ryan whispered, almost to himself as he cautiously scanned the curve of the corridor before leading the party around.

It was there. "Got it!"

Mac frowned and looked around. "Think I must be double or triple stupe, but I can't see what you're getting excited about," he said quizzically.

"Up there..." Ryan gestured with his H&K toward a maintenance hatch on the ceiling.

"What good does that do us?" Abner sniffed.

"The maintenance ducts follow the line of the corridors. We can come out onto the elevator shaft, get down into one of the cars, then surprise these fireblasted stupes when we get to the right level."

Abner grinned. "I like it, even though it sounds like it's going to be hard work."

"No one said it was going to be easy," Ryan replied.

Jak was the first to climb into the duct. Ryan cupped his hands to give the albino teen a foothold, and then he sprung up to the hatch with grace and ease, using the end of one of his knives to loosen the screws that held the hatch in place. Once it was open, he pulled himself inside and wriggled around, reaching down to give Dean a helping hand as the boy was next up.

Inside the ducts there was enough room for them to kneel without being cramped, and they had soon assisted the ville dwellers into the space, having a little trouble with Abner as the old baron wasn't as fit as he would have liked to think. But, like Mac, he was still surprisingly agile for a man of his age and weight.

Ryan was the last man up, having elected to go last

in order to help J.B., who was still having niggling doubts about how his ankle would hold up. Before he jumped and caught hold of Jak and J.B.'s hands, he passed up the hatch cover. When the two friends had helped Ryan into the duct, he placed the hatch cover over the hole, so at least it would look undisturbed at a cursory glance.

It was dingy and dusty inside the duct. The air was thick, and difficult to breathe. It was obvious that the duct had been neglected by the techs for some time.

Ryan let Jak take the lead, the albino having a sure idea of the direction of the duct. They crawled in silence, unwilling to speak in the dust and heat that clawed at their throats. It seemed to take forever, but couldn't have been more than a few minutes before a cold blast of air swept across them.

"Elevator shaft," Jak croaked. "Ahead."

There was a blackness in front of them, where the lighting ceased, and a grille hatch covered the exit of the duct into the elevator shaft.

Now they came to the one part of the plan that relied on chance—if either of the elevator cars was below the level of the grille, then they could climb down and through the emergency hatch on top of the car. If both cars were above them, then they had a real problem.

Fortune favored them, and the far car was just at the level below them. It did mean, however, that they had to scale across the cables before dropping down to its roof. Jak went first, dropping catlike onto the car, and lifting the emergency hatch with one hand, the other grasping the .357 Magnum Colt Python, poised to blow away any opposition below.

The car was empty, the doors shut.

Jak beckoned to the others, and they made their way

across to the car, dropping down into the well-lit interior.

Without a word, Ryan pressed the button that would take them down to armory and the comp room that controlled the redoubt.

"What about Doc?" Mildred asked as the elevator started its descent.

"We look for him later. Best to try and secure first," Ryan said tersely. He didn't want to forget Doc, but first things first.

The elevator arrived at the right level, and everyone checked their blasters as the doors began to whirr open.

"This is it," Ryan said.

WALLACE SAT behind his desk, tapping his finger on its surface as he fixed the young private opposite him with a stony stare.

"Sir, don't do that," said the private, unable to keep the tremor from his voice. Like all those in the redoubt, he had been brought up to believe in the innate superiority of the Gen, and even though he had faith in the sarj, there was something that ran deeper.

"Do you really want those outsiders to make fools of us all?" Wallace said softly.

"No sir, the Sarj says—"

"Screw that stupe. Hand that to me, boy, and we'll say no more about it," Wallace interrupted. He held out his hand for the H&K the private held. Mesmerized by the charisma of the Gen, the private handed it over.

Wallace smiled grimly and shot the boy in the chest, the force of the slug throwing his already dead body off the chair.

"Never trust anyone, especially in times of war—and

that's what this is," Wallace stated before making his way into the anteroom.

Surveying the screens, he saw the mayhem that had broken out. He laughed gently to himself, a laugh that bespoke his slide into insanity.

He'd teach the sarj to mess with him.

WHEN RYAN'S raiding party had emerged from the elevator, it had been a swift and bloody race to the armory. They had emerged around the back of Murphy's men, taking them by complete surprise. The sec men had been blasted before they even had the chance to turn and face their attackers. The sec men farther down the corridor had retreated until they were holed up in the armory. Put on the defensive, they had retreated until the only secure place was the armory itself. There was no other way in. Alternatively there was no other way out.

Murphy and ten sec men were in the room, surrounded on both sides by Ryan's raiders, one group led by Jak and one by the one-eyed warrior himself.

With Murphy pinned down, Mildred and J.B. had set off with their small party to secure the main comp center and close down the comp systems controlling the redoubt.

It was here that they got the biggest shock. Arriving at the door Wallace had guided them past during his tour, they found that it wasn't guarded.

J.B. directed two of the ville dwellers to cover the corridor, while he and Mildred took the door. The third man in their party was to cover them as they went in.

The Armorer could only presume that Wallace had been so certain of his plan working that he had left this section manned only by the techs and whitecoats who worked here. Still, in a redoubt they could probably all use blasters. He wasn't going to take chances.

Bracing on his weaker ankle, J.B. used his good foot to kick open the door. Unlike most of the others in this section, it was a simple wooden door, which puzzled him.

The door crashed back on its hinges, and J.B. sprayed a short burst into the room. There was the small explosion of destroyed equipment, and the squeal of a tech mowed down at the knees.

J.B. and Mildred stepped into the room. Immediately the Armorer could see why the door was a simple wooden barrier—this was only an outer room, with the inner chamber protected by the usual sec door.

"Dark night, what has that madman done?" J.B. whispered as he caught sight of the Plexiglas window that lined one wall.

"What is it, John?" Mildred asked as she followed him into the room. "Wha—Oh, my God…"

J.B. and Mildred stood in front of the window, staring at the rat king.

And their eyes were drawn to Doc.

"Sweet Jesus," Mildred husked, resisting the urge to gag. "How could they—? No, scratch that." She turned to J.B. "We can't pull the plug until I see how Doc's connected. Leave me here with two for cover. Take one and get back to Ryan, let him know what's going on, then get back here."

"Okay."

J.B. left. He trusted Mildred's medical skills to get Doc out of there if it was possible. Otherwise he knew she would pull the plug if she couldn't get Doc out.

Ignoring the weeping tech, lost in his pain, Mildred went through the sec door and anteroom, into the main comp room where the skein of cables and wires connecting the rat king slithered across the floor.

"Let's see if I can get you detached, you damn crazy old fool," she whispered to Doc, smoothing back his hair.

"I wouldn't be too sure about that," said a level female voice from across the chamber.

Chapter Twenty-Two

Mildred froze. She recognized the voice, but couldn't see the owner as she was bent over Doc. Where the hell was that idiot ville dweller when she needed her?

The outsider was standing in the anteroom, her blaster raised. A cobbled-together mix of a Smith & Wesson stock with a homemade barrel welded to it, it hadn't been tested in combat as of yet. A rifle of indeterminate origin, lost in a welter of remakes and remodels, was on her shoulder, now out of ammo.

"What happened to my cover?" Mildred grated.

"Missy, I can't see her!" exclaimed the outsider, her speech snuffled and punctuated by heavy breathing through her deformed nose.

"Of course she can't see me," whispered the velvet voice. "You don't think I'm just going to walk in the most obvious door and be chilled, do you?"

Mildred allowed herself the risk of raising her head—slowly, so as not to rattle her captor.

"Shit, I should have figured you'd be protecting this monstrosity," Mildred said as she caught sight of Dr. Tricks, standing in a shadowed corner of the computer room, a 5-shot, two-inch Smith & Wesson .38 snubbie in her grip. It was trained steadily on Mildred.

Tricks shrugged. "This is my territory. If Sarj takes over, then I get to devote all my time to this while he streamlines things. That suits me. I hate wasting my time on those other projects that are going nowhere. Let's be honest. Most of the people I have under me now are stupes. That's not their fault. I'm just a freak in a different way. But if I could can all the other junk and just work on this—'' her liquid brown eyes lit up with a fanaticism Mildred recognized all too well ''—then we might just have the power to take this pest-hole of a country and put it back where it belongs. That would be wonderful. Did you realize that the mechanism operates at less than a thousandth of its potential?''

"I didn't," Mildred said calmly. "You know what I think?''

Tricks shook her head.

"I think you're mistaking me for someone who gives a fuck,'' Mildred said calmly. "Now, you can have your damn fool mechanism, and you and Murphy can do what the hell you want. But I'm going to disconnect Doc and get the hell out.'' She stopped speaking and leaned over the old man.

"Don't touch him,'' Tricks yelled, an edge of hysteria creeping into her voice. "You just don't get it. The Moebius cannot operate unless it has six linked minds. He's the only match we could find, and it was only divine interventions that brought him to us at the right time. You can't disconnect him. I won't let you.''

Mildred moved to cover Doc with her body and hoped that the scientist was ignorant of firearms. "Lady, that isn't a military-issue blaster you've got there. I'd guess it's been in your line since before skydark, and I'd also guess that you've never used it. You do know that if you fire at me now, the bullet will go right through and into Doc?''

"You're lying," Tricks snapped, her voice betraying her real indecision.

"Your choice," Mildred told her, feigning distraction as she examined the wires and electrodes attached to Doc. Her mind was racing, and she found it hard to focus on her task, knowing that Tricks might just fire from panic.

It was that panic that saved Mildred. Unsure of what to do, Tricks stepped forward with the wiggle that had driven the males in the redoubt mad with desire. Her intention was to bring the blaster down on Mildred's head as a club. But in order to do that, she had to step into the line of fire from the woman who was covering Mildred.

In her confusion Tricks had forgotten about her. The ville dweller raised her blaster and fired.

Tricks got lucky one time. There was a deafening report that made Mildred wince as the blaster exploded in the ville dweller's hand, separating it from her arm near the elbow. The flash from the explosion seared the skin from her face, enlarging the snuffling hole that should have been a nose, her ragged and matted hair catching fire and forming a halo of flame around her head. Her scream was piercing.

Tricks looked in horror, momentarily forgetting Mildred. It was all the distraction she needed. Spinning, her foot followed through the momentum and caught Tricks on the wrist, knocking the blaster from her hand and cracking the fragile bones in her mutie wrist. Tricks's own scream joined in awful harmony with the ville dweller.

As Mildred prepared to follow through with another attack, she heard a shot that sounded like another explosion in the contained space. Tricks's face took on a pained, surprised expression, her perfect mouth forming an O of surprise, her brown eyes bulging from the sockets as her whitecoated torso became a mass of red, her back blossoming red in an outward spray as a load of shot from a homemade blaster ripped through her.

The shot continued across the room, striking the mainframe, which exploded in a fury of sparks and flame.

"Oh, shit," Mildred whispered before turning to the ville dweller who had entered the chamber on hearing his companion's blaster explode. He was looking at the mewling, burned frame of his dead compatriot.

"Thanks for that," Mildred said tersely, "but we've just really screwed things. I should've been more alert, and that shot...no, never mind, it was the right thing. Just pray I can get Doc disconnected and us out of here before the damn thing blows."

WALLACE MADE HIS WAY from his office to the armory. There was confusion all around him, scared techs and whitecoats running around aimlessly, not knowing what they were supposed to be doing. There were no orders anymore, and no regs drilled into them that allowed for such a situation.

The Gen waited patiently for the elevator car to reach his level, stepped in and pressed the button for the level he wanted. His mind had completely snapped, and there was only one thing on that mind—the destruction of Murphy. The chaos all around told him that without the regs, there was only confusion. Murphy had trashed those regs, and all that remained was the court-martial and sentence. As commanding officer, Wallace had already run the procedures in his mind, and arrived at the only possible conclusion.

Death. Murphy had to die.

And if it took him, as well, what did that matter? He had failed in his position and wasn't worthy of living. He had let down his country and his forefathers. There was no one to carry on the line. Somehow he'd never got around to it. So why shouldn't it all end with him?

The elevator arrived at the required level. The doors creaked open, and Wallace stepped out. With a disdainful sniff he smelled the cordite and stench of death in the air. He took in the corpses of his own sec men, chilled by the surprise attack of the outsiders.

So much for Murphy's tactics. This was the mark of a good leader?

Even more reason for him to die.

Wallace strode down the corridor, his bulky waddle lessened by the length of strides. If he looked like a man in a hurry, then maybe that was because he had an agenda that made it urgent. If he didn't achieve his objective soon, then he felt as though all reason would snap.

That's if there was any reason left.

The sporadic bursts of blasterfire became louder as he walked through the mayhem. The armory was up ahead. He could see two groups of outsiders clustered around the entrance to the room, covering the corridor that led, at its terminus, to the armory. The entry was protected by a barricade of boxes, stacked to provide cover for the sec force holed up within.

Wallace strode through the outsiders as though they weren't there, ignoring the blasterfire that rang out around him.

"SIR, IT'S THE GEN."

Murphy, lurking at the back of the armory, didn't at

first realize what was being said. He was engrossed in his task, searching for a gren that would be powerful enough to take out the outsiders but wouldn't endanger his own men or the redoubt. A lifetime of learning about the caverns and fault lines that surrounded the enclave and the redoubt had led him to believe that triggering a large explosion would cause a disturbance that could endanger the stability of the redoubt's structure.

"Sir, the Gen..." The soldier's voice was more insistent. Murphy snapped back from his preoccupation, suddenly aware of what was being said to him. He also noted that the firing had virtually ceased.

"What did you say, boy?" he asked, turning to look over the barricade. "Holy shit..."

RYAN SIGNALED his force to hold its fire. On the opposite side Jak gestured for his force to also cease fire.

"Who the fuck is that dipshit?" Mac whispered in awed tones, not knowing whether to think Wallace mad or brave to the point of reckless insanity.

"Used to be in charge here," Ryan said tersely. "We were the excuse for him to be deposed by Murphy."

"So what's he doing?"

Ryan shrugged. "Your guess is as good as mine."

"Fucked if is," Jak replied grimly.

Krysty saw Wallace remove the gren from his pocket, and she whispered in Ryan's ear, "We've got big trouble, lover."

"You're telling me," the one-eyed warrior replied. "If he lets a gren loose in the armory, we need to be two levels up, or at least get that sec door down," he added, nodding toward the raised door that would close off the route to the armory.

"No, it's worse than that, lover. It's almost as if the

Earth Mother herself is screaming a warning to me. When he lets that gren go, we need to be as far away from here as possible.''

MURPHY WAS at the front of the barricade, looking over the top as Wallace approached.

"What's that crazy...?" he whispered to himself before raising his voice. "Gen, what do you want?"

"Even the score, Sarj. You have been tried under Reg 17B, Subsection A. You're guilty as hell, boy."

"Shit, what are you talking about? What trial? There is no trial. I'm in command here."

Wallace laughed, loud and harsh. "Command? You call this command, boy? Look at you—holed up with nowhere to run. You've lost, boy. Face it."

"Bullshit. I've got the arms right here to win."

"All you've got is your own sad chilling, boy," Wallace said coldly.

Murphy saw the Gen hand out a gren, saw him pull the pin and lob the gren over the barricade so that it landed in the center of the room. He watched as the Gen turned and punched in the code on the sec door that made it start to close with a creak and a moan.

"You bastard, you fucker," Murphy yelled, realizing that it was too late for him to scoop up the gren and throw it through the rapidly lessening gap where the sec door was closing. He raised his blue Beretta and drilled three holes in Wallace's back, throwing the Gen against the wall.

Wallace turned as he slumped to the corridor floor. His eyes were fogged with the approach of death, but he still managed to force a grin and a small chuckle from his throat. His voice bubbled as the blood rose in his throat, the words little more than a whisper.

"Never could get it right, Murphy. Not as smart as you thought, boy...not born to lead..."

Murphy heard the words with an awful clarity as he turned to watch the gren.

There was a flash as the gren exploded, milliseconds later triggering the waiting boxes of grens.

Murphy was already dead by the time the sound of the explosions rippled through the crumbling corridor, a fraction of a second later.

MILDRED HEARD the explosions as she attempted to remove the first electrode from a shaved portion of Doc's skull. It seemed to be held only with tape, but she was wary lest it be attached in some other way beneath. She heard the explosions as one—a dull whump that made everything in the room shake.

Mildred braced herself against the couch on which Doc lay, seemingly comatose. She swore to herself, shook her head to clear it, then proceeded to strip off the tape. The electrode underneath wasn't attached directly to the brain through a trepanned hole in the skull, as she could see on the others in the room, but it did seem to have some kind of hook that bit into Doc's scalp.

"Sorry if this hurts, you old buzzard," she murmured, "but your hide is so damn thick that I seriously doubt it."

Gritting her teeth, she pulled the electrode free, prying the hook from the scalp. It seemed to be nothing more than a securing mechanism, coming free with just a slight twist, a trickle of blood marking the spot where it had been attached.

Doc twitched.

"WE ARE BEING DIVIDED. Another leaving so soon?"

The mass of men who comprised the rat king stood in the comp room, watching Mildred detach Doc. The mainframe was still sparking, small fires flaring and dying as the transistor circuits on the motherboard burned out piece by piece.

"We are all leaving," Doc replied. He was able to walk away from them, to stand apart. He no longer had the need to mask his thoughts. "By the Three Kennedys, that feels good," he said aloud. "For all that I had thought about it, I do not think I would ever truly appreciated the joys of individuality before now."

"We can no longer read your thoughts, as you are moving away from us," said the Air Force general, stepping forward. "What do you mean, we are all leaving?"

"Look at yourself," Doc answered. "You are speaking on your own, and you have moved away from the block. Just as you were when I was first joined to you. Face the facts. Without a full complement, you are separating of your own accord. Look how your imaging has focused on things as they really are. This the first time you have not been through a simulation or a model. Look at the computer." Doc pointed a bony finger at the gently smoldering mainframe. "If that ceases operation, then nature will take the course denied it for so long, and you will die. As you should. If you stop and think about it, it should be a blessed relief to you."

The Air Force general frowned. "But if we die, then the mechanism dies. And if the mechanism dies, then those who are dependent upon us will also die."

Doc craned forward, his body language registering the bewilderment he suddenly felt. "Those who are dependent?"

"Of course. Do we not spend our time in futility, using a fraction of our capability to keep the life-support systems of the redoubt in working order?"

"Oh, mercy me, has the good Dr. Wyeth thought of this?" Doc blurted, realizing what it could mean.

MILDRED HAD REMOVED almost all the electrodes and was keeping half an eye on the tubes feeding Doc and cleaning his blood, wondering which she should disconnect first, when he started to writhe and moan on the couch, seemingly desperate to fight his way back to consciousness.

"It's okay, Doc. Don't rush it, you old coot—more haste, less speed, as they always used to say."

Doc's eyes opened, staring and unfocused, but still alert. "Haste and speed are of the essence, my dear Doctor," he croaked unexpectedly.

"Calm down, you old buzzard," Mildred said softly, trying to hide the relief in her voice that he was still alive. The tubes seemed to detach easily enough, and Mildred silently thanked the recently chilled Tricks for her efficiency.

"I fear you do not understand," Doc continued hoarsely. "The mainframe is dying…By leaving the others I am killing them."

Mildred paused, looking at the desiccated, barely living zombielike corpses on the other couches. What had Doc been through when he was linked to that machine?

"They belong dead," she said shortly.

"Perhaps." Doc managed the ghost of a smile. "But they control the redoubt. When they die, it dies."

"Shit," Mildred said softly, "including the mat-trans."

"Exactly," Doc said with a weak nod.

It was then that the first tremor began to rock the redoubt, making the couches move on their mountings, screws and bolts protesting as the floor heaved beneath their solid grip.

Mildred looked up. "Oh, yeah, this is all we need."

"FIREBLAST! The stupe bastard! Get down!"

Ryan roared across the corridor, pushing to the ground as many people in his party as he could lay hands on, exhorting Jak to do the same, and barely believing what he had just seen.

The sec door groaned into place and was dented almost immediately by the force of the explosion. The displacement of air was at such a force and speed that it bent the metal, testing its strength to the utmost.

"Dark night, what was that?" the Armorer asked, arriving on the scene scant moments after the initial blast and skidding to a halt beside Ryan, who was getting to his feet.

"That triple-stupe madman Wallace just blew himself and Murphy out of existence, taking the armory with them," Krysty said, her voice hushed by the immensity of the action.

J.B. pushed back his fedora, ran his hand over his face and fixed Ryan with a worried look. "That's bad news," he said quietly.

Krysty frowned, noticing the unspoken agreement between the two old friends. She, too, felt the sense of impending danger, but for the moment the link between the feeling and hard reality was evading her.

It was Mac who voiced the question. "Friends, I might sound stupe, but why is it bad news? With Murphy and Wallace chilled, there's no one left to lead, and we can mop them up. Right?"

"Wrong," J.B. answered flatly. "First thing, an explosion in the armory is bad—spectacularly bad. Mebbe there's nerve-gas grens, all sorts of shit in there."

"But the door's closed, it's sealed," Mac interjected.

"The air-conditioning system," Ryan said simply.

"Right," the Armorer continued. "If that's still working in there, and there's no reason to think it isn't, then the gas released will spread through the entire redoubt."

"How long that take?" Jak questioned. He and the other assault party had made their way across to join the others. Abner was looking particularly worried. Mac knew that the old man always looked that way when he didn't understand what was going on.

"Depends on how much the system was damaged in there, and how much gas, if any, was in the armory."

"So there might not be any?" Abner said, his voice tinged with relief.

"We can't guarantee either way," J.B. stated. You can close off parts of the system if you can get to the right control panel, but where that is... Anyhow, it's not just the air-conditioning that could be a problem."

Krysty felt the earth shift beneath her feet, even though she knew logically that nothing was happening. It was a chill premonition.

"Earthquake," she whispered. "Of course, the faults that formed the valley. And we're just deep enough for it to probably take effect if such a force started a shift."

"Dark night," J.B. said softly, 'Millie and Doc—"

"Found him?" Jak asked sharply. When J.B. nodded, the albino looked at Ryan and said, "Let's find, get the fuck out."

THE FLIGHT to the comp room was bloodless and swift. There was no resistance from the remaining sec men, who were having more trouble fighting off whitecoats and techs who saw the military as responsible for the downfall of their little civilization, and had turned on them, grabbing makeshift weapons and chilled men's blasters to fight back. As was always the way with the community, they were so self-obsessed as to ignore the small party that made its way between them. They didn't have to fire a shot in anger, which was surprising but pleasing, as it enabled them all to conserve ammo.

They were almost on the comp room when the first series of tremors struck. Out in the corridors Ryan and his party stumbled as fissures appeared in the concrete floors, and dust and plaster spilled from the ceilings in a fine mist.

The whole structure of the deeply buried redoubt seemed to move around them, stressed concrete groaning and complaining as the steel within started to buckle. Weaknesses along fault lines began to spread cracks that threatened to separate corridors.

"We've got to get Doc and Millie and get out," J.B. said through gritted teeth, pressing on despite the fear that started to build within him.

Krysty detected that note in his voice. "Me, too," she whispered to him, "but we can fight that. It's just the remnants of the torture."

"I know," gritted the Armorer, worries about his ankle holding up feeding into the remains of the psychological torture they had all received at Tricks's hands. "But what if nerve gas has been released, and that's fueling it?"

"Then we need to stay alert and move it," Krysty replied.

J.B. nodded, wiping dust from his glasses. The comp room and lab were ahead. Almost there...

THE VILLE DWELLER who had been standing guard for Mildred entered the comp room, his eyes wild with panic and fear.

"This place is falling apart. We'll all be trapped," he yelled at her.

Mildred ignored him for a second as she helped Doc to his feet. He looked older, frailer than he had for some time, and it was only his immense power of will that kept him from blacking out. When he was steady, she turned to the ville dweller.

"We'll all get out of here if we stay calm. Otherwise we're finished. Do you understand?"

The tall, muscled man with the pockmarked complexion nodded, for all his years and scarring looking like an innocent and frightened child. Which, in some ways, he was. He had never encountered anything like this before.

"Okay," he breathed, keeping the tremor from his voice, "what do we do now?"

Mildred looked at Doc.

"The mat-trans," Doc croaked in a trembling and tired voice. "The Moebius will shut down soon, and then we will not be able to get out that way."

"What about...?" Mildred asked, indicating the frightened ville dweller.

"True, my good Doctor. We can not leave this poor soul to his fate. If we can locate Ryan and the others, his people should be with them—"

"We're here, Doc," Ryan said as his party reached the comp room. "This place is falling apart, and we need to get out."

"Certainly do," Mildred said quickly, explaining what Doc had told her.

"Shit—we have to move," Ryan spit. "Mac, Abner, we'll lead you back to the wags, then we'll make our own way."

"How will you do that?" Mac asked in bemusement.

"Never mind. It'd take too long to explain. But trust me, we'll be okay. Now let's go. Jak, Dean, you help Doc."

As the albino slipped around to assist Doc, he handed him the LeMat and lion's-head swordstick.

"Where did you get these, lad?" Doc asked with a beatific smile.

"Leave things lying around, someone bound to pick up," the albino said, grinning. "Now quit talking. Let's move."

THE ELEVATORS WERE still working, but it was a rough ride up to the level where the wags had been left. The elevator shafts were reinforced against such movements of the earth, but the shock waves spread out by the explosion in the armory had started a series of tremors that were threatening to destroy the redoubt.

They reached the wags without incident. Most of the infighting was concentrated on the lower levels. Mac and Abner marshaled their few people into one of the wags, and Ryan hit the outer-door sec code, praying that the door wasn't too warped by the earth shifts to be jammed.

It lifted with an agonized and protesting squeal.

"Are you sure you won't come with us?" Abner asked. "It's not much of a life, but mebbe we could move out with your assistance, settle beyond the valley."

Ryan shook his head. "Thanks, but we always go our own way. Now move before the door comes down on you."

"Can you manage this?" he asked Mac.

The sec man nodded shortly and ground the wag into gear as another tremor shook the floor beneath them, the sec door dropping inches as the concrete frame split.

"Goodbye, friend Ryan," he yelled over the roar of the engine and the moaning of the earth. "It hasn't been fun, but it's been good."

Without looking back, he gunned the wag and drove it out into the enclave, weaving around the rocks and boulders that were tumbling down the sides of the rock walls.

Ryan had already turned away, before the wag had even left the redoubt.

"Let's move. Usual formation, and quick."

They moved to the elevator in single file. There was no one around at that level, but they could never afford to let caution lapse.

The elevator half dropped to the level of the mat-trans, the cable snagging as the car hit the buckling walls. It was time for them all to sweat, except for Doc. He was too wasted and drained by his experience to truly, at that point, take in what was happening.

Ryan and Jak forced the elevator doors back as it reached the level they wanted, the door mechanism opening too slowly for their liking as the earth shook and the walls started to shed shards of concrete and plastic. The metal lining of the air-conditioning shafts had come down through one point in the corridor, and they had to weave around it, stepping over the chilled corpses of sec men, whitecoats and techs.

"Ritual culling," Doc murmured to no one but himself.

Finally, hearts pounding and sweat pouring from them in exertion and fear, they reached the outer chamber of the mat-trans.

Krysty went straight to the comps in the control room.

"Still working, lover," she murmured as she hit the code to start the mat-trans, using the knowledge they had picked up from the few units they had seen that didn't use the door closing as a jump trigger.

They entered the chamber, taking their positions on the floor and preparing for the jump. Jak and Dean helped Doc to a sitting position, then huddled themselves against the wall. Mildred and J.B. sat together, holding hands, blasters close by.

Krysty sat and waited for Ryan as the one-eyed warrior closed the door and spun the wheel. He turned to join Krysty, and was thrown across the chamber as the redoubt screamed in agony, walls beginning to crumble and cave in under the pressure of the shifting earth.

As Ryan hit the floor, the disks began to glow, the air crackling around them with electrostatic discharge, and a white mist rose and formed around them in curling tendrils.

He reached out for Krysty as the nausea rose, and everything began to fade to black. The chamber shook around them, and his last thought was a hope that the jump would be made before the chamber was destroyed by the earthquakes.

Gold Eagle brings you high-tech action and mystic adventure!

THE Destroyer™

#121 A POUND OF PREVENTION

Created by

MURPHY
and SAPIR

Organized crime lords are converging in the East African nation of Luzuland, for what looks like an underworld summit. Remo—with his own problems—is just not in the mood to be killing his way up the chain of command in East Africa. Chiun has gone AWOL, and unless he can beat some sense into his pupil's skull, Remo's bent on nuking a mob-infested Third World city to deliver a pound of prevention to wipe out a generation of predators....

Available in October 2000 at your favorite retail outlet.

Or order your copy now by sending your name, address, zip or postal code, along with a check or money order (please do not send cash) for $5.99 for each book ordered ($6.99 in Canada), plus 75¢ postage and handling ($1.00 in Canada), payable to Gold Eagle Books, to:

In the U.S.

Gold Eagle Books
3010 Walden Ave.
P.O. Box 9077
Buffalo, NY 14269-9077

In Canada

Gold Eagle Books
P.O. Box 636
Fort Erie, Ontario
L2A 5X3

Please specify book title with your order.
Canadian residents add applicable federal and provincial taxes.

GDEST121

James Axler

OUTLANDERS®

DOOM DYNASTY

Kane, once a keeper of law and order in the new America, is part of the driving machine to return power to the true inheritors of the earth. California is the opening salvo in one baron's savage quest for immortality—and a fateful act of defiance against earth's dangerous oppressors. Yet their sanctity is grimly uncertain as an unseen force arrives for a final confrontation with those who seek to rule, or reclaim, planet Earth.

End game begins for rogue arms dealers....

DON PENDLETON's

MACK BOLAN®

War SEASON

America reels in horror and shock when terrorists slaughter hundreds in Philadelphia, using a prototype weapon of megadeath called the Annihilator. The blood trail leads to a private arms dealer on the U.S. military payroll, selling hardware off the books. Mack Bolan's orders are sanctioned by the President and to the point: take down Amazon arms!!!

Available in September 2000 at your favorite retail outlet.

Or order your copy now by sending your name, address, zip or postal code, along with a check or money order (please do not send cash) for $5.99 for each book ordered ($6.99 in Canada), plus 75¢ postage and handling ($1.00 in Canada), payable to Gold Eagle Books, to:

In the U.S.	In Canada
Gold Eagle Books	Gold Eagle Books
3010 Walden Avenue	P.O. Box 636
P.O. Box 9077	Fort Erie, Ontario
Buffalo, NY 14269-9077	L2A 5X3

Please specify book title with your order.
Canadian residents add applicable federal and provincial taxes.

GOLD EAGLE®

GSB74

DON PENDLETON'S

STONY

AMERICA'S ULTRA-COVERT INTELLIGENCE AGENCY

MAN®

DRAGON FIRE

The President orders Stony Man to place its combat teams on full alert when top-secret data for U.S. missile technology is stolen. Tracing the leads to Chinese agents, Phoenix Force goes undercover deep in Chinese territory, racing against time to stop China from taking over all of Asia!

Available in November 2000 at your favorite retail outlet.

A journey to the dangerous frontier
known as the future...
Don't miss these titles!

JAMES AXLER

DEATH
LANDS®

#89008-7	NORTHSTAR RISING	$5.99 U.S.☐	$6.99 CAN.☐
#89007-9	RED EQUINOX	$5.99 U.S.☐	$6.99 CAN.☐
#89006-0	ICE AND FIRE	$5.99 U.S.☐	$6.99 CAN.☐
#89005-2	DECTRA CHAIN	$5.99 U.S.☐	$6.99 CAN.☐
#89004-4	PONY SOLDIERS	$5.99 U.S.☐	$6.99 CAN.☐

(limited quantities available on certain titles)

TOTAL AMOUNT	$	
POSTAGE & HANDLING	$	
($1.00 for one book, 50¢ for each additional)		
APPLICABLE TAXES*	$	_____
TOTAL PAYABLE	$	_____

(check or money order—please do not send cash)

To order, complete this form and send it, along with a check or money order for the total above, payable to Gold Eagle Books, to: **In the U.S.:** 3010 Walden Avenue, P.O. Box 9077, Buffalo, NY 14269-9077; **In Canada:** P.O. Box 636, Fort Erie, Ontario, L2A 5X3.

Name: _____

Address: _____ City: _____

State/Prov.: _____ Zip/Postal Code: _____

*New York residents remit applicable sales taxes.
Canadian residents remit applicable GST and provincial taxes.

GOLD
EAGLE®

GDLBACK2